Lose yourself

in the

magical world of

Cecelia
Ahern

Before embarking on her writing career, Cecelia Ahern completed a degree in Journalism and Media Communications. At twenty-one years old she wrote her first novel *PS, I Love You* which instantly became an international bestseller and was adapted into a major motion picture starring Hilary Swank. Her successive novels *Where Rainbows End, If You Could See Me Now* and *A Place Called Here* were also number one bestsellers. Her books are published in forty-six countries and have collectively sold over nine million copies. Cecelia has also co-created the hit ABC Network comedy series *Samantha Who?* which stars Christina Applegate. Her sixth and latest book *The Gift* is a Christmas story out in hardback next month. Cecelia lives in Dublin, Ireland.

To sign up for the exclusive Cecelia Ahern HarperCollins newsletter and discover all about Cecelia's books, as well as interviews, photographs and much more, log onto **www.cecelia-ahern.com**. You can also turn to the back of this book for more details about the website.

PS - don't forget to read Cecelia's other novels:
PS, I Love You
Where Rainbows End
If You Could See Me Now
A Place Called Here
The Gift (coming soon)

Acclaim for
Thanks for the Memories

'Cecelia Ahern is queen of the modern fairytale ... In *Thanks for the Memories*, Ahern has given her readers exactly what they want: love, magic, happy endings. And most of all, hope.' *Irish Times*

'You'll love this sweet and very readable tale' *Heat*

'An absorbing heart-warming story' *Glamour*

'The key to Ahern's success is her ability to not just tell a good story, but sprinkle it with plenty of laughs, tears, and a little bit of magic' *Mirror*

'Unputdownable' *Grazia*

'The legendary Ahern will keep you guessing what binds these stories... a classic' *Company*

'Another masterpiece' *OK!*

'The writing is ambitious and, in parts, poetic' *Daily Telegraph*

Acclaim for Cecelia's previous bestsellers

'There's more than a touch of fairytale about
Cecelia Ahern's novels' *Glamour*

'A sensational debut novel that proves true love never dies'
Cosmopolitan

'A wonderfully life-affirming debut' *Company*

'Like an Irish Sleepless in Seattle and almost certainly
the chick-lit bestseller of the year' *In Style*

'A fun, fresh read' *Marie Claire*

'Wild humour and heartbreak tangled up in one great road'
Cathy Kelly

'Insightful and true' Deirdre Purcell, *Irish Independent*

'Heartwarmingly good' *Heat*

'Everything she writes comes from the heart' *Sunday Tribune*

'A wonderfully warm and witty debut from
a terrific new writer …' *Daily Express*

HarperCollinsPublishers
77–85 Fulham Palace Road,
Hammersmith, London W6 8JB

www.harpercollins.co.uk

Published by HarperCollinsPublishers 2008
1

Copyright © Cecelia Ahern 2008

Cecelia Ahern asserts the moral right to
be identified as the author of this work

A catalogue record for this book
is available from the British Library

ISBN: 978 0 00 7233694

This novel is entirely a work of fiction.
The names, characters and incidents portrayed in it are
the work of the author's imagination. Any resemblance to
actual persons, living or dead, events or localities is
entirely coincidental.

TYPESET in Sabon by Palimpsest Book
Production Limited, Grangemouth, Stirlingshire

Printed and bound in Great Britain by Clays Ltd, St Ives plc

Mixed Sources
Product group from well-managed
forests and other controlled sources
www.fsc.org Cert no. SW-COC-1806
© 1996 Forest Stewardship Council

FSC is a non-profit international organisation established
to promote the responsible management of the world's forests.
Products carrying the FSC label are independently certified to
assure consumers that they come from forests that are
managed to meet the social, economic and ecological needs
of present and future generations.

Find out more about HarperCollins and the environment at
www.harpercollins.co.uk/green

Sources

www.tcd.ie
www.ibts.ie
www.rotunda.ie

Cecelia
Ahern

Thanks for the Memories

HARPER

Thanks to my precious people for their love, guidance and support; David, Mimmie, Dad, Georgina, Nicky, Rocco, Jay, Breda and Neil. To Marianne for her Midas touch and for her 'clatter' of vision. Thanks to Lynne Drew, Amanda Ridout, Claire Bord, Moira Reilly, Tony Purdue, Fiona McIntosh and the whole team at HarperCollins. Huge thanks as always to Vicki Satlow with the incredible HV, and Pat Lynch. I'd like to thank all my friends for supporting and sharing the adventure with me. Special thanks to Sarah for being the godliest of all godlies. Thanks to Mark Monahan at Trinity College, Karen Breen at the Irish Blood Transfusion Service and Bernice at Viking Splash Tours.

Dedicated, with love, to my grandparents,
Olive & Raphael Kelly and Julia & Con Ahern,
Thanks for the Memories

PROLOGUE

Close your eyes and stare into the dark.

My father's advice when I couldn't sleep as a little girl. He wouldn't want me to do that now but I've set my mind to the task regardless. I'm staring into that immeasurable blackness that stretches far beyond my closed eyelids. Though I lie still on the ground, I feel perched at the highest point I could possibly be; clutching at a star in the night sky with my legs dangling above cold black nothingness, I take one last look at my fingers wrapped around the light and let go. Down I go, falling, then floating, and, falling again, I wait for the land of my life.

I know now, as I knew as that little girl fighting sleep, that behind the gauzed screen of shut-eye, lies colour. It taunts me, dares me to open my eyes and lose sleep. Flashes of red and amber, yellow and white speckle my darkness. I refuse to open them. I rebel and I squeeze my eyelids together tighter to block out the grains of light, mere distractions that keep us awake but a sign that there's life beyond.

But there's no life in me. None that I can feel, from where I lie at the bottom of the staircase. My heart beats quicker now, the lone fighter left standing in the ring, a red boxing glove pumping victoriously into the air, refusing to give up. It's the only part of me that cares, the only part that ever cared. It fights to pump the blood around to heal, to replace what I'm losing. But it's all leaving my body as quickly as it's sent; forming a deep black ocean of its own around me where I've fallen.

Rushing, rushing, rushing. We are always rushing. Never have enough time here, always trying to make our way there. Need to have left here five minutes ago, need to be there now. The phone rings again and I acknowledge the irony. I could have taken my time and answered it now.

Now, not then.

I could have taken all the time in the world on each of those steps. But we're always rushing. All, but my heart. That slows now. I don't mind so much. I place my hand on my belly. If my child is gone, and I suspect this is so, I'll join it there. There . . . where? Wherever. It; a heartless word. He or she so young; who it was to become, still a question. But there, I will mother it.

There, not here.

I'll tell it: I'm sorry, sweetheart, I'm sorry I ruined your chances, my chance – our chance of a life together. But close your eyes and stare into the darkness now, like Mummy is doing, and we'll find our way together.

2

There's a noise in the room and I feel a presence.

'Oh God, Joyce, oh God. Can you hear me, love? Oh God. Oh God. Oh, please no, Good Lord, not my Joyce, don't take my Joyce. Hold on, love, I'm here. Dad is here.'

I don't want to hold on and I feel like telling him so. I hear myself groan, an animal-like whimper and it shocks me, scares me. I have a plan, I want to tell him. I want to go, only then can I be with my baby.

Then, not now.

He's stopped me from falling but I haven't landed yet. Instead he helps me balance on nothing, hover while I'm forced to make the decision. I want to keep falling but he's calling the ambulance and he's gripping my hand with such ferocity it's as though it is *he* who is hanging on to dear life. As though I'm all he has. He's brushing the hair from my forehead and weeping loudly. I've never heard him weep. Not even when Mum died. He clings to my hand with all of the strength I never knew his old body had and I remember that I am all he has and that he, once again just like before, is my whole world. The blood continues to rush through me. Rushing, rushing, rushing. We are always rushing. Maybe I'm rushing again. Maybe it's not my time to go.

I feel the rough skin of old hands squeezing mine, and their intensity and their familiarity force me to open my eyes. Light fills them and I glimpse his face, a look I never want to see again. He clings to his baby. I know I've lost mine; I can't let him lose his. In making my decision I already begin to grieve. I've landed now, the land of my life. And, still, my heart pumps on.

Even when broken it still works.

One Month Earlier

ONE

'Blood transfusion,' Dr Fields announces from the podium of a lecture hall in Trinity College's Arts building, 'is the process of transferring blood or blood-based products from one person into the circulatory system of another. Blood transfusions may treat medical conditions, such as massive blood loss due to trauma, surgery, shock and where the red-cell-producing mechanism fails.

'Here are the facts. Three thousand donations are needed in Ireland every week. Only three per cent of the Irish population are donors, providing blood for a population of almost four million. One in four people will need a transfusion at some point. Take a look around the room now.'

Five hundred heads turn left, right and around. Uncomfortable sniggers break the silence.

Dr Fields elevates her voice over the disruption. 'At least one hundred and fifty people in this room will need a blood transfusion at some stage in their lives.'

That silences them. A hand is raised.

'Yes?'

'How much blood does a patient need?'

'How long is a piece of string, dumb-ass,' a voice from the back mocks, and a scrunched ball of paper flies at the head of the young male enquirer.

'It's a very good question.' She frowns into the darkness, unable to see the students through the light of the projector. 'Who asked that?'

'Mr Dover,' someone calls from the other side of the room.

'I'm sure Mr Dover can answer for himself. What's your first name?'

'Ben,' he responds, sounding dejected.

Laughter erupts. Dr Fields sighs.

'Ben, thank you for your question – and to the rest of you, there is no such thing as a stupid question. This is what Blood For Life Week is all about. It's about asking all the questions you want, learning all you need to know about blood transfusions before you possibly donate today, tomorrow, the remaining days of this week on campus, or maybe regularly in your future.'

The main door opens and light streams into the dark lecture hall. Justin Hitchcock enters, the concentration on his face illuminated by the white light of the projector. Under one arm are multiple piles of folders, each one slipping by the second. A knee shoots up to hoist them back in place. His right hand carries both an overstuffed briefcase and a dangerously balanced Styrofoam cup of

8

coffee. He slowly lowers his hovering foot down to the floor, as though performing a t'ai chi move, and a relieved smile creeps onto his face as calm is restored. Somebody sniggers and the balancing act is once again compromised.

Hold it, Justin. Move your eyes away from the cup and assess the situation. Woman on podium, five hundred kids. All staring at you. Say something. Something intelligent.

'I'm confused,' he announces to the darkness, behind which he senses some sort of life form. There are twitters in the room and he feels all eyes on him as he moves back towards the door to check the number.

Don't spill the coffee. Don't spill the damn coffee.

He opens the door, allowing shafts of light to sneak in again and the students in its line shade their eyes.

Twitter, twitter, nothing funnier than a lost man.

Laden down with items, he manages to hold the door open with his leg. He looks back to the number on the outside of the door and then back to his sheet, the sheet that, if he doesn't grab it that very second, will float to the ground. He makes a move to grab it. Wrong hand. Styrofoam cup of coffee falls to the ground. Closely followed by sheet of paper.

Damn it! There they go again, twitter, twitter. Nothing funnier than a lost man who's spilled his coffee and dropped his schedule.

'Can I help you?' The lecturer steps down from the podium.

Justin brings his entire body back into the classroom and darkness resumes.

'Well, it says here . . . well, it said there,' he nods his head towards the sodden sheet on the ground, 'that I have a class here now.'

'Enrolment for international students is in the exam hall.'

He frowns. 'No, I—'

'I'm sorry.' She comes closer. 'I thought I heard an American accent.' She picks up the Styrofoam cup and throws it into the bin, over which a sign reads 'No Drinks Allowed'.

'Ah . . . oh . . . sorry about that.'

'Mature students are next door.' She adds in a whisper, 'Trust me, you don't want to join this class.'

Justin clears his throat and corrects his posture, tucking the folders tighter under his arm. 'Actually I'm lecturing the History of Art and Architecture class.'

'You're lecturing?'

'Guest lecturing. Believe it or not.' He blows his hair up from his sticky forehead. *A haircut, remember to get a haircut. There they go again, twitter, twitter. A lost lecturer, who's spilled his coffee, dropped his schedule, is about to lose his folders and needs a haircut. Definitely nothing funnier.*

'Professor Hitchcock?'

10

'That's me.' He feels the folders slipping from under his arm.

'Oh, I'm so sorry,' she whispers. 'I didn't know . . .' She catches a folder for him. 'I'm Dr Sarah Fields from the IBTS. The Faculty told me that I could have a half-hour with the students before your lecture, your permission pending, of course.'

'Oh, well, nobody informed me of that, but that's no problemo.' *Problemo?* He shakes his head at himself and makes for the door. *Starbucks, here I come.*

'Professor Hitchcock?'

He stops at the door. 'Yes.'

'Would you like to join us?'

I most certainly would not. There's a cappuccino and cinnamon muffin with my name on them. No. Just say no.

'Um . . . nn–es.' *Nes?* 'I mean yes.'

Twitter, twitter, twitter. Lecturer caught out. Forced into doing something he clearly didn't want to do by attractive young woman in white coat claiming to be a doctor of an unfamiliar initialised organisation.

'Great. Welcome.'

She places the folders back under his arm and returns to the podium to address the students.

'OK, attention, everybody. Back to the initial question of blood quantities. A car accident victim may require up to thirty units of blood. A bleeding ulcer could require anything between three and thirty units of blood. A coronary artery bypass may use between one and five units of blood. It varies, but with such quantities needed, now you see why we *always* want donors.'

Justin takes a seat in the front row and listens with horror to the discussion he's joined.

'Does anybody have any questions?'

Can you change the subject?

'Do you get paid for giving blood?'

More laughs.

'Not in this country, I'm afraid.'

'Does the person who is given blood know who their donor is?'

'Donations are usually anonymous to the recipient but products in a blood bank are always individually traceable through the cycle of donation, testing, separation into components, storage and administration to the recipient.'

'Can anyone give blood?'

'Good question. I have a list here of contra-indications to being a blood donor. Please all study it carefully and take notes if you wish.' Dr Fields places her sheet under the projector and her white coat lights up with a rather graphic picture of someone in dire need of a donation. She steps away and instead it fills the screen on the wall.

People groan and the word 'gross' travels around the tiered seating like a Mexican wave. Twice by Justin. Dizziness overtakes him and he averts his eyes from the image.

'Oops, wrong sheet,' Dr Fields says cheekily, slowly replacing it with the promised list.

Justin searches with great hope for needle or blood phobia in an effort to eliminate himself as a possible blood donor. No such luck – not that it mattered, as the chances of him donating a drop of blood to anyone are as rare as ideas in the morning.

'Too bad, Dover.' Another scrunched ball of paper goes flying from the back of the hall to hit Ben's head again. 'Gay people can't donate.'

Ben coolly raises two fingers in the air.

'That's discriminatory,' one girl calls out.

'It is also a discussion for another day,' Dr Fields responds, moving on 'Remember, your body will replace the liquid part of the donation within twenty-four hours. With a unit of blood at almost a pint and everyone having eight to twelve pints of blood in their body, the average person can easily spare giving one.'

Pockets of juvenile laughter at the innuendo.

'Everybody, please.' Dr Fields claps her hands, trying desperately to get attention. 'Blood For Life Week is all about education as much as donation. It's all well and good that we can have a laugh and a joke but at this time I think it's important to note the fact that someone's *life*, be it woman, man or child, could be depending on you right now.'

How quickly silence falls upon the class. Even Justin stops talking to himself.

TWO

'Professor Hitchcock.' Dr Fields approaches Justin, who is arranging his notes at the podium while the students take a five-minute break.

'Please call me Justin, Doctor.'

'Please call me Sarah.' She holds out her hand.

Very 'Nice to meet you, Sarah.'

'I just want to make sure we'll see each other later?'

'Later?'

'Yes, later. As in . . . after your lecture,' she smiles.

Is she flirting? It's been so long, how am I supposed to tell? Speak, Justin, speak.

'Great. A date would be great.'

She purses her lips to hide a smile. 'OK, I'll meet you at the main entrance at six and I'll bring you across myself.'

'Bring me across where?'

'To where we've got the blood drive set up. It's

15

beside the rugby pitch but I'd prefer to bring you over myself.'

'The blood drive . . .' He's immediately flooded with dread. 'Ah, I don't think that—'

'And then we'll go for a drink after?'

'You know what? I'm just getting over the flu so I don't think I'm eligible for donating.' He parts his hands and shrugs.

'Are you on antibiotics?'

'No, but that's a good idea, Sarah. Maybe I *should* be . . .' He rubs his throat.

'Oh, I think you'll be OK,' she grins.

'No, you see, I've been around some pretty infectious diseases lately. Malaria, smallpox, the whole lot. I was in a very tropical area.' He remembers the list of contraindications. 'And my brother, Al? Yeah, he's a leper.' *Lame, lame, lame.*

'Really.' She lifts an eyebrow and though he fights it with all his will, he cracks a smile. 'How long ago did you leave the States?'

Think hard, this could be a trick question. 'I moved to London three months ago,' he finally answers truthfully.

'Oh, lucky for you. If it was two months you wouldn't be eligible.'

'Now hold on, let me think . . .' He scratches his chin and thinks hard, randomly mumbling months of the year aloud. 'Maybe it *was* two months ago. If I work backwards from when I arrived . . .' He trails off, while counting his fingers and staring off into the distance with a concentrated frown.

'Are you afraid, Professor Hitchcock?' she smiles.

'Afraid? No!' He throws his head back and guffaws. 'But did I mention I have malaria?' He sighs at her failure to take him seriously. 'Well, I'm all out of ideas.'

'I'll see you at the entrance at six. Oh, and don't forget to eat beforehand.'

'Of course, because I'll be *ravenous* before my date with a giant homicidal needle,' he mumbles as he watches her leave.

The students begin filing back into the room and he tries to hide the smile of pleasure on his face, mixed as it is. Finally the class is his.

OK, my little twittering friends. It's pay-back time.

They're not yet all seated when he begins.

'Art,' he announces to the lecture hall, and he hears the sounds of pencils and notepads being extracted from bags, loud zips and buckles, tin pencil cases rattling; all new for the first day. Squeaky-clean and untarnished. Shame the same can not be said for the students. 'The products of human creativity.' He doesn't stall to allow them time to catch up. In fact, it is time to have a little fun. His speech speeds up.

'The creation of beautiful or significant things.' He paces as he speaks, still hearing zipping sounds and rattling.

'Sir, could you say that again ple—'

'No,' he interrupts. 'Engineering,' he moves on, 'the practical application of science to commerce or industry.' Total silence now.

'Creativity and practicality. The fruit of their merger is architecture.'

Faster, Justin, faster!

'Architecture-is-the-transformation-of-ideas-into-a-physical-reality. The-complex-and-carefully-designed-structure-of-something-especially-with-regard-to-a-specific-period. To-understand-architecture-we-must-examine-the-relationship-between-technology-science-and-society.'

'Sir, can you—'

'No.' But he slows slightly. 'We examine how architecture through the centuries has been shaped by society, how it continues to be shaped, but also how it, in turn, shapes society.'

He pauses, looking around at the youthful faces staring up at him, their minds empty vessels waiting to be filled. So much to learn, so little time to do it in, such little passion within them to understand it truly. It is his job to give them passion. To share with them his experiences of travel, his knowledge of all the great masterpieces of centuries ago. He will transport them from the stuffy lecture theatre of the prestigious Dublin college to the rooms of the Louvre Museum, hear the echoes of their footsteps as he walks them through the Cathedral of St-Denis, to St-Germain-des-Prés and St-Pierre de

18

Montmartre. They'll know not only dates and statistics but the smell of Picasso's paints, the feel of baroque marble, the sound of the bells of Notre-Dame Cathedral. They'll experience it all, right here in this classroom. He will bring it all to them.

They're staring at you, Justin. Say something.

He clears his throat. 'This course will teach you how to analyse works of art and how to understand their historical significance. It will enable you to develop an awareness of the environment while also providing you with a deeper sensitivity to the culture and ideals of other nations. You will cover a broad range: history of painting, sculpture and architecture from Ancient Greece to modern times; early Irish art; the painters of the Italian Renaissance; the great Gothic cathedrals of Europe; the architectural splendours of the Georgian era and the artistic achievements of the twentieth century.'

He allows a silence to fall.

Are they filled with regret on hearing what lay ahead of them for the next four years of their lives? Or do their hearts beat wildly with excitement as his does, just thinking about all that is to come? Even after all these years, he still feels the same enthusiasm for the buildings, paintings and sculptures of the world. His exhilaration often leaves him breathless during lectures; he has to remember to slow down, not to tell them everything at once. Though he wants them to know everything, right now!

He looks again at their faces and has an epiphany.

You have them! They're hanging on your every word, just waiting to hear more. You've done it, they're in your grasp!

Someone farts and the room explodes with laughter.

He sighs, his bubble burst, and continues his talk in a bored tone. 'My name is Justin Hitchcock and in my special guest lectures scattered throughout the course, you will study the introduction to European painting such as the Italian Renaissance and French Impressionism. This includes the critical analysis of paintings, the importance of iconography and the various technical methods used by artists from the Book of Kells to modern day. There'll also be an introduction to European architecture. Greek temples to the present day, blah blah blah. Two volunteers to help me hand these out, please.'

And so it was another year. He wasn't at home in Chicago now; he had chased his ex-wife and daughter to live in London and was flying back and forth between there and Dublin for his guest lectures. A different country perhaps but another class of the same. First week and giddy. Another group displaying an immature lack of understanding of his passions; a deliberate turning of their backs on the possibility – no, not the possibility, the *surety* – of learning something wonderful and great.

20

It doesn't matter what you say now, pal, from here on in the only thing they'll go home remembering is the fart.

THREE

'What is it about fart jokes, Bea?'

'Oh, hi, Dad.'

'What kind of a greeting is that?'

'Oh, gee whizz, wow, Dad, so great to hear from you. It's been, what, ah shucks, three hours since you last phoned?'

'Fine, you don't have to go all porky pig on me. Is your darling mother home yet from a day out at her new life?'

'Yes, she's home.'

'And has she brought the delightful Laurence back with her?' He can't hold back his sarcasm, which he hates himself for but, unwilling to withdraw it and incapable of apologising, he does what he always does, which is to run with it, therefore making it worse. 'Laurence,' he drawls, 'Laurence of A— inguinal hernia.'

'Oh, you're such a geek. Would you ever give up talking about his trouser leg,' she sighs with boredom.

Justin kicks off the scratchy blanket of the cheap Dublin hotel he's staying in. 'Really, Bea, check it next time he's around. Those trousers are far too tight for what he's got going on down there. There should be a name for that. Something-itis.'

Balls-a-titis.

'There are only four TV channels in this dump, one in a language I don't even understand. It sounds like they're clearing their throats after one of your mother's terrible coq-au-vins. You know, in my wonderful home back in Chicago, I had over two hundred channels.' *Dick-a-titis. Dickhead-a-titis. Ha!*

'Of which none you watched.'

'But one had a choice not to watch those deplorable house-fixer-upper channels and music channels of naked women dancing around.'

'I appreciate *one* going through such an upheaval, Dad. It must be very traumatic for you, a sort-of grown man, while I, at sixteen years old, had to take this huge life adjustment of parents getting divorced and a move from Chicago to London all in my stride.'

'You got two houses and extra presents, what do you care?' he grumbles. 'And it was your idea.'

'It was my idea to go to *ballet school* in London, not for your marriage to end!'

'Oh, *ballet school*. I thought you said, "Break up, you *fool*." My mistake. Think we should move back to Chicago and get back together?'

'Nah.' He hears the smile in her voice and knows it's OK.

'Hey, you think I was going to stay in Chicago while you're all the way over this side of the world?'

'You're not even in the same country right now,' she laughs.

'Ireland is just a work trip. I'll be back in London in a few days. Honestly, Bea, there's nowhere else I'd rather be,' he assures her.

Though a Four Seasons would be nice.

'I'm thinking of moving in with Peter,' she says far too casually.

'So what is it about fart jokes?' he asks again, ignoring her. 'I mean what is it about the sound of expelling air that can stop people from being interested in some of the most incredible master-pieces ever created?'

'I take it you don't want to talk about me moving in with Peter?'

'You're a child. You and Peter can move into the wendy house, which I still have in storage. I'll set it up in the living room. It'll be real nice and cosy.'

'I'm eighteen. Not a child any more. I've lived alone away from home for two years now.'

'One year alone. Your mother left *me* alone the second year to join you, remember.'

'You and Mum met at my age.'

'And we did not live happily ever after. Stop imitating us and write your own fairy tale.'

'I would, if my overprotective father would stop

butting in with his version of how the story should go.' Bea sighs and steers the conversation back to safer territory. 'Why are your students laughing at fart jokes, anyway? I thought your seminar was a one-off for postgrads who'd elected to choose your boring subject. Though why anybody would do that, is beyond me. You lecturing me on Peter is boring enough and I love him.'

Love! Ignore it and she'll forget what she said.

'It wouldn't be beyond you, if you'd listen to me when I talk. Along with my postgraduate classes, I was asked to speak to first-year students throughout the year too, an agreement I may live to regret, but no matter. On to my day job and far more pressing matters, I'm planning an exhibition at the Gallery on Dutch painting in the seventeenth century. You should come see it.'

'No, thanks.'

'Well, maybe my postgrads over the next few months will be more appreciative of my expertise.'

'You know, your students may have laughed at the fart joke but I bet at least a quarter of them donated blood.'

'They only did it because they heard they'd get a free KitKat afterward,' Justin huffs, rooting through the insufficiently filled mini-bar. 'You're angry at me for not giving blood?'

'I think you're an asshole for standing up that woman.'

'Don't use the word "asshole", Bea. Anyway, who told you that I stood her up?'

'Uncle Al.'

'Uncle Al is an asshole. And you know what else, honey? You know what the good doctor said today about donating blood?' He struggles with opening the film on the top of a Pringles box.

'What?' Bea yawns.

'That the donation is anonymous to the recipient. Hear that? *Anonymous*. So what's the point in saving someone's life if they don't even know you're the one who saved them?'

'Dad!'

'What? Come on, Bea. Lie to me and tell me you wouldn't want a bouquet of flowers for saving someone's life?'

Bea protests but he continues.

'Or a little basket of those, whaddaya call 'em muffins that you like, coconut—'

'Cinnamon,' she laughs, finally giving in.

'A little basket of cinnamon muffins outside your front door with a little note tucked into the basket saying, "Thanks, Bea, for saving my life. Anytime you want anything done, like your dry cleaning picked up, or your newspaper and a coffee delivered to your front door every morning, a chauffeur-driven car for your own personal use, front-row tickets to the opera . . ." Oh the list could go on and on.'

He gives up pulling at the film and instead picks up a corkscrew and stabs the top. 'It could be like one of those Chinese things; you know the way someone saves your life and then you're forever indebted to them. It could be nice having someone tailing you everyday; catching pianos flying out of windows and stopping them from landing on your head, that kind of thing.'

Bea calms herself. 'I hope you're joking.'

'Yeah, of course I'm joking.' Justin makes a face. 'The piano would surely kill them and that would be unfair.'

He finally pulls open the Pringles lid and throws the corkscrew across the room. It hits a glass on top of the minibar and it smashes.

'What was that?'

'House-cleaning,' he lies. 'You think I'm selfish, don't you?'

'Dad, you uprooted your life, left a great job, nice apartment and flew thousands of miles to another country just to be near me, of course I don't think you're selfish.'

Justin smiles and pops a Pringle into his mouth.

'But if you're not joking about the muffin basket, then you're definitely selfish. And if it was Blood For Life Week in my college, I would have taken part. But you have the opportunity to make it up to that woman.'

'I just feel like I'm being bullied into this entire thing. I was going to get my hair cut tomorrow, not have people stab at my veins.'

'Don't give blood if you don't want to, I don't care. But remember, if you do it, a tiny little needle isn't gonna kill you. In fact, the opposite may happen, it might save someone's life and you never

28

know, that person could follow you around for the rest of your life leaving muffin baskets outside your door and catching pianos before they fall on your head. Now wouldn't that be nice?'

FOUR

In a blood drive beside Trinity College's rugby pitch, Justin tries to hide his shaking hands from Sarah, while handing over his consent form and 'Health and Lifestyle' questionnaire, which frankly discloses far more about him than he'd reveal on a date. She smiles encouragingly and talks him through everything as though giving blood is the most normal thing in the world.

'Now I just need to ask you a few questions. Have you read, understood and completed the health and lifestyle questionnaire?'

Justin nods, words failing him in his clogged throat.

'And is all the information you've provided true and accurate to the best of your knowledge?'

'Why?' he croaks. 'Does it not look right to you? Because if it doesn't I can always leave and come back again another time.'

She smiles at him with the same look his mother

31

wore before tucking him into bed and turning off the light.

'OK, we're all set. I'm just going to do a haemo-globin test,' she explains.

'Does that check for diseases?' He looks around nervously at the equipment in the van. *Please don't let me have any diseases. That would be too embarrassing. Not likely anyway. Can you even remember the last time you had sex?*

'No, this just measures the iron in your blood.' She takes a pinprick of blood from the pad of his finger. 'Blood is tested later for diseases and STDs.'

'Must be handy for checking up on boyfriends,' he jokes, feeling sweat tickle his upper lip. He studies his finger.

She quietens as she carries out the quick test.

Justin lies supine on a cushioned bench and extends his left arm. Sarah wraps a pressure cuff around his upper arm, making the veins more prominent, and she disinfects his inner elbow.

Don't look at the needle, don't look at the needle.

He looks at the needle and the ground swirls beneath him. His throat tightens.

'Is this going to hurt?' Justin swallows hard as his shirt clings to his saturated back.

'Just a little sting,' she smiles, approaching him with a cannula in her hand.

He smells her sweet perfume and it distracts him momentarily. As she leans over, he sees down her V-neck sweater. A black lace bra.

'I want you to take this in your hand and squeeze it repeatedly.'

'What?' he laughs nervously.

'The ball,' she smiles.

'Oh.' He takes a small soft ball into his hand. 'What does this do?' His voice shakes.

'It's to help speed up the process.'

He pumps at top speed.

Sarah laughs. 'Not yet. And not that fast, Justin.'

Sweat rolls down his back. His hair sticks to his sticky forehead. *You should have gone for the haircut, Justin. What kind of a stupid idea was this—* 'Ouch.'

'That wasn't so bad, was it?' she says softly, as though talking to a child.

Justin's heart beats loudly in his ears. He pumps the ball in his hand to the rhythm of his heartbeat. He imagines his heart pumping the blood, the blood flowing through his veins. He sees it reach the needle, go through the tube and he waits to feel faint. But the dizziness never comes and so he watches his blood run through the tube and down under the bed into the collection bag she has thoughtfully hidden below the bed on a scale.

'Do I get a KitKat after this?'

She laughs. 'Of course.'

'And then we get to go for drinks or are you just using me for my body?'

'Drinks are fine, but I must warn you against doing anything strenuous today. Your body needs to recover.'

He catches sight of her lace bra again. *Yeah, sure.*

Fifteen minutes later, Justin looks at his pint of blood with pride. He doesn't want it to go to some stranger, he almost wants to bring it to the hospital himself, survey the wards and present it to someone he really cares about, someone special, for it's the first thing to come straight from his heart in a very long time.

Present Day

FIVE

I open my eyes slowly.

White light fills them. Slowly, objects come into focus and the white light fades. Orangey pink now. I move my eyes around. I'm in a hospital. A television high up on the wall. Green fills its screen. I focus more. Horses. Jumping and racing. Dad must be in the room. I lower my eyes and there he is with his back to me in an armchair. He thumps his fists lightly on the chair's arms, I see his tweed cap appearing and disappearing behind the back of the chair as he bounces up and down. The springs beneath him squeak.

The horse racing is silent. So is he. Like a silent movie being carried out before me, I watch him. I wonder if it's my ears that aren't allowing me to hear him. He springs out of his chair now faster than I've seen him move in a long time, and he raises his fist at the television, quietly urging his horse on.

The television goes black. His two fists open and he raises his hands up in the air, looks up to the ceiling and beseeches God. He puts his hands in his pockets, feels around and pulls the material out. They're empty and the pockets of his brown trousers hang inside out for all to see. He pats down his chest, feeling for money. Checks the small pocket of his brown cardigan. Grumbles. So it's not my ears.

He turns to feel around in his overcoat beside me and I shut my eyes quickly.

I'm not ready yet. Nothing has happened to me until they tell me. Last night will remain a nightmare in my mind until they tell me it was true. The longer I close my eyes, the longer everything remains as it was. The bliss of ignorance.

I hear him rooting around in his overcoat, I hear change rattling and I hear the clunk as the coins fall into the television. I risk opening my eyes again and there he is back in his armchair, cap bouncing up and down, pounding his fists against the air.

My curtain is closed to my right but I can tell I share a room with others. I don't know how many. It's quiet. There's no air in the room; it's stuffy with stale sweat. The giant windows that take up the entire wall to my left are closed. The light is so bright I can't see out. I allow my eyes to adjust and finally I see. A bus stop across the road. A woman waits by the stop, shopping bags by her feet and on her hip sits a baby, bare chubby legs bouncing in the Indian summer sun. I look away immediately. Dad is watching me. He is leaning out over the side of the armchair, twisting his head around, like a child from his cot.

'Hi, love.'

'Hi.' I feel I haven't spoken for such a long time, and I expect to croak. But I don't. My voice is pure, pours out like honey. Like nothing's happened. But nothing has happened. Not yet. Not until they tell me.

With both hands on the arms of the chair he slowly pulls himself up. Like a seesaw, he makes his way over to the side of the bed. Up and down, down and up. He was born with a leg length discrepancy, his left leg longer than his right. Despite the special shoes he was given in later years, he still sways, the motion instilled in him since he learned to walk. He hates wearing those shoes and, despite our warnings and his back pains, he goes back to what he knows. I'm so used to the sight of his body going up and down, down and up. I recall as a child holding his hand and going for walks. How my arm would move in perfect rhythm with him. Being pulled up as he stepped down on his right leg, being pushed down as he stepped on his left.

He was always so strong. Always so capable. Always fixing things. Lifting things, mending things. Always with a screwdriver in his hand, taking things apart and putting them back together – remote controls, radios, alarm clocks, plugs. A handyman for the entire street. His legs were uneven, but his hands, always and for ever, steady as a rock.

He takes his cap off as he nears me, clutches it with both hands, moves it around in circles like a steering wheel as he watches me with concern. He steps onto his right leg and down he goes. Bends his left leg. His position of rest.

'Are you . . . em . . . they told me that . . . eh.' He clears his throat. 'They told me to . . .' He swallows hard and his thick messy eyebrows furrow and hide his glassy eyes. 'You lost . . . you lost, em . . .'

My lower lip trembles.

His voice breaks when he speaks again. 'You lost a lot of blood, Joyce. They . . .' He lets go of his cap with one hand and makes circular motions with his crooked finger, trying to remember. 'They did a transfusion of the blood thingy on you so you're em . . . you're OK with your bloods now.'

My lower lip still trembles and my hands automatically go to my belly, not long enough gone to even show swelling under the blankets. I look to him hopefully, only realising now how much I am still holding on, how much I have convinced myself the awful incident in the labour room was all a terrible nightmare. Perhaps I imagined my baby's silence that filled the room in that final moment. Perhaps there were cries that I just didn't hear. Of course it's possible – by that stage I had little energy and was fading away – maybe I just didn't hear

40

the first little miraculous breath of life that everybody else witnessed.

Dad shakes his head sadly. No, it had been me that had made those screams instead.

My lip trembles more now, bounces up and down and I can't stop it. My body shakes terribly and I can't stop it either. The tears; they well, but I stop them from falling. If I start now I know I will never stop.

I'm making a noise. An unusual noise I've never heard before. Groaning. Grunting. A combination of both. Dad grabs my hand and holds it hard. The feel of his skin brings me back to last night, me lying at the end of the stairs. He doesn't say anything. But what can a person say? I don't even know.

I doze in and out. I wake and remember a conversation with a doctor and wonder if it was a dream. Lost your baby, Joyce, we did all we could . . . blood transfusion . . . Who needs to remember something like that? No one. Not me.

When I wake again the curtain beside me has been pulled open. There are three small children running around, chasing one another around the bed while their father, I assume, calls to them to stop in a language I don't recognise. Their mother, I assume, lies in bed. She looks tired. We catch eyes and smile at one another.

I know how you feel, her sad smile says, I know how you feel.

What are we going to do? my smile says back to her.

I don't know, her eyes say. I don't know.

Will we be OK?

She turns her head away from me, her smile gone.

Dad calls over to them. 'Where are you lot from then?'

'Excuse me?' her husband asks.

'I said where are you lot from then?' Dad repeats. 'Not from around here, I see.' Dad's voice is cheery and pleasant. No insults intended. No insults ever intended.

'We are from Nigeria,' the man responds.

'Nigeria,' Dad replies. 'Where would that be then?'

'In Africa.' The man's tone is pleasant too. Just an old man starved of conversation, trying to be friendly, he realises.

'Ah, Africa. Never been there myself. Is it hot there? I'd say it is. Hotter than here. Get a good tan, I'd say, not that you need it,' he laughs. 'Do you get cold here?'

'Cold?' the African smiles.

'Yes, you know.' Dad wraps his arms around his body and pretends to shiver. 'Cold?'

'Yes,' the man laughs. 'Sometimes I do.'

'Thought so. I do too and I'm from here,' Dad explains. 'The chill gets right into my bones. But I'm not a great one for heat either. Skin goes red, just burns. My daughter, Joyce, goes brown. That's her over there.' He points at me and I close my eyes quickly.

'A lovely daughter,' the man says politely.

'Ah, she is.' Silence while I assume they watch me. 'She was on one of those Spanish islands a few months back and came back black, she did. Well, not as black as you, you know, but she got a fair ol' tan on her. Peeled, though. You probably don't peel.'

The man laughs politely. That's Dad. Never means any harm but has never left the country in his entire life. A fear of flying holds him back. Or so he says.

'Anyway, I hope your lovely lady feels better soon. It's an awful thing to be sick on your holliers.'

With that I open my eyes.

'Ah, welcome back, love. I was just talking to these nice neighbours of ours.' He seesaws up to me again, his cap in his hands. Rests on his right leg, goes down, bends his left leg. 'You know I think we're the only Irish people in this hospital. The nurse that was here a minute ago, she's from Sing-a-song or someplace like that.'

'Singapore, Dad,' I smile.

'That's it.' He raises his eyebrows. 'You met her already, did you? They all speak English, though, the foreigners do. Sure, isn't that better than being on your holidays and having to do all that signed-languagey stuff.' He puts his cap down on the bed and wiggles his fingers around.

43

'Dad,' I smile, 'you've never been out of the country in your life.'

'Haven't I heard the lads at the Monday Club talking about it? Frank was away in that place last week – oh, what's that place?' He shuts his eyes and thinks hard. 'The place where they make the chocolates?'

'Switzerland.'

'No.'

'Belgium.'

'No,' he says, frustrated now. 'The little round ball-y things all crunchy inside. You can get the white ones now but I prefer the original dark ones.'

'Maltesers?' I laugh, but feel pain and stop.

'That's it. He was in Maltesers.'

'Dad, it's Malta.'

'That's it. He was in Malta.' He is silent. 'Do they make Maltesers?'

'I don't know. Maybe. So what happened to Frank in Malta?'

He squeezes his eyes shut again and thinks. 'I can't remember what I was about to say now.'

Silence. He hates not being able to remember. He used to remember everything.

'Did you make any money on the horses?' I ask.

'A few bob. Enough for a few rounds at the Monday Club tonight.'

'But today is Tuesday.'

'It's on a Tuesday on account of the bank holiday,' he explains, seesawing around to the other side of the bed to sit down.

44

I can't laugh. I'm too sore and it seems some of my sense of humour was taken away with my child.

'You don't mind if I go, do you, Joyce? I'll stay if you want, I really don't mind, it's not important.'

'Of course it's important. You haven't missed a Monday night for twenty years.'

'Apart from bank holidays!' He lifts a crooked finger and his eyes dance.

'Apart from bank holidays,' I smile, and grab his finger.

'Well,' he takes my hand, 'you're more important than a few pints and a singsong.'

'What would I do without you?' My eyes fill again.

'You'd be just fine, love. Besides . . .' he looks at me warily, 'you have Conor.'

I let go of his hand and look away. What if I don't want Conor any more?

'I tried to call him last night on the hand phone but there was no answer. But maybe I tried the numbers wrong,' he adds quickly. 'There are so many more numbers on the hand phones.'

'Mobiles, Dad,' I say distractedly.

'Ah, yes. The mobiles. He keeps calling when you're asleep. He's going to come home as soon as he can get a flight. He's very worried.'

'That's nice of him. Then we can get down to the business of spending the next ten years of our married life trying to have babies.' Back to business. A nice little distraction to give our relationship some sort of meaning.

'Ah now, love . . .'

The first day of the rest of my life and I'm not sure I want to be here. I know I should be thanking somebody for this but I really don't feel like it. Instead I wish they hadn't bothered.

SIX

I watch the three children playing together on the floor of the hospital, little fingers and toes, chubby cheeks and plump lips – the faces of their parents clearly etched on theirs. My heart drops into my stomach and it twists. My eyes fill again and I have to look away.

'Mind if I have a grape?' Dad chirps. He's like a little canary swinging in a cage beside me.

'Of course you can. Dad, you should go home now, go get something to eat. You need your energy.'

He picks up a banana. 'Potassium,' he smiles, and moves his arms rigorously. 'I'll be jogging home tonight.'

'How did you get here?' It suddenly occurs to me that he hasn't been into the city for years. It all became too fast for him, buildings suddenly sprouting up where there weren't any, roads with traffic going in different directions from before. With great sadness he sold his car too, his failing eyesight too much of a danger for him and others on the roads. Seventy-five years old, his wife dead ten years. Now he has a routine of his own, content to stay around the local area, chatting to his neighbours, church every Sunday and Wednesday, Monday Club every Monday (apart from the bank holidays when it's on a Tuesday), butchers on a Tuesday, his crosswords, puzzles and TV shows during the days, his garden all the moments in between.

'Fran from next door drove me in.' He puts the banana down, still laughing to himself about his jogging joke, and pops another grape into his mouth. 'Almost had me killed two or three times. Enough to let me know there is a God if ever there was a time I doubted. I asked for seedless grapes; these aren't seedless,' he frowns. Liver-spotted hands put the bunch back on the side cabinet. He takes seeds out of his mouth and looks around for a bin.

'Do you still believe in your God now, Dad?' It comes out crueller than I mean to but the anger is almost unbearable.

'I do believe, Joyce.' As always, no offence taken. He puts the pips in his handkerchief and places it back in his pocket. 'The Lord acts in mysterious ways, in ways we often can neither explain nor understand, tolerate nor bear. I understand how you can question Him now – we all do at times. When your mother died I . . .' he trails off and abandons the sentence as always, the furthest he will go to being disloyal about his God, the furthest he will go to discussing the loss of his wife. 'But this time God answered all my prayers. He sat up and heard me calling last night. He said to me,' Dad puts on a broad Cavan accent, the accent he had as a child before moving to Dublin in his teens, '"No problem, Henry. I hear you loud and clear. It's all in hand so don't you be worrying. I'll do this for you, no bother at all." He saved you. He kept my girl alive and for that I'll be forever grateful to Him, sad as we may be about the passing of another.'

I have no response to that, but I soften.

He pulls his chair closer to my bedside and it screeches along the floor.

'And I believe in an afterlife,' he says a little quieter now. 'That I do. I believe in the paradise of heaven, up there in the clouds, and everyone that was once here is up there. Including the sinners, for God's a forgiver, that I believe.'

'Everyone?' I fight the tears. I fight them from falling. If I start I know I will never stop. 'What about my baby, Dad? Is my baby there?'

He looks pained. We hadn't spoken much about my pregnancy. Early days and we were all worried, nobody more than he. Only days ago we'd had a minor falling-out over my asking him to store our spare bed in his garage. I had started to prepare the nursery, you see . . . Oh dear, the nursery. The spare bed and junk just cleared out. The cot already purchased. Pretty yellow on the walls. 'Buttercup Dream' with a little duckie border.

Five months to go. Some people, my father included, would think preparing the nursery at four months is premature but we'd been waiting six years for a baby, for this baby. Nothing premature about that.

'Ah, love, you know I don't know . . .'

'I was going to call him Sean if it was a boy,' I hear myself finally say aloud. I have been saying these things in my head all day, over and over, and here they are, spilling out of me instead of the tears.

'Ah, that's a nice name. Sean.'

'Grace, if it was a girl. After Mum. She would have liked that.'

His jaw sets at this and he looks away. Anyone who doesn't know him would think this has angered him. I know this is not the case. I know it's the emotion gathering in his jaw, like a giant reservoir, storing and locking it all away until absolutely necessary, waiting for those rare moments when the drought within him calls for those walls to break and for the emotions to gush.

'But for some reason I thought it was a boy. I don't know why but I just felt it somehow. I could have been wrong. I was going to call him Sean,' I repeat.

Dad nods. 'That's right. A fine name.'

'I used to talk to him. Sing to him. I wonder if he heard.' My voice is far away. I feel like I'm calling out from the hollow of a tree, where I hide.

Silence while I imagine a future that will never be with little imaginary Scan. Of singing to him every night, of marshmallow skin and splashes at bath time. Of kicking legs and bicycle rides. Of sandcastle architecture and football-related hot-headed tantrums. Anger at a missed life – no, worse – a lost life, overrides my thoughts.

'I wonder if he even knew.'

'Knew what, love?'

'What was happening. What he would be missing. Did he think I was sending him away? I hope he doesn't blame me. I was all he had and—' I stop. Torture over for now. I feel seconds away from screaming with such terror, I must stop. If I start my tears now I know I will never stop.

'Where is he now, Dad? How can you even die when you haven't even been born yet?'

'Ah, love.' He takes my hand and squeezes it again.

'Tell me.'

This time he thinks about it. Long and hard. He pats my hair, with steady fingers takes the strands from my face and tucks them behind my ears. He hasn't done that since I was a little girl.

'I think he's in heaven, love. Oh, there's no thinking involved – I know so. He's up there with your mother, yes he is. Sitting on her lap while she plays rummy with Pauline, robbing her blind and cackling away. She's up there all right.' He looks up and wags his forefinger at the ceiling.

51

'Now you take care of baby Sean for us, Gracie, you hear? She'll be tellin' him all about you, she will, about when you were a baby, about the day you took your first steps, about the day you got your first tooth. She'll tell him about your first day of school and your last day of school and every day in between, and he'll know all about you so that when you walk through those gates up there, as an old woman far older than me now, he'll look up from rummy and say, "Ah, there she is now. The woman herself. My mammy." Straight away he'll know.'

The lump in my throat, so huge I can barely swallow, prevents me from saying the thank you I want to express, but perhaps he sees it in my eyes as he nods in acknowledgement and then turns his attention back to the TV while I stare out the window at nothing.

'There's a nice chapel here, love. Maybe you should go visit, when you're good and ready. You don't even have to say anything, He won't mind. Just sit there and think. I find it helpful.'

I think it's the last place in the world I want to be.

'It's a nice place to be,' Dad says, reading my mind. He watches me and I can almost hear him praying for me to leap out of bed and grab the rosary beads he's placed by the bedside.

'It's a rococo building, you know,' I say suddenly, and have no idea what I'm talking about.

'What is?' Dad's eyebrows furrow and his eyes

disappear underneath, like two ____ ____ into their shells. 'This hospital?'

I think hard. 'What were we talki____

Then he thinks hard. 'Maltesers. No!

He's silent for a moment, then starts answ____ as though in a quick-fire round of a quiz.

'Bananas! No. Heaven! No. The chapel! We were talking about the chapel.' He flashes a million-dollar smile, jubilant he succeeded in remembering the conversation of less than one minute ago. He goes further now. 'And then you said it's a rickety building. But honestly it felt fine to me. A bit old but, sure, there's nothin' wrong with being old and rickety.' He winks at me.

'The chapel is a *rococo* building, not rickety,' I correct him, feeling like a teacher. 'It's famous for the elaborate stucco work which adorns the ceiling. It's the work of French stuccadore, Barthelemy Cramillion.'

'Is that so, love? When did he do that, then?' He moves his chair in closer to the bed. Loves nothing more than a *scéal*.

'In 1762.' So precise. So random. So natural. So inexplicable that I know it.

'That long? I didn't know the hospital was here since then.'

'It's been here since 1757,' I reply, and then frown. How on earth do I know that? But I can't stop myself, almost like my mouth is on autopilot, completely unattached to my brain. 'It was designed by the same man who did Leinster House.

53

Cassells was his name. One of the most famous architects of the time.'

'I've heard of him, all right,' Dad lies. 'If you'd said Dick I'd have known straight away.' He chuckles.

'It was Bartholomew Mosse's brainchild,' I explain and I don't know where the words are coming from, don't know where the knowledge is coming from. From where else, I don't know. Like a feeling of *déjà vu* – these words, this feeling is familiar but I haven't heard them or spoken them in this hospital. I think maybe I'm making it up but I know somewhere deep inside that I'm correct. A warm feeling floods my body.

'In 1745 he purchased a small theatre called the New Booth and he converted it into Dublin's first lying-in hospital.'

'It stood here, did it? The theatre?'

'No, it was on George's Lane. This was all just fields. But eventually that became too small and he bought the fields that were here, consulted with Richard Cassells and in 1757 the new lying-in hospital, now known as the Rotunda, was opened by the Lord Lieutenant. On the eighth of December, if I recall correctly.'

Dad is confused. 'I didn't know you had an interest in that kind of thing, Joyce. How do you know all that?'

I frown. I didn't know I knew that either. Suddenly frustration overwhelms me and I shake my head aggressively.

'I want a haircut,' I add angrily, blowing my fringe off my forehead. 'I want to get out of here.'

'OK, love.' Dad's voice is quiet. 'A little longer, is all.'

SEVEN

Get a haircut! Justin blows his fringe out of his eyes and glares with dissatisfaction at his reflection in the mirror.

Until his image caught his eye, he was packing his bag to go back to London while whistling the happy tune of a recently divorced man who'd just been laid by the first woman since his wife. Well, the second time that year, but the first that he could recall with some small degree of pride. Now, standing before the full-length mirror, his whistling stalls, the image of his Fabio self failing miserably against the reality. He corrects his posture, sucks in his cheeks and flexes his muscles, vowing that now that the divorce cloud has lifted, he will get his body back in order. Forty-three years old, he is handsome and he knows it, but it's not a view that is held with arrogance. His opinions on his looks are merely understood with the same logic he applies to tasting a fine wine. The grape was merely grown in the right place, under the right conditions. Some degree of nurturing and love mixed with later moments of being completely trampled on and walked all over. He possesses the common sense enabling him to recognise he was born with good genes and features that were in proportion, in the right places. He should be neither praised nor blamed for this just as a less attractive person should not be viewed with flared nostrils and a media-obsessed induced smirk. It's just how it is.

At almost six feet, he is tall, his shoulders broad, his hair still thick and chestnut brown, though greying at the sides. This he does not mind, he's had grey hairs since his twenties and has always felt they give him a distinguished look. Though there were some, afraid of the very nature of life, that viewed his salt-and-pepper sideburns as a thorn that would burst the bubble of their pretend life every time he was in their presence. They would come at him, bowing over and hunchbacked, and taking on the appearance of a sixteenth-century black-toothed tramp, thrusting hair dye at him as though it were a carafe of precious water from the fountain of eternal life.

For Justin, moving on and change are what he expects. He is not one for pausing, for becoming stuck in life, though he didn't expect his particular philosophy of ageing and greying to apply to his marriage. Jennifer left him two years ago to ponder this, though not just this, but for a great many other reasons too. So many, in fact, he wishes he had taken out a pen and notepad and listed them as she bellowed at him in her tirade of hate. In the initial dark lonely nights that followed, Justin held the bottle of dye in his hand and wondered if he gave in to his solid tight philosophy, would he make things all right? Would he wake up in the morning and Jennifer be in their bed; would the light scar on his chin have healed from where the wedding ring had landed; would the list of things about him she hated so much be the very things she loved? He sobered up then and emptied the dye down his rented accommodation kitchen sink, blackened stainless steel that proved a reminder to him everyday of his decision to stay rooted in reality, until he moved to London to be closer to his daughter, much to his ex-wife's disgust.

Through strands of his long fringe hanging over his eyes, he has a vision of the man he expects to see. Leaner, younger, perhaps with fewer wrinkles around the eyes. Any faults, such as the expanding waistline, are partly due to age and partly of his own doing, because he took to beer and takeaways for comfort during his divorce process rather than walking or the occasional jog.

Repeated flashbacks of the previous night draw his eyes back to the bed, where he and Sarah finally got to know one another intimately. All day he definitely felt like the big man on campus and he was just seconds away from interrupting his talk on Dutch and Flemish painting to give details of his previous night's performance.

First-year students in the midst of Rag Week, only three-quarters of the class had shown up after the previous night's foam party and those that were in attendance he was sure wouldn't notice if he launched into a detailed analysis of his lovemaking skills. He didn't test his assumptions, all the same.

Blood For Life Week is over, much to Justin's relief, and Sarah has moved on from the college, back to her base. On his return to Dublin this month he coincidentally bumped into her in a bar, that he just happened to know she frequented, and they went from there. He wasn't sure if he would see her again though his inside jacket pocket was safely padded with her number.

He has to admit that while the previous night was indeed delightful – a few too many bottles of Château Olivier, which, until last night he's always found disappointing despite its ideal location in Bordeaux, in a lively bar on the Green, followed by a trip to his hotel room – he feels much was missing from his conquest. He acquired some Dutch courage from his hotel mini-bar before calling round to see her, and by the time he arrived, he was already incapable of serious conversation or, more seriously, incapable of conversation – *Oh, for Christ's sake, Justin, what man do you know cares about the damn conversation?* But, despite ending up in his bed, he feels that Sarah did care about the conversation. He feels that perhaps there were things she wanted to say to him and perhaps did say while he saw those sad blue eyes boring into his and her rosebud lips opening and closing, but his Jameson whiskey wouldn't allow him to hear, instead singing over her words in his head like a petulant child.

With his second seminar in two months complete, Justin throws his clothes into his bag, happy to see the back of his miserable musty room. Friday afternoon, time to fly back to London. Back to his daughter, and his younger brother, Al, and sister-in-law, Doris, visiting from Chicago. He departs the hotel, steps out onto the cobbled side streets of Temple Bar and into his waiting taxi.

'The airport, please.'

'Here on holidays?' the driver asks immediately.

'No.' Justin looks out the window, hoping this will end the conversation.

'Working?' The driver starts the engine.

'Yes.'

'Where do you work?'

'A college.'

'Which one?'

Justin sighs. 'Trinity.'

'You the janitor?' Those green eyes twinkle playfully at him in the mirror.

'I'm a lecturer on Art and Architecture,' he says defensively, folding his arms and blowing his floppy fringe from his eyes.

'Architecture, huh? I used to be a builder.'

Justin doesn't respond and hopes the conversation will end there.

'So where are ye off to? Off on holiday?'

'Nope.'

'What is it then?

'I live in London.' *And my US social security number is . . .*

'And you work here?'

'Yep.'

'Would you not just live here?'

'Nope.'

'Why's that then?'

'Because I'm a guest lecturer here. A previous colleague of mine invited me to give a seminar once a month.'

'Ah.' The driver smiles at him in the mirror as though he'd been trying to fool him. 'So what do you do in London?' His eyes interrogate him.

I'm a serial killer who preys on inquisitive cab drivers.

'Lots of different things.' Justin sighs and caves in as the driver waits for more. 'I'm the editor of the *Art and Architectural Review*, the only truly international art and architectural publication,' he says proudly. 'I started it ten years ago and still we're unrivalled. Highest selling magazine of its kind.' *Twenty thousand subscribers, you liar.*

There's no reaction.

'I'm also a curator.'

The driver winces. 'You've to touch dead bodies?'

Justin scrunches his face in confusion. 'What? No.' Then adds unnecessarily, 'I'm also a regular panelist on a BBC art and culture show.'

Twice in five years doesn't quite constitute regular, Justin. Oh, shut up.

The driver studies Justin now, in the rearview mirror. 'You're on TV?' He narrows his eyes. 'I don't recognise you.'

'Well, do you watch the show?'

'No.'

Well, then.

Justin rolls his eyes. He throws off his suit jacket, opens another of his shirt buttons and lowers the window. His hair sticks to his forehead. Still. A few weeks have gone by and he still hasn't been to the barber. He blows his fringe out of his eyes.

They stop at a red light and Justin looks to his left. A hair salon.

'Hey, would you mind pulling over on the left just for a few minutes?'

'Look, Conor, don't worry about it. Stop apologising,' I say into the phone tiredly. He exhausts me. Every little word with him drains me. 'Dad is here with me now and we're going to get a taxi to the house together, even though I'm perfectly capable of sitting in a car by myself.'

Outside the hospital, Dad holds the door open for me and I climb into the taxi. Finally I'm going home but I don't feel the relief I was hoping for. There's nothing but dread. I dread meeting people I know and having to explain what has happened, over and over again. I dread walking into my house and having to face the half-decorated nursery. I dread having to get rid of the nursery, having to replace it with a spare bed and filling the wardrobes with my own overflow of shoes and bags I'll never wear. As though a bedroom for them alone is as good a replacement as a child. I dread having to go to work instead of taking the leave I had planned. I dread seeing Conor. I dread going back to a loveless marriage with no baby to distract us. I dread living every day of the rest of my life while Conor drones on and on down the phone about wanting to be here for me, when it seems my telling him *not* to come home has been my mantra for the past few days. I know it would be common sense for me to want my husband to come rushing home to me – in fact, for my husband to want to come rushing home to me – but there are many buts in our marriage and this *incident* is not a regular normal occurrence. It deserves outlandish behaviour. To behave the right way, to do the adult thing feels wrong to me because I don't want anybody around me. I've been poked and prodded psychologically and physically. I want to be on my own to grieve. I want to feel sorry for myself without sympathetic words and clinical explanations. I want to be illogical, self-pitying, self-examining, bitter and lost for just a few more days, please, world, and I want to do it alone.

Though that is not unusual in our marriage.

Conor's an engineer. He travels abroad to work for months before coming home for one month and going off again. I used to get so used to my own company and routine that for the first week of him being home I'd be irritable and wish he'd go back. That changed over time, of course. Now that irritability stretches to the entire month of him being home. And it's become glaringly obvious I'm not alone in that feeling.

When Conor took the job all those years ago, it was difficult being away from one another for so long. I used to visit him as much as I could but it was difficult to keep taking time off work. The visits got shorter, rarer, then stopped.

I always thought our marriage could survive anything as long as we both tried. But then I found myself having to try to try. I dug beneath the new layers of complexities we'd created over the years to get to the beginning of the relationship. What was it, I wondered, that we had then that we could revive? What was the thing that could make two people want to promise one another to spend every day of the rest of their lives together? Ah, I found it. It was a thing called love. A small simple word. If only it didn't mean so much, our marriage would be flawless.

My mind has wandered much while lying in that hospital bed. At times it has stalled in its wandering, like when entering a room and then forgetting what for. It stands alone dumbstruck. At those times it has been numb, and when staring at the pink walls I have thought of nothing but of the fact that I am staring at pink walls.

My mind has bounced from numbness to feeling too much, but on an occasion while wandering far, I dug deep to find a memory of when I was six years old and I had a favourite tea set given to me by my grandmother Betty. She kept it in her house for me to play with when I called over on Saturdays, and during the afternoons when my grandmother was 'taking tea' with her friends I would dress in one of my mother's pretty dresses from when she was a child and have afternoon tea with Aunt Jemima, the cat. The dresses never quite fit but I wore them all the same, and Aunt Jemima and I never did take to tea but we were both polite enough to keep up the pretence until my parents came to collect me at the end of the day. I told this story to Conor a few years ago and he laughed, missing the point.

It was an easy point to miss – I won't hold him accountable for that – but what my mind was shouting at him to understand was that I've increasingly found that people never truly tire of playing games and dressing up, no matter how many years pass. Our lies now are just more sophisticated; our words to deceive, more eloquent. From cowboys and Indians, doctors and nurses, to husband and wife, we've never stopped pretending. Sitting in the taxi beside Dad, while listening to Conor over the phone, I realise I've stopped pretending.

'Where is Conor?' Dad asks as soon as I've hung up.

He opens the top button of his shirt and loosens

his tie. He dresses in a shirt and tie every time he leaves his house, never forgets his cap. He looks for the handle on the car door, to roll the window down.

'It's electronic, Dad. There's the button. He's still in Japan. He'll be home in a few days.'

'I thought he was coming back yesterday.' He puts the window all the way down and is almost blown away. His cap topples off his head and the few strands of hair left on his head stick up. He fixes the cap back on his head, has a mini battle with the button before finally figuring out how to leave a small gap at the top for air to enter the stuffy taxi.

'Ha! Gotcha,' he smiles victoriously, thumping his fist at the window.

I wait until he's finished fighting with the window to answer. 'I told him not to.'

'You told who what, love?'

'Conor. You were asking about Conor, Dad.'

'Ah, that's right, I was. Home soon, is he?'

I nod.

The day is hot and I blow my fringe up from my sticky forehead. I feel my hair sticking to the back of my clammy neck. Suddenly it feels heavy and greasy on my head. Brown and scraggy, it weighs me down and once again I have the over-whelming urge to shave it all off. I become agitated in my seat and Dad, sensing it again, knows not to say anything. I've been doing that all week: experiencing anger beyond comprehension, so that

I want to drive my fists through the walls and punch the nurses. Then I become weepy and feel such loss inside me it's as if I'll never be filled again. I prefer the anger. Anger is better. Anger is hot and filling and gives me something to cling on to.

We stop at a set of traffic lights and I look to my left. A hair salon.

'Pull over here, please.'

'What are you doing, Joyce?'

'Wait in the car, Dad. I'll be ten minutes. I'm just going to get a quick haircut. I can't take it any more.'

Dad looks at the salon and then to the taxi driver and they both know not to say anything. The taxi directly in front of us indicates and moves over to the side of the road too. We pull up behind it.

A man ahead of us gets out of the car and I freeze with one foot out of the car, to watch him. He's familiar and I think I know him. He pauses and looks at me. We stare at one another for a while. Search each other's face. He scratches at his left arm; something that holds my attention for far too long. The moment is unusual and goose bumps rise on my skin. The last thing I want is to see somebody I know, and I look away quickly.

He looks away from me too and begins to walk.

'What are you doing?' Dad asks far too loudly, and I finally get out of the car.

I start walking towards the hair salon and it

becomes clear that our destination is the same. My walk becomes mechanical, awkward, self-conscious. Something about him makes me disjointed. Unsettled. Perhaps it's the possibility of having to tell somebody there will be no baby. Yes, a month of non-stop baby talk and there will be no baby to show for it. Sorry, guys. I feel guilty for it, as though I've cheated my friends and family. The longest tease of all. A baby that will never be. My heart is twisted at the thought of it.

He holds open the door to the salon and smiles. Handsome. Fresh-faced. Tall. Broad. Athletic. Perfect. Is he glowing? I must know him.

'Thank you,' I say.

'You're welcome.'

We both pause, look at one another, back to the two identical taxis waiting for us by the pavement and back to one another. I think he's about to say something else but I quickly look away and step inside.

The salon is empty and two staff members are sitting down chatting. They are two men; one has a mullet, the other is bleached blond. They see us and spring to attention.

'Which one do you want?' the American says out of the side of his mouth.

'The blond,' I smile.

'The mullet it is then,' he says.

My mouth falls open but I laugh.

'Hello there, loves.' The mullet man approaches us. 'How can I help you?' He looks back and forth

69

from the American to me. 'Who is getting their hair done today?'

'Well, both of us, I assume, right?' American man looks at me and I nod.

'Oh, pardon me, I thought you were together.'

I realise we are so close our hips are almost touching. We both look down at our adjoined hips, then up to join eyes and then we both take one step away in the opposite direction.

'You two should try synchronised swimming,' the hairdresser laughs, but the joke dies when we fail to react. 'Ashley, you take the lovely lady. Now come with me.' He leads his client to a chair. The American makes a face at me while being led away and I laugh again.

'Right, I just want two inches off, please,' the American says. 'The last time I got it done they took, like, twenty off. Please, just two inches,' he stresses. 'I've got a taxi waiting outside to take me to the airport, so as quick as possible too, please.'

His hairdresser laughs. 'Sure, no problem. Are you going back to America?'

The man rolls his eyes. 'No, I'm not going to America, I'm not going on holiday and I'm not going to meet anyone at arrivals. I'm just going to take a flight. Away. Out of here. You Irish ask a lot of questions.'

'Do we?'

'Y—' he stalls and narrows his eyes at the hairdresser.

'Gotcha,' the hairdresser smiles, pointing the scissors at him.

'Yes you did.' Gritted teeth. 'You got me good.'

I chuckle aloud and he immediately looks at me. He seems slightly confused. Maybe we do know each other. Maybe he works with Conor. Maybe I went to school with him. Or college. Perhaps he's in the property business and I've worked with him. I can't have; he's American. Maybe I showed him a property. Maybe he's famous and I shouldn't be staring. I become embarrassed and I turn away again quickly.

My hairdresser wraps a black cape around me and I steal another glance at the man beside me, in the mirror. He looks at me. I look away, then back at him. He looks away. And our tennis match of glances is played out for the duration of our visit.

'So what will it be for you, madam?'

'All off,' I say, trying to avoid my reflection but I feel cold hands on the sides of my hot cheeks, raising my head, and I am forced to stare at myself face to face. There is something unnerving about being forced to look at yourself when you are unwilling to come to terms with something. Something raw and real that you can't run away from. You can lie to yourself, to your mind and in your mind all of the time but when you look yourself in the face, well, you know that you're lying. I am not OK. That, I did not hide from myself, and the truth of it stared me in the face. My cheeks are

71

sunken, small black rings below my eyes, red lines like eyeliner still sting from my night tears. But apart from that, I still look like me. Despite this huge change in my life, I look exactly the same. Tired, but me. I don't know what I'd expected. A totally changed woman, someone that people would look at and just know had been through a traumatic experience. Yet the mirror told me this: you can't know everything by looking at me. You can *never* know by looking at someone.

I'm five foot five, with medium-length hair that lands on my shoulders. My hair colour is midway between blonde and brown. I'm a medium kind of person. Not fat, not skinny; I exercise twice a week, jog a little, walk a little, swim a little. Nothing to excess, nothing not enough. Not obsessed, addicted to anything. I'm neither out-going nor shy, but a little of both, depending on my mood, depending on the occasion. I never overdo anything and enjoy most things I do. I'm seldom bored and rarely whine. When I drink I get tipsy but never fall over or get ill. I like my job, don't love it. I'm pretty, not stunning, not ugly; don't expect too much, am never too disappointed. I'm never overwhelmed or under it either; just nicely whelmed. I'm OK. Nothing spectacular but sometimes special. I look in the mirror and see this medium average person. A little tired, a little sad, but not falling apart. I look to the man beside me and I see the same.

'Excuse me?' the hairdresser breaks into my

thoughts. 'You want it *all* off? Are you sure? You've such healthy hair.' He runs his fingers through it. 'Is this your natural colour?'

'Yes, I used to put a little colour in it but I stopped because of the—' I'm about to say 'baby'. My eyes fill and I look down but he thinks I'm nodding to my stomach, which is hidden under the gown.

'Stopped because of what?' he asks.

I continue to look at my feet, pretend to be doing something with my foot. An odd shuffle manoeuvre. I can't think of anything to say to him and so I pretend not to hear him. 'Huh?'

'You were saying you stopped because of something?'

'Oh, em . . .' Don't cry. Don't cry. If you start now you will never stop. 'Oh, I don't know,' I mumble, bending over to play with my handbag on the ground. It will pass, it will pass. Someday it will all pass, Joyce. 'Chemicals. I stopped because of chemicals.'

'Right, this is what it'll look like,' he takes my hair and ties it back. 'How about we do a Meg Ryan in *French Kiss*?' He pulls hairs out in all directions and I look like I've stuck my fingers in an electric socket. 'It's the sexy messy bed-head look. Or else we can do this.' He messes about with my hair some more.

'Can we hurry this along? I've got a taxi waiting outside too.' I look out the window. Dad is chatting to the taxi driver. They're both laughing and I relax a little.

73

'O . . . K. Something like this really shouldn't be rushed. You have a lot of hair.'

'It's fine. I'm giving you permission to hurry. Just cut it all off.' I look back to the car.

'Well, we must leave a few inches on it, darling.' He directs my face back towards the mirror. 'We don't want Sigourney Weaver in *Aliens*, do we? No GI Janes allowed in this salon. We'll give you a side-swept fringe, very sophisticated, very now. It'll suit you, I think, show off those high cheekbones. What do you think?'

I don't care about my cheekbones. I want it all off.

'Actually, how about we just do this?' I take the scissors from his hand, cut my ponytail, and then hand them both back to him.

He gasps. But it sounds more like a squeak. 'Or we could do that. A . . . bob.'

American man's mouth hangs open at the sight of my hairdresser with a large pair of scissors and ten inches of hair dangling from his hand. He turns to his and grabs the scissors before he makes another cut. 'Do not,' he points, 'do *that* to me!'

Mullet man sighs and rolls his eyes. 'No, of course not, sir.'

The American starts scratching his left arm again. 'I must have got a bite.' He tries to roll up his shirtsleeve and I squirm in my seat, trying to get a look at his arm.

'Could you please sit still?'

'Could you please sit still?'

The hairdressers speak in perfect unison. They look to one another and laugh.

'Something funny in the air today,' one of them comments and American man and I look at one another. Funny, indeed.

'Eyes back to the mirror, please, sir.' He looks away.

My hairdresser places a finger under my chin and tips my face back to the centre. He hands me my ponytail.

'Souvenir.'

'I don't want it.' I refuse to take my hair in my hands. Every inch of that hair was from a moment that has now gone. Thoughts, wishes, hopes, desires, dreams that are no longer. I want a new start. A new head of hair.

He begins to shape it into style now and as each strand falls I watch it drift to the ground. My head feels lighter.

The hair that grew the day we bought the cot. Snip.

The hair that grew the day we picked the nursery paint colours, bottles, bibs and baby grows. All bought too soon, but we were so excited . . . Snip.

The hair that grew the day we decided the names. Snip.

The hair that grew the day we announced it to friends and family. Snip.

The day of the first scan. The day I found out I was pregnant. The day my baby was conceived. Snip. Snip. Snip.

75

The more painful recent memories will remain at the root for another little while. I will have to wait for them to grow until I can be rid of them too and then all traces will be gone and I will move on.

I reach the till as the American pays for his cut.

'That suits you,' he comments, studying me.

I go to tuck some hair behind my ear self-consciously but there's nothing there. I feel lighter, light-headed, delighted with giddiness, giddy with delight.

'So does yours.'

'Thank you.'

He opens the door for me.

'Thank you.' I step outside.

'You're far too polite,' he tells me.

'Thank you,' I smile. 'So are you.'

'Thank you,' he nods.

We laugh. We both gaze at our taxis queuing up waiting, and look back at one another curiously. He gives me a smile.

'The first taxi or the second taxi?' he asks.

'For me?'

He nods. 'My driver won't stop talking.'

I study both taxis, see Dad in the second, leaning forward and talking to the driver.

'The first. My dad won't stop talking.'

He studies the second taxi where Dad has now pushed his face up against the glass and is staring at me as though I'm an apparition.

'The second taxi it is, then,' the American says, and walks to his taxi, glancing back twice.

'Hey,' I protest, and watch him, entranced.

I float to my taxi and we both pull our doors closed at the same time. The taxi driver and Dad look at me like they've seen a ghost.

'What?' My heart beats wildly. 'What happened? Tell me?'

'Your hair,' Dad simply says, his face aghast. 'You're like a boy.'

EIGHT

As the taxi gets closer to my home in Phisboro, my stomach knots tighter.

'That was funny how the man in front kept his taxi waiting too, Gracie, wasn't it?'

'Joyce. And yes,' I reply, my leg bouncing with nerves.

'Is that what people do now when they get their hairs cut?'

'Do what, Dad?'

'Leave taxis waiting outside for them.'

'I don't know.'

He shuffles his bum to the edge of the seat and pulls himself closer to the taxi driver. 'I say, Jack, is that what people do when they go to the barbers now?'

'What's that?'

'Do they leave their taxis outside waiting for them?'

'I've never been asked to do it before,' the driver explains politely.

Dad sits back satisfied. 'That's what I thought, Gracie.'

'It's Joyce,' I snap.

'Joyce. It's a coincidence. And you know what they say about coincidences?'

'Yep.' We turn the corner onto my street and my stomach flips.

'That there's no such thing as a coincidence,' Dad finishes, even though I've already said yes. 'Indeedy no,' he says to himself. 'No such thing. There's Patrick,' he waves. 'I hope he doesn't wave back.' He watches his friend from the Monday Club with two hands on his walking-frame. 'And David out with the dog.' He waves again although David is stopping to allow his dog to poop and is looking the other way. I get the feeling Dad feels rather grand in a taxi. It's rare he's in one, the expense being too much and everywhere he needs to go being within walking distance or a short bus hop away.

'Home sweet home,' he announces. 'How much do I owe you, Jack?' He leans forward again. He takes two five-euro notes out of his pocket.

'The bad news, I'm afraid . . . twenty euro, please.'

'What?' Dad looks up in shock.

'I'll pay, Dad, put your money away.' I give the driver twenty-five and tell him to keep the change. Dad looks at me like I've just taken a pint out of his hand and poured it down the drain.

Conor and I have lived in the red-brick terraced

house in Phisboro since our marriage ten years ago. The houses have been here since the forties, and over the years we've pumped our money into modernising it. Finally it's how we want it, or it was until this week. A black railing encloses a small patch of a front garden where the rose bushes my mother planted preside. Dad lives in an identical house two streets away, the house I grew up in, though we're never done growing up, continually learning, and when I return to it I regress to my youth.

The front door to my house opens just as the taxi drives off. Dad's neighbour Fran smiles at me from my own front door. She looks at us awkwardly, failing to make eye contact with me each time she looks in my direction. I'll have to get used to this.

'Oh, your hair!' she says first, then gathers herself. 'I'm sorry, love, I meant to be out of here by the time you got home.' She opens the door fully and pulls a checked trolley-bag behind her. She is wearing a single Marigold glove on her right arm.

Dad looks nervous and avoids my eye.

'What were you doing, Fran? How on earth did you get into my house?' I try to be as polite as I can but the sight of someone in my house without my permission both surprises and infuriates me.

She pinks and looks to Dad. Dad looks at her hand and coughs. She looks down, laughs nervously and pulls off her single Marigold. 'Oh, your dad gave me a key. I thought that . . . well, I put down a nice rug in the hallway for you. I hope you like it.'

I stare at her with utter confusion.

'Never mind, I'll be off now.' She walks by me, grabs my arm and squeezes hard but still refuses to look at me. 'Take care of yourself, love.' She walks on down the road, dragging her trolley-bag behind her, her Nora Batty tights in rolls around her thick ankles.

'Dad,' I look at him angrily, 'what the hell is this?' I push into the house, looking at the disgusting dusty rug on my beige carpet. 'Why did you give a near-stranger my house keys so she could come in and leave a rug? I am not a charity!'

He takes off his cap and scrunches it in his hands. 'She's not a stranger, love. She's known you since the day you were brought home from the hospital—'

Wrong story to tell at this moment, and he knows it.

'I don't care!' I splutter. 'It's *my* house, not yours! You cannot just do that. I hate this ugly piece of shit rug!' I pick up one side of the clashing carpet, I drag it outside and then slam the door shut. I'm fuming and I look at Dad to shout at him again. He is pale and shaken. He is looking at the floor sadly. My eyes follow his.

Various shades of faded brown stains, like red wine, splatter the beige carpet. It has been cleaned in some places but the carpet hairs have been brushed in the opposite direction and give away that something once lay there. My blood.

I put my head in my hands.

Dad's voice is quiet, injured. 'I thought it would be best for you to come home with that gone.'

'Oh, Dad.'

'Fran has been here for a little while everyday now and has tried different things on it. It was me that suggested the rug,' he adds in a smaller voice. 'You can't blame her for that.'

I despise myself.

'I know you like all the nice new matching things in your house,' he looks around, 'but Fran or I wouldn't have the likes of that.'

'I'm sorry, Dad. I don't know what came over me. I'm sorry I shouted at you. You've been nothing but helpful this week. I'll . . . I'll call around to Fran at some stage and thank her properly.'

'Right,' he nods, 'I'll leave you at it, so. I'll bring the rug back to Fran. I don't want any of the neighbours seeing it outside on the path and telling her so.'

'No, I'll put it back where it was. It's too heavy for you to bring all the way around. I'll keep it for the time being and return it to her soon.' I open the front door and retrieve it from the outside path. I drag it back into the house with more respect, laying it down so that it hides the scene where I lost my baby.

'I'm so sorry, Dad.'

'Don't worry.' He seesaws up to me and pats

my shoulder. 'You're having a hard time, that I know. I'm only round the corner if you need me for anything.'

With a flick of his wrist, his tweed cap is on his head and I watch him seesaw down the road. The movement is familiar and comforting, like the motion of the sea. He disappears round the corner and I close the door. Alone. Silence. Just me and the house. Life continues as though nothing has happened.

It seems as though the nursery upstairs vibrates through the walls and floor. Thump-thump. Thump-thump. As though like a heart, it's trying to push out the walls and send blood flowing down the stairs, through the hallways to reach every little nook and cranny. I walk away from the stairs, the scene of the crime, and wander around the rooms. It appears everything is exactly as it was, though on further inspection I see that Fran has tidied around. The cup of tea I was drinking is gone from the coffee table in the living room. The galley kitchen hums with the sound of the dishwasher Fran has set. The taps and draining boards glisten, the surfaces are gleaming. Straight through the kitchen the door leads to the back garden. My mum's rose bushes line the back wall. Dad's geraniums peep up from the soil.

Upstairs the nursery still throbs.

I notice the red light on the answering machine in the hall flashing. Four messages. I flick through the list of registered phone numbers and recognise friends' numbers. I leave the answering machine, not able to listen to their condolences quite yet. Then I freeze. I go back. I flick through the list again. There it is. Monday evening. 7.10 p.m. Again at 7.12 p.m. My second chance to take the call. The call I had foolishly rushed down the stairs for and sacrificed my child's life.

They have left a message. With shaking fingers, I press play.

'Hello, this is Xtra-vision, Phisboro calling about the DVD *The Muppet Christmas Carol*. It says on our system that it's one week late. We'd appreciate it if you could return it as soon as possible, please.'

I inhale sharply. Tears spring in my eyes. What did I expect? A phone call worthy of losing my baby? Something so urgent that I was right to rush for it? Would that somehow warrant my loss?

My entire body trembles with rage and shock. Breathing in shakily, I make my way into the living room. I look straight ahead to the DVD player. On top, is the DVD I rented while minding my goddaughter. I reach for the DVD, hold it tightly in my hands, squeeze it as though I can stop the life in it. Then I throw it hard across the room. It knocks our collection of photographs off the top of the piano, cracking the glass on our wedding photo, chipping the silver coating of another.

I open my mouth. And I scream. I scream at the top of my lungs, the loudest I can possibly go. It's deep and low and filled with anguish. I scream again and hold it for as long as I can. One scream after another from the pit of my stomach, from the depths of my heart. I let out deep howls that border on laughter, that are laced with frustration. I scream and I scream until I am out of breath and my throat burns.

Upstairs, the nursery continues to vibrate. Thump-thump, thump-thump. It beckons me, the heart of my home beating wildly. I go to the staircase, step over the rug and onto the stairs. I grab the banister, feeling too weak even to lift my legs. I pull myself upstairs. The thumping gets louder and louder with every step until I reach the top and face the nursery door. It stops throbbing. All is still now.

I trace a finger down the door, press my cheek to it, willing all that happened not to be so. I reach for the handle and open the door.

A half-painted wall of Buttercup Dream greets me. Soft pastels. Sweet smells. A cot with a mobile of little yellow ducks dangling above. A toy box decorated with giant letters of the alphabet. On a little rail hang two baby grows. Little booties on a dresser.

A bunny rabbit sits up enthusiastically inside the cot. He smiles stupidly at me. I take my shoes off and step barefoot onto the soft shagpile carpet, try to root myself in this world. I close the door behind me. There's not a sound. I pick up the rabbit and carry it around the room with me while I run my hands over the shiny new furniture, clothes and toys. I open a music box and watch as the little mouse inside begins to circle round and round after a piece of cheese to a mesmerising tinkling sound.

'I'm sorry, Sean,' I whisper, and my words catch in my throat. 'I'm so, so sorry.'

I lower myself to the soft floor, pull my legs close to me and hug the blissfully unaware bunny. I look again to the little mouse whose very being revolves around eternally chasing a piece of cheese he will never ever reach, let alone eat.

I slam the box shut and the music stops and I am left in silence.

NINE

'I can't find any food in the apartment; we're going to have to get take-out,' Justin's sister-in-law, Doris, calls into the living room as she roots through the kitchen cabinets.

'So maybe you know the woman,' Justin's younger brother, Al, sits on the plastic garden furniture chair in Justin's half-furnished living room.

'No, you see, that's what I'm trying to explain. It's *like* I know her but at the same time, I didn't know her at all.'

'You recognised her.'

'Yes. Well, no.' *Kind of.*

'And you don't know her name.'

'No. I definitely don't know her name.'

'Hey, is anyone listening to me in there or am I talking to myself?' Doris interrupts again. 'I said there's no food here so we're going to have to get take-out.'

'Yeah, sure, honey,' Al calls automatically. 'Maybe she's a student of yours or she went to one of your talks. You usually remember people you give talks to?'

'There's hundreds of people at a time,' Justin shrugs. 'And mostly they sit in darkness.'

'So that's a no then.' Al rubs his chin.

'Actually, forget the take-out,' Doris calls. 'You don't have any plates or cutlery – we're going to have to eat out.'

'And just let me get this clear, Al. When I say "recognise", I mean I didn't actually know her face.'

Al frowns.

'I just got a feeling. Like she was familiar.' *Yeah, that's it, she was familiar.*

'Maybe she just looked like someone you know.' *Maybe.*

'Hey, is anybody listening to me?' Doris interupts them, standing at the living-room door with her inch-long leopard-print nails on her skin-tight leather-trouser-clad hips. Thirty-five-year-old Italian-American fast-talking Doris had been married to Al for the past ten years and is regarded by Justin as a lovable but annoying younger sister. Without an ounce of fat on her bones, everything she wears looks like it comes out of the closet of *Grease*'s Sandy post makeover.

'Yes, sure, honey,' Al says again, not taking his eyes off Justin. 'Maybe it was that *déjà vu* thingy.'

'Yes!' Justin clicks his fingers. 'Or perhaps *vécu*, or *senti*,' he rubs his chin, lost in thought. 'Or *visité*.'

'What the heck is that?' Al asks as Doris pulls over a cardboard box filled with books, to sit on, and joins them.

'*Déjà vu* is French for "already seen" and it describes the experience of feeling that one has witnessed or experienced a new situation previously. The term was coined by a French psychic researcher Emile Boirac, which expanded upon an essay that he wrote while at the University of Chicago.'

'Go the Maroons!' Al raises Justin's old trophy cup that he's drinking from, in the air, and then gulps down his beer.

Doris looks at him with disdain. 'Please continue, Justin.'

'Well, the experience of *déjà vu* is usually accompanied by a compelling sense of familiarity, and also a sense of eeriness or strangeness. The experience is most frequently attributed to a dream, although in some cases there is a firm sense that the experience genuinely happened in the past. *Déjà vu* has been described as remembering the future.'

'Wow,' Doris says breathily.

'So what's your point, bro?' Al belches.

'Well, I don't think this thing today with me and the woman was *déjà vu*,' Justin frowns and sighs.

'Why not?'

'Because *déjà vu* relates to just *sight* and I felt . . . oh, I don't know.' I *felt*. '*Déjà vécu* is translated as "already lived", which explains the experience that involves more than sight, but of having a weird knowledge of what is going to happen next. *Déjà senti* specifically means "already felt", which is exclusively a mental happening and *déjà visité* involves an uncanny knowledge of a new place, but that's less common. No,' he shakes his head, 'I definitely didn't feel like I had been at the salon before.'

They all go quiet.

Al breaks the silence. 'Well, it's definitely *déjà* something. Are you sure you didn't just sleep with her before?'

'Al.' Doris hits her husband across the arm. 'Why didn't you let me cut your hair, Justin, and who are we talking about anyway?'

'You own a doggie parlour.' Justin frowns.

'Dogs have hair,' she shrugs.

'Let me try to explain this,' Al interrupts. 'Justin saw a woman yesterday at a hair salon in Dublin and he says he recognised her but didn't know her face, and he felt that he knew her but didn't actually know her.' He rolls his eyes melodramatically, out of Justin's view.

'Oh my God,' Doris sings, 'I know what this is.'

'What?' Justin asks, taking a drink from a toothbrush holder.

'It's obvious.' She holds her hands up and looks from one brother to another for dramatic effect. 'It's past-life stuff.' Her face lights up. 'You knew the woman in a *paaast liiife*,' she pronounces the words slowly. 'I saw it on *Oprah*.' She nods her head, eyes wide.

'Not more of this crap, Doris. It's all she talks about now. She sees somethin' about it on TV and that's all I get, all the way from Chicago on the plane.'

'I don't think it's past-life stuff, Doris, but thanks.'

Doris tuts. 'You two need to have open minds about this kind of thing because you never know.'

'Exactly, you *never* know,' Al fires back.

'Oh, come on, guys. The woman was familiar, that's all. Maybe she just looked like someone I knew at home. No big deal.' *Forget about it and move on.*

'Well, you started it with your *déjà* stuff,' Doris huffs. 'How do you explain it?'

Justin shrugs. 'The optical pathway delay theory.'

They both stare at him, dumb-faced.

'One theory is that one eye may record what is seen fractionally faster than the other, creating that strong recollection sensation upon the same scene being viewed milliseconds later by the other eye. Basically it's the product of a delayed optical input from one eye, closely followed by the input from the other eye, which should be simultaneous. This misleads conscious awareness and suggests a sensation of familiarity when there shouldn't be one.'

Silence.

Justin clears his throat.

'Believe it or not, honey, I prefer your past-life thing,' Al snorts, and finishes his beer.

'Thanks, sweetie.' Doris places her hands on her heart, overwhelmed. 'Anyway as I was saying when I was *talking to myself* in the kitchen, there's no food, cutlery or crockery here so we'll have to eat out tonight. Look at how you're living, Justin. I'm worried about you,' Doris looks around the room with disgust and her back-combed hair-sprayed dyed red hair follows the movement. 'You've moved all the way over to this country on your own, you've got nothing but garden furniture and unpacked boxes in a basement that looks like it was built for students. Clearly Jennifer also got all the *taste* in the settlement too.'

'This is a Victorian masterpiece, Doris. It was a real find, and it's the only place I *could* find with a bit of history as well as having affordable rent. This is an expensive town.'

'I'm sure it was a gem hundreds of years ago but now it gives me the creeps and whoever built it is probably still hanging around these rooms. I can feel him watching me.' She shudders.

'Don't flatter yourself.' Al rolls his eyes.

'All the place needs is a bit of TLC and it'll be fine,' Justin says, trying to forget the apartment he loved and has recently sold in the affluent and historic neighbourhood of Old Town Chicago.

'Which is why I'm here.' Doris claps her hands with glee.

'Great.' Justin's smile is tight. 'Let's go get some dinner now. I'm in the mood for a steak.'

'But you're vegetarian, Joyce.' Conor looks at me as though I've lost my mind. I probably have. I can't remember the last time I've eaten red meat but I have a sudden craving for it now that we've sat down at the restaurant.

'I'm not vegetarian, Conor. I just don't like red meat.'

'But you've just ordered a medium-rare steak!'

'I know,' I shrug. 'I'm just one crazy cat.'

He smiles as if remembering there once was a wild streak in me. We are like two friends meeting up after years apart. So much to talk about but not having the slightest clue where to start.

'Have you chosen the wine yet?' the waiter asks Conor.

I quickly grab the menu. 'Actually I would like to order this one, please.' I point to the menu.

'Sancerre 1998. That's a very good choice, madam.'

'Thank you.' I have no idea whatsoever why I've chosen it.

Conor laughs. 'Did you just do eeny-meeny-miny-mo?'

I smile but get hot under the collar. I don't know why I've ordered that wine. It's too expensive and I usually drink white, but I act naturally because I don't want Conor to think I've lost my mind. He already thought I was crazy when he saw I'd chopped all my hair off. He needs to think I'm back to my normal self in order for me to say what I'm going to say tonight.

The waiter returns with the bottle of wine.

'You can do the tasting,' Al says to Justin, 'seeing as it was your choice.'

Justin picks up the glass of wine, dips his nose into the glass and inhales deeply.

I inhale deeply and then swivel the wine in the glass, watching for the alcohol to rise and sweep the sides. I take a sip and hold it on my tongue, suck it in and allow the alcohol to burn the inside of my mouth. Perfect.

'Lovely, thank you.' I place the glass on the table again.

Conor's glass is filled and mine is topped up.

'It's beautiful wine.' I begin to tell him the story.

'I found it when Jennifer and I went to France years ago,' Justin explains. 'She was there performing in the Festival des Cathédrales de Picardie with the orchestra, which was a memorable experience. In Versailles, we stayed in Hôtel du Berry, an elegant 1634 mansion full of period furniture. It's practically a museum of regional history – you probably remember my telling you about it. Anyway, on one of her nights off in Paris we found this beautiful little fish restaurant tucked away down one of the cobbled alleys of Montmartre. We ordered the special, seabass, but you know how much of a red wine fanatic I am – even with fish I prefer to drink red – so the waiter suggested we go for the Sancerre.

'You know I always thought of Sancerre as a white wine, as it's famous for using the Sauvignon grape, but as it turns out it also uses some Pinot Noir. *And* the great thing is that you can drink the red Sancerre cooled exactly like white, at twelve degrees. But when not chilled, it's also good with meat. Enjoy.' He toasts his brother and sister-in-law.

Conor is looking at me with a frozen face. 'Montmartre? Joyce, you've never been to Paris before. How do you know so much about wine? And who the hell is Jennifer?'

I pause, snap out of my trance and suddenly hear the words of the story I had just explained. I do the only thing I can do under the circumstances. I start laughing. 'Gotcha.'

'Gotcha?' he frowns.

'They're the lines to a movie I watched the other night.'

'Oh.' Relief floods his face and he relaxes. 'Joyce, you scared me there for a minute. I thought somebody had possessed your body.' He smiles. 'What film is it from?'

'Oh, I can't remember,' I wave my hand dismissively, wondering what on earth is going on with me and try to recall if I even watched a film any night during the past week.

'You don't like anchovies now?' he interrupts my thoughts, and looks down at the little collection of anchovies I've gathered in a pile at the side of my plate.

'Give them to me, bro,' Al says, lifting his plate closer to Justin's. 'I love 'em. How you can have a Caesar salad without anchovies is beyond me. Is it OK that I have anchovies, Doris?' he asks sarcastically. 'The doc didn't say anchovies are going to kill me, did he?'

'Not unless somebody stuffs them down your throat, which is quite possible,' Doris says through gritted teeth.

'Thirty-nine years old and I'm being treated like a kid.' Al looks wistfully at the pile of anchovies.

'Thirty-five years old and the only kid I have is my husband,' Doris snaps, picking an anchovy from the pile and tasting it. She ruffles her nose and looks around the restaurant. 'They call this an Italian restaurant? My mother and her family would roll in their graves if they knew this.' She blesses herself quickly. 'So, Justin, tell me about this lady you're seeing.'

Justin frowns. 'Doris, it's really no big deal, I told you I just thought I knew her.' *And she looked like she thought she knew you too.*

'No, not her,' Al says loudly with a mouthful

of anchovies. 'She's talking about the woman you were banging the other night.'

'Al!' Food wedges in Justin's throat.

'Joyce,' Conor says with concern, 'are you OK?'

My eyes fill as I try to catch my breath from coughing.

'Here, have some water.' He pushes a glass in my face.

People around us are staring, concerned.

I'm coughing so much I can't even take a breath to drink. Conor gets up from his chair and comes around to me. He pats my back and I shrug him off, still coughing with tears running down my face. I stand up in panic, overturning my chair behind me in the process.

'Al, Al, do something. Oh, Madonn-ina Santa!' Doris panics. 'He's going purple.'

Al untucks his napkin from his collar and coolly places it on the table. He stands up and positions himself behind his brother. He wraps his arms around his waist, and pumps hard on his stomach.

On the second push, the food is dislodged from Justin's throat.

As a third person races to my aid, or rather to join the growing panicked discussion of how to perform the Heimlich manoeuvre, I suddenly stop coughing. Three faces stare at me in surprise while I rub my throat with confusion.

'Are you OK?' Conor asks, patting my back again.

'Yes,' I whisper, embarrassed by the attention we are receiving. 'I'm fine, thank you. Everyone, thank you so much for your help.'

They are slow to back away.

'Please go back to your seats and enjoy your dinner. Honestly, I'm fine. Thank you.' I sit down quickly and rub my streaming mascara from my eyes, trying to ignore the stares. 'God, that was embarrassing.'

'That was odd; you hadn't even eaten anything. You were just talking and then, bam! You started coughing.'

I shrug and rub my throat. 'I don't know, something caught when I inhaled.'

The waiter comes over to take our plates away. 'Are you all right, madam?'

'Yes, thank you, I'm fine.'

I feel a nudge from behind me as our neighbour leans over to our table. 'Hey, for a minute there I thought you were going into labour, ha-ha! Didn't we, Margaret?' He looks at his wife and laughs.

'No,' Margaret says, her smile quickly fading and her face turning puce. 'No, Pat.'

'Huh?' He's confused. 'Well, *I* did anyway. Congrats, Conor.' He gives a suddenly pale Conor a wink. 'There goes sleep for the next twenty years, believe you me. Enjoy your dinner.' He turns back to face his table, and we hear murmured squabbling.

Conor's face falls and he reaches for my hand across the table. 'Are you OK?'

'That's happened a few times now,' I explain, and instinctively place my hand over my flat stomach. 'I've barely looked in the mirror since I've come home. I can't stand to look.'

Conor makes appropriate sounds of concern and I hear the words 'beautiful' and 'pretty' but I silence him. I need for him to listen and not to try to solve anything. I want him to know that I'm not trying to be pretty or beautiful but for once just to appear as I am. I want to tell him how I feel when I force myself to look in the mirror and study my body that now feels like a shell.

'Oh, Joyce.' His grip on my hand tightens as I speak, he squeezes my wedding ring into my skin and it hurts.

A wedding ring but no marriage.

I wriggle my hand a little to let him know to loosen his grip. Instead he lets go. A sign.

'Conor,' is all I say. I give him a look and I know he knows what I'm about to say. He's seen this look before.

'No, no, no, no, Joyce, not this conversation now.' He withdraws his hand from the table completely and holds his hands up in defence. 'You – *we* – have been through enough this week.'

'Conor, no more distractions.' I lean forward with urgency in my voice. 'We have to deal with us *now* or before we know it, ten years on we'll be wondering every single day of our miserable lives what *might* have been.'

We've had this conversation in some form or another on an annual basis over the last five years and I wait for the usual retort from Conor. That no one says marriage is easy, we can't expect it to be so, we promised one another, marriage is for life and he's determined to work at it. Salvage from the skip what's worth saving, my itinerant husband preaches. I focus on the centre flame's reflection in my dessert spoon while I wait for his usual comments. I realise minutes later they still haven't come. I look up and see he is battling tears and is nodding in what looks like agreement.

I take a breath. This is it.

Justin eyes the dessert menu.

'You can't have any, Al.' Doris plucks the menu out of her husband's hands and snaps it shut.

'Why not? Am I not allowed to even read it?'

'Your cholesterol goes up just reading it.'

Justin zones out as they squabble. He shouldn't be having any either. Since his divorce he's started to let himself go, eating as a comfort instead of his usual daily workout. He really shouldn't, but his eyes hover above one item on the menu like a vulture watching its prey.

'Any dessert for you, sir?' the waiter asks.

Go on.

'Yes. I'll have the . . .'

*　　*　　*

'Banoffee pie, please,' I blurt out to the waiter, to my own surprise.

Conor's mouth drops.

Oh dear. My marriage has just ended and I'm ordering dessert. I bite my lip and stop a nervous smile from breaking out.

To new beginnings. To the pursuit of . . . some-thingness.

TEN

A grand chime welcomes me to my father's humble home. It's a sound far more than deserving of the two up-two down, but then, so is my father.

The sound teleports me back to my life within these walls and how I'd identified visitors by the sound of their call at the door. As a child, short piercing sounds told me that friends, too short to reach, were hopping up to punch the button. Fast and weak snippets of sound alerted me to boyfriends cowering outside, terrified of announcing their very existence, never mind their arrival, to my father. Late night unsteady, uncountable rings sang Dad's homecoming from the pub without his keys. Joyful, playful rhythms were family calls on occasions, and short, loud, continuous bursts like machine-gun fire warned us of door-to-door salespeople. I press the bell again, but not just because at ten a.m. the house is quiet and nothing stirs; I want to know what my call sounds like.

Apologetic, short and clipped. Almost doesn't

105

want to be heard but needs to be. It says, sorry, Dad, sorry to disturb you. Sorry the thirty-three-year-old daughter you thought you were long ago rid of is back home after her marriage has fallen apart.

Finally I hear sounds inside and I see Dad's seesaw movement coming closer, shadowlike and eerie, in the distorted glass.

'Sorry, love,' he opens the door, 'I didn't hear you the first time.'

'If you didn't hear me then how did you know I rang?'

He looks at me blankly and then down at the suitcases around my feet. 'What's this?'

'You . . . you told me I could stay for a while.'

'I thought you meant till the end of *Countdown*.'

'Oh . . . well, I was hoping to stay for a bit longer than that.'

'Long after I'm gone, by the looks of it.' He surveys his doorstep. 'Come in, come in. Where's Conor? Something happen to the house? You haven't mice again, have you? It's the time of the year for them all right, so you should have kept the windows and doors closed. Block up all the openings, that's what I do. I'll show you when we're inside and settled. Conor should know.'

'Dad, I've never called around to stay here because of mice.'

'There's a first time for everything. Your mother used to do that. Hated the things. Used

106

to stay at your grandmother's for the few days while I ran around here like that cartoon cat trying to catch them. Tom or Jerry, was it?' He squeezes his eyes closed tight to think, then opens them again, none the wiser. 'I never knew the difference but by God they knew it when I was after them.' He raises a fist, looks feisty for a moment while captured in the thought and then he stops suddenly and carries my suitcases into the hall.

'Dad?' I say, frustrated. 'I thought you understood me on the phone. Conor and I have separated.'

'Separated what?'

'Ourselves.'

'From what?'

'From each other!'

'What on earth are you talking about, Gracie?'

'Joyce. We're not together any more. We've split up.'

He puts the bags down by the hall's wall of photographs, there to provide any visitor who crosses the threshold with a crash course of the Conway family history. Dad as a boy, Mum as a girl, Dad and Mum courting, married, my christening, communion, débutant ball and wedding. Capture it, frame it, display it; Mum and Dad's school of thought. It's funny how people mark their lives, the benchmarks they choose to decide when a moment is more of a moment than any other. For life is made of them. I like to think the best ones of all are in my mind, that they run through my blood in their own memory bank for no one else but me to see.

Dad doesn't pause for a moment at the revelations of my failed marriage and instead works his way into the kitchen. 'Cuppa?'

I stay in the hall looking around at the photos and breathe in that smell. The smell that's carried around everyday on every stitch of Dad's back, like a snail carries its home. I always thought it was the smell of Mum's cooking that drifted around the rooms and seeped into every fibre, including the wallpaper, but it's ten years since Mum has passed away. Perhaps the scent was her; perhaps it's still her.

'What are you doin' sniffin' the walls?'

I jump, startled and embarrassed at being caught, and make my way into the kitchen. It hasn't changed since I lived here and it's as spotless as the day Mum left it, nothing moved, not even for convenience's sake. I watch Dad move slowly about, resting on his left foot to access the cupboards below, and then using the extra inches of his right leg as his own personal footstool to reach above. The kettle boils too loudly for us to have a conversation and I'm glad of that because Dad grips the handle so tightly his knuckles are white. A teaspoon is cupped in his left hand, which rests on his hip, and it reminds me of how he used to stand with his cigarette, shielded in his cupped hand that'd be stained yellow from nicotine. He looks out to his immaculate garden and grinds his teeth. He's angry and I feel like a teenager once again, awaiting my talking-down.

'What are you thinking about, Dad?' I finally ask as soon as the kettle stops hopping about like a crammed Hill 16 in Croke Park during an All-Ireland Final.

'The garden,' he replies, his jaw tightening once again.

'The garden?'

'That bloody cat from next door keeps pissing on your mother's roses.' He shakes his head angrily. 'Fluffy,' he throws his hands up, 'that's what she calls him. Well, Fluffy won't be so fluffy when I get my hands on him. I'll be wearin' one of them fine furry hats the Russians wear and I'll dance the *hopak* outside Mrs Henderson's front garden while she wraps a shiverin' *Baldy* up in a blanket inside.'

'Is that what you're really thinking about?' I ask incredulously.

'Well, not really, love,' he confesses, calming down. 'That and the daffodils. Not far off from planting season for spring. And some crocuses. I'll have to get some bulbs.'

Good to know my marriage breakdown isn't my dad's main priority. Nor his second. On the list after crocuses.

'Snowdrops too,' he adds.

It's rare I'm around the area so early on in the day. Usually I'd be at work showing property around the city. It's so quiet now with everyone

109

at work, I wonder what on earth Dad does in this silence.

'What were you doing before I came?'

'Thirty-three years ago or today?'

'Today.' I try not to smile because I know he's serious.

'Quiz.' He nods at the kitchen table where he has a page full of puzzles and quizzes. Half of them are completed. 'I'm stuck on the number six. Have a look at that.' He brings the cups of tea to the table, managing not to spill a drop despite his swaying. Always steady.

'"Which of Mozart's operas was not well received by one especially influential critic who summed up the work as having 'Too many notes'?"' I read the clue aloud.

'Mozart,' Dad shrugs. 'Haven't a clue about that lad at all.'

'Emperor Joseph the Second,' I say.

'What's that now?' Dad's caterpillar eyebrows go up in surprise. 'How did you know that, then?'

I frown. 'I must have just heard it somwh— do I smell smoke?'

He sits up straight and sniffs the air like a bloodhound. 'Toast. I made it earlier. Had the setting on too high and burned it. They were the last two slices, as well.'

'Hate that.' I shake my head. 'Where's Mum's photograph from the hall?'

'Which one? There are thirty of her.'

'You've counted?' I laugh.

110

'Nailed them up there, didn't I? Forty-four photos in total, that's forty-four nails I needed. Went down to the hardware store and bought a pack of nails. Forty nails it contained. They made me buy a second packet just for four more nails.' He holds up four fingers and shakes his head. 'Still have thirty-six of them left over in the toolbox. What is the world comin' to at all, at all.'

Never mind terrorism or global warming. The proof of the world's downfall, in his eyes, comes down to thirty-six nails in a toolbox. He's probably right too.

'So where is it?'

'Right where it always is,' he says unconvincingly.

We both look at the closed kitchen door, in the direction of the hall table. I stand up to go out and check. These are the kinds of things you do when you have time on your hands.

'Ah ah,' he jerks a floppy hand at me, 'sit yourself down.' He rises. 'I'll go out and check.' He closes the kitchen door behind him, blocking me from seeing out. 'She's there all right,' he calls to me. 'Hello, Gracie, your daughter was worried about you. Thought she couldn't see you but sure, haven't you been there all along watchin' her sniffin' the walls, thinkin' the paper's on fire. But sure isn't it only madder she's gettin', leaving her husband and packing in her job.'

I haven't mentioned anything to him about

taking leave from my job, which means Conor has spoken to him, which means Dad knew my exact intentions for being here from the very first moment he heard the doorbell ring. I have to give it to him, he plays stupid very well. He returns to the kitchen and I catch a glimpse of the photo on the hall table.

'Ah!' He looks at his watch in alarm. 'Ten twenty-five! Let's go inside quick!' He moves faster than I've seen him in a long time, grabbing his weekly television guide and his cup of tea and rushing into the television room.

'What are we watching?' I follow him into the living room, watching him with amusement.

'*Murder, She Wrote*, you know it?'

'Never seen it.'

'Oh, wait'll you see, Gracie. That Jessica Fletcher is a quare one for catching the murderers. Then over on the next channel we'll watch *Diagnosis Murder*, where the dancer solves the cases.' He takes a pen and circles it on the TV page.

I'm captivated by Dad's excitement. He sings along with the theme tune, making trumpet noises with his mouth.

'Come in here and lie on the couch and I'll put this over you.' He picks up a tartan blanket draped over the back of the green velvet couch and places it gently over me, tucking it in around my body so tightly I can't move my arms. It's the same blanket I rolled on as a baby, the same blanket they covered me with when I was home sick from school and was allowed to watch television on the couch. I watch Dad with fondness, remembering the tenderness he always showed me as a child, feeling right back there again.

Until he sits at the end of the couch and squashes my feet.

ELEVEN

'What do you think, Gracie – will Betty be a millionaire by the end of the show?'

I have sat through an endless amount of half-hour morning shows over the last few days and now we are watching the *Antiques Roadshow*.

Betty is seventy years old, from Warwickshire, and is currently waiting with anticipation as the dealer tries to price the old teapot she has brought with her.

I watch the dealer handling the teapot delicately and a comfortable, familiar feeling overwhelms me. 'Sorry, Betty,' I say to the television, 'it's a replica. From the eighteenth century. The French used them but Betty's one was made in the early twentieth century. You can see from the way the handle is shaped. Clumsy craftsmanship.'

'Is that so?' Dad looks at me with interest.

We watch the screen intently and listen as the dealer repeats my remarks. Poor Betty is devastated but tries to pretend it was too precious a gift from her grandmother for her to have sold anyhow.

'Liar,' Dad shouts. 'Betty already had her cruise booked and her bikini bought. How do you know all that about the pots and the French, Gracie? Read it in one of your books maybe?'

'Maybe.' I have no idea. I get a headache thinking about this new-found knowledge.

Dad catches the look on my face. 'Why don't you call a friend or something? Have a chat.'

I don't want to but I know I should. 'I should probably give Kate a call.'

'The big-boned girl? The one who ploughed you with poteen when you were sixteen?'

'That's Kate,' I laugh. He has never forgiven her for that.

'What kind of a name is that, at all, at all. She was a messer, that girl. Has she come to anything?'

'No, not at all. She just sold her shop in the city for two million to become a stay-at-home mother.' I try not to laugh at the shock on his face.

His ears prick up. 'Ah, sure, give her a call. Have a chat. You women like to do that. Good for the soul, your mother always said. Your mother loved talking, was always blatherin' on to someone or other about somethin' or other.'

'Wonder where she got that from,' I say under my breath but just as if by a miracle, my father's rubbery-looking ears work.

'Her star sign is where she got it from. Taurus. Talked a lot of bull.'

'Dad!'

'What? Is it an admittance of hate? No. Nothing of the sort. I loved her with all my heart but the woman talked a lot of bull. Not enough to talk about a thing, I had to hear about how she felt about it too. Ten times over.'

'You don't believe in star signs,' I nudge him.

'I do too. I'm Libra. Weighing scales.' He rocks from side to side. 'Perfectly balanced.'

I laugh and escape to my bedroom to phone Kate. I enter the room, practically unchanged since the day I left it. Despite the rare occasion of guests staying over after I'd gone, my parents never removed my leftover belongings. The Cure stickers were still on the door and parts of the wallpaper were ripped from the tape that had secured my posters. As a punishment for ruining the walls, Dad forced me to cut the grass in the back garden, but while doing so I ran the lawnmower over a shrub in the bedding. He refused to speak to me for the rest of the day. Apparently it was the first year the shrub had blossomed since he'd planted it. I couldn't understand his frustration then, but after spending years of hard work cultivating a marriage, only for it to wither and die, I can now understand his plight. But I bet he didn't feel the relief I feel right now.

My box bedroom can only fit a bed and a wardrobe but it was my whole world. My only personal space to think and dream, to cry and laugh and wait until I became old enough to do all the things I wasn't allowed to do. My only space in the world then and, at thirty-three years old, my only space now. Who knew I'd find myself back again without any of the things I'd yearned for, and, even worse, still yearning for them? Not to be a member of The Cure or married to Robert Smith, but with no baby and no husband. The wallpaper is floral and wild; completely inappropriate for a space of rest. Millions of tiny brown flowers cluster together with tiny splashes of faded green stalks. No wonder I'd covered them with posters. The carpet is brown with lighter brown swirls, stained from spilled perfume and make-up. New additions to the room are old and faded brown leather suitcases lying on top of the wardrobe, gathering dust since Mum died. Dad never goes anywhere, a life without Mum, he decided long ago, enough of a journey for him.

The duvet cover is the newest introduction. New, as in, over ten years old; Mum purchased it when my room became the guest room. I moved out a year before she died, to live with Kate, and I wish everyday since that I hadn't, all those precious days of not waking up to hear her long yawns that turned into songs, talking to herself as she made her verbal diary with Gay Byrne's radio show on in the background. She loved Gay Byrne; her sole ambition in life being to meet him. The closest she got to that dream was when she and Dad got tickets to sit in the audience of *The Late Late Show* and she spoke about it for years. I think she had a thing for him. Dad hated him. I think he knew about her thing.

He likes to listen to him now, though, whenever he's on. I think he reminds him of a precious time spent with Mum, as though when we all hear Gay Byrne's voice, he hears Mum's instead. When she died, he surrounded himself with all the things she adored. He put Gay on the radio every morning, watched Mum's television shows, bought her favourite biscuits in his weekly shopping trip even though he never ate them. He liked to see them on the shelf when he opened the cupboard, liked to see her magazines beside his newspaper. He liked her slippers staying beside her armchair by the fire. He liked to remind himself that his entire world hadn't fallen apart. Sometimes we need all the glue we can get, just to hold ourselves together.

At sixty-five years old, he was too young to lose his wife. At twenty-three I was too young to lose my mother. At fifty-five she shouldn't have lost her life, but cancer, the thief of seconds, undetected until far too late, stole it from her and us all. Dad married late in life for that time, and didn't have me until he was forty-two years old. I think that there was somebody that broke his heart back then that he has never spoken of and that I've never asked about, but what he does say about that period is that he spent more days of his life waiting for Mum than actually being with her, but that every second spent looking for her and, eventually, remembering her, was worth it for all the moments in between.

Mum never met Conor but I don't know whether she would have liked him, though she was too polite ever to have shown it. Mum loved all kinds of people but particularly those with high spirit and energy, people that lived and exuded that life. Conor is pleasant. Always just pleasant. Never overexcited. Never, in fact, excited at all. Just pleasant, which is just another word for nice. Marrying a nice man gives you a nice marriage but never anything more. And nice is OK when it's among other things but never when it stands alone.

Dad would talk to anyone anywhere and not have a feeling about them one way or another. The only negative thing he ever said about Conor was, 'Sure, what kind of man likes *tennis*?' A GAA and soccer man, Dad had spat the word out as though just saying it had dirtied his mouth.

Our failure to produce a child didn't do much to sway Dad's opinion. He blamed it on the tennis but particularly on the little white shorts Conor sometimes wore, whenever pregnancy test after pregnancy test failed to show blue. I know he said it all to put a smile on my face; sometimes it worked, other times it didn't, but it was a safe joke because we all knew it wasn't the tennis shorts or the man wearing them that was the problem.

I sit down on the duvet cover bought by Mum,

not wanting to crease it. A two-pillow and duvet cover set from Dunnes with a matching candle for the windowsill, which has never been lit and has lost its scent. Dust gathers on the top, incriminating evidence that Dad is not keeping up with his duties, as if at seventy-five years old the removal of dust from anywhere but his memory shelf should be a priority. But the dust has settled and so let it stay.

I turn on my mobile, which has been switched off for days, and it begins to beep as a dozen messages filter through. I have already made my calls to those near, dear and nosy. Like pulling off a Band-Aid; don't think about it, move quickly and it's almost painless. Flip open the phonebook and bam, bam, bam: three minutes each. Quick snappy phone calls made by a strangely upbeat woman who'd momentarily inhabited my body. An incredible woman, in fact, positive and perky, yet emotional and wise at all the right times. Her timing impeccable, her sentiments so poignant I almost wanted to write them down. She even attempted a bit of humour, which some members of the near, dear and nosy coped well with while others seemed almost insulted – not that she cared, for it was her party and she was crying if she wanted to. I've met her before, of course; she whizzes around to me for the occasional trauma, steps into my shoes and takes over the hard parts. She'll be back again, no doubt.

No, it will be a long time before I can speak in

my own voice to people other than the woman I am calling now.

Kate picks up on the fourth ring.

'Hello,' she shouts and I jump. There are manic noises in the background, as though a mini-war has broken out.

'Joyce!' she yells and I realise I'm on speaker-phone. 'I've been *calling* you and *calling* you. Derek, SIT DOWN. MUMMY IS NOT HAPPY! Sorry, I'm just doing the school run. I've to bring six kids home, then a quick snack before I bring Eric to basketball and Jayda to swimming. Want to meet me there at seven? Jayda is getting her ten-metre badge today.'

Jayda howls in the background about hating ten-metre badges.

'How can you hate it when you've never had one?' Kate snaps. Jayda howls even louder and I have to move the phone from my ear. 'JAYDA! GIVE MUMMY A BREAK! DEREK, PUT YOUR SEATBELT ON! If I have to brake suddenly, you will go FLYING through the windscreen and SMASH YOUR FACE IN. Hold on, Joyce.'

There is silence while I wait.

'Gracie!' Dad yells. I run to the top of the stairs in panic, not used to hearing him shout like that since I was a child.

'Yes? Dad! Are you OK?'

'I got seven letters,' he shouts.

'You got *what*?'

'Seven letters!'

'What does that mean?'

122

'In *Countdown*!'

I stop panicking and sit on the top stair in frustration. Suddenly Kate's voice is back and it sounds as though calm has been restored.

'OK, you're off speakerphone. I'll probably be arrested for holding the phone, not to mention cast off the car-pool list, like I give a flying fuck about that.'

'I'm telling my mammy you said the f word,' I hear a little voice.

'Good. I've been wanting to tell her that for years,' Kate murmurs to me and I laugh.

'FUCK, FUCK, FUCK, FUCK,' I hear a crowd of kids chanting.

'Jesus, Joyce, I better go. See you at the leisure centre at seven? It's my only break. Or else I have tomorrow. Tennis at three or gymnastics at six? I can see if Frankie is free to meet up too.'

Frankie. Christened Francesca but refuses to answer to it. Dad was wrong about Kate. She may have sourced the poteen but technically it was Frankie that held my mouth open and poured it down my throat. As a result of this version of the story never being told, he thinks Frankie's a saint, very much to Kate's annoyance.

'I'll take gymnastics tomorrow,' I smile as the children's chanting gets louder. Kate's gone and there's silence.

'GRACIE!' Dad calls again.

'It's *Joyce*, Dad.'

'I got the conundrum!'

I make my way back to my bed and cover my head with a pillow.

A few minutes later Dad arrives at the door, scaring the life out of me.

'I was the only one that got the conundrum. The contestants hadn't a clue. Simon won anyway, goes through to tomorrow's show. He's been the winner for three days now and I'm half bored lookin' at him. He has a funny-looking face; you'd have a right laugh if you saw it. Don't think Carol likes him much either and she's after losin' loads of weight again. Do you want a HobNob? I'm going to make another cuppa.'

'No, thanks.' I put the pillow back over my head. He uses so many *words*.

'Well, I'm having one. I have to eat with my pills. Supposed to take it at lunch but I forgot.'

'You took a pill at lunch, remember?'

'That was for my heart. This is for my memory. Short-term memory pills.'

I take the pillow off my face to see if he's being serious. 'And you forgot to take it?'

He nods.

'Oh, Dad.' I start to laugh while he looks on as though I'm having an episode. 'You are medicine enough for me. Well, you need to get stronger pills. They're not working, are they?'

He turns his back and makes his way down the hall, grumbling, 'They'd bloody well work if I remembered to take them.'

'Dad,' I call to him and he stops at the top of

the stairs. 'Thanks for not asking any questions about Conor.'

'Sure, I don't need to. I know you'll be back together in no time.'

'No we won't,' I say softly.

He walks a little closer to my room. 'Is he stepping out with someone else?'

'No he's not. And I'm not. We don't love each other. We haven't for a long time.'

'But you married him, Joyce. Didn't I bring you down the aisle myself?' He looks confused.

'What's that got to do with anything?'

'You both promised each other in the house of our Lord, I heard you myself with my own ears. What is it with you young people these days, breaking up and remarrying all the time? What happened to keeping promises?'

I sigh. How can I answer that? He begins to walk away again.

'Dad.'

He stops but doesn't turn round.

'I don't think you're thinking of the alternative. Would you rather I kept my promise to spend the rest of my life with Conor, but not love him and be unhappy?'

'If you think your mother and I had a perfect marriage then you're wrong because there's no such thing. No one's happy all the time, love.'

'I understand that, but what if you're *never* happy. Ever.'

He thinks about that for what looks like the

first time and I hold my breath until he finally speaks. 'I'm going to have a HobNob.'

Halfway down the stairs he shouts back rebelliously, 'A *chocolate* one.'

TWELVE

'I'm on a vacation, bro, why are you dragging me to a gym?' Al half-walks half-skips alongside Justin in an effort to keep up with his lean brother's long strides.

'I have a date with Sarah next week,' Justin power-walks from the tube station, 'and I need to get back into shape.'

'I didn't realise you were *out* of shape,' Al pants, and wipes trickles of sweat from his brow.

'The divorce cloud was preventing me from working out.'

'The divorce cloud?'

'Never heard of it?'

Al, unable to speak, shakes his head and wobbles his chins like a turkey.

'The cloud moves to take the shape of your body, wraps itself nice and tight around you so that you can barely move. Or breathe. Or exercise. Or even *date*, let alone *sleep* with other women.'

127

'Your divorce cloud sounds like my marriage cloud.'

'Yeah, well, that cloud has moved on now.' Justin looks up at the grey London sky, closes his eyes for a brief moment and breathes in deeply. 'It's time for me to get back into action.' He opens his eyes and walks straight into a lamppost. 'Jesus, Al!' He doubles over, head in his hands. 'Thanks for the warning.'

Al's beetroot face wheezes back at him, words not coming easily. Or at all.

'Never mind *my* having to work out, look at yourself. Your doctor's already told you to drop a few hundred pounds.'

'Fifty pounds . . .' gasp, 'aren't exactly . . .' gasp, 'a few *hundred*, and don't start on me too.' Gasp. 'Doris is bad enough.' Wheeze. Cough. 'What she knows about dieting is beyond me. The woman doesn't eat. She's afraid to bite a nail in case they've too many calories.'

'Doris's nails are real?'

'Them and her hair is about all. I gotta hold on to something.' Al looks around, flustered.

'Too much information,' Justin says, misunderstanding. 'I can't believe Doris's *hair* is real too.'

'All but the colour. She's a brunette. Italian, of course. Dizzy.'

'Yeah, she is a bit dizzy. All that past-life talk about the woman at the hair salon,' Justin laughs. *So how do you explain it?*

'I meant *I'm* dizzy.' Al glares at him and reaches out to hold on to the nearby railing.

'Oh . . . I knew that, I was kidding. It looks like we're almost here. Think you can make it another hundred yards or so?'

'Depends on the "or so",' Al snaps.

'It's about the same as the week *or so* vacation that you and Doris were planning on taking. Looks like that's turning into a month.'

'Well, we wanted to surprise you, and Doug is well able to take care of the shop while I'm gone. The doc advised me to take it easy, Justin. With heart conditions being in the family history, I really need to rest up.'

'You told the doctor there's a history of heart conditions in the family?' Justin asks.

'Yeah, Dad died of a heart attack. Who else would I be talkin' about?'

Justin is silent.

'Besides, you won't be sorry, Doris will have your apartment done up so nice that you'll be glad we stayed. You know she did the doggie parlour all by herself?'

Justin's eyes widen.

'I know,' Al beams proudly. 'So, how many of these seminars will you be doing in Dublin? Me and Doris might accompany you on one of your trips over there, you know, see the place Dad was from.'

'Dad was from Cork.'

'Oh. Does he still have family there? We could go and trace our roots, what do you think?'

'That's not such a bad idea.' Justin thinks of his schedule. 'I have a few more seminars ahead. You probably won't be here that long, though.' He eyes Al sideways, testing him. 'And you can't come next week because I'm mixing that trip with a date with Sarah.'

'You're really hot on this girl?'

His almost forty-year-old brother's vocabulary never ceases to amaze Justin. 'Am I hot on this girl?' he repeats, amused and confused all at the same time. *Good question. Not really, but she's company. Is that an acceptable answer?*

'Did she have you at "I vant your blood"?' Al chuckles.

'Wow, that was uncanny,' Justin says. 'Sarah, too, is a vampire from Transylvania. Let's do an hour at the gym.' He changes the subject. 'I don't think "resting up" is going to make you any better. That's what got you into this state in the first place.'

'*One hour?*' Al almost explodes. 'What are you planning on doing on the date, rock-climbing?'

'It's just lunch.'

Al rolls his eyes. 'What, you have to chase and kill your food? Anyway, you wake up tomorrow morning after your first work-out for a whole year, you won't be able to *walk*, never mind screw.'

I wake up to the sound of banging pots and pans coming from downstairs. I expect to be in my own bedroom at home and it takes me a moment to remember. And then I remember everything, all over again. My daily morning pill as usual, hard to swallow. One of these days I'll wake up and I'll just know. I'm not sure which scenario I prefer; the moments of forgetfulness are such bliss.

I didn't sleep well last night between the thoughts in my head and the sound of the cistern flushing every hour after Dad's toilet breaks. When he was asleep, his snores rattled through the walls of the house.

Despite the interruptions, my dreams during my rare moments of sleep are still vivid in my mind. They almost feel real, like memories, though who's to know how real even they are, with all the altering our minds do? I remember being in a park, though I don't think I was me. I twirled a young girl with white-blonde hair around in my arms while a woman with red hair looked on smiling, with a camera in her hand. The park was colourful with lots of flowers and we had a picnic . . . I try to remember the song I'd been hearing all night but it fails me. Instead I hear Dad downstairs singing 'The Auld Triangle', an old Irish song he has sung at parties all of my life and probably most of his too. He'd stand there, eyes closed, pint in hand, a picture of bliss as he sang his story of how 'the auld triangle went jingle jangle'.

I swing my legs out of the bed and groan with pain, suddenly feeling an ache in both legs from my hips, right down my thighs, all the way down to my calf muscles. I try to move the rest of my body and feel paralysed with the pain too; my shoulders, biceps, triceps, back muscles and torso. I massage my muscles with complete confusion and make a note in my head to go to the doctor, just in case it's something to be worried about. I'm sure it's my heart, either looking for more attention, or so full of pain it has needed to ooze its ache around the rest of my body just to relieve itself. Each throbbing muscle is an extension of the pain I feel inside, though a doctor will tell me it's due to the thirty-year-old bed I slept on, manufactured before the time people claimed nightly back support as their God-given right. Potayto, potato.

I throw a dressing gown around me and slowly, as stiff as a board, make my way downstairs, trying my best not to bend my legs.

The smell of smoke is in the air again and I notice as I'm passing the hall table that Mum's photograph once again isn't there. Something urges me to slide open the drawer beneath the table and there she is, lying face down in the drawer. Tears spring in my eyes, angry that something so precious has been hidden away. It has always meant more than a photograph to the both of us; it represents her presence in the house, pride of place to greet us whenever we come in the front door or down the stairs. I take deep breaths and decide to say nothing for now, assuming Dad has his reasons, though I can't think of any acceptable examples at this point. I slide the drawer closed and leave her where Dad has placed her, feeling like I'm burying her all over again.

When I limp into the kitchen, chaos greets me. There are pots and pans everywhere, tea towels, egg shells and what looks like the contents of the cupboards covering the counters. Dad is wearing an apron with an image of a woman in red lingerie and suspenders, over his usual sweater, shirt and trousers. On his feet are Manchester United slippers, shaped as large footballs.

'Morning, love.' He sees me and steps up onto his left leg to give me a kiss on the forehead.

I realise it's the first time in years somebody has made my breakfast for me, but it's also the first time for many years that Dad has had somebody to cook breakfast for. Suddenly the singing, the mess, the clattering pots and pans all make sense. He's excited.

'I'm making waffles!' he says with an American accent.

'Ooh, very nice.'

'That's what the donkey says, isn't it?'

'What donkey?'

'The one . . .' he stops stirring whatever is in the frying pan and closes his eyes to think, 'the story with the green man.'

'The Incredible Hulk?'

'No.'

'Well, I don't know any other green people.'

'You do, you know the one . . .'

'The Wicked Witch of the West?'

'No! There's no donkey in that! Think about stories with donkeys in them.'

'Is it a biblical tale?'

'Were there talking donkeys in the Bible, Gracie? Did Jesus eat waffles, do you think? Christ, we have it all wrong: it was waffles he was breaking at supper to share with the lads, and not bread after all!'

'My name is Joyce.'

'I don't remember Jesus eating waffles but, sure, won't I ask the crowd at the Monday Club? Maybe I've been reading the wrong Bible all my life.' He laughs at his own joke.

I look over his shoulder. 'Dad, you're not even making waffles!'

He sighs with exasperation. 'Am I a donkey? Do I look like a donkey to you? Donkeys make waffles, *I* make a good fry-up.'

I watch him poking the sausages around, trying to get all sides evenly cooked. 'I'll have sausages too.'

'But you're one of those vegetarianists.'

'Vegetarian. And I'm not any more.'

'Sure of course you're not. You've only been one since you were fifteen years old after seeing that show about the seals. Tomorrow I'll wake up and you'll be tellin' me you're a man. Saw it on the telly once. This woman, about the same age as you, brought her husband live on the telly in front of an audience to tell him that she decided that she wanted to turn her—'

134

Feeling frustrated with him, I blurt out, 'Mum's photo isn't on the hall table.'

Dad freezes, a reaction of guilt, and this makes me somewhat angry, as though before I had convinced myself that the mysterious midnight photograph-mover had broken in and done the dirty deed himself. I'd almost prefer that.

'Why?' is all I say.

He keeps himself busy, clattering with plates and cutlery now. 'Why what? Why are you walking like that is what I want to know?' Dad eyes my walk curiously.

'I don't know,' I snap, and limp across the room to take a seat at the table. 'Maybe it runs in the family.'

'Hoo hoo hoo,' Dad hoots and looks up at the ceiling, 'we've got a live one here, boss! Set the table like a good girl.'

He brings me right back and I can't help but smile. And so I set the table and Dad makes the breakfast and we both limp around the kitchen pretending everything is as it was and forever shall be. World without end.

THIRTEEN

'So, Dad, what are your plans for the day? Are you busy?'

A forkful of sausage, egg, bacon, pudding, mushroom and tomato stops on its way into my dad's open mouth. Amused eyes peer out at me from under his wildly wiry eyebrows.

'Plans, you say? Well, let's see, Gracie, while I go through the ol' schedule of events for the day. I was thinking of after I finish my fry in approximately fifteen minutes, I'd have another cuppa tea. Then while I'm drinking me tea I might sit down in this chair at this table, or maybe that chair where you are, the exact venue is TBD, as my schedule would say. Then I'll go through yesterday's answers of the crossword to see what we got correct and what was incorrect and then I'll find out the answer to the ones I couldn't figure out yesterday. Then I'll do the Dusoku, then the word game. I see we've to try and find *nautical* words today. *Seafaring, maritime, yachting,* yes,

I'll be able to do that, sure I can see the word "boating" there on the first line already. Then I'm going to cut out my coupons and all that will fill my early morning right up, Gracie. Then I'd say I'll have another cuppa after all of that and then my programmes start. If you'd like to make an appointment, talk to Maggie.' He finally shovels the food into his mouth and egg drips down his chin. He doesn't notice and leaves it there.

I laugh. 'Who's Maggie?'

He swallows and smiles, amused at himself. 'I don't know why I said it.' He thinks hard and finally laughs. 'There was a fella I used to know in Cavan, this is goin' back sixty years now, Brendan Brady was his name. Whenever we'd be tryin' to make arrangements he'd say,' Dad deepens his voice, '"Talk to Maggie," like he was someone awful important.' She was either his wife or his secretary, I hadn't a clue. "Talk to Maggie,"' he repeats. 'Maggie was probably his mother,' he laughs, and continues eating.

'So basically, according to your schedule, you're doing exactly the same thing as yesterday.'

'Oh, no, it's not the same at all.' He thumbs through his TV guide and stabs a greasy finger on today's page. He looks at his watch and slides his finger down the page. He picks up his highlighter and marks another show. '*Animal Hospital* is on instead of the *Antiques Roadshow*. Not exactly the same day as yesterday at all, at all, how's about that. It'll be doggies and bunnies today instead of

Betty's fake teapots. We might see her trying to sell the family dog for a few shillings. You might get that bikini on you after all, Betty.' He continues to draw a design around his shows on the TV page, his tongue licking the corners of his mouth in concentration as though he was decorating a manuscript.

'The Book of Kells,' I blurt out of nowhere, though that is nothing odd these days. My random ramblings are becoming something of the norm.

'What are you talking about now?' Dad stops his colouring and resumes eating.

'Let's go into town today. Do a tour of the city, go to Trinity College and look at the Book of Kells.'

Dad stares at me and munches. I'm not sure what he's thinking. He's probably thinking the same of me.

'You want to go to Trinity College. The girl who never wanted to set foot near the place for either studies or excursions with me and your mother, suddenly out of the blue wants to go. Sure, aren't "suddenly" and "out of the blue" one and the same? They shouldn't go together in a sentence, Henry,' he corrects himself.

'Yes, I want to go.' I suddenly, out of the blue, very much want to go to Trinity College.

'If you don't want to watch the *Animal Hospital* show just say so. You don't have to go darting into the city. There's such a thing as changing channels.'

139

'You're right, Dad, and I've been doing some of that recently.'

'Is that so? I hadn't noticed, what with your marriage breaking up, your not being a vegetarianist any more, your not mentioning a word about your job and your moving in with me, and all. There's been so much action around here, how's a man to tell if a channel's been changed or if a new show has just begun?'

'I need to do something new,' I explain. 'I have time for Frankie and Kate but everybody else . . . I'm just not ready right now. We need a change of schedule, Dad. I've got the big remote control of life in my hands and I'm ready to start pushing some buttons.'

He stares at me for a moment and puts a sausage in his mouth in response.

'We'll get a taxi into town and catch one of those tour buses, what do you think? MAGGIE!' I shout out at the top of my voice and it makes Dad jump. 'MAGGIE, DAD IS COMING INTO TOWN WITH ME TO HAVE A LOOK AROUND. IS THAT OK?'

I cock my ear and wait for a response. Happy I've received one, I nod and stand up. 'Right, Dad, it's been decided. Maggie says it's fine if you go into town. I'll have a shower and we'll leave in an hour. Ha! That rhymes.' I limp out of the kitchen, leaving my bewildered father behind with egg on his chin.

*   *   *

140

'I doubt Maggie said yes to me walkin' at this speed, Gracie,' Dad says, trying to keep up with me as we dodge pedestrians on Grafton Street.

'Sorry, Dad.' I slow down and link his arm. Despite his corrective footwear he still sways and I sway with him. Even if he was operated on to equal the length of his legs, I'd imagine he'd still sway, it's so much a part of who he is.

'Dad, are you ever going to call me Joyce?'

'What are you talkin' about? Sure, isn't that your name?'

I look at him with surprise. 'Do you not notice you always call me Gracie?'

He seems taken aback but makes no comment and keeps walking. Up and down, down and up.

'I'll give you a fiver, every time you call me Joyce today,' I smile.

'That's a deal, Joyce, Joyce, Joyce. Oh, how I love you, Joyce,' he chuckles. 'That's twenty quid already!' He nudges me and says seriously, 'I didn't notice I called you that, love. I'll do my best.'

'Thank you.'

'You remind me so much of her, you know.'

'Ah, Dad, really?' I'm touched; I feel my eyes prick with tears. He never says that. 'In what way?'

'You both have little piggy noses.'

I roll my eyes.

'I don't know why we're walking further away from Trinity College. Wasn't it there that you wanted to go to?'

'Yes, but the tour buses leave from Stephen's

Green. We'll see it as we're passing. I don't really want to go in there now anyway.'

'Why not?'

'It's lunchtime.'

'And the Book of Kells goes off for an hour's break, does it?' Dad rolls his eyes. 'A ham sambo and a flask of tea and then it props itself back up on display, right as rain for the afternoon. Is that what you think happens? Because, not going just because it's lunchtime doesn't make any sense to me.'

'Well, it does to me.' And I don't know why it does but it just feels like the right direction to go in. Internal compass says so.

Justin darts through the front arch of Trinity College and bounds up the road to Grafton Street. Lunchtime with Sarah. He beats away the nagging voice within him telling him to cancel her. *Give her a chance. Give yourself a chance.* He needs to try, he needs to find his feet again, he needs to remember that not every meeting with a woman is going to be the same as the first time he laid eyes on Jennifer. The thump-thump, thump-thump feeling that made his entire body vibrate, the butterflies that did acrobatics in his stomach, the tingle when he brushed off her skin. He thought about how he'd felt on his date with Sarah. Nothing. Nothing but flattery that she was attracted to him and excitement that he was back out in the dating world again. Plenty of feelings about her and the situation but nothing *for* her.

He had more of a reaction to the woman in the hair salon a few weeks ago and that was saying something. *Give her a chance. Give yourself a chance.*

Grafton Street is crowded at lunchtime, as though the gates to Dublin zoo have been opened and all the animals have flooded out, happy to escape confinement for an hour. He has finished work for the day, his seminar on his specialist subject, Copper as Canvas: 1575–1775, being a success with the third-year students who had elected to hear him speak.

Conscious that he'll be late for Sarah, he attempts to break into a run, but the aches and pains in his over-exercised body almost cripple him. Hating that Al's warnings were correct, instead he limps along, trailing behind what seem to be the two slowest people on Grafton Street. His plan to overtake them on either side is botched as people-traffic prevent him from leaving his lane. With impatience he slows, surrendering to the speed of the two before him, one of whom is singing happily to himself and swaying.

Drunk at this hour, honestly.

Dad takes his time, meandering up Grafton Street as though he has all the time in the world. I suppose he does, compared to everybody else, though a younger person would think differently. Sometimes he stops and points at things, joins circles of spectators to watch a street act and when we continue on, he steps out of line to really

143

confuse the situation. Like a rock in a stream, he sends people flowing around him; he's a small diversion yet he's completely oblivious. He sings as we move up and down, down and up.

'Grafton Street's a wonderland,
There's magic in the air,
There's diamonds in the ladies' eyes and gold-
    dust in their hair.
And if you don't believe me,
Come and see me there,
In Dublin on a sunny summer morning.'

He looks at me and smiles and sings it all over again, forgetting some words and humming them instead.

During my busiest days at work, twenty-four hours just don't seem enough. I almost want to hold my hands out in the air and try to grasp the seconds and minutes as if I could stop them from moving on, like a little girl trying to catch bubbles. You can't hold on to time but somehow Dad appears to. I always wondered how on earth he filled his moments, as though my opening doors and talking about sunny angles, central heating and wardrobe space was worth so much more than his pottering. In truth, we're all just pottering, filling the time that we have here, only we like to make ourselves feel bigger by compiling lists of importance.

So this is what you do when it all slows down and the minutes that tick by feel a little longer than before. You take your time. You breathe slowly. You open your eyes a little wider and look at everything. Take it all in. Rehash stories of old, remember people, times and occasions gone by. Allow everything you see to remind you of something. Talk about those things. Stop and take your time to notice things and make those things you notice matter. Find out the answers you didn't know to yesterday's crosswords. *Slow down*. Stop trying to do everything now, now, now. Hold up the people behind you for all you care, feel them kicking at your heels but maintain your pace. Don't let anybody dictate your speed.

Though if the person behind me kicks my heels one more time . . .

The sun is so bright it's difficult to look straight ahead. It's as though it's sitting on the top of Grafton Street, another bowling ball ready to knock us all down. Finally we near the top of the street and escape of the human current is in sight. Dad suddenly stops walking, enthralled by the sight of a mime artist nearby. As I'm linking his arm, I'm forced to a sudden stop too, causing the person behind to run straight into me. One grand final kick of my heels. That is it.

'Hey!' I spin around. 'Watch it!'

He grunts at me in frustration and power-walks off. 'Hey yourself,' an American accent calls back.

I'm about to shout again but his voice silences me.

'Look at that,' Dad marvels, watching the mime trapped in an invisible box. 'Should I give him an invisible key to get out of that box?' He laughs again. 'Wouldn't that be funny, love?'

'No, Dad.' I examine the back of my road-rage nemesis, trying to recall the voice.

'You know de Valera escaped prison by using a key that was smuggled in to him in a birthday cake. Someone should tell this fella that story. Now where do we go from here?' He spins round beside me, looking about. He walks off in another direction, straight through a group of parading Hare Krishnas, without taking the slightest bit of notice.

The sandy duffel coat turns round again, throws me one last dirty look before he hurries on in a huff.

Still, I stare. If I was to reverse the frown. That smile. Familiar.

'Gracie, this is where you get the tickets. I've found it,' he shouts from afar.

'Hold on, Dad.' I watch after the duffel coat. Turn round one more time and show me your face, I plead.

'I'll just go get the tickets, so.'

'OK, Dad.' I continue to watch the duffel coat moving further away. I don't – correction, *can't* – move my eyes away from him. I mentally throw a cowboy's rope around his body and begin to pull him back towards me. His strides become smaller, his speed gradually slows.

He suddenly stops dead in his tracks. Yee-ha. Please turn. I pull on the rope.

He spins round, searches the crowd. For me?

'Who are you?' I whisper.

'It's me!' Dad is beside me again. 'You're just standing in the middle of the street.'

'I know what I'm doing,' I snap. 'Here, go get the tickets.' I hold out some money.

I step away from the Hare Krishnas, keeping my eye on the duffel coat, hoping he'll see me. The crisp pale wool of his coat almost glows among the dark and gloomy colours of others around him. Around his sleeves, down his front like an autumn St Nicholas. I clear my throat and smooth down my shortened hair.

His eyes continue to search the street and then they ever so slowly fall upon mine. I remember him in the second it takes them to register me. 'Him' from the hair salon.

What now? Perhaps he won't recognise me at all. Perhaps he's just still angry that I shouted at him. I'm not sure what to do. Should I smile? Wave? Neither of us moves.

He holds up a hand. Waves. I look behind me first, to ensure it's me that his attention is on. Though I was so sure anyway, I would have bet my father on it. Suddenly Grafton Street is empty. And silent. Just me and him. Funny how that happened. How thoughtful of everyone. I wave back. He mouths something to me.

Hungry? Horny? No.

Sorry. He's sorry. I try to figure out what to mouth back but I'm smiling. Nothing can be mouthed when smiling, it's as impossible as whistling through a smile.

'I got the tickets!' Dad shouts. 'Twenty euro each – it's a crime, that is. Seeing is for free, I don't know how they can charge us to use our eyes. I'm planning to write a strongly worded letter to somebody about that. Next time you ask me why I stay in and watch my programmes I'll have it in mind to remind you that it's free. Two euro for my TV guide, one hundred and fifty for a *yearly* licence fee is better value than a *day* out with you,' he huffs. 'Expensive taxis into the town, lookin' at things in a city I've lived in and have looked at for free for sixty years.'

Suddenly I hear the traffic again, see the people crowding around, feel the sun and breeze on my face, feel my heart beating wildly in my chest as my blood rushes around in frenzied excitement. I feel Dad tugging on my arm.

'It's leaving now. Come on, Gracie, it's leaving. It's a bit of a walk up the road, we have to go. Near the Shelbourne Hotel. Are you OK? You look like you've seen a ghost and don't tell me you have because I've dealt with enough today already. Forty euro,' he mutters to himself.

A steady flow of pedestrians gather at the top of Grafton Street to cross the road, blocking my view of him. I feel Dad pulling me back and so I begin to move with him down Merrion

Row, walking backwards, trying to keep him in sight.

'Damn it!'

'What's wrong, love? It's not far up the road at all. What on earth are you doing, walking backwards?'

'I can't see him.'

'Who, love?'

'A guy I think I know.' I stop walking backwards and stand in line with Dad, continuing to look down the street and scouring the crowds.

'Well, unless you know that you know him for sure, I wouldn't be stopping to chat in the city,' Dad says protectively. 'What kind of a bus is this at all, Gracie? It looks a bit odd, I'm not sure about this. I don't come to the city for a few years and look what the CIE do.'

I ignore him and let him lead the way onto the bus, while I'm busy looking the other way, searching furiously through the, curiously, plastic windows. The crowd finally move on from in front of where he stood to reveal nothing.

'He's gone.'

'Is that so? Can't have known him too well then, if he just ran off.'

I turn my attention to my father. 'Dad, that was the weirdest thing.'

'I don't care what you say, there's nothing weirder than this.' Dad looks around us in bewilderment.

Finally I too look around the bus and take in

my surroundings. Everyone else is wearing a Viking helmet, with life jackets on their laps.

'OK, everybody,' the tour guide speaks into the microphone, 'we finally have everyone on board. Let's show our new arrivals what to do. When I say the word I want you all to rooooooar just like the Vikings did! Let me hear it!'

Dad and I jump in our seats, and I feel him cling to me, as the entire bus roars.

FOURTEEN

'Good afternoon, everybody, I'm Olaf the White, and welcome aboard the Viking Splash bus! Historically known as DUKWS, or Ducks, as they're more affectionately known. We are sitting in the amphibious version of the General Motors vehicle built during World War Two. Designed to withstand being driven onto beaches in fifteen-foot seas to deliver cargo or troops from ship to shore, they are now more commonly used as rescue and underwater recovery vehicles in the US, UK and other parts of the world.'

'Can we get off?' I whisper in Dad's ear.

He swats me away, enthralled.

'This particular vehicle weighs seven tonnes, is thirty-one feet long and eight feet wide. It has six wheels and can be driven in rear-wheel or all-wheel drive. As you can see, it has been mechanically rebuilt and outfitted with comfortable seats, a roof, roll down sides to protect you from the elements, because as you all know, after we see the sites around the city, we have a "splashdown" into the water with a fantastic trip around the Grand Canal Docklands!'

Everyone cheers and Dad looks at me, eyes wide like a little boy.

'Sure, no wonder it was twenty euro. A bus that goes into the water. A *bus*? That goes into the *water*? I've never seen the likes of it. Wait till I tell the lads at the Monday Club about this. Big mouth Donal won't be able to beat this story for once.' He turns his attention back to the tour operator, who, like everyone else on the bus, is wearing a Viking helmet with horns. Dad collects two, props one on his head and hands the other, which has blonde side plaits attached, to me.

'Olaf, meet Heidi.' I pop it on my head and turn to Dad.

He roars quietly in my face.

'Sights along the way include our famous city cathedrals, St Patrick's and Christchurch, Trinity College, Government buildings, Georgian Dublin . . .'

'Ooh, you'll like this one,' Dad elbows me.

'. . . and of course *Viking Dublin*!'

Everyone roars again, including Dad, and I can't help but laugh.

'I don't understand why we're celebrating a bunch of oafs who raped and pillaged their way around our country.'

'Oh, would you ever lighten up, at all, and have the craic?'

'And what do we do when we see a *rival* DUKW on the road?' the tour guide asks.

There's a mixture of boos and roars.

'OK, let's go!' Olaf says enthusiastically.

Justin frantically searches over the shaven heads of a group of Hare Krishnas who have begun to parade by him and obstruct his view of his woman in the red coat. A sea of orange togas, they smile at him merrily through their bell-ringing and drum-beating. He hops up and down on the spot, trying to get a view down Merrion Row.

Before him, a mime artist, dressed in a black leotard, with a painted white face, red lips and a striped hat, appears suddenly. They stand opposite one another, each waiting for the other to do something, Justin praying for the mime to grow bored and leave. He doesn't. Instead, the mime squares his shoulders, looks mean, parts his legs and lets his fingers quiver around his holster area.

Keeping his voice down, Justin speaks politely, 'Hey, I'm really not in the mood for this. Would you mind playing with someone else, please?'

Looking forlorn, the mime begins to play an invisible violin.

Justin hears laughter and realises he has an audience. *Great.*

'Yeah, that's funny. OK, enough now.'

Ignoring the antics, Justin distances himself from the growing crowd and continues to search down Merrion Row for the red coat.

153

The mime appears beside him again, holds his hand to his forehead and searches the distance as though at sea. His herd of spectators follow, bleating and snap-happy. An elderly Japanese couple take a photograph.

Justin grits his teeth and speaks quietly, hoping nobody but the mime can hear. 'Hey, asshole, do I look like I'm having fun?'

With lips of a ventriloquist, a gruff Dublin accent responds, 'Hey, asshole, do I look like I give a shit?'

'You wanna play like this? Fine. I'm not sure whether you're trying to be Marcel Marceau or Coco the clown but your little pantomime street performance is insulting to both of them. This crowd might find your stolen routines from Marceau's repertoire amusing but I don't. Unlike me, they're not aware that you've failed to notice the fact that Marceau used these routines to tell a story or sketch a theme or character. He did not just randomly stand on a street trying to get out of a box nobody could see. Your lack of creativity and technique gives a bad name to mimes all over the world.'

The mime blinks once and proceeds to walk against an invisible strong wind.

'Here I am!' a voice calls beyond the crowd.

There she is! She recognised me!

Justin shuffles from foot to foot, trying to catch sight of her red coat.

The crowd turns and parts, to reveal Sarah, looking excited by the scene.

The mime mimicks Justin's obvious disappointment, plastering a look of despair on his face and hunching his back so that his arms hang low and his hands almost scrape the ground.

'Oooooooo,' go the crowd, and Sarah's face falls.

Justin nervously replaces his look of disappointment with a smile. He makes his way through the crowd, greets Sarah quickly and leads her speedily away from the scene while the crowd clap and some drop coins into a container nearby.

'Don't you think that was a bit rude? Maybe you should have given him some change or something,' she says, looking over her shoulder apologetically at the mime, who is covering his face and moving his shoulders up and down violently in a false fit of tears.

'I think the gentleman in the leotard was a bit rude.' Distracted, Justin continues to look around for the red coat as they make their way to the restaurant for lunch, which Justin now definitely wants to cancel.

Tell her you feel sick. No. She's a doctor, she'll ask too many questions. Tell her you have unfortunately made a mistake and that you have a lecture, right now. Tell her, tell her!

But instead he finds himself continuing to walk with her, his mind as active as Mount St Helens, his eyes jumping around like an addict needing a fix. In the basement restaurant, they are led to a quiet table in the corner. Justin eyes the door.

Yell 'FIRE' and run!

Sarah shuffles her coat off her shoulders to reveal much flesh, and pulls her chair closer to his.

Such a coincidence he bumped, quite literally, into the woman from the salon again. Though maybe it wasn't such a big deal; Dublin's a small town. Since being here he's learned that everyone pretty much knows everyone, or somebody related to somebody, that someone once knew. But the woman, he would definitely have to stop calling her that. He should give her a name. *Angelina.*

'What are you thinking about?' Sarah leans across the table and gazes at him.

Or Lucille. 'Coffee. I'm thinking about coffee. I'll have a black coffee, please,' he says to the waitress clearing their table. He looks at her name badge. *Jessica.* No, his woman wasn't a Jessica.

'You're not eating?' Sarah asks, disappointed and confused.

'No, I can't stay as long as I'd hoped. I have to get back to the college earlier than planned.' His leg bounces beneath the table, hitting the surface and rattling the cutlery. The waitress and Sarah eye him peculiarly.

'Oh, OK, well,' she studies the menu, 'I'll have a chef's salad and a glass of the house white, please,' she says to the waitress and then to Justin, 'I have to eat or I'll collapse, I hope you don't mind.'

'No problem,' he smiles. *Even though you*

ordered the biggest fucking salad on the menu.
How about the name, Susan? Does my woman
look like a Susan? My woman? *What the hell is*
wrong with me?

'We are now turning into Dawson Street, so
named after Joshua Dawson, who also designed
Grafton, Anne and Henry Streets. On your right
you will see the Mansion House, which houses
the Lord Mayor of Dublin.'

All horned Viking helmets turn to the right.
Video cameras, digital cameras and camera
phones are suspended from the the open windows.

'You think this is what the Vikings did, way
back when, Dad? Went clickety-click with their
cameras at buildings that weren't even built yet?'
I whisper.

'Oh, shut up,' he says loudly, and the tour
operator stops speaking, shocked.

'Not you.' Dad waves a hand at him. 'Her.' He
points, and the entire bus looks at me.

'To your right you will see St Anne's Church,
which was designed by Isaac Wells in 1707. The
interior dates back to the seventeenth century,'
Olaf continues to the thirty-strong crew of Vikings
aboard.

'Actually the Romanesque façade wasn't
added until 1868, and that was designed by
Thomas Newenham Deane,' I whisper to Dad.

'Oh,' Dad says slowly at this, eyes widening.
'I didn't know that.'

My eyes widen at my own piece of information. 'Me neither.'

Dad chuckles.

'We are now on Nassau Street, we will pass Grafton Street on the left in just a moment.'

Dad starts singing, 'Grafton Street's a wonderland.' Loudly.

The American woman in front of us turns around, her face beaming. 'Oh, do you know that song? My father used to sing that song. He was from Ireland. Oh, I would love to hear it again; can you sing it for us?'

A chorus of, 'Oh, yes, please do . . .' from around us.

No stranger to singing in public, the man who sings weekly at the Monday Club begins singing and the entire bus joins in, moving from side to side. Dad's voice reaches out beyond the plastic fold-up windows of the DUKW and into the ears of pedestrians and traffic going by.

I take another mental photograph of Dad sitting beside me, singing with his eyes closed, two horns propped on top of his head.

Justin watches with growing impatience as Sarah slowly picks at her salad. Her fork playfully pokes at a piece of chicken; the chicken hangs on, falls off, grabs on again and manages to hang on while she waves it around, using it as a sledgehammer to knock pieces of lettuce over to see what's beneath. Finally she stabs a piece of tomato and as she lifts the fork to her mouth, the same piece of chicken falls off again. That was the third time she'd done that.

'Are you sure you're not hungry, Justin? You seem to be really studying this plate,' she smiles, waving another forkful of food around, sending red onion and cheddar cheese tumbling back to the plate. It was like one step forward, two steps back every time.

'Yeah, sure, I wouldn't mind having some.' He'd already ordered and finished a bowl of soup in the time it had taken her to have five mouthfuls.

'You want me to feed it to you?' she flirts, moving it in circular motions towards his mouth.

'Well, I want more on it than that, for a start.'

She spears a few other pieces of food.

'More,' he says, keeping an eye on his watch. The more food he can squeeze in his mouth, the quicker this frustrating experience will be over. He knows that his woman, *Veronica*, is probably long gone by now, but sitting here, watching Sarah burn more calories playing with her food than ingesting them, isn't going to confirm that for him.

'OK, here comes the aeroplane,' she sings.

'More.' At least half of it has fallen again during its 'take-off'.

'More? How can you possibly fit more on the fork, never mind in your mouth?'

'Here, I'll show you.' Justin takes the fork from

159

her and begins stabbing at as much as he can. Chicken, corn, lettuce, beetroot, onion, tomato, cheese; he manages it all. 'Now, if the lady pilot would like to bring her plane in to land . . .'

She giggles. 'This is *not* going to fit in your mouth.'

'I have a pretty big mouth.'

She shovels it in, laughing all the while, barely fitting it all into Justin's mouth. When he's finally swallowed it all, he looks at his watch and then again at her plate.

'OK, now you do it.' *You're such a shit, Justin.*

'No way,' she laughs.

'Come on.' He gathers as much food as possible, including the same piece of chicken she's deserted four times and 'flies' it into her open mouth.

She laughs while trying to fit it all in. Barely able to breathe, chew, swallow or smile, she still tries to look pretty. For almost a full minute she's unable to speak in her attempts to chew as lady-like as possible. Juices, dressing and food dribble down her chin and when she finally swallows, her lipstick-smudged mouth smiles at him to reveal a great big piece of lettuce stuck between her teeth.

'That was fun,' she smiles.

Helen. Like Helen of Troy, so beautiful she could start a war.

'Are you finished? Can I take the plate?' the waitress asks.

Sarah begins to answer, 'N—' but Justin jumps in.

'Yes, we are, thank you.' He avoids Sarah's stare.

'Actually I'm not quite finished, thank you,' Sarah says sternly. The plate is replaced.

Justin's leg bounces beneath the table, his impatience growing. *Salma. Sexy Salma.* An awkward silence falls between them.

'I'm sorry, Salma, I don't mean to be rude—'

'Sarah.'

'What?'

'My name is Sarah.'

'I know that. It's just that—'

'You called me Salma.'

'Oh. What? Who's Salma? God. Sorry. I don't even know a Salma, honestly.'

She speeds up her eating, obviously dying to get away from him now.

He says more softly, 'It's just that I have to get back to the college—'

'Earlier than planned. You said.' She smiles quickly and her face falls immediately as she looks back down at her plate. She pierces the food with purpose now. Playtime over. Time to eat. Food fills her mouth instead of words.

Justin cringes inside, knowing his behaviour is uncharacteristically rude. *Now say it like you mean it, you jerk.* He stares at her: beautiful face, great body, intelligent woman. Dressed smartly in a trouser suit, long legs, big lips. Long elegant fingers, neat French-manicured nails, a smart bag to match her shoes by her feet. Professional, confident, intelligent. There is absolutely nothing wrong with this woman at all. It is Justin's own distraction that is the problem, the feeling that a part of him is somewhere else. A part of him, in fact, that feels so nearby, he is almost compelled to run out and catch it. Right now running seems like a good idea but the problem is he doesn't know what he is trying to catch, or who. In a city of one million people, he can't expect to walk outside this door and find the same woman standing on the pavement. And is it worth leaving the beautiful woman sitting with him in this restaurant, in order just to chase a good idea?

He stops bouncing his leg up and down and settles back into his chair, no longer at the edge of his seat or ready to dive for the door the second she puts down her knife and fork.

'Sarah,' he sighs, and means it this time when he says, 'I'm very sorry.'

She stops forking food into her mouth and looks up at him, chews quickly, dabs at her lips with a napkin and swallows. Her face softens. 'OK.'

She wipes away the crumbs around her plate, shrugging. 'I'm not looking for a marriage here, Justin.'

'I know, I know.'

'Lunch is all this is.'

'I know that.'

'Or shall we say just coffee, in case mentioning the former sends you running out the fire exit yelling "Fire"?' She acknowledges his empty cup and flicks at imaginary crumbs now.

He reaches out to grab her hand and stop her fidgeting. 'I'm sorry.'

'OK,' she repeats.

The air clears, the tension evaporates, her plate is cleared away.

'I suppose we should get the check—'

'Have you always wanted to be a doctor?'

'Whoa.' She pauses midway opening her wallet. 'It's just intense either way with you, isn't it?' But she's smiling.

'I'm sorry.' Justin shakes his head. 'Let's have a coffee before we leave. Hopefully I'll have time to stop this from being the worst date you've ever been on.'

'It's not.' She shakes her head, smiling. 'But it's a close second. It was almost the worst but you pulled it right back there with the doctor question.'

Justin smiles. 'So. Have you?'

She nods. 'Ever since James Goldin operated on me when I was in Junior Infants. What do you call it, kindergarten? Anyway, I was five years old and he saved my life.'

'Wow. That's young for a serious operation. It must have had a huge effect.'

'Profound. I was in the yard at lunch break, I fell during a game of hopscotch and hurt my knee.

The rest of my friends were discussing amputation but James Goldin came running over and straight away gave me mouth-to-mouth. Just like that, the pain went away. And that's when I knew.'

'That you wanted to be a doctor?'

'That I wanted to marry James Goldin.'

Justin smiles. 'And did you?'

'Nah. Became a doctor instead.'

'You're good at it.'

'Yes, because you can tell that from a needle insertion at a blood donation,' she smiles. 'Everything OK in that department?'

'My arm's a little itchy but it's fine.'

'Itchy? It shouldn't be itchy, let me see.'

He goes to roll up his sleeve and stops. 'Could I ask you something?' He squirms a little in his chair. 'Is there any way that I can find out where my blood went?'

'Where? As in, which hospital?'

'Well, yeah, or even better, do you know *who* it went to?'

She shakes her head. 'The beauty of this is that it's completely anonymous.'

'But someone, somewhere would know, wouldn't they? In hospital records or even *your* office records?'

'Of course. Products in a blood bank are always individually traceable. It's documented throughout the entire process of donation, testing, separation into components, storage and administration to the recipient but—'

'There's a word I hate.'

'Unfortunately for you, you can't know who received your donation.'

'But you just said that it's documented.'

'That information can't be released. But all our details are kept in a secure computerised database where all your donor details are kept. Under the Data Protection Act you have the right to access your donor records.'

'Will those records tell me who received my blood?'

'No.'

'Well, then, I don't want to see them.'

'Justin, the blood you donated was not transfused directly into somebody's body exactly as it came from your vein. It was broken up and separated into red blood cells, white blood cells, platelets—'

'I know, I know, I know all of that.'

'I'm sorry that there's nothing I can do. Why are you so keen to know?'

He thinks about it for a while, drops a brown sugar cube into his coffee and stirs it around. 'I'm just interested to know who I helped, if I helped them at all and if I did, how they are. I feel like . . . no, it sounds stupid, you'll think I'm insane. It doesn't matter.'

'Hey, don't be silly,' she says soothingly. 'I already think you're insane.'

'I hope that's not your medical opinion.'

'Tell me.' Her piercing blue eyes watch him over the brim of her coffee cup as she sips.

165

'This is the first time I've said this aloud, so forgive me for speaking while I think. At first, it was a ridiculous macho ego trip. I wanted to know whose life I saved. Which lucky person I'd sacrificed my precious blood for.'

Sarah smiles.

'But then over the last few days I haven't been able to stop thinking about it. I feel differently. Genuinely different. Like I've given something away. Something precious.'

'It is precious, Justin. We need more donors all the time.'

'I know, but not – not like that. I just feel like there's someone out there walking around with something inside them that I gave them and now I'm missing something—'

'The body replaces the liquid part of your donation within twenty-four hours.'

'No, I mean, I feel like I've given something away, a part of me, and that somebody else has been completed because of that part of me and . . . my God, this sounds crazy. I just want to know who that person is. I just feel like there's a part of me missing and I need to get out there and grab it.'

'You can't get your blood back, you know,' Sarah jokes weakly, and they both fall into deep thought; Sarah looking sadly into her coffee, Justin trying to make sense of his jumbled words.

'I should never try to discuss something so illogical with a doctor, I suppose,' he says.

166

'You sound like a lot of people I know, Justin. You're just the first person I've heard blame it on a blood donation.'

Silence.

'Well,' Sarah reaches behind her chair to get her coat, 'you're in a rush so we should really move now.'

They make their way down Grafton Street in a comfortable silence that's occasionally dotted with small talk. They automatically stop walking at the Molly Malone statue, across the road from Trinity College.

'You're late for your class.'

'No, I've got a little while before I—' He looks at his watch and then remembers his earlier excuse. He feels his face redden. 'Sorry.'

'It's OK,' she repeats.

'I feel like this whole lunch date has been me saying sorry and you saying that it's OK.'

'It really is OK,' she laughs.

'And I really am—'

'Stop!' She holds her hand to his mouth to hush him. 'Enough.'

'I really had a lovely time,' he says awkwardly. 'Should we . . . you know, I'm feeling really uncomfortable right now with her watching us.'

They look to their right and Molly stares down at them with her bronze eyes.

Sarah laughs. 'You know maybe we could make arrangements to—'

'Rooooooaaaaaaaaarrrrrrrrrr!!'

Justin almost leaps out of his skin with fright, startled by the intense screaming coming from the bus stopped at the traffic lights beside him. Sarah yelps with fright and her hand flies to her chest. Beside them more than a dozen men, women and children, all wearing Viking helmets, are waving their fists in the air and laughing and roaring at passers-by. Sarah and the dozens of others crowded around them on the pavement start laughing, some roar back, most ignore them.

Justin, whose breath has caught in his throat, is silent, for he can't take his eyes off the woman laughing uproariously with an old man; a helmet on her head, long blonde plaits flowing each side.

'We certainly got them, Joyce,' the old man laughs, roaring lightly in her face and waving his fist.

She looks surprised at first, then hands him a five-euro note, much to his delight, and they both continue laughing.

Look at me, Justin wills her. Her eyes stay on the old man's as he holds the note up to the light to check its authenticity. Justin looks to the traffic lights, which are still red. He has time yet for her to see him. *Turn around! Look at me just once!* The pedestrian lights flash to amber. He doesn't have much time.

Her head remains turned, completely lost in conversation.

The lights turn green and the bus slowly moves off up Nassau Street. He starts to walk alongside it, willing her with everything he has to look at him.

'Justin!' Sarah calls. 'What are you doing?'

He keeps on walking alongside the bus, quickening his pace and finally breaking out into a jog. He can hear Sarah calling after him but he can't stop.

'Hey!' he calls.

Not loud enough; she doesn't hear him. The bus picks up speed and Justin's jog breaks out into a run, the adrenalin surging through his body. The bus is beating him, speeding up. He's losing her.

'Joyce!' he blurts out. The surprising sound of his own yell is enough to stop him in his tracks. What on earth is he doing? He doubles over to rest his hands on his knees, tries to catch his breath, tries to centre himself in the whirlwind he feels caught up in. He looks back at the bus one last time. A Viking helmet appears from the window, blonde plaits moving from side to side like a pendulum. He can't make out the face but with just one head, just one person looking out from that bus and back at him, he knows it has to be her.

The whirlwind stops momentarily while he holds up a hand in salute.

A hand appears out the window and the bus rounds the corner onto Kildare Street, leaving Justin to, once again, watch her disappear from sight with his heart beating so wildly, he's sure the pavement is pounding beneath him. He may not have the slightest clue what is going on but there is one thing he knows now for sure.

Joyce. Her name is Joyce.

He looks down the empty street.

But who are you, Joyce?

'Why are you hanging your head out of the window?' Dad pulls me in, wild with worry. 'You might not have much to live for but, for Christ-sake, you owe it to yourself to live it.'

'Did you hear somebody calling my name?' I whisper to Dad, my mind a whirl.

'Oh, she's hearing voices now,' he grumbles. '*I* said your bloody name and you gave me a fiver for it, don't you remember?' He snaps it before her face and turns his attention back to Olaf.

'On your left is Leinster House, the building that now houses the National Parliament of Ireland.'

Snappedy-snap, clickety-click, flash-flash, record.

'Leinster House was originally known as Kildare House after the Earl of Kildare commissioned it to be built. On his becoming the Duke of Leinster, it was renamed. Parts of the building, which was formerly the Royal College of Surgeons—'

'Science,' I say loudly, still largely lost in thought.

'Pardon me?' He stops talking and heads turn once again.

'I was just saying that,' my face flushes, 'it was the Royal College of Science.'

'Yes, that's what I said.'

'No, you said "surgeons",' the American woman in front of me speaks out.

'Oh,' he gets flustered. 'Excuse me, I'm mistaken. Parts of the building, which was formerly the . . . the Royal College of,' he looks pointedly at me, '*Science*, have served as the seat of the Irish government since 1922 . . .'

I tune out.

'Remember I told you about the guy who designed the Rotunda hospital?' I whisper to Dad.

'I do. Dick somebody.'

'Richard Cassells. He designed this too. It's been claimed that it formed a model for the design of the White House.'

'Is that so?' Dad says.

'Really?' The American woman twists around in her seat to face me. She speaks loudly. Very loudly. Too loudly. 'Honey, did you hear that? This lady says the guy who designed this, designed the White House.'

'No, I didn't actually—'

Suddenly I notice the tour operator has stopped talking and is currently glaring at me with as much love as a Viking Dragon for a Sea Cat. All eyes, ears and horns are on us.

'Well, I said it's been *claimed* that it formed a *model* for the design of the White House. There aren't any certainties as such,' I say quietly, not wanting to be dragged into this. 'It's just that James Hoban, who won the competition for the design of the White House in 1792, was an Irishman.'

They stare expectantly at me.

'Well, he studied architecture in Dublin and would have more than likely studied the design of Leinster House,' I finish off quickly.

The people around me ooh, aah and talk amongst one another about that titbit of information.

'We can't hear you!' someone at the top of the bus shouts out.

'Stand up, Gracie.' Dad pushes me up.

'Dad . . .' I slap him away.

'Hey, Olaf, give her the microphone!' the woman shouts to the tour operator. He grudgingly hands it over and folds his arms.

'Eh, hello.' I tap it with my finger and blow into the mike.

'You have to say, "Testing one, two, three," Gracie.'

'Eh, testing one, two—'

'We can hear you,' Olaf the White snaps.

'OK, well,' I repeat my comments, and the people up front nod with interest.

'And this is all part of your government's buildings too?' the American woman points to the buildings either side.

I look uncertainly at Dad and he nods at me with encouragement. 'Well, actually no. The building to the left is the National Library and the National Museum is on the right.' I go to sit down again and Dad whooshes my backside back up. They are all still looking at me for more. The tour guide looks sheepish.

'Well, a bit of interesting information *may be* that the National Library and the National Museum were originally home of the Dublin Museum of Science and Art, which opened in 1890. Both were designed by Thomas Newenham Deane and his son Thomas Manly Deane after a competition held in 1885 and were constructed by the Dublin contractors J. and W. Beckett, who demonstrated the best of Irish craftsmanship in their construction. The Museum is one of the best surviving examples of Irish decorative stonework, woodcarving and ceramic tiling. The National Library's most impressive feature is the entrance rotunda. Internally this space leads up an impressive staircase to the magnificent reading room with its vast vaulted ceiling. As you can see for yourselves, the exterior of the building is characterised by its array of columns and pilasters in the Corinthian order and the rotunda with its open veranda and corner pavilions framing the composition. In the—'

Loud clapping interrupts my talk – single, loud clapping, coming only from one person: Dad. The rest of the bus is silent. A child, asking her mother if they can roar again, breaks it. An imaginary piece of tumbleweed blows down the aisle, landing at a grinning Olaf the White.

'I, em, I wasn't finished,' I say quietly.

Dad claps louder in response, and one man, who is sitting alone in the back row, joins in nervously.

'And . . . that's all I know,' I say quickly, sitting down.

'How do you know all that?' the woman in front asks.

'She's an estate agent,' Dad says proudly.

The woman's brow creases, she makes an 'oh' shape with her mouth and turns around again to face an extremely satisfied-looking Olaf. He grabs the microphone from me.

'Now everybody, let's rooooooooaaaaaar!'

The silence is broken as everybody comes to life again, while each muscle and organ in my body cringes into a foetal position.

Dad leans into me and crushes me against the window. He moves his head close to whisper in my ear and our helmets knock against one another.

'How did you know all that, love?'

As though I'd used all of my words up in that tirade, my mouth opens and closes but nothing comes out. How on earth did I know all of that?

FIFTEEN

My ears immediately sizzle as soon I enter the school gymnasium that same evening, and spy Kate and Frankie huddled together on the bleachers, looking deep in conversation with concern etch-a-sketched across their faces. Kate looks as though Frankie's just told her that her father's passed away, a face I'm familiar with as I was the one to give her that look, with that very news, five years ago at Arrivals in Dublin airport when she'd cut short her holiday to rush to his side. Now Kate is talking and Frankie looks as though her dog's been hit by a car, a face I'm also familiar with, as I was once again the one to deliver the news, and the blow, that broke three of the sausage dog's legs. Now Kate looks as though she's been caught in the act as she glances in my direction. Frankie freezes too. Looks of surprise, then guilt and then a smile to make me think they've just been discussing the weather, rather than the events in my life, which are as changeable as.

I wait for the usual Lady of Trauma to fill my shoes. To give me a little break while she offers the usual insightful comments that keep inquisitors at bay; explaining one's recent loss as more of a continuous journey rather than a dead end, giving one the invaluable opportunity to gain strength and learn about oneself, and thereby turning this terribly tragic affair into something hugely positive. Usual Lady of Trauma does not arrive, knowing this is no easy gig for her. She is well aware the two people who currently hug me tight can see through her words and right to the heart of me.

My friends' hugs are longer and tighter; consist of extra squeezes and pats, which alternate between a circular rubbing motion and a light pitter-pattering on the back, both of which I find surprisingly comforting. The pity in their faces hammers home my great loss and my stomach feels queasy and my head fully loaded again. I realise that swaddling myself in a nest with Dad does not hold the super healing powers I'd hoped for, for every time I leave the house and meet somebody new, I have to go through it over again. Not just the entire rigmarole, but I have to feel it all, all over again, which is a far more tiring thing than words. Wrapped in Kate and Frankie's arms I could easily morph into the baby that they in their minds are coddling, but I don't, because if I start now, I know I'll never stop.

We sit on the bleachers away from the other

parents where few sit together but most take time that is precious and rare to be alone to read or think or watch their children doing unimpressive sideways tumbles on the blue rubber mats. I spot Kate's children, six-year-old Eric and my five-year-old goddaughter, Jayda, the *Muppet Christmas Carol* fanatic I have sworn not to hold anything against. They are enthusiastically hopping about and chirping like crickets, pulling their underwear from in between the cheeks of their behinds and tripping over untied shoelaces. Eleven-month-old Sam sleeps beside us in a stroller, blowing bubbles from his chubby lips. I watch him fondly, then remember again and look away. Ah, remembering. That old chestnut.

'How's work, Frankie?' I ask, wanting everything to be as it was.

'Busy as usual,' she responds, and I detect guilt, perhaps even embarrassment.

I envy her normality, possibly even her boredom. I envy that her today was the same as her yesterday.

'Still buying low, selling high?' Kate pipes up.

Frankie rolls her eyes. 'Twelve years, Kate.'

'I know, I know,' Kate bites her lip and tries not to laugh.

'Twelve years, I've had this job and twelve years you've being saying that. It's not even funny any more. In fact I don't recall it *ever* being, and yet you persist.'

Kate laughs. 'It's just that, I have absolutely no idea what it is that you do. Something in the stock market?'

'Manager, deputy head corporate treasury and investor solutions desk,' Frankie tells her.

Kate stares back blankly, then sighs. 'So many words to say that you work at a desk.'

'Oh, I'm sorry, what do you do all day, again? Wipe shitty asses and make organic banana sandwiches?'

'There are other aspects to being a mother, Frankie,' Kate puffs. 'It is my responsibility to prepare three human beings so that if, God forbid, something happens to me, or when they are adults, they will be able to live and function and succeed responsibly in the world all by themselves.'

'And you mush organic bananas,' Frankie adds. 'No, no, hold on, is that before or after the preparation of three human beings? Before.' She nods to herself. 'Yes, definitely mush bananas and *then* prepare human beings. Got it.'

'All I'm saying is, you have, what, *seven* words to describe your paper-pushing job?'

'I believe it's eight.'

'I have one. *One*.'

'Well, I don't know. Is "car-pooler" one or two words? Joyce, what do you think?'

I stay out of it.

'The point I'm trying to make is that the word "mum",' she says, irritated, 'a teeny, tiny little word that *every* woman with a child is called, fails to describe the plethora of duties. If I was doing what I do everyday in your company, I'd be running the fucking place.'

Frankie shrugs nonchalantly. 'Sorry, but I don't think I care. And I can't speak for my colleagues, but personally I like to make my own banana sandwiches and wipe my own behind.'

'Really?' Kate lifts an eyebrow. 'I'm surprised you don't have some poor man you picked up along the way, do that for you.'

'Nope, I'm still searching for that special one,' Frankie smiles back sweetly.

They do this all the time: talk at each other, never to each other, in an odd bonding ritual that seems to pull them closer when it would do the opposite to anybody else. In the silence that follows they both have time to figure out what exactly they were talking about in my company. Ten seconds later Kate kicks Frankie. Oh, yes. The mention of children.

When something tragic has happened, you'll find that you, the tragic*ee*, become the person that has to make everything comfortable for everyone else.

'How's Crapper?' I fill their uncomfortable silence and ask after Frankie's dog.

'He's doing well; his legs are healing nicely. Still howls when he sees your photograph, though. Sorry I had to move it from the fireplace.'

'Doesn't matter. In fact I was going to ask you to move it. Kate, you can get rid of my wedding photo too.'

Divorce talk. Finally.

'Ah, Joyce,' she shakes her head and looks at me sadly, 'that's my favourite photo of me. I looked

179

so good at your wedding. Can I not just cut Conor out?'

'Or draw a little moustache on him,' Frankie adds. 'Or better yet, give him a personality. What colour should that be?'

I bite my lip guiltily to hide a smile that threatens to crawl from the corner of my lips. I'm not used to this kind of talk of my ex. It's disrespectful and I'm not sure I'm completely comfortable with it. But it is funny. Instead I look away to the children on the floor.

'OK, everybody.' The gymnastics instructor claps his hands for attention and the crickets' hopping and chirping momentarily subsides. 'Spread out on the mat. We're going to do backwards rolls. Place your hands flat on the floor, fingers pointing towards your shoulders as you roll back to a stand. Like this.'

'Well, looky-look at our little flexible friend,' Frankie remarks.

One by one the children roll backwards to a perfect stand. Until it gets to Jayda, who rolls over one side of her head in the most awkward way, kicks another child in the shins and then gets onto her knees before finally jumping to a stand. She strikes a Spice Girl pose in all of her pink sparkling glory, with peace fingers and all, thinking nobody has noticed her error. The instructor ignores her.

'Preparing a human being for the world,' Frankie repeats smartly. 'Yip. You'd be running the fucking place all right.' Frankie turns to me and softens her voice. 'So, Joyce, how are you?'

I have debated whether to tell them, whether to tell anyone. Short of carting me off to the madhouse I have no idea how anybody will react to what's been happening to me, or even how they should react. But after today's experience, I side with the part of my brain that is anxious to reveal.

'This is going to sound really odd so bear with me on this.'

'It's OK.' Kate grabs my hand. 'You say whatever you want. Just release.'

Frankie rolls her eyes.

'Thanks.' I slowly slip my hand out of hers. 'I keep seeing this guy.'

Kate tries to register this. I can see her trying to link it with the loss of my baby or my looming divorce, but she can't.

'I think I know him but at the same time, I know I don't. I've seen him precisely three times now, the most recent being today, when he chased after my Viking bus. And I think he called out my name. Though I may have imagined that because how on earth could he know my name? Unless he knows me, but that brings me back to my being sure that he really doesn't. What do you think?'

'Hold on, I'm way back at the Viking bus part,' Frankie slows me down. 'You say you have a Viking bus.'

'I don't *have* one. I was on one. With Dad. It goes into the water too. You wear helmets with horns and go "aaaagh" at everyone.' I go close to their faces and wave my fists at them.

They stare back blankly.

I sigh and slide back on the bench. 'So anyway, I keep seeing him.'

'OK,' Kate says slowly, looking at Frankie.

There's an awkward silence as they worry about my sanity. I join with them on that.

Frankie clears her throat. 'So this man, Joyce, is he young, old, or indeed a Viking upon your magic bus that travels the high waters?'

'Late thirties, early forties. He's American. We got our hair cut together. That's where I saw him first.'

'Which is lovely, by the way.' Kate gently fingers a few front strands.

'Dad thinks I look like Peter Pan,' I smile.

'So maybe he remembers you from the hair salon,' Frankie reasons.

'It even felt weird at the salon. There was a . . . recognition or a *something*.'

Frankie smiles. 'Welcome to the world of singledom.' She turns to Kate, whose face is scrunched up in disagreement. 'When's the last time Joyce allowed herself a little flirt with someone? She's been married for so long.'

'Please,' Kate says patronisingly to Frankie. 'If you think that's what happens when you're married then you're sorely mistaken. No wonder you're afraid to get married.'

'I'm not afraid, I just don't agree with it. You

know, just today I was watching a make-up show—'

'Oh, here we go.'

'Shut up and listen. And the make-up expert said that because the skin is so sensitive around the eye, you must apply cream with your *ring finger* because it is the finger with the *least power*.'

'Wow,' Kate says drily. 'You sure have revealed us married folk for the fools that we are.'

I rub my eyes wearily. 'I know I sound insane, I'm tired and probably imagining things where there is nothing to be imagined. The man I'm supposed to have on the brain is Conor and he's not. He's really not at all. I don't know if it's a delayed reaction and next month I'm going to fall apart, start drinking and wear black everyday—'

'Like Frankie,' Kate butts in.

'But right now, I feel nothing but relieved,' I continue. 'Isn't that terrible?'

'Is it OK for me to feel relieved too?' Kate asks.

'You hated him?' I ask sadly.

'No. He was fine. He was nice. I just hated you not being happy.'

'I hated him,' Frankie chirps up.

'We spoke briefly yesterday. It was odd. He wanted to know if he could take the espresso machine.'

'The bastard,' Frankie spits.

'I really don't care about the espresso machine. He can have it.'

'It's mind games, Joyce. Be careful. First it's the

183

espresso machine and then it's the house and then it's your soul. And then it's that emerald ring that belonged to his grandmother that he claims you stole but that you recall more than clearly that when you first went to his house for lunch he said, "help yourself" and there it was.' She scowls.

I look to Kate for help.

'Her break-up with Lee.'

'Ah. Well, it's not going to get like your break-up with Lee.'

Frankie grumbles.

'Christian went for a pint with Conor last night,' Kate says. 'Hope you don't mind.'

'Of course I don't. They're friends. Is he OK?'

'Yeah, he seemed fine. He's upset about the, you know . . .'

'Baby. You can say the word. I'm not going to fall apart.'

'He's upset about the baby and disappointed the marriage didn't work but I think he thinks it's the right thing to do. He's going back to Japan in a few days. He also said you're both putting the house on the market.'

'I don't like being there any more and we bought it together, so it's the right thing to do.'

'But are you sure? Where will you live? Is your dad not driving you insane?'

As a tragicee and future divorcee, you'll also find that people will question you on the biggest decision you've ever made in your life as though you hadn't thought about it at all before, as though, through their twenty questions and many dubious faces, they're going to shine light on something that you missed the first time or hundredth time round during your darkest hours.

'Funnily enough, no,' I smile as I think about him. 'He's actually having the opposite effect. Though he's only managed to call me Joyce once in a week. I'm going to stay with him until the house is sold and I find somewhere else to live.'

'That story about the man . . . apart from him, how are you *really*? We haven't seen you since the hospital and we were so worried.'

'I know. I'm sorry about that.' I'd refused to see them when they came to visit, and I'd sent Dad out to the corridor to send them home, which of course he didn't, and so they'd sat by my side for a few minutes while I stared at the pink wall, thinking about the fact I was staring at a pink wall, and then they left. 'I really appreciated you coming, though.'

'No you didn't.'

'OK, I didn't then, but I do now.'

I think about that, about how I am now, *really*. Well, they asked.

'I eat meat now. And I drink red wine. I hate anchovies and I listen to classical music. I particularly love the *JK Ensemble* with John Kelly on Lyric FM, who doesn't play Kylie and I don't mind. Last night I listened to Handel's "*Mi restano le lagrime*" from Act Three Scene One of *Alcina* before going to sleep, and I actually knew the

185

words but have no idea how. I know a lot about Irish architecture but not as much as I know about French and Italian. I've read *Ulysses* and can quote from it *ad nauseam* when I couldn't even finish the audio book before. Only today I wrote a letter to the council telling them how their cramming yet another new ugly modern block into an area in which its buildings are mostly older, less fashionable constructs means that not only is the nation's heritage seriously under threat but the sanity of its citizens too. I thought my father was the only person who wrote strongly worded letters. That's not such a big deal in itself, the big deal is that two weeks ago I'd have been *excited* about the prospect of showing these properties. Today I'm particularly vexed about talk of bulldozing a hundred-year-old building in Old Town, Chicago, and so I plan to write another letter. I bet you're wondering how I knew about that. Well, I read it in the recent edition of the *Art and Architectural Review*, the only truly international art and architectural publication. I'm a subscriber now.' I take a breath. 'Ask me anything, because I'll probably know the answer and I've no idea how.'

Stunned, Kate and Frankie look at one another.

'Maybe with the stress of constantly worrying about you and Conor over with, you're able to concentrate on things more,' Frankie suggests.

I consider that but not for long. 'I dream almost every night about a little girl with white-blonde hair who every night gets bigger. And I hear music

– a song I don't know. When I'm not dreaming about her I have vivid dreams of places I've never been, eating foods I've never tasted and surrounded by strange people that I seem to know so well. A picnic in a park with a woman with red hair. A man with green feet. And sprinklers.' I think hard. 'Something about sprinklers.

'When I wake up I have to remember all over again that my dreams are not real and that my reality is not a dream. I find that next to impossible, but not completely, because Dad is there with a smile on his face and sausages on the frying pan, chasing a cat called Fluffy around the garden and for some unknown reason hiding Mum's photograph in the hall drawer. And after the first few moments of my waking day when everything is crap, all those other things become the only things on my mind. And a man I can't get out of my head, but not Conor, as you'd assume, the love of my life that I've just separated from. No, I keep thinking about an American man that I don't even know.'

The girls' eyes are filled, their faces a mixture of sympathy, worry and confusion.

I don't expect them to say anything – they probably think I'm crazy – and so I look out to the kids again on the gymnasium floor and watch as Eric takes to the balance beam, a four-inch-wide beam covered in thin leather. The instructor calls out to him to do aeroplane arms. Eric's face is a picture of nervous concentration. He stops walking as he slowly lifts his arms. The instructor offers words of encouragement and a small proud smile lifts onto Eric's face. He raises his eyes briefly to see if his mother is watching and in that one moment, loses balance and falls straight down, the beam quite unfortunately landing between his legs. His face is one of horror.

Frankie snorts again. Eric howls. Kate runs to her child. Sam continues to blow bubbles.

I leave.

SIXTEEN

Driving back to Dad's, I try not to glance at my house as I pass. My eyes lose the battle with my mind and I see Conor's car parked outside. Since our final meal together at the restaurant we have talked a few times, each conversation varying in degrees of affection for one another, the last, at the lower end of the scale. The first call came late at night the day after our final meal; Conor asking just one last time if we were doing the right thing. His slurred words and soft voice drifted in my ear as I lay on my bed in my childhood box bedroom and stared at the ceiling, just as I did during those all-night phone calls when we first met. Living with my father at thirty-three years of age after a failed marriage, and a vulnerable husband on the other end of the phone . . . it was so easy right then to remember the greatest times we'd ever spent together and go back on our decision. But more often than not, the easy decisions are the wrong decisions, and sometimes we feel like we're going backwards when we're actually moving forward.

The next phone call was a little more stern, an embarrassed apology and a mention of something legal related. The next, a frustrated enquiry into why my solicitor hadn't replied to his solicitor yet. The next, him telling me his newly pregnant sister was going to take the cot, something that made me fly into a jealous rage as soon as I rang off and throw the phone in the bin. The last was to tell me he'd boxed everything up, he was leaving for Japan in a few days. And could he have the espresso machine?

But each time I hung up the phone, I felt that my weak goodbye wasn't a goodbye. It was more of a 'see you around'. I knew that there was always a chance to back out, that he'd be around for a little while longer, that our words weren't really final.

I pull the car over and stare up at the house we've lived in for almost ten years. Didn't it deserve more than a few weak goodbyes?

I ring the doorbell and there's no answer. Through the front window I can see everything in boxes, the walls naked, the surfaces bare, the stage set for the next family to move in and tread the boards. I turn my key in the door and step inside, making a noise so as not to surprise him. I'm about to call his name when I hear the soft tinkle of music drifting from upstairs. I make my way up to the half-decorated nursery and find Conor sitting on the soft carpet, tears streaming down his face as he watches the mouse chase the cheese. I cross the room and reach for him. On the floor, I hold him close and rock him gently. I close my eyes and drift away.

He stops crying and looks up at me slowly. 'What?'

'Hmm?' I snap out of my trance.

'You said something. In Latin.'

'No, I didn't.'

'Yes you did. Just there.' He dries his eyes. 'Since when do you speak Latin?'

'I don't.'

'Right,' he says sharply. 'Well, what does the one phrase that you do know mean?'

'I don't know.'

'You must know, you just said it.'

'Conor, I don't recall saying anything.' He glares at me, something pretty close to hate and I swallow hard.

A stranger stares back at me in a tense silence.

'OK.' He gets to his feet and moves towards the door. No more questions, no more trying to understand me. He no longer cares. 'Patrick will be acting as my solicitor now.'

Fantastic, his shit-head brother.

'OK,' I whisper.

He stops at the door and turns round, grinds his jaw as his eyes take in the room. A last look at everything, including me, and he's gone.

The final goodbye.

* * *

I have a restless night in bed at Dad's as more images flash through my mind like lightning, so fast and sharp they light up my head with an urgent bolt and then are gone again. Back to black.

A church. Bells ringing. Sprinklers. A tidal wave of red wine. Old buildings with shop fronts. Stained glass.

A view through banisters of a man with green feet, closing a door behind him. A baby in my arms. A girl with white-blonde hair. A familiar song.

A casket. Tears. Family dressed in black.

Park swings. Higher and higher. My hands pushing a child. Me swinging as a child. A seesaw. A chubby young boy raising me higher in the air, as he lowers himself to the ground. Sprinklers again. Laughter. Me and the same boy in swimming togs. Suburbs. Music. Bells. A woman in a white dress. Cobbled streets. Cathedrals. Confetti. Hands, fingers, rings. Shouting. Slamming.

The man with green feet closing the door.

Sprinklers again. A chubby young boy chasing me and laughing. A drink in my hand. My head down a toilet. Lecture halls. Sun and green grass. Music.

The man with green feet outside in the garden, holding a hose in his hand. Laughter. The girl with the white-blonde hair playing in the sand. The girl laughing on a swing. Bells again.

View from the banisters of the man with green feet closing a door. A bottle in his hand.

192

A pizza parlour. Ice-cream sundaes.

Pills in his hand too. The man's eyes seeing mine before the door closes. My hand on a doorknob. The door opening. Empty bottle on the ground. Bare feet with green soles. A casket.

Sprinklers. Rocking back and forth. Humming that song. Long blonde hair covering my face and in my small hand. Whispers of a phrase . . .

I open my eyes with a gasp, heart drumming in my chest. The sheets are wet beneath me; my body is soaked in sweat. I fumble in the darkness for the bedside lamp. With tears in my eyes that I refuse to allow to fall, I reach for my mobile and dial with trembling fingers.

'Conor?' My voice is shaking.

He mumbles incoherently for a little while until he awakens. 'Joyce, it's three a.m.,' he croaks.

'I know, I'm sorry.'

'What's wrong? Are you OK?'

'Yes, yes, I'm fine, it's just that, well, I – I had a dream. Or a nightmare or maybe it was neither, there were flashes of, well . . . lots of places and people and things and,' I stop myself and try to focus. '*Perfer et obdura; dolor hic tibi proderit olim?*'

'What?' he says groggily.

'The Latin that I said earlier, is that what I said?'

'Yeah, it sounds like it. Jesus, Joyce—'

'Be patient and tough; someday this pain will be useful to you,' I blurt out. 'That's what it means.'

He is quiet and then he sighs. 'OK, thanks.'

'Somebody told me that, if not when I was a child, but tonight, they told me.'

'You don't have to explain.'

Silence.

'I'm going back to sleep now.'

'OK.'

'Are you OK, Joyce? Do you want me to call someone for you or . . . ?'

'No, I'm fine. Perfect.' My voice catches in my throat. 'Good night.'

He's gone.

A single tear rolls down my cheek and I wipe it away before it reaches my chin. Don't start, Joyce. Don't you dare start now.

SEVENTEEN

As I make my way downstairs the following morning, I spy Dad placing Mum's photograph back on the hall table. He hears me approaching, whips out his handkerchief from his pocket and pretends he's dusting it.

'Ah, there she is. Muggins has risen from the dead.'

'Yes, well, the toilet flushing every fifteen minutes kept me awake for most of the night.' I kiss the top of his almost hairless head and go into the kitchen. I sniff the smoky atmosphere again.

'I'm very sorry that my prostate is bothering *your* sleep.' He studies my face. 'What's wrong with your eyes?'

'My marriage is over and so I decided to spend the night crying,' I explain matter-of-factly, hands on hips, sniffing the air.

He softens a bit but sticks the knife in regardless. 'I thought that's what you wanted.'

'Yes, Dad, you're absolutely right, the past few weeks have been every girl's dream.'

He moves up and down, down and up to the kitchen table, takes his usual seat in the path of the sun's beam, props his glasses on the base of his nose and continues his Sudoku. I watch him for a while, feeling mesmerised by his simplicity and then continue my sniffing mission.

'Did you burn toast again?' He doesn't hear me and keeps scribbling away. I check the toaster. 'It's on the right setting, I don't understand how it's still burning.' I look inside. No crumbs. I check the bin, no toast thrown out. I sniff the air again, grow suspicious and watch Dad from the corner of my eye. He fidgets.

'You're like that Fletcher woman or that Monk man, snooping around. You'll find no corpses here,' he says without looking up from his puzzle.

'Yes, but I'll find *something*, won't I?'

His head jerks up, quickly. Nervously. Aha. I narrow my eyes.

'What's up with you at all, at all?'

I ignore him, and race around the kitchen, opening presses, searching inside each of them.

He looks worried. 'Have you lost your mind? What are you doing?'

'Did you take your pills?' I ask, coming across the medicine cabinet.

'What pills?'

With a response like that, there's definitely something up.

'Your heart pills, memory pills, vitamin pills.'

'No, no and . . .' he thinks for a while, 'no.'

I bring them over to him, line them up on the table. He relaxes a little. Then I continue searching the cupboards and I feel him tense. I pull on the cereal cupboard knob—

'Water!' he shouts, and I jump and bang the door closed.

'Are you OK?'

'Yes,' he says calmly. 'I just need a glass of water for my pills. Glasses are in that cupboard over there.' He points to the other end of the kitchen.

Suspiciously, I fill a glass with water and deliver it to him. I return to the cereal cupboard.

'Tea!' he shouts. 'Sure, we'll have a cup of tea. Sit down there and I'll make it for you. You've been through such a tough time and you've been great about it all. So brave. Trophy brave, as a man says. Now sit down there and I'll fetch you a cuppa. A nice bit of cake as well. Battenburg – you liked that as a wee one. Always tried to take the marzipan off when no one was lookin', the greedy goat that you were.' He tries to steer me away.

'Dad,' I warn. He stops dithering and sighs in surrender.

I open the cupboard door and look inside. Nothing odd, or out of place, just the porridge I eat every morning and Sugar Puffs that I never touch. Dad looks satisfied, lets out a hearty harrumph-ing sound and makes his way back to the table. Hold on a minute. I open the press again and reach for the Sugar Puffs that I never eat and never see Dad eat. As soon as I lift it I know that it's empty of cereal. I look inside.

'Dad!'

'Ah what, love?'

'Dad, you promised me!' I hold the packet of cigarettes in front of his face.

'I only had one, love.'

'You have not had *only* one. That smell of smoke every morning is not burned toast. You lied to me!'

'One a day is hardly going to kill me.'

'That's exactly what it's going to do. You've had bypass surgery, you're not supposed to smoke at all! I turn a blind eye to your morning fry-ups but this, this is unacceptable,' I tell him.

Dad rolls his eyes and he holds his hand up like a puppet's mouth, mimicking me as he snaps it open and closed in my face.

'That's it, I'm calling your doctor.'

His mouth drops, he jumps out of his chair. 'No, love, don't do that.'

I march out to the hall and he chases after me. Up, down, down, up, up, down. Goes down on his right, bends his left.

'Ah, you wouldn't do that to me. If the cigarettes don't kill me, she will. She's a battleaxe, that woman.'

I pick up the phone that's beside Mum's photograph and dial the emergency number I've memorised. The first number that comes to my mind when I need to help the most important person in my life.

'If Mum knew what you were doing she would go berserk – oh.' I stall. 'That's why you hide the photograph?'

Dad looks down at his hands and nods sadly. 'She made me promise I'd stop. If not for me, for her. I didn't want her to see,' he adds in a whisper as though she can hear us.

'Hello?' There's a response on the other end of the phone. 'Hello? Is that you, Dad?' a young girl with an American accent says.

'Oh,' I snap out of it and Dad looks pleading at me. 'Pardon me,' I speak into the phone. 'Hello?'

'Oh, I'm sorry, I saw an Irish number and thought you were my dad,' the voice on the other end explains.

'That's OK,' I say, confused.

Dad is standing before me with his hands together in prayer.

'I was looking for . . .' Dad shakes his head wildly and I stall.

'Tickets to the show?' the girl asks.

I frown. 'To what show?'

'The Royal Opera House.'

'Sorry, who is this? I'm confused.'

Dad rolls his eyes and sits on the bottom stair. 'I'm Bea.'

'Bea.' I look at Dad questioningly and he shrugs. 'Bea who?'

'Well, who is this?' Her tone is harder.

'My name is Joyce. I'm sorry, Bea, I think I've dialled the wrong number. You said you saw an Irish number? Have I called America?'

'No, don't worry.' Happy there isn't a stalker at the other end, her tone is friendly again. 'You've called London,' she explains. 'I saw the Irish number and thought you were my dad. He's flying back tonight to make it to my show tomorrow and I was worried because I'm still a student and it's such a huge deal and I thought he was . . . sorry, I have absolutely no idea why I'm explaining this to you but I'm so nervous,' she laughs and takes a deep breath. 'Technically, this is his emergency number.'

'Funny, I dialled my emergency number too,' I say faintly.

We both laugh.

'Oh, weird,' she says.

'Your voice is familiar, Bea. Do I know you?'

'I don't think so. Don't know anyone in Ireland apart from my dad, who is a man and American, so unless you're my dad trying to be funny . . .'

'No, no, I'm not trying to be . . .' I feel weak at the knees. 'This may sound like a stupid question but, are you blonde?'

Dad holds his head in his hands and I hear him groan.

'Yeah! Why, do I sound blonde? Maybe that's not such a good thing,' she laughs.

I have a lump in my throat and must stop speaking. 'Just a silly guess,' I force out.

'Good guess,' she says curiously. 'Well, I hope everything's OK. You said you dialled your emergency number?'

'Yes, thanks, everything's fine.'

Dad looks relieved.

She laughs. 'Well, this is weird. I better go. Nice talking to you, Joyce.'

'Nice talking to you too, Bea. Best of luck with your ballet show.'

'Oh, sweet, thank you.'

We say our goodbyes and with a shaking hand I replace the handset.

'You silly dope, did you just dial the Americas?' Dad says, putting his glasses on and pressing a button on the phone. 'Joseph down the road showed me how to do this when I was getting the cranky calls. You can see who's called you and who you've called too. Turns out it was Fran bumping off her hand phone. The grandchildren got it for her last Christmas and she's done nothing with it but wake me up at all hours. Anyway, there it is. First few numbers are 0044. Where's that?'

'That's the UK.'

'Why on earth did you do that? Were you trying to trick me? Christ, that alone was enough to give me a heart attack.'

'Sorry, Dad.' I lower myself to the bottom stair, feeling shaky. 'I don't know where I got that number from.'

'Well, that sure taught me a lesson,' he says insincerely. 'I'll never smoke again. No siree, Bob.

Give me those cigarettes and I'll throw them out.'

I hold my hand out, feeling dazed.

He snaps the packet up and shoves it deep into his trouser pocket. 'I hope you'll be paying for that phone call because my pension certainly won't be.' He narrows his eyes. 'What's up with you?'

'I'm going to London,' I blurt out.

'What?' His eyes almost pop out of his head. 'Christ Almighty, Gracie, it's just one thing after another with you.'

'I have to find some answers to . . . something. I have to go to London. Come with me,' I urge, standing up and stepping towards him.

He begins to walk backward with his hand held protectively over his pocket containing the cigarettes.

'I can't go,' he says nervously.

'Why not?'

'Sure, I've never been away from here in my life!'

'All the more reason to go away now,' I urge him intensely. 'If you're going to smoke, you might as well see outside of Ireland before you kill yourself.'

'There are numbers I can call about being spoken to like that. Don't you think that I haven't heard about all of that abuse carry-on that children do to their elderly parents?'

'Don't play the victim, you know I'm looking out for you. Come to London with me, Dad. Please.'

'But, but,' he keeps moving backward, his eyes wide, 'I can't miss the Monday Club.'

'We'll go tomorrow morning, be back before Monday, I promise.'

'But, I don't have a passport.'

'You just need photo ID.'

We're approaching the kitchen now.

'But we've nowhere to stay.' He passes through the door.

'We'll book a hotel.'

'It's too expensive.'

'We'll share a room.'

'But I won't know where anything is in London.'

'I know my way; I've been plenty of times.'

'But . . . but,' he bumps into the kitchen table and can move back no further. His face is a picture of terror. 'I've never been on a plane before.'

'There's nothing to it. You'll probably have a great time up there. And I'll be right beside you, talking to you the whole time.'

He looks unsure.

'What is it?' I ask gently.

'What will I pack? What will I need for over there? Your mother usually packed all my going-away bags.'

'I'll help you pack,' I smile, getting excited. 'This is going to be so much fun – you and me on our first overseas holiday!'

Dad looks excited for a moment, then the excitement fades. 'No, I'm not going. I can't swim. If the plane goes down, I can't swim. I don't want

203

to go over the seas. I'll fly with you somewhere but not over the seas.'

'Dad, we live on an island; *everywhere* we go outside of this country, has to be over the sea. And there are life jackets on the plane.'

'Is that so?'

'Yeah, you'll be fine,' I assure him. 'They show you what to do in case of emergencies, but believe me there won't be one. I've flown dozens of times without so much as a hiccup. You'll have a great time. And imagine all the things you'll have to tell the gang at the Monday Club? They'll hardly believe their ears, they'll want to hear your stories all day.'

A smile slowly creeps onto Dad's lips and he concedes, 'Big mouth Donal would have to listen to someone else tell a more interesting story, for a change. I think Maggie might be able to clear a spot for me in the schedule, all right.'

EIGHTEEN

'Fran's outside, Dad. We have to go!'

'Hold on, love, I'm just making sure everything's OK.'

'Everything's fine,' I assure him. 'You've checked five times already.'

'You can never be too sure. You hear these stories of televisions malfunctioning and toasters exploding and people coming back from their holidays to a pile of smouldering ashes instead of their house.' He checks the socket switches in the kitchen for the umpteenth time.

Fran beeps the horn again.

'I swear one of these days I'm going to throttle that woman. Beep, beep, beep yourself,' he calls back, and I laugh.

'Dad,' I take his hand, 'we really have to go now. The house will be fine. All your friends that live around will keep an eye on it. Any little noise outside and their noses are pressed up against their windows. You know that.'

He nods and looks about, his eyes watering.

'We'll have great fun, really we will. What are you worried about?'

'I'm worried about that damn Fluffy cat, comin' into my garden and pissin' on my plants. I'm worried that the stranglers will suffocate my poor petunias and snapdragons, and that there'll be no one to keep an eye on my chrysanthemums. What if there's wind and rain when we're away? I haven't staked them yet and the flowers get heavy and might break. Do you know how long the magnolia took to settle? Planted it when you were a wee one, while your mother was lying out catchin' the sun on her legs and laughin' at Mr Henderson, God rest his soul, who was peekin' out the curtains at her from next door.'

Beep, beeeeeeep. Fran presses down on the horn.

'It's only a few days, Dad. The garden will be fine. You can get to work on it as soon as you get back.'

'OK, so.' He takes a last look around and makes his way to the door.

I watch his figure swaying. Dressed in his Sunday finest; a three-piece suit, shirt and tie, extra-shined shoes and his tweed cap, of course, which he'd never be seen without outside the house. He looks as though he's jumped straight from the photographs on the wall beside him. He stalls at the hall table and reaches for the photograph of Mum.

'You know your mother was always at me to go to London with her.' He pretends to wipe a smudge on the glass but really he runs his finger over Mum's face.

'Bring her with you, Dad.'

'Ah, no, that'd be silly,' he says confidently, but looks at me unsurely. 'Wouldn't it?'

'I think it'd be a great idea. The three of us will go and have a great time.'

His eyes tear up again and with a simple nod of the head, he slides the photo frame into his overcoat pocket and exits the house to more of Fran's beeping.

'Ah, there you are, Fran,' he calls to her as he sways down the garden path. 'You're late, we've been waiting for you for ages.'

'I was beeping, Henry – did you not hear me?'

'Were you now?' He gets into the car. 'You should press it a little harder the next time; we couldn't hear a thing in there.'

As I slide the key into the lock the phone sitting just inside the hall begins ringing. I look at my watch. Seven a.m. Who on earth would be calling at seven a.m.?

Fran's car beeps again and I turn round angrily and see Dad leaning over Fran's shoulder, pushing his hand down on the steering wheel.

'There you go now, Fran. We'll hear you the next time. Come on, love, we've a plane to catch!' he laughs uproariously.

I ignore the ringing phone and hurry to the car with the bags.

*   *   *

'There's no answer.' Justin paces the living room in a panic. He tries the number again. 'Why didn't you tell me about this yesterday, Bea?'

Bea rolls her eyes. 'Because I didn't think it'd be such a big deal. People get wrong numbers all the time.'

'But it wasn't a wrong number.' He stops walking and taps his foot impatiently to the sound of the rings.

'That's exactly what it was.'

Answering machine. Damn it! Do I leave a message?

He hangs up and frantically dials again.

Bored with his antics, Bea sits on the garden furniture in the living room and looks around the dust-sheet-covered room and the walls filled with dozens of colour samples. 'When is Doris going to have this place finished?'

'After she starts,' Justin snaps, dialling again.

'My ears are burning,' Doris sings, appearing at the door in a pair of leopard-print overalls, her face heavily made up as usual. 'Found these yesterday, aren't they adorable?' she laughs. 'Buzzy-Bea, sweetie, so lovely to see you!' She rushes to her niece and they embrace. 'We are so excited about your performance tonight, you have no idea. Little Buzzy-Bea all grown up and performing in the *Royal Opera House*.' Her voice rises to a screech. 'Oh, we are so proud, aren't we, Al?'

Al enters the room with a chicken leg in his hand. 'Mmm hhm.'

Doris looks him up and down with disgust, and then back to her niece. 'A bed for the spare room arrived yesterday morning so you'll actually have something to sleep on when you stay, won't that be a treat?' She glares at Justin. 'Also, I got some paint and fabric samples so we can start planning your room design but I'm only designing according to feng shui rules. I won't hear of anything else.'

Bea freezes. 'Oh gee, great.'

'I know we'll have such fun!'

Justin glares at his daughter. 'That's what you get for withholding information.'

'What information? What's going on?' Doris ties her hair up in a cerise-pink scarf and makes a bow at the top of her head.

'Dad is having a conniption fit,' Bea explains.

'I told him to go to the dentist already. He has an abscess, I'm sure of it,' Doris says matter-of-factly.

'I told him too,' Bea agrees.

'No, not that. The woman,' Justin says intensely. 'Remember the woman I was telling you about?'

'Sarah?' Al asks.

'No!' Justin responds as though that was the most ridiculous answer ever given.

'Who can keep up with you?' Al shrugs him off. 'Certainly not Sarah, especially when you're running at top speed after buses, leaving her behind.'

Justin cringes. 'I apologised.'

'To her voice mail,' he chuckles. 'She is never going to answer your calls again.'

I wouldn't blame her.

'The *déjà vu* woman?' Doris gasps, realising.

'Yes.' Justin gets excited. 'Her name is Joyce and she called Bea yesterday.'

'She *may not* have.' Bea's protests falls on deaf ears. '*A* woman named Joyce rang yesterday. But I do believe there's more than one Joyce in the world.'

Ignoring her, Doris gasps again. 'How can this be? How do you know her name?'

'I heard somebody call her that on a Viking bus. And *yesterday* Bea got a *phone call*, on her *emergency* number, that no one but me has, from a *woman in Ireland.*' Justin pauses for dramatic effect. 'Called Joyce.'

There's a silence. Justin nods his head knowingly. 'Yep, I know, Doris. Spooky, huh?'

Frozen in place, Doris widens her eyes. 'Spooky, all right. Besides from the Viking bus.' She turns to Bea. 'You're eighteen years old and you've given your father an *emergency* number?'

Justin groans with frustration and starts dialling again.

Bea's cheeks pink. 'Before he moved over, Mum wouldn't let him call at certain hours because of the time difference. So I got another number. It's not technically an emergency number but he's the only one that has it and every time he calls he seems to have done something wrong.'

'Not true,' Justin objects.

'Sure,' Bea responds breezily, flicking through a magazine. 'And I'm not moving in with Peter.'

'You're right, you're *not*. Peter,' he spits out the name, 'picks strawberries for a living.'

'I love strawberries,' Al offers his support. 'If it wasn't for Petey, I wouldn't eat 'em.'

'Peter is an *IT consultant*.' Bea holds her hands out in confusion.

Choosing this moment to butt in, Doris turns to Justin. 'Sweetie, you know I'm all for this stuff with the *déjà vu* lady—'

'Joyce, her name is Joyce.'

'Whatever, but you got nothing but a coincidence. And I'm all for coincidences but this is . . . well, a pretty dumb one.'

'I have not got nothing, Doris, and that sentence is atrociously wrong on so many grammatical levels, you wouldn't believe. I have got a *name* and now I have a *number*.' He kneels before Doris and squeezes her face in his hands, pushing her cheeks together so that her lips puff out. 'And that, Doris Hitchcock, means that I got something!'

'It also makes you a stalker,' Bea says under her breath.

You are now leaving Dublin. We hope you enjoyed your stay.

Dad's rubber ears go back on his head, his bushy eyebrows lift upward.

'You'll tell all the family that I'm asking for them, won't you, Fran?' Dad says a little nervously.

'Of course I will, Henry. You'll have a great

time.' Fran's eyes smile at me knowingly in the rearview mirror.

'I'll see them all when I come back,' Dad adds, closely watching a plane as it disappears to the skies. 'It's off behind the clouds now,' he says, looking at me unsurely.

'The best part,' I smile.

He relaxes a little.

Fran pulls over at the drop-off section, busy with people conscious they can't stay for more than a minute and are quickly unloading bags, hugging, taxi drivers being paid, other drivers being moved on. Dad stands still, like the rock thrown into the stream again, and takes it all in, as I lift the bags from the boot. Eventually he snaps out of it and turns his attention to Fran, suddenly filled with warm affection for a woman he usually can't stop bickering about. Then he surprises us all by offering her a hug, awkward as it is.

Once inside, in the hustle and bustle of one of Europe's busiest airports, Dad holds on to my arm tightly with one hand and with the other, pulls along the weekend bag I've lent him. It had taken me the entire day and night to convince him it wasn't anything like the tartan trolley-bags Fran and all the other older ladies use for their shopping. He looks around now and I see him registering men with similar bags. He looks happy, if not a little confused. We go to the computers to check in.

'What are you doing? Getting the sterling pounds out?'

'It's not an ATM, this is check-in, Dad.'

'Do we not speak to a person?'

'No, this machine does it for us.'

'I wouldn't trust this yoke.' He looks over the shoulder of the man beside us. 'Excuse me, is your yokey-mabob working for you?'

'*Scusi?*'

Dad laughs. 'Scoozy-woozy to you too.' He looks back at me with a grin on his face. 'Scoozy. That's a good one.'

'*Mi dispiace tanto, signore, la prego di ignorarlo, è un vecchio sciocco e non sa cosa dice,*' I apologise to the Italian man, who seemed more than taken aback by Dad's comments. I have no idea what I've said but he returns my smile and continues checking in.

'You speak Italian?' Dad looks surprised but I haven't time to respond as he hushes me as an announcement is made. 'Whisht, Gracie, it might be for us. We better hurry.'

'We have two hours until our flight.'

'Why did we come so early?'

'We have to.' I'm already getting tired now and the tireder I get, the shorter the answers get.

'Who says?'

'Security.'

'Security who?'

'Airport security. Through there.' I nod in the direction of the metal detectors.

'Where do we go now?' he asks once I retrieve our boarding passes from the machine.

'To check our bags in.'

'Can we not carry them on?'

'No.'

'Hello,' the lady behind the counter smiles, and takes my passport and Dad's ID.

'Hello,' Dad says chirpily, a saccharine smile forcing itself through the wrinkles of his permanently grumpy face.

I roll my eyes. Always a sucker for the ladies.

'How many bags are you checking in?'

'Two.'

'Did you pack your own bags?'

'Yes.'

'No.' Dad nudges me and frowns. 'You packed my bag for me, Gracie.'

I sigh. 'Yes, but you were with me, Dad. We packed it together.'

'Not what she asked.' He turns back to the lady. 'Is that OK?'

'Yes.' She continues, 'Did anybody ask you to carry anything for them on the plane?'

'N—'

'Yes,' Dad interrupts me again. 'Gracie put a pair of her shoes in my bag because they wouldn't fit in hers. We're only going for a couple of days, you know, and she brought three pairs. *Three*.'

'Do you have anything sharp or dangerous in your hand luggage – scissors, tweezers, lighters or anything like that?'

'No,' I say.

Dad squirms and doesn't respond.

'Dad,' I elbow him, 'tell her no.'

'No,' he finally says.

'Well done,' I snap.

'Have a pleasant trip.' She hands us back our IDs.

'Thank you. You have very nice lipstick,' Dad adds before I pull him away.

I take deep breaths as we approach the security gates and I try to remind myself that this is Dad's first time in an airport and that if you've never heard the questions before, particularly if you're a seventy-five-year-old, I agree they would seem quite strange.

'Are you excited?' I ask, trying to make the moment enjoyable.

'Delirious, love.'

I give up and keep to myself.

I collect a clear plastic bag and fill it with my make-up and his pills, and we make our way through the maze that is the security queue.

'I feel like a little mouse,' Dad comments. 'Will there be cheese at the end of this?' He gives a wheezy laugh. Then we are through to the metal detectors.

'Just do what they say,' I tell him while taking off my belt and jacket. 'You won't cause any trouble, will you?'

'Trouble? Why would I cause trouble? What are you doing? Why are you taking your clothes off, Gracie?'

I groan quietly.

'Sir, could you please remove your shoes, belt, overcoat and cap?'

'What?' Dad laughs at him.

'Remove your shoes, belt, overcoat and cap.'

'I will do no such thing. You want me walking around in my socks?'

'Dad, just do it,' I tell him.

'If I take my belt off, my trousers will fall down,' he says angrily.

'You can hold them up with your hands,' I snap.

'Christ Almighty,' he says loudly.

The young man looks round to his colleagues.

'Dad, just do it,' I say more firmly now. An extremely long queue of irritated seasoned travellers who already have their shoes, belts and coats off, is forming behind us.

'Empty your pockets, please.' An older and angrier-looking security man steps in.

Dad looks uncertain.

'Oh my God, Dad, this is not a joke. Just do it.'

'Can I empty them away from her?'

'No, you'll do it right here.'

'I'm not looking.' I turn away, baffled.

I hear clinking noises as Dad empties his pockets.

'Sir, you were told you could not bring these things through with you.'

I spin round to see the security man holding a lighter and toe-nail clippers in his hands, the packet of cigarettes is in the tray with the photograph of Mum. And a banana.

'Dad!' I say.

'Stay out of this, please.'

'Don't speak to my daughter like that. I didn't know I couldn't bring them. She said scissors and tweezers and water and—'

'OK, we understand, sir, but we're going to have to take these from you.'

'But that's my good lighter, you can't take it from me! And what'll I do without my clippers?'

'We'll buy new ones,' I say through gritted teeth. 'Now just do what they say.'

'OK,' he waves his hands rudely at them, 'keep the damn things.'

'Sir, please remove your cap, jacket, shoes and belt.'

'He's an old man,' I say to the security guard in a low voice so that the gathering crowd behind us don't hear. 'He needs a chair to sit on to take off his shoes. And he shouldn't have to take them off as they're corrective footwear. Can you not just let him through?'

'The nature of his right shoe means that we must check it,' the man begins to explain but Dad overhears and explodes.

'Do you think I have a BOMB IN MY SHOE? Sure, what kind of eejit would do that? Do you think I have a BOMB sittin' on my head under my cap or in my belt? Is my banana really a GUN, do you think?' He waves the banana around at the staff, making shooting sounds. 'Are you all gone loony in here?'

Dad reaches for his cap. 'Or maybe I've a GRENADE under my—'

He doesn't have the opportunity to finish as everything goes crazy. He is whisked away before my eyes and I am taken to a small cell-like room and ordered to wait.

NINETEEN

After fifteen minutes of sitting alone in the sparse interrogation room with nothing but a table and chair, I hear the door in the next room open, then close. I hear the squeak of chair legs and then Dad's voice, as always, louder than everyone else's. I move closer to the wall and press my ear up against it.

'Who are you travelling with?'

'Gracie.'

'Are you sure about that, Mr Conway?'

'Of course! She's my daughter, ask her yourself!'

'Her passport tells us her name is Joyce. Is she lying to us, Mr Conway? Or are you lying?'

'I'm not lying. Oh, I meant Joyce, I meant to say Joyce.'

'Are you changing your story now?'

'What story? I got the name wrong, is all. My wife is Gracie, I get confused.'

'Where is your wife?'

'She's not with us any more. She's in my pocket.

219

I mean the photograph of her is in my pocket. At least, it *was* in my pocket until the lads out there took her and put her in the tray. Will I get my toe-nail clippers back, do you think? They cost me a bit.'

'Mr Conway, you were told sharp items and lighter fluid is not permitted on the flights.'

'I know that, but my daughter, Gracie, I mean, Joyce, went mad at me yesterday when she found my pack of smokes hidden in the Sugar Puffs and I didn't want to take the lighter out of my pocket or she'd lose the head again. I apologise for that, though. I wasn't intending to blow up the plane or anything.'

'Mr Conway, please refrain from using such language. Why did you refuse to take off your shoes?'

'I have holes in me socks!'

There is a silence.

'I'm seventy-five years old, young man. Why on earth do I have to take my shoes off? Did you think I was going to blow the plane up with a rubber shoe? Or maybe it's the insoles you're worried about. Maybe you're right, you can never tell the damage a man can do with a good insole—'

'Mr Conway, please don't use such language and refrain from smart-aleck behaviour or you will not be allowed on the plane. What was the reason for your refusal to remove your belt?'

'My trousers would have fallen down! I'm not like all these kids now, I don't wear a belt to look *groovy*, as they say. Where I come from you wear it because it keeps your pants up. And you'd be arrestin' me for a whole lot more than this, if it didn't, believe you me.'

'You haven't been arrested, Mr Conway. We just need to ask you some questions. Behaviour such as yours is prohibited at this airport, so we need to ascertain if you are a threat to the safety of our passengers.'

'What do you mean, a threat?'

The security officer clears his throat. 'Well, it means finding out if you are a member of any gangs or terrorist organisations before we reconsider allowing you through.'

I hear Dad roar with laughter.

'You must understand that planes are very confined spaces and we can't allow anybody on that we aren't sure of. We have the right to choose who we allow onboard our aircraft.'

'The only threat I'd be in a confined space is when I've had a good curry from my local. And terrorist organisations? I am, all right. The Monday Club is all I'm a member of. Meet every Monday except on bank holidays when we meet on a Tuesday. A bunch of lads and lasses like me gettin' together for a few pints and a singsong is all it is. Though if you're lookin' for juice, Donal's family were pretty heavily involved in the IRA all right.'

I hear the man questioning him clear his throat again.

'Donal?'

'Donal McCarthy. Ah, leave him alone, he's ninety-seven, and I'm talkin' about way back when his dad fought. The only rebellious thing he's able to do now is whack the chessboard with his cane and that's only because he's frustrated he can't play. Arthritis in both his hands. Could do with gettin' it in his mouth, if you ask me. Talkin' is all he does. Annoys Peter no end but they've never gotten along since he courted his daughter and broke her heart. She's seventy-two. Have you ever heard anything more ridiculous? Had a wandering eye, she claimed, but sure, he's as cock-eyed as they come. His eye wanders without him even knowing it. I wouldn't blame the man for that, though he does like to dominate the conversations every week. I can't wait for him to listen to me for a change.' Dad laughs and sighs in the long pause that follows. 'Do you think I could get a cuppa?'

'We won't be much longer, Mr Conway. What is the nature of your visit to London?'

'I'm going because my daughter dragged me here, last minute. She gets off the phone yesterday morning and looks at me with a face as white as a sheet. I'm off to London, she says, like it's somethin' you just do last minute. Ah, maybe it is what you young people do, but not for me. Not what I'm used to at all, at all. Never been on a plane before, you see. So she says wouldn't it be fun if we both go away? And usually I'd say no, I've loads to be doin' in my garden. Have to put down

222

the lilies, tulips, daffodils and hyacinths in time for the spring, you see, but she says live a little and I felt like peltin' her because it's more livin' I've been doing than her. But because of recent, well, troubles, shall we say, I decided to come with her. And that's no crime, is it?'

'What recent troubles, Mr Conway?'

'Ah, my Gracie—'

'Joyce.'

'Yes, thank you. My Joyce, she's been goin' through a rough patch. Lost her little baby a few weeks back, you see. Had been years trying to have one with a fella that plays tennis in little white shorts and things finally looked great but she had an accident, fell, you see and she lost the little one. Lost a little of herself too, if I'm to be honest with you. Lost the husband too just last week, but don't you be feelin' sorry for her about that. She lost somethin' all right but, mind you, she got a little somethin' she never had before. Can't put my finger on exactly what, but whatever it is, I don't think it's such a bad thing. Generally things aren't goin' right for her and sure, what kind of a father would I be to let her go off on her own in this state? She's got no job, no baby, no husband, no mother and soon no house, and if she wants to go to London for a break, even if it is last minute, then she sure as hell is entitled to go without any more people stopping her from what she wants.

'Here, take my bloody cap. My Joyce wants to

223

go to London and you fellows should let her. She's a good girl, never did a thing wrong in her life. She has nothing right now but me and this trip, as far as I can see. So here, take it. If I have to go without my cap and my shoes and my belt and my coat, well then, that's fine by me, but my Joyce isn't going to London without me.'

Well, if that isn't enough to break a girl.

'Mr Conway, you do know that you get your clothing back once you go through the metal detector?'

'What?' he shouts. 'Why the hell didn't she tell me that? All this feckin' nonsense for nothing. Honestly, you'd think she almost *wants* the trouble sometimes. OK, lads, you can take my things. Will we still make the flight, do you think?'

Any tears that had welled very quickly dried.

Finally the door to my cell opens and, with a single nod, I'm a free woman.

'Doris, you cannot move the stove in the kitchen. Al, tell her.'

'Why not?'

'Honey, first of all it's heavy and second of all, it's gas. You are not qualified to move around kitchen appliances,' Al explains, and prepares to bite into a doughnut.

Doris whisks it away from him, leaving him to lick dribbles of jam from his fingers. 'You two don't seem to understand that it's bad feng shui to have a stove facing a door. The person at the stove may instinctively want to glance back at the door, which creates a feeling of unease, which can lead to accidents.'

'Perhaps removing the stove altogether will be a safer option for Dad.'

'You have to give me a break,' Justin sighs, sitting down at the new kitchen table and chairs. 'All the place needs is furniture and a lick of paint, not for you to restructure the entire place according to yoda.'

'It is not according to yoda,' Doris huffs. 'Donald Trump follows feng shui, you know.'

'Oh, *well then*,' Al and Justin say in unison.

'Yes, well then. Maybe if you did what he did, you'd be able to walk up the stairs without having to take a lunch-break halfway up,' she snaps at Al. 'Just because you sell tyres, sweetie, it doesn't mean you have to wear them too.'

Bea's mouth drops and Justin tries not to laugh. 'Come on, sweetheart, let's get out of here before it turns to violence.'

'Where are you two going? Can I come?' Al asks.

'I'm going to the dentist and Bea has rehearsals for tonight.'

'Good luck, Blondie.' Al ruffles her hair. 'We'll be cheering for you.'

'Thanks.' She grinds her teeth and fixes her hair. 'Oh, that reminds me. One more thing about the woman on the phone, Joyce?'

What, what, what? 'What about her?'

225

'She knows that I'm blonde.'

'How did she know?' Doris asks, with surprise.

'She said she just guessed. But that's not it. Before she hung up she said, "Best of luck with your ballet show."'

'So she's a thoughtful lucky-guesser,' Al shrugs.

'Well, I was thinking about it afterward and I don't remember telling her anything about my show being specifically ballet.'

Justin immediately looks to Al, a little more concerned now that it involves his daughter, but adrenalin still surges. 'What do you think?'

'I think, watch your back, bro. She could be a fruit cake.' He stands up and heads to the kitchen, rubbing his stomach. 'Actually, that's not a bad idea. Fruit cake.'

Deflated, Justin looks hopefully at his daughter. 'Did she sound like a fruit cake?'

'I dunno,' Bea shrugs. 'What does a fruit cake sound like?'

Justin, Al and Bea all turn to stare at Doris.

'What?' she squeals.

'No,' Bea shakes her head wildly at her father. 'Nothing like that, at all.'

'What's this for, Gracie?'

'It's a sick bag.'

'What does this do?'

'It's for hanging your coat up.'

'Why is that there?'

'It's a table.'

'How do you get it down?'

'By unlatching it, at the top.'

'Sir, please leave your table-top up until after take-off.'

Silence.

'What are they doing outside?'

'Loading the bags.'

'What's that yoke?'

'An ejector seat for people who ask three million questions.'

'What's it, really?'

'For reclining your chair.'

'Sir, could you stay upright until after take-off, please?'

Silence.

'What does that do?'

'Air conditioning.'

'What about that?'

'A light.'

'And that one?'

'Yes, sir, can I help you?'

'Eh, no, thanks.'

'You pressed the button for assistance.'

'Oh, is that what that little woman on the button is for? I didn't know. Can I have a drink of water?'

'We can't serve drinks until after take-off, sir.'

'Oh, OK. That was a fine display you did earlier. You were the image of my friend Edna when you had that oxygen mask on. She used to smoke sixty a day, you see.'

The air stewardess makes an *oh* shape with her mouth.

'I feel very safe now, but what if we go down over land?' He raises his voice and the passengers around us look our way. 'Surely the life jackets are hopeless, unless we blow our whistles while we're flying through the air and hope someone below hears us and catches us. Do we not have parachutes?'

'There's no need to worry, sir, we won't go down over land.'

'OK. That's very reassuring, indeed. But if we do, tell the pilot to aim for a hay stack or something.'

I take deep breaths and pretend that I don't know him. I continue reading my book, *The Golden Age of Dutch Painting: Vermeer, Metsu and Terborch*, and convince myself this was not the bad idea it's turning out to be.

'Where are the toilets?'

'To the top and on the left but you can't go until after take-off.'

Dad's eyes widen. 'And when will that be?'

'In just a few minutes.'

'In just a few minutes, that,' he takes the sick bag out from the seat pocket, 'won't be used for what it's supposed to be used for.'

'We will be in the air in just a few minutes more, I assure you.' The stewardess quickly leaves before he asks another question.

I sigh.

'Don't you be sighing until after take-off,' Dad says, and the man next to me laughs and pretends to turn it into a cough.

Dad looks out the window and I revel in the moment of silence.

'Oh oh oh,' he sings, 'we're moving now, Gracie.'

As soon as we're off the ground, the wheels moan as they're brought back up and then we are light in the air. Dad is suddenly quiet. He is turned sideways in his chair, head filling the window, watching as we reach the beginning of the clouds, mere wisps at first. The plane bumps around as it pushes through the clouds. Dad is agog as we're surrounded by white on all sides of the plane, his head darts around looking at every window possible, and then suddenly it is blue and calm above the fluffy world of clouds. Dad blesses himself. He pushes his nose up against the window, his face lit by the nearby sun, and I take a mental photograph for my own hall of memories.

The seatbelt fasten sign goes off with a bing and cabin crew announce that we may now use electronic devices, the facilities, and that food and refreshments will be served shortly. Dad takes down the table-top, reaches into his pocket and takes out his photograph of Mum. He places her down on the table, facing out the window. He reclines his chair and they both watch the endless sea of white clouds disappear further below us and don't say a word for the remainder of the flight.

TWENTY

'Well, I must say, that was absolutely marvellous. Marvellous indeed.' Dad pumps the pilot's hand up and down enthusiastically.

We are standing by the just-opened door of the plane, with a queue of hundreds of irritated passengers huffing and puffing down our necks. They are like greyhounds whose trap has opened, the bunny has been fired off ahead of them and all that blocks their path is, well, Dad. The usual rock in the stream.

'And the *food*,' Dad continues to the cabin crew, 'it was excellent, just excellent.'

He's eaten a ham roll and a cup of tea.

'I can't believe I was eating in the sky,' he laughs. 'Well done again, just marvellous. Nothing short of miraculous, I'd say. My Lord.' He pumps the pilot's hand again, as though he's meeting JFK.

'OK, Dad, we should move on now. We're holding everybody up.'

'Oh, is that so? Thanks again, folks. 'Bye now.

Might see you on the way back,' he shouts over his shoulder, as I pull him away.

We make our way through the tunnel adjoining the plane to the terminal and Dad says hello and tips his hat to everyone we pass.

'You really don't have to say hello to everybody, you know.'

'It's nice to be important, Gracie, but it's more important to be nice. Particularly when in another country,' says the man who hasn't left the province of Leinster for ten years.

'Will you stop shouting?'

'I can't help it. My ears feel funny.'

'Either yawn or hold your nose and blow. It will help your ears to pop.'

He stands by the conveyor belt, purple-faced, with his cheeks puffed out and his fingers over his nose. He takes a deep breath and pushes. He lets out a fart.

The conveyor belt jerks into motion and like flies around a carcass, people suddenly swoop in front of us to block our view, as though their life depends on grabbing their bags this very second.

'There's your bag.' I step forward.

'I'll get it, love.'

'No, I will. You'll hurt your back.'

'Step back, love, I can do it.' He passes over the yellow line and grabs his bag, only to realise that the strength he once had is gone and he finds himself walking alongside it, while tugging away. Ordinarily I would rush to help him but I'm doubled over laughing. All I can hear is Dad saying, 'Excuse me, excuse me,' to people who are standing over the yellow line, as he tries to keep up with his moving luggage. He does a full lap of the conveyor belt and by the time he gets back to where I stand (though I'm still doubled over) somebody has the common sense to help the out-of-breath grumbling old man.

He pulls his bag over to me, his face scarlet, his breathing heavy.

'I'll let you get your own bag,' he says, pulling his cap further down over his eyes with embarrassment.

I wait for our bags while Dad wanders around baggage claim 'acquainting himself with London'. After the incident at Dublin airport, the satellite navigational voice in my head has continuously nagged at me to make a U-turn *right now* but somewhere inside, another part of me is under strict orders to soldier on, feeling convinced this trip is the right thing to do. Now I'm wondering what exactly *this* is. As I collect my bag from the belt, I am aware that there is not a clear purpose for this trip at all. A wild-goose chase is all it is. Instinct alone, caused by a confusing conversation with a girl named Bea, has caused me to fly to another country with my seventy-five-year-old father, who has never left Ireland in his life. Suddenly what seemed like the 'only thing to do' at the time, has now occurred to me as being completely irrational behaviour.

What does it mean to dream about somebody you've never met, almost every night, and then have a chance encounter with them over the phone? I had called my dad's emergency number; she had answered her dad's emergency phone number. What message is in that? What am I supposed to learn? Is it a mere coincidence that an ordinary right-thinking person would ignore or am I right to think and feel that something more lies beneath this? My hope is that this trip will have some answers for me. Panic begins to build as I watch Dad reading a poster on the far side of the room. I have no idea what to do with him.

Suddenly Dad's hand flies to his head and then his chest and he darts towards me with a manic look in his eyes. I make a grab for his pills.

'Gracie,' he gasps.

'Here, quickly, take these.' My hand trembles as I hold out the pills and bottle of water.

'What on earth are you doing?'

'Well, you looked . . .'

'I looked what?'

'Like you were going to have a heart attack!'

'That's because I bloody well will, if we don't get out of here quick.' He grabs my arm and starts to pull me along.

'What's wrong? Where are we going?'

'We're going to Westminster.'

'What? Why? No! Dad, we have to go to the hotel to leave our bags.'

He stops walking and whips around, pushes his

face close to mine, almost aggressively. His voice shakes with the adrenalin. 'The *Antiques Roadshow* are having a valuation day today from nine thirty to four thirty in the afternoon in a place called Banqueting House. If we leave now we can start queuing. I'm not going to miss seeing it on the telly and then come all the way to London just to miss seeing it in the flesh. Sure we might even get to see Michael Aspel. *Michael Aspel*, Gracie. Christ Almighty, let's get out of here.'

His pupils are dilated, he's all fired up. He shoots off through the sliding doors, with nothing to declare but temporary insanity, and takes a confident left.

I stand in the arrivals hall, while men in suits approach me with placards from all sides. I sigh and wait. Dad appears from the direction he went in, seesawing and pulling his bag behind him at top speed.

'You could have told me that was the wrong way,' he says, passing me and heading in the opposite direction.

Dad rushes through Trafalgar Square, pulling his suitcase behind him and scattering a flock of pigeons into the sky. He's not interested in acquainting himself with London any more; he has only Michael Aspel and the treasures of the blue-rinse brigade in sight. Finally, after we've taken a few wrong turns since surfacing from the tube station, Banqueting House is eventually in view, a seventeenth-century former royal palace, and though I am sure I have never visited it before, it stands before me, a familiar sight.

Once deep in the queue, I study the single drawer that is in the hands of the old man in front of us. Behind us, a woman is rolling out a tea cup from a pile of newspapers to show somebody else in the queue. All around me there is excited and rather innocent and polite chatter, and the sun is shining as we wait outside to enter the reception area of Banqueting House. There are TV vans, camera and sound people going in and out of the building, and cameras filming the long queue while a woman with a microphone picks people out of the crowd to interview. Many people in the queue have brought deck chairs, picnic baskets of scones and finger sandwiches, and canteens of tea and coffee, and as Dad looks around with a grumbling stomach I feel like a guilty mother who hasn't properly equipped her child. I'm also concerned for Dad that we won't make it past the front door.

'Dad, I don't want to worry you but I really think that we're supposed to have something with us.'

'What do you mean?'

'Like an object. Everybody else has things with them to be valued.'

Dad looks around and notices for the first time. His face falls.

'Maybe they'll make an exception for us,' I add quickly but I doubt it.

'What about these cases?' He looks down at our bags.

I try not to laugh. 'I got them in TK Maxx; I don't think they'll be interested in valuing them.'

Dad laughs. 'Maybe I'll give them my undies, Gracie, what you think? There's a fine bit of history in them.'

I make a face and he waves his hand dismissively.

We shuffle along slowly in the queue and Dad has a great time chatting to everybody about his life and his exciting trip with his daughter. After queuing for an hour and a half, we have been invited to two houses for afternoon tea and Dad has taken note from the gentleman behind us on how to stop the mint in his garden from taking over his rosemary. Up ahead, just beyond the doors, I see an elderly couple being turned away due to having no items with them. Dad sees this too and looks at me, his eyes worried. It will be us next.

'Eh . . .' I look around quickly for something.

Both entrance doors have been held open for the flowing crowd. Just inside the main entrance, behind the opened door is a wooden waste basket posing as an umbrella stand, holding a few forgotten and broken umbrellas. While no one is looking I turn it upside down, emptying the few scrunched balls of paper and broken umbrellas out. I kick them behind the door just in time to hear, 'Next.'

I carry it up to the reception desk and Dad's eyes almost pop out of his head at the sight of me.

'Welcome to Banqueting House,' the young woman greets us.

'Thank you,' I smile innocently.

'How many objects have you brought today?' she asks.

'Oh, just the one.' I raise the bin onto the table.

'Oh, wow, fantastic.' She runs her fingers along it and Dad gives me a look, that if for any second I had forgotten which of us was the parent, I am quickly reminded. 'Have you been to a valuation day before?'

'No.' Dad shakes his head wildly. 'But I see it on the telly all the time. Big fan, I am. Even when Hugh Scully was host.'

'Wonderful,' she smiles. 'Once you enter the hall you'll see there are many queues. Please join the queue for the appropriate discipline.'

'What queue should we join for this thing?' Dad looks at the item as though there's a bad smell.

'Well, what is it?' she smiles.

Dad looks at me baffled.

'We were hoping you'd tell us that,' I say politely.

'I'd suggest miscellaneous, and though that is the busiest table, we try to move it along as quickly as possible for you by having four experts. Once you reach the expert's table, simply show your item and he or she will tell you all about it.'

'Which table do we go to for Michael Aspel?'

'Unfortunately Michael Aspel isn't actually an

expert, he is the host, so he doesn't have a table of his own, but we do have twenty other experts that will be available to answer your questions.'

Dad looks devastated.

'There is the chance that your item may be chosen for television,' she adds quickly, sensing Dad's disappointment. 'The expert shows the object to the television team and a decision is made whether to record it, depending on rarity, quality, what the expert can say about the object and, of course, value. If your object is chosen, you'll be taken to our waiting room and made up before talking to the expert about your object in front of the camera for about five minutes. You would meet Michael Aspel under those circumstances. And the exciting news is that for the first time, we are broadcasting the show live, in, ooh let's see,' she examines her watch, 'in one hour.'

Dad's eyes widen. 'But five *minutes*? To talk about that thing?' Dad explodes and she laughs.

'Do bear in mind that we have to see two thousand people's items before the show,' she says to me with a knowing look.

'We understand. We're just here to enjoy the day, isn't that right, Dad?'

He doesn't hear; he's busy looking around for Michael Aspel.

'Do enjoy your day,' the woman says finally, calling the next person in line forward.

As soon as we enter the busy hall, I immediately look up at the ceiling of the double-cubed room, already knowing what to expect: nine huge canvases commissioned by Charles I, to fill the panelled ceiling.

'Here you go, Dad.' I hand him the waste basket. 'I'm going to take a look around this beautiful building while you look at the junk people are putting inside it.'

'It's not junk, Gracie. I once saw the show where a man's collection of walking sticks went for sixty thousand sterling pounds.'

'Wow, in that case you should show them your shoe.'

He tries not to laugh.

'Off you go to have a look around and I'll meet you back here.' He starts to wander away before he even finishes the sentence. Dying to get rid of me.

'Have fun,' I wink.

He smiles broadly and looks around the hall with such happiness, my mind takes another photograph.

As I wander the rooms of the only part of White-hall Palace to survive a fire, the feeling that I've been here before comes over me in a giant wave and I find a quiet corner and secretly produce my mobile.

'Manager, deputy head corporate treasury and investor solutions desk, Frankie speaking.'

'My God, you weren't lying. That's a ridiculous amount of words.'

'Joyce! Hi!' Her voice is hushed and behind her, the stock-trading in the Irish Financial Services Centre offices, sounds manic.

'Can you talk?'

'For a little bit, yeah. How are you?'

'I'm fine. I'm in London. With Dad.'

'What? With your dad? Joyce, I've told you before it's not polite to bind and gag your father. What are you doing there?'

'I just decided to come over last minute.' For what, I have no idea. 'We're currently at the *Antiques Roadshow*. Don't ask.'

I leave the quiet rooms behind me and enter the gallery of the main hall. Below me I can see Dad wandering around the crowded hall with the bin in his hands. I smile as I watch him.

'Have we ever been to Banqueting House together?'

'Refresh my memory, where is it, what is it and what does it look like?'

'It's at the Trafalgar Square end of Whitehall. It's a seventeenth-century former royal palace designed by Inigo Jones in 1619. Charles I was executed on a scaffold in front of the building. I'm in a room now, with nine canvases covering the panelled ceiling.' What does it look like? I close my eyes. 'From memory, the roofline is balustrade. The street façade has two orders of engaged columns, Corinthian over Ionic, above a rusticated basement, which lock together in a harmonious whole.'

'Joyce?'

'Yes?' I snap out of it.

'Are you reading from a tourist guide?'

'No.'

'Our last trip to London consisted of Madame Tussaud's, a night in G-A-Y and a party back in a man named Gloria's flat. It's happening again, isn't it? That thing you were talking about?'

'Yes.' I slump into a chair in the corner, feel a rope beneath me and jump back up. I quickly move away from the antique chair, looking around for security cameras.

'Has your being in London got anything to do with the American man?'

'Yes,' I whisper.

'Oh, Joyce—'

'No, Frankie, listen. Listen and you'll understand. I hope. Yesterday I panicked about something and called Dad's doctor, a number that is practically engraved in my head, as it should be. I couldn't possibly get it wrong, right?'

'Right.'

'Wrong. I ended up dialling a UK number and a girl named Bea answered the phone. She'd seen an Irish number and thought it was her dad calling. So from our short conversation I figure out that her dad is American but was in Dublin and was travelling to London last night to see her in a show today. And she has blonde hair. I think Bea is the little girl I keep dreaming about seeing on the swings and playing in the sand, all at different ages.'

Frankie is quiet.

'I know I sound insane, Frankie, but this is what's happening. I have no explanation for it.'

'I know, I know,' she says quickly. 'I've known you practically all my life – this is *not* something you'd be inclined to make up – but even as I take you seriously please do keep in consideration the fact that you've had a traumatic time and what you're currently experiencing could be due to high levels of stress.'

'I've already considered that.' I groan and hold my head in my hands. 'I need help.'

'We'll only consider insanity as a last resort. Let me think for a second.' She sounds as though she's writing it down. 'So basically, you have seen this girl, Bea—'

'Maybe Bea.'

'OK, OK, let's just say it is Bea. You've seen her grow up?'

'Yes.'

'To what age?'

'From birth to I don't know . . .'

'Teenager, twenties, thirties?'

'Teenager.'

'OK, so who else is in the scenes with Bea?'

'Another woman. With a camera.'

'But never your American man?'

'No. So he probably has nothing to do with this at all.'

'Let's not rule anything out. So when you view Bea and the lady with the camera, are you part of the scene or viewing them as an outsider?'

I close my eyes and think hard, see my hands pushing the swing, holding hands, taking a photograph of the girl and her mother in the park, feeling the water from the sprinklers spray and tickle my skin . . . 'No, I'm part of it. They can see me.'

'OK.' She is silent.

'What, Frankie, what?'

'I'm figuring it out. Hold on. OK. So you see a child, a mother and they both see you?'

'Yes.'

'Would you say that in your dreams you're viewing this girl grow up through the eyes of a father?'

Goose bumps form on my skin.

'Oh my God,' I whisper. The American man?

'I take it that's a yes,' Frankie says. 'OK, we're on to something here. I don't know what, but it's something very weird and I can't believe I'm even entertaining these thoughts. But what the hell, I only have a million other things to do. What else do you dream about?'

'It's all very fast, images just flashing by.'

'Try and remember.'

'Sprinklers in a garden. A chubby young boy. A woman with long red hair. I hear bells. See old buildings with shop fronts. A church. A beach. I'm at a funeral. Then at college. Then with the woman and young girl. Sometimes she's smiling and holding my hand, sometimes she's shouting and slamming doors.'

'Hmm . . . she must be your wife.'

I bury my head in my hands. 'Frankie, this sounds so ridiculous.'

'Who cares? When has life ever made sense? Let's keep going.'

'I don't know, the images are all so abstract. I can't make any sense of it.'

'What you should do is, every time you get a flash of something, or suddenly know something you never knew, then write it down and tell me. I'll help you figure this out.'

'Thank you.'

'So apart from the place you're in now, what kinds of things do you suddenly just know about?'

'Em . . . mostly buildings.' I look around and then up at the ceiling. 'And art. I spoke Italian to a man at the airport. And Latin, I spoke Latin to Conor the other day.'

'Oh God.'

'I know. I think he wants to have me sent away.'

'Well, we won't let him do that. Yet. OK so, buildings, art, languages. Wow, Joyce, it's like you've gotten a crash course in an entire college education you never had. Where is the culturally ignorant girl I once knew and loved?'

I smile. 'She's still here.'

'OK, one more thing. My boss has called me for a meeting this afternoon. What is it about?'

'Frankie, I don't have psychic powers!'

The door to the gallery opens and a flustered-looking young girl with a headset over her head rushes in. She approaches almost every woman on her way in, asking for me.

'Joyce Conway?' she asks me, out of breath.

'Yes.' My heat beats a mile a minute. Please let Dad be OK. Please, God.

'Is your father Henry?'

'Yes.'

'He wants you to join him in the green room.'

'He *what*? In the *what*?'

'He's in the green room. He's going live with Michael Aspel in just a few minutes with his item and he wants you to join him because he says you know more about it. We really have to move now, there's very little time and we need to get you made up.'

'Live with Michael Aspel . . .' I trail off. I realise I'm still holding the phone. 'Frankie,' I say, dazed, 'put on BBC, quick. You're about to witness me getting into very big trouble.'

TWENTY-ONE

I half-walk, half-run behind the girl with the headset, to get to the green room, and arrive panting and nervous to see Dad sitting on a make up chair facing a mirror lit up by bulbs, tissue tucked into his collar, a cup and saucer in his hand, his bulbous nose being powdered for his close-up.

'Ah, there you are, love,' Dad says grandly. 'Everybody, this is my daughter and she'll be the one to tell us all about my lovely piece here that caught the eye of Michael Aspel.' This is followed by a chuckle and he sips on his tea. 'There's Jaffa Cakes over there if you want them.'

Evil little man.

I look around the room at all the interested, nodding heads, and force a smile onto my face.

Justin squirms uncomfortably in his chair in the dentist's waiting room, with his throbbing swollen cheek, sandwiched between two old dears carrying on a conversation about someone they know called Rebecca, who should leave a man called Timothy.

Shut up, shut up, shut up!

The 1970s television in the corner, which is covered by a lace cloth and fake flowers, announces that the *Antiques Roadshow* is about to begin.

Justin groans. 'Does anybody mind if I change the channel?'

'I'm watching it,' says a young boy no older than seven years old.

'Charming,' Justin smiles at him with loathing, then looks to his mother for backup.

Instead she shrugs. 'He's watching it.'

Justin grunts in frustration.

'Excuse me.' Justin finally interrupts the women to his right and left. 'Would one of you ladies like to swap places with me, so that you can continue this conversation more privately?'

'No, don't worry, love, there's nothing private about this conversation, believe you me. Eavesdrop all you like.'

The smell of her breath silently tiptoes under his nostrils again, tickles them with a feather duster and runs off with an evil giggle.

'I wasn't eavesdropping. Your *lips* were quite literally in my *ear*, and I'm not sure if Charlie or Graham or Rebecca would appreciate that.' He turns his nose away.

'Oh, Ethel,' one laughs, 'he thinks we're talking about *real* people.'

How foolish I am.

Justin turns his attention back to the television in the corner, which the other six people in the room are glued to.

'. . . And welcome to our first *live Antiques Roadshow* special . . .'

Justin sighs loudly again.

The little boy narrows his eyes at him and raises the volume with the remote control that is firmly within his grasp.

'. . . coming to you from Banqueting House, London.'

Oh, I've been there. A nice example of Corinthian and Ionic locked together in a harmonious whole.

'We have had over two thousand people spilling through our doors since nine thirty this morning, and only moments ago those doors have closed, leaving us to display the best pieces for you to view at home. Our first guests come from—'

Ethel leans across Justin and rests her elbow on his thigh. 'So anyway, Margaret—'

He zones in on the television so as not to grab both their heads and smash them together.

'So what do we have here?' Michael Aspel asks. 'Looks like a designer waste basket to me,' he says as the camera takes a close-up on the piece propped on the table.

Justin's heart begins to palpitate.

'Do you want me to change it now, mister?' The boy flicks through the channels at top speed.

249

'No!' he shouts, breaking through Margaret and Ethel's conversation and reaching out dramatically into thin air as though he can stop the waves from changing the channel. He falls to the carpet on his knees, before the television. Margaret and Ethel jump and go silent. 'Go back, go back, go back!' he shouts at the boy.

The boy's lower lip begins to tremble as he looks to his mother.

'There's no need to shout at him.' She holds his head to her chest, protectively.

He grabs the remote control from the boy and flicks through the channels at top speed. He stops when he comes upon the close-up of Joyce, whose eyes are looking uncertainly to the left and right, as though she has just landed in the cage of a Bengal tiger at feeding time.

In the Irish Financial Services Centre, Frankie is racing through the offices searching for a television. She finds one, surrounded by dozens of suits studying the figures that are racing by on the screen.

'Excuse me! Coming through!' she shouts, pushing her way through. She rushes to the TV and starts fiddling with the buttons to cries of abuse from the men and women around her.

'I'll just be one minute, the market won't crash in all of the *two minutes* this will take.' She flicks around and finds Joyce and Henry live on BBC.

She gasps and holds her hands up to her mouth.

250

And then she laughs and throws her fist at the screen. 'You go, Joyce!'

The team around her quickly shuffles off to find another screen, apart from one man who seems pleased by the change in channel and decides to stay and watch.

'Oh, that's a nice piece,' he comments, leaning back against the desk and folding his arms.

'*Em . . .*' Joyce is saying, 'well, we found it . . . I mean we *put* it, put this beautiful . . . extraordinarily . . . eh, wooden . . . bucket, outside of our house. Well, not *outside*,' she quickly withdraws that statement on seeing the appraiser's reaction. '*Inside*. We put it inside our front porch so that it's protected from the weather, you see. For umbrellas.'

'Yes, and it may have been used for that too,' he says. 'Where did you get it from?'

Joyce's mouth opens and closes for a few seconds and Henry jumps in. He is standing upright with his hands clasped over his belly. His chin is raised, there is a glint in his eye and he ignores the expert and takes on a posh accent to direct his answer at Michael Aspel, whom he addresses as though he's the Pope.

'Well, Michael, I was given this by my great-great-grandfather Joseph Conway, who was a farmer in Tipperary. He gave it to my grandfather Shay, who was also a farmer. My grandfather gave it to my father, Paddy-Joe, who was also a farmer in Cavan and then when he died, I took it.'

251

'I see, and do you have any idea where your great-great- grandfather may have got this?'

'He probably stole it from the Brits,' Henry jokes, and is the only one to laugh. Joyce elbows her father, Frankie snorts, and on the floor before the television in a dentist's waiting room in London, Justin throws his head back and laughs loudly.

'Well, the reason I ask is because this is a fabulous item you have. It's a rare nineteenth-century English Victorian era upright jardinière planter—'

'I love gardening, Michael,' Henry interrupts the expert, 'do you?'

Michael smiles at him politely and the expert continues, 'It has wonderful hand-carved Black Forest-style plaques set in the Victorian ebonised wood framing on all four sides.'

'Country English or French décor, what do you think?' Frankie's work colleague asks her.

She ignores him, concentrating on Joyce.

'Inside it has what looks like an original tole-painted tin liner. Superb condition, ornate patterns carved into the solid wood panels. We can see here that two of the sides have a floral motif and the other two sides are figural, one with the centre lion's head and the other with griffin figures. Very striking indeed and an absolutely wonderful piece to have by your front door too.'

'Worth a few quid, is it?' Henry asks, dropping the posh accent.

'We'll get to that part,' the expert says. 'While

it is in good condition, it appears there would have been feet, quite likely wooden. There are no splits or warping in the sides, there is an original tole-painted tin removable liner and the finger ring handles on the sides are intact. So bearing all that in mind, how much do you think it's worth?'

'Frankie!' Frankie hears her boss calling her from across the room. 'What's this I hear about you messing with the monitors?'

Frankie stands up, turns her back and while blocking the television with her body, attempts to turn the channel back.

'Ah,' her colleague tuts. 'They were just about to announce the value. That's the best bit.'

'Step aside,' her boss frowns.

Frankie moves to display the stock market figures racing across the screen. She smiles brightly, showing all her teeth, and then sprints back to her desk.

In the dental surgery's waiting room, Justin is glued to the television, glued to Joyce's face.

'Is she a friend, love?' Ethel asks.

Justin studies Joyce's face and smiles, 'Yes she is. Her name is Joyce.'

Margaret and Ethel ooh and aah.

On screen, Joyce's father or at least who Justin assumes him to be, turns to Joyce and shrugs.

'What would you say, love? How much lolly for Dolly?'

Joyce smiles tightly. 'I really wouldn't have the slightest idea how much it's worth.'

'How does between one thousand five hundred to one thousand seven hundred pounds sound to you?' the expert asks.

'Sterling pounds?' the old man asks, flabbergasted.

Justin laughs.

The camera zooms in on Joyce and her father's face. They are both astonished, so gobsmacked, in fact, that neither of them can say anything.

'Now there's an impressive reaction,' Michael laughs. 'Good news from this table, let's go over to our porcelain table to see if any of our other collectors here in London, have been as lucky.'

'Justin Hitchcock,' the receptionist announces.

The room is quiet. They all look around at one another.

'Justin,' she repeats, raising her voice.

'That must be him on the floor,' Ethel says. 'Yoohoo!' she sings and gives him a kick with her comfortable shoe. 'Are you Justin?'

'Somebody's in love, ooohey-ooohey,' Margaret sings while Ethel makes kissing noises.

'Louise,' Ethel says to the receptionist, 'why don't I go in now while this young man runs down to Banqueting House to see his lady? I'm tired of waiting.' She stretches her left leg out and makes pained expressions.

Justin stands and wipes the carpet hairs from his trousers. 'I don't know why you're both waiting here anyway, at your age. You should just leave your teeth here and then come back later when the dentist's finished with them.'

He exits the room as a year-old copy of *Homes and Gardens* flies at his head.

TWENTY-TWO

'Actually, that's not a bad idea.' Justin stops following the receptionist down the hallway to the surgery, as adrenalin once again surges through his body. 'That's exactly what I'll do.'

'You're going to leave your teeth here?' she says drily, in a strong Liverpool accent.

'No, I'm going to Banqueting House,' he says, hopping about with excitement.

'Great, Dick. Can Anne come too? Let's be sure to ask Aunt Fanny first.' She glares at him, killing his excitement. 'I don't care what's going on with you, you're not escaping again. Come now. Dr Montgomery won't be happy if you don't show for your appointment again,' she urges him along.

'OK, OK, hold on. My tooth is fine now.' He holds out his hands and shrugs like it's all no big deal. 'All gone. No pain at all. In fact, chomp, chomp, chomp,' he says as he snaps his teeth together. 'Look, completely gone. What am I even doing here? Can't feel a thing.'

'Your eyes are watering.'

'I'm emotional.'

'You're delusional. Come on.' She continues to lead him down the corridor.

Dr Montgomery greets him with a drill in his hand, 'Hello, Clarisse,' he says, and breaks his heart laughing. 'Just joking. Trying to run off on me again, Justin?'

'No. Well, yes. Well, no, not run off exactly but I realised that there's somewhere else I should be and . . .'

All throughout his explanation, the firm-handed Dr Montgomery and his equally strong assistant manage to usher him into the chair, and by the time he's finished his excuse he realises he's wearing a protective gown and reclining.

'Blah blah blah, was all I heard, I'm afraid, Justin,' Dr Montgomery says cheerily.

He sighs.

'You're not going to fight me today?' Dr Montgomery snaps two surgical gloves onto his hands.

'As long as you don't ask me to cough.'

Dr Montgomery laughs as Justin reluctantly opens his mouth.

The red light on the camera goes off and I grab Dad's arm.

'Dad, we have to go now,' I say with urgency.

'Not now,' Dad responds in a David Attenborough-style loud whisper. 'Michael Aspel is right over there. I can see him, standing behind the porcelain table, tall, charming, more handsome than I thought. He's looking around for someone to talk to.'

'Michael Aspel is very busy in his natural habitat, presenting a live television show.' I dig my fingernails into Dad's arm. 'I don't think talking to you is very high on his priority list right now.'

Dad looks slightly wounded, and not from my fingernails. He lifts his chin high in the air, which I know from down the years has an invisible string attached to his pride. He prepares to approach Michael Aspel, who is standing alone by the porcelain table with his finger in his ear.

'Must get waxy build-up, like me,' Dad whispers. 'He should use that stuff you got for me. Pop! Comes right out.'

'It's an earpiece, Dad. He's listening to the people in the control room.'

'No, I think it's a hearing aid. Let's go over to him and remember to speak up and mouth your words clearly. I have experience with this.'

I block his path and leer over him in the most intimidating way possible. Dad steps onto his left leg and immediately rises near enough to my eyelevel.

'Dad, if we do not leave this place right now, we will find ourselves locked in a cell. Again.'

Dad laughs, 'Ah, don't exaggerate, Gracie.'

'I'm *bloody* Joyce,' I hiss.

'All right, bloody Joyce, no need to get your bloody knickers in a twist.'

'I don't think you understand the seriousness of our situation. We have just stolen a seventeen-hundred-pound Victorian waste basket from a once-upon-a-time royal palace and talked about it live on air.'

Dad looks at me quickly, his bushy eyebrows raised halfway up his forehead. For the first time in a long time I can see his eyes. They look alarmed. And rather watery and yellow at the corners, and I make a note to ask him about that later, when we are not running from the law. Or the BBC.

The production girl I chased in order to find Dad gives me wide eyes from across the room. My heart beats in panic and I look around quickly. Heads are turning to stare at us. They know.

'OK, we have to go now. I think they know.'

'It's no big deal. We'll put it back.' He speaks as though it *is* a big deal. 'We haven't even taken it off the premises – that's no crime.'

'OK, it's now or never. Grab it quick, so we can put it back and get out of here.'

I scan the crowd to make sure nobody big and burly is coming towards us, cracking their knuckles and swinging a baseball bat. Just the young girl with the headset, and I'm sure I can take her on, and if not, Dad can hit her on the head with his clunky corrective shoe.

Dad grabs the waste basket from the table and tries to hide it in the inside of his coat. The coat barely makes it a third of the way around and I look at him bizarrely and he removes it. We make our way through the crowd, ignoring congrats and well-wishes from those who seem to think we've won the lottery. I see the young girl with the headset pushing her way through the crowd too.

'Quick, Dad, quick.'

'I'm going as fast as I can.'

We make it to the door of the hall, leaving the crowd behind, and start towards the main entrance. I look back before closing it behind me, and catch the girl with the headset, talking into her mike, urgently. She starts to run but gets caught behind two men in brown overalls carrying a wardrobe across the floor. I grab the wooden bin from Dad's hands and immediately we speed up. Down the stairs, we grab our bags from the cloakroom and then up and down, down and up, all the way along the marble-floored hallway.

Dad reaches for the gold oversized handle on the main door and we hear, 'Stop! Wait!'

We stop abruptly and slowly turn to look at one another, fearfully. I mouth 'Run' at Dad. He sighs dramatically, rolls his eyes and steps down on his right leg, bending his left as a way of reminding me of his struggles with walking, let alone running.

'Where are you two going in such a hurry?' the man asks, making his way towards us.

We slowly turn round, and I prepare to defend our honour.

'It was her,' Dad says straight away, thumb pointed at me.

My mouth falls open.

'It was both of you, I'm afraid,' he smiles. 'You left your microphone and packs on. Worth a bit, these are.' He fiddles around the back of Dad's trousers and unclips his battery pack. 'Could have gotten into a bit of trouble if you'd escaped with this,' he laughs.

Dad looks relieved until I ask nervously, 'Were these turned on, the entire time?'

'Eh,' he studies the pack and flicks the switch to the 'off' position. 'They were.'

'Who would have heard us?'

'Don't worry, they wouldn't have broadcasted your sound while they went to the next item.'

I breath a sigh of relief.

'But internally, whoever was wearing head-phones on the floor would have heard,' he explains, removing Dad's mike. 'Oh, and the control room too,' he adds.

He turns to me next and I get into an embarrassing muddle as he pulls the pack from the waistband of my trousers and in doing so tugs the string of my thong, which it's mistakenly attached to.

'Ooowwwwwww!' I yelp, and it echoes around the corridor.

'Sorry.' The sound man's face reddens while I fix myself. 'Pitfall of the job.'

'Perk, my friend, perk,' Dad smiles.

After he shuffles back to the fair, we place the umbrella stand back by the entrance door while no one is looking, fill it with the broken umbrellas and exit the scene of the crime.

'So, Justin, any news?' Dr Montgomery asks.

Justin, who is reclined in the chair, with two surgically gloved hands *and* apparatus shoved in his mouth, is unsure of how to answer, and decides to blink once having seen that on television. Then unsure of what exactly that signal means, he blinks twice to confuse matters.

Dr Montgomery misses his code and chuckles, 'Cat got your tongue?'

Justin rolls his eyes.

'I might start getting offended one of these days, if people continue to ignore me when I ask questions.' He chuckles again and leans in over Justin, giving him a good view up his nostrils.

'Arrrgggh,' he flinches as the cool prong hits his sore point.

'Hate to say I told you so,' Dr Montgomery continues, 'but that would be a lie. The cavity that you wouldn't let me look at during your last visit has become infected and now the tissue is inflamed.'

He taps around some more.

'Aaaahh.' Justin makes some gurgling sounds from the back of his throat.

'I should write a book on dentistry language. Everybody makes all sorts of sounds that only I can understand. What do you think, Rita?'

Rita with the glossy lips doesn't care much.

Justin gurgles some expletives.

'Now, now,' Dr Montgomery's smile fades for a moment. 'Don't be rude.'

Startled, Justin concentrates on the television suspended from the wall in the corner of the room. Sky News's red banner at the bottom of the screen screams it's breaking news again and though it's muted and too far away for him to read what exactly it is that they are breaking, it provides a welcome distraction from Dr Montgomery's dismal jokes and calms his urge to jump out of the chair and grab the first taxi he can find, straight to Banqueting House.

The broadcaster is currently standing outside Westminster, but as Justin can't hear a thing he has no idea what it's related to. He studies the man's face and tries to lip-read while Dr Montgomery comes at him with what looks like a needle. His eyes widen as he catches sight of something on the television. His pupils melt into his eyes, blackening them.

Dr Montgomery smiles as he holds it before Justin's face. 'Don't worry, Justin. I know how much you hate needles but it's necessary for a numbing effect. You need a filling in another tooth before that gets an abscess as well. It won't hurt, it will just feel slightly odd.'

Justin's eyes grow wider as he watches the television and he tries to sit up. For once, Justin doesn't care about the needle. He must try to communicate this as best as possible. Unable to move or close his mouth, he begins to make deep noises from the back of his throat.

'OK, don't panic. Just one more minute. I'm nearly there.'

He leans over Justin again, blocking his view of the television, and Justin squirms in his seat, trying to see the screen.

'My goodness, Justin, please stop it. The needle won't kill you, but I might if you don't stop wriggling.' Chuckle, chuckle.

'Ted, I think maybe we should stop,' his assistant says, and Justin looks at her with grateful eyes.

'Is he having a fit of some sort?' Dr Montgomery asks her and then raises his voice at Justin as though he has suddenly become hearing-impaired. 'I say, are you having a fit of some sort?'

Justin rolls his eyes and makes more noises from the back of his throat.

'TV? What do you mean?' Dr Montgomery looks up at Sky News and finally removes his fingers from Justin's mouth.

All three focus on the television screen, the other two concentrating on the news while Justin watches the background where Joyce and her father have wandered into the path of the camera's angle, them in the forefront, Big Ben in the background. Seemingly unaware, they carry out what looks like a seriously heated conversation, their hands gesturing wildly.

'Look at those two idiots at the back,' Dr Montgomery laughs.

Suddenly Joyce's father pushes his suitcase over to Joyce and then storms off in the other direction, leaving Joyce alone with two bags, and throwing her hands up with frustration.

'Yeah, thanks, that's very mature,' I shout after Dad who has just stormed off, leaving his suitcase behind with me. He is going in the wrong direction. Again. Has been since we left the Banqueting House but refuses to admit it and also refuses to get a taxi to the hotel as he is on a penny-saving mission.

He is still within my sights and so I sit on my case and wait for him to realise the error of his ways and come back. It's evening now and I just want to get to the hotel and have a bath. My phone rings.

'Hi, Kate.'

She is laughing hysterically.

'What's up with you?' I smile. 'Well, it's nice to hear *somebody* is in a good mood.'

'Oh, Joyce,' she catches her breath and I imagine she's wiping her teared-up eyes. 'You are the best dose of medicine, you really are.'

'What do you mean?' I can hear children's laughter in the background.

'Do me a favour and raise your right hand.'

'Why?'

'Just do it. It's a game the kids taught me,' she giggles.

'OK,' I sigh, and raise my right hand.

I hear the kids howl with laughter in the back.

'Tell her to wiggle her right foot,' Jayda shouts down the phone.

'OK,' I laugh. This is putting me in a much better mood. I wiggle my right foot and they laugh again. I can even hear Kate's husband howling in the background, which suddenly makes me uncomfortable again. 'Kate, what exactly is this?'

Kate can't answer, she's laughing so much.

'Tell her to hop up and down!' Eric shouts.

'No.' I'm irritated now.

'She did it for Jayda,' he begins to whinge, and I sense tears.

I quickly hop up and down.

They howl again.

'By any chance,' Kate wheezes through her laugher, 'is there anyone around you who has the time?'

'What are you talking about?' I frown, looking around. I see Big Ben behind me, still not sure of the joke, and as I turn back round only then see the camera crew in the distance. I stop hopping.

'What on earth is that woman doing?' Dr Montgomery steps closer to the television. 'Is she dancing?'

'Oo han ee ha?' Justin says, feeling the effects of his numbed mouth.

'Of course I can see her,' he responds. 'I think she's doing the hokey cokey. See? You put your left leg in,' he begins to sing. 'Left leg out. In. Out.

267

In. Out. Shake it all about.' He dances around. Rita rolls her eyes.

Justin, relieved that his sightings of Joyce aren't all in his mind, begins to bounce up and down in his seat, impatiently. *Hurry! I need to get to her.*

Dr Montgomery glances at him curiously, pushes Justin back in the chair and places the instruments in his mouth again. Justin gurgles and makes noises from the back of his throat.

'It's no good explaining it to me, Justin, you're not going anywhere until I have filled this cavity. You'll have to take antibiotics for the abscess, then when you come back I'll either extract it or use endodontic treatment. Whatever I'm in the mood for,' he laughs girlishly. 'And whoever this Joyce lady is, you can thank her for curing your fear of needles. You didn't even notice I'd injected you.'

'Aah haa ooo aaa aa ee a.'

'Oh, well, good for you, old boy. I donated blood before too, you know. Satisfying isn't it?'

'Aa. Ooo aaa iii uuuu.'

Dr Montgomery throws his head back and laughs. 'Oh, don't be silly, they'll never tell you who the blood has gone to. Besides it's been separated into different parts, platelets, red blood cells and what have you.'

Justin gurgles again.

The dentist laughs again. 'What kind of muffins do you want?'

'Aa.'

'Banana,' he considers this. 'Prefer chocolate, myself. Air, Rita, please.'

A bewildered Rita puts the tube into Justin's mouth.

TWENTY-THREE

I succeed in hailing a black cab and I send the driver in the direction of the dapper old man who is easily spotted on the pavement swaying in horizontal motions like a drunken sailor, amidst the crowd's vertical stream. Like a salmon, he swims upstream, pushing against the throngs of people going in the opposite direction. Not doing it just for the sake of it, not to be deliberately different, or even noticing he's the odd one out.

Seeing him now reminds me of a tale he told me when I was so small he seemed to me to be as gigantic as our neighbour's oak tree that loomed over our garden wall, raining acorns onto our grass. This, during the months when outside playtime was interrupted by afternoons spent staring out the window at the grey world, and, outside, wearing mitts that hung from strings through my coat sleeves. The howling wind would blow the giant oak tree's branches from side to side, leaves going swish swash, left to right, just like my dad,

271

a skittle wavering at the end of a bowling alley. But neither of them fell under the wind's force. Not like the acorns, that leapt from their branches like panicked parachutist pushed out unawares or excited wind worshippers falling to their knees.

When my dad was as sturdy as an oak tree and when I was bullied at school for sucking my thumb, he recalled the Irish myth of how an ordinary salmon had eaten hazelnuts that had fallen into the Fountain of Wisdom. In doing so, the salmon gained all the knowledge in the world, and the first to eat the salmon's flesh would, in turn, gain this knowledge. The poet Finneces spent seven long years fishing for this salmon and when he'd finally caught it, he instructed his young apprentice, Fionn, to prepare it for him. When spattered with hot fat from the cooking salmon, Fionn immediately sucked on his burned thumb to ease his pain. In doing so, he gained incredible knowledge and wisdom. For the rest of his life, when he didn't know what to do, all he had to do was suck on his thumb and the knowledge would come.

He told me that story way back when I sucked my thumb and when he was as big as an oak tree. When Mum's yawns sounded like songs. When we were all together. When I had no idea there would ever come a time when we wouldn't be. When we used to have chats in the garden, under the weeping willow. Where I always used to hide and where he always found me. When nothing was impossible and when the three of us, together forever, was a given.

I smile now as I watch my great big salmon of knowledge moving upstream, weaving in and out of the pedestrians pounding the pavements towards him.

Dad looks up, sees me, gives me two fingers and keeps walking.

Ah.

'Dad,' I call out the open window, 'come on, get in the car.'

He ignores me and holds a cigarette to his mouth, inhaling long and hard, so much so that his cheeks concave.

'Dad, don't be like this. Just get in the car and we'll go to the hotel.'

He continues walking, looks straight ahead, as stubborn as anything. I've seen this face so many times before, arguing with Mum over spending too late and too often at the pub, arguments with the Monday Club gang about the political state of their country, at a restaurant when his beef is handed to him not resembling a piece of charcoal as he so wishes. The 'I'm right, you're wrong' look that has set his chin in that defiant stance, jutting outward like Cork and Kerry's rugged coastline to the rest of the land. A defiant chin, a troubled head.

'Look, we don't even have to talk. You can ignore me in the car too. And in the hotel. Don't talk to me all night, if it'll make you feel better.'

'You'd like that, wouldn't you?' he huffs.

'Honestly?'

He looks at me.

'Yes.'

He tries not to smile. Scratches the corner of his mouth with his yellow-stained cigarette fingers to hide how he softens. The smoke rises into his eyes and I think of his yellow eyes, think of how piercingly blue they used to be when, as a little girl, legs swinging, chin on my hands, I'd watch him sitting at the kitchen table, while he dismantled a radio or a clock or a plug. Piercing blue eyes, alert, busy, like a CAT scan sourcing a tumour. His cigarette squashed between his lips, to the side of his mouth like Popeye, the smoke drifting into his squinted eyes, perhaps staining them the yellow that he sees through now. The colour of age, like old newspapers dipped in time.

I'd watch him, transfixed, afraid to speak, afraid to breathe, afraid to break the spell he'd cast on the contraption he was fixing. Like the surgeon who'd operated on his heart during his bypass surgery ten years ago, there he was, youth on his side, connecting wires, clearing blockages, his shirt-sleeves rolled to just below his elbows, the muscles in his arms tanned from the gardening, flexing and unflexing as his fingers tackled the problem. His fingernails, always with a trace of dirt under the surface. His right forefinger and middle finger, yellow from the nicotine. Yellow, but steady. Uneven, but steady.

Finally he stops walking. He throws his cigarette on the ground and stomps it out with his chunky shoe. The cab stops. I throw the life-saving ring around his body and we pull him out of his stream of defiance and into the boat. Always a chancer, always lucky, he'd fall into a river and come out dry, with fish in his pockets. He sits in the car without a word to me, his clothes, breath and fingers smelling of smoke. I bite my lip to stop from saying anything and prepare to have my thumb burned.

He is silent for a record amount of time. Ten, maybe fifteen, minutes. Finally words start spilling out of his mouth, as though they'd been queuing up impatiently behind his closed lips during the rare silence. As though they'd been fired from his heart and, as usual, not from his head, catapulted to his mouth, only this time to find themselves bounce against the walls of closed lips. Instead of being allowed out into the world, they build up like paranoid fat cells, afraid of the food never coming. But now the lips open and the words fly out in all directions like projectile vomit.

'You may have got a sherbet but I hope you know that I haven't a sausage.' He raises his chin, which pulls on the invisible string attached to his pride. He appears pleased with the collection of words that have strung themselves together for him on this particular occasion.

'What?'

'You heard me.'

'Yes, but . . .'

'Sherbet dab, *cab*. Sausage and mash, *cash*,' he explains. 'It's the ol' Chitty Chitty.'

I try to work that out in my head.

'Bang Bang, *rhyming slang*,' he finishes. 'He knows exactly what I'm talking about,' he nods at the driver.

'He can't hear you.'

'Why? Is he Mutt and Jeff?'

'What?'

'Deaf.'

'No,' I nod my head, feeling dazed and tired. 'When the red light is off, they can't hear you.'

'Like Joe's hearing aid,' Dad responds. He leans forward and flicks the switch in the back of the cab. 'Can you hear me?' he shouts.

'Yeah, mate.' The driver looks at him in the mirror. 'Loud and clear.'

Dad smiles and flicks the switch again. 'Can you hear me now?'

There is no response, the driver quickly glances at him in the rearview mirror, concern wrinkling his forehead, while trying also to keep an eye on the road.

Dad chuckles.

I bury my face in my hands.

'This is what we do to Joe,' he says mischievously. 'Sometimes he can go a whole day without realising we turned his hearing aid off. He just thinks that no one's saying anything. Every half-hour he shouts,

"JAYSUS, IT'S VERY QUIET IN HERE!"' Dad laughs and flicks the switch again, ''Allo, guv,' Dad says pleasantly.

'All right, Paddy,' the driver responds.

I wait for Dad's gnarled fist to go through the slit in the window. It doesn't. Instead his laughter filters through.

'I feel like being on my tod tonight. I say, could you tell me where there's a good jack near my hotel, so I can go for a pig without my teapot.'

The young driver studies Dad's innocent face in the mirror, always meaning well, never intending insults. But he doesn't respond and continues driving.

I look away so Dad isn't embarrassed, but I feel rather superior and hate myself for it. Moments later, at a set of traffic lights, the hatch opens and the driver passes a piece of paper through.

'There's a list of a few there, mate. I'd suggest the first one, that's my favourite. Does good loop and tucker right about now, if you know what i mean,' he smiles and winks.

'Thank you.' Dad's face lights up. He studies the paper closely as though it's the most precious thing he's ever been given, then folds it carefully and slides it into his top pocket, proudly. 'It's just that this one here, is being a merry ol' soul, if you know what *I* mean. Make sure she gives you a good bit of rifle.'

The driver laughs and pulls over at our hotel. I examine it from the cab and am pleasantly surprised. The three-star hotel is right in the heart of the city, only ten minutes' walk from main theatres, Oxford Street, Piccadilly and Soho. Enough to keep us either out of trouble. Or right in it.

Dad gets out of the car and pulls his case along to the revolving doors at the hotel entrance. I watch him while waiting for my change. The doors are going around so fast, I can see him trying to time his entrance. Like a dog afraid to jump into the cold sea, he inches forward, then stops, jerks forward again and stops. Finally he makes a run for it and his suitcase gets stuck outside, jamming the revolving doors and trapping him inside.

I take my time getting out of the cab. I lean in the passenger's side window to the sound of Dad rapping on the glass behind me.

'Help! Someone!' I hear Dad call.

'By the way, what did he call me?' I ask the driver, calmly ignoring the calls behind me.

'A merry old soul?' he asks with a grin. 'You don't want to know.'

'Tell me,' I smile.

'It means arsehole,' he laughs, and then he pulls away, leaving me at the side of the street with my mouth gaping.

I notice the knocking has quietened and turn to see that Dad has been freed at last. I hurry inside.

'I can't give you a credit card, but I can give you my word,' Dad is saying slowly and loudly to the woman behind the reception desk. 'And my word is as good as my honour.'

'It's OK, here you go.' I slide my credit card across the counter to the young lady.

'Why can't people just pay with paper money these days?' Dad says, leaning further over the counter. 'It's more trouble that the youth of today are getting themselves into, debt after debt because they want this, they want that, but they don't want to work for it so they use those plastic thingies. Well, that's not free money, I can tell you that.' He nods his head with finality. 'You'll only ever lose with one of those.'

No one responds.

The receptionist smiles at him politely and taps away on the computer. 'You're sharing a room?' she asks.

'Yes,' I respond with dread.

'Two Uncle Teds, I hope?'

She frowns.

'Beds,' I say quietly. 'He means beds.'

'Yes, they're twin beds.'

'Is it an en-suite?' He leans in, trying to see her name badge. 'Breda, is it?' he asks.

'Aakaanksha. And, yes, sir, all our rooms are en-suite,' she says politely.

'Oh,' he looks impressed. 'Well, I hope your lifts are working because I can't take the apples, my Cadbury's playin' up.'

I squeeze my eyes together tightly.

'Apples and pears, *stairs*. Cadbury snack, *back*,'

he says with the same voice he used to say nursery rhymes to me as a little girl.

'I see. Very good, Mr Conway.'

I take the key and head towards the elevator, hearing his little voice repeating a question over and over again as he follows me through the foyer. I hit the button for the third floor and the doors close.

The room is standard and it's clean, and that's good enough for me. Our beds are far enough apart for my liking, there's a television and a mini-bar, which hold Dad's attention while I run a bath.

'I wouldn't mind a drop of fine,' he says, his head disappearing into the mini-bar.

'You mean wine.'

'Fine and dandy, *brandy*.'

I finally slide down into the hot soothing bath-water, the suds rise like the foam atop an ice-cream float. They tickle my nose and cover my body, overflow and float to the ground, where they slowly fade with a crackling sound. I lie back and close my eyes, feeling tiny bubbles all over my body pop as soon as they touch my skin . . . There's a knock on the door.

I ignore it.

Then it goes again, a little more loudly this time.

Still I don't answer.

BANG! BANG!

'What?' I shout.

'Oh, sorry, thought you'd fallen asleep or something, love.'

'I'm in the bath.'

'I know that. You have to be careful in those things. Could nod off and slip under the water and drown. Happened to one of Amelia's cousins. You know Amelia. Visits Joseph sometimes, down the road. But she doesn't drop by as much as before on account of the bath accident.'

'Dad, I appreciate your concern but I'm fine.'

'OK.'

Silence.

'Actually, it's not that, Gracie. I'm just wonderin' how long you'll be in there for?'

I grab the yellow rubber duck sitting at the side of the bath and I strangle it.

'Love?' he asks in a little voice.

I hold the duck under the water, trying to drown it. Then I let go, it bobs to the top again, the same silly eyes staring back at me. I take a deep breath, breathe out slowly.

'About twenty minutes, Dad, is that OK?'

Silence.

I close my eyes again.

'Eh, love. It's just that you've been in there twenty minutes already and you know how my prostate is—'

I don't hear any more, because I'm climbing out of the bath with all the gracefulness of a piranha at feeding time. My feet squeak on the bathroom floor, water splashes in all directions.

'Everything OK in there, Shamu?' Dad laughs uproariously at his own joke.

I throw a towel around me and open the door. 'Ah, Willy's been freed,' he smiles.

I bow and hold my arm out to the toilet. 'Your chariot awaits you, sir.'

Embarrassed, he shuffles inside and closes the door behind him. It locks.

Wet and shivering, I browse through the half-bottles of red wine in the mini-bar. I pick one up and study the label. Immediately an image flashes through my mind, so vivid, I feel like my body has been transported.

A picnic basket with this bottle inside, an identical label, red and white chequered cloth laid out on the grass, a little girl with blonde hair twirling, twirling in a pink tutu. The wine swirling, swirling in a glass. The sound of her laughter. Birds twittering. Children's laughter far off, a dog barking. I am lying on the chequered cloth, barefoot, trousers rolled above my ankles. *Hairy* ankles. I feel a hot sun beating down on my skin, the little girl dances and twirls before the sun, sometimes blocking the harshness of light, other times spinning in the other direction to send the glare into my eyes. A hand appears before me, a glass of red wine in it. I look to her face. Red hair, lightly freckled, smiling adoringly. At me.

'Justin,' she's singing. 'Earth to Justin!'

The little girl is laughing and twirling, the wine is swirling, the long red hair is blowing in the light breeze . . .

Then it's gone. I'm back in the hotel room,

282

standing before the mini-bar, my hair dripping bath water onto the carpet. Dad is studying me, watching me curiously, hand suspended in the air as though he's not sure whether to touch me or not.

'Earth to Joyce,' he's singing.

I clear my throat. 'You're done?'

Dad nods and his eyes follow me to the bathroom. On the way there, I stop and turn. 'By the way, I've booked a ballet show for tonight if you'd like to come. We need to leave in an hour.'

'OK, love,' he nods softly, and watches after me with a familiar look of worry in his eyes. I've seen that look as a child, I've seen it as an adult and a million times in between. It's as though I've taken the stabilisers off my bicycle for the very first time and he's running along beside me, holding on tight, afraid to let me go.

TWENTY-FOUR

Dad breathes heavily beside me and links my arm tightly as we slowly make our way to Covent Garden. Using my other hand I pat down my pockets, feeling for his heart pills.

'Dad, we're definitely getting a taxi back to the hotel and I'm not taking no for an answer.'

Dad stops and stares ahead, he takes deep breaths.

'Are you OK? Is it your heart? Should we sit down? Stop and take a rest? Go back to the hotel?'

'Shut up and turn round, Gracie. It's not just my heart that takes my breath away, you know.'

I spin round and there it is, the Royal Opera House, its columns illuminated for the evening performance, a red carpet lining the pavement outside and crowds filing through the doors.

'You have to take your moments, love,' Dad says, taking in the sight before him. 'Don't just go head first into everything, like a bull seeing red.'

Having booked our tickets so late we are seated

in the lower slips almost at the top of the tremendous theatre. The position is unlucky, yet we are fortunate to have got tickets at all. The view of the stage is restricted, yet the view of the boxes opposite is perfect. Squinting through the binoculars situated beside the seat, I spy on the people filling the boxes. No sign of my American man. *Earth to Justin?* I hear the woman's voice in my head and wonder if Frankie's theory about seeing the world from his eyes was correct.

Dad is enthralled by our view. 'We've got the best seats in the house, love, look.' He leans over the balcony and his tweed cap almost falls off his head. I grab his arm and pull him back. He takes the photograph of Mum from his pocket and places her on the velvet balcony ledge. 'Best seat in the house, indeed,' he says, his eyes filling.

The voice over the intercom system counts latecomers down and finally the cacophony of the orchestra dies down, the lights dim and there is silence before the magic begins. The conductor taps and the orchestra play the opening bars of Tchaikovsky's ballet. Apart from Dad snorting when the male principal dancer appears on stage wearing tights, it runs smoothly and we are both entranced by the story of *Swan Lake*. I look away from the prince's coming-of-age party and study those sitting in the boxes. Their faces are lit, their eyes dancing along with the dancers they follow. It's as though a music box has been opened, spilling music and light from it and all those watching have been enchanted, captured by its magic. I continue to spy at them through my opera glasses, moving from left to right, a row of unfamiliar faces until . . . My eyes widen as I reach the familiar face, the man from the hair salon I now know from Bea's biography in the programme, to be Mr Hitchcock. *Justin Hitchcock?* He watches the stage, entranced, leaning so far over the balcony it looks as though he'll topple over the ledge.

Dad elbows me. 'Would you stop looking around you, and keep your eye on the stage. He's about to kill her.'

I turn to face the stage and try to hold my eyes on the prince leaping about with his crossbow, but I can't. A magnetic pull turns my face back down to the box, anxious to see who Mr Hitchcock is sitting with. My heart is drumming so loudly I only realise now it's not part of Tchaikovsky's score. Beside him is the woman with long, red hair and lightly freckled face, who holds the camera in my dreams. Beside her is a sweet-looking gentleman and behind them, squashed together are a young man pulling uncomfortably at his tie, a woman with big curly red hair and a large round man. I flick through my memory files like I'm going through Polaroids. The chubby boy from the sprinkler scene and seesaw? Perhaps. But the other two, I don't know. I move my eyes back to Justin Hitchcock and smile, finding his face more entertaining than the action on stage.

Suddenly the music changes, the light reflecting

on his face flickers and his expression changes. I know instantly that Bea is on stage, and I turn to watch. There she is among the flock of swans, moving about so gracefully in perfect unison, dressed in a white fitted corset dress with raggedy long white tutu, similar to feathers. Her long blonde hair is tied up in a bun, covered by a neat headdress. I recall the image of her in the park as a little girl, twirling and twirling in her tutu and I'm filled with pride. How far she has come. How grown up she is now. My eyes fill.

'Oh, look, Justin,' Jennifer says breathily beside him.

He is looking. He can't take his eyes off his daughter, a vision in white, dancing in perfect unison with the flock of swans, not a movement out of place. She looks so grown up, so . . . how did that happen? It seems like only yesterday she was twirling for him and Jennifer in the park across from their house, a little girl with a tutu and dreams and now . . . His eyes fill and he looks beside him to Jennifer, to share a look, share the moment but at the same time, she reaches for Laurence's hand. He looks away quickly, back to his daughter. A tear falls and he reaches into his front pocket for his handkerchief.

A handkerchief is raised to my face, catches my tear before it drips from my chin.

'What are you crying for?' Dad says loudly,

dabbing at my chin roughly, as the curtain lowers for the interval.

'I'm just so proud of Bea.'

'Who?'

'Oh, nothing . . . I just think it's a beautiful story. What do you think?'

'I think those lads have definitely got socks down their tights.'

I laugh and wipe my eyes. 'Do you think Mum's enjoying it?'

He smiles and stares at the photo. 'She must be, she hasn't turned round once since it started. Unlike you, who's got ants in her pants. If I'd known you were so keen on binoculars I'd have taken you out bird-watching long ago.' He sighs and looks around. 'The lads at the Monday Club won't believe this at all. Donal McCarthy, you better watch out,' he chuckles.

'Do you miss her?'

'It's been ten years, love.'

It stings that he can be so dismissive. I fold my arms and look away, silently fuming.

Dad leans closer and nudges me. 'And everyday, I miss her more than I did the day before.'

Oh. I immediately feel guilty for wishing that on him.

'It's like my garden, love. Everything grows. Including love. And with that growing everyday how can you expect missing her to ever fade away? Everything builds, including our ability to cope with it. That's how we keep going.'

I shake my head, in awe of some of the things he comes out with. Philosophical and otherwise. And this from a man who's been calling me his teapot (lid, *kid*) since we landed.

'And I just thought you liked pottering,' I smile.

'Ah, there's a lot to be said for pottering. You know Thomas Berry said that gardening is an active participation in the deepest mysteries of the universe? There are lessons in pottering.'

'Like what?' I try not to smile.

'Well, even a garden grows stranglers, love. It grows them naturally, all by itself. They creep up and choke the plants that are growing from the very same soil as they are. We each have our demons, our self-destruct button. Even in gardens. Pretty as they may be. If you don't potter, you don't notice them.'

He eyes me and I look away, choosing to clear my already-clear throat.

Sometimes I wish he'd just stick to laughing at men in tights.

'Justin, we're going to the bar, are you coming?' Doris asks.

'No,' he says, in a huff like a child, folding his arms.

'Why not?' Al squeezes further into the box to sit beside him.

'I just don't want to.' He picks up the opera glasses and starts fiddling with them.

'But you'll be here on your own.'

'So?'

'Mr Hitchcock, would you like me to get you a drink?' Bea's boyfriend, Peter, asks.

'Mr Hitchcock was my father, you can call me Al. Like the song.' He punches him playfully on the shoulder but it knocks him back a few steps.

'OK, Al, but I actually meant Justin.'

'*You* can call me Mr Hitchcock.' Justin looks at him like there's a bad smell in the room.

'We don't have to sit with Laurence and Jennifer, you know.'

Laurence. Laurence of Ahernia who has elephantitis of the—

'Yes we do, Al, don't be ridiculous,' Doris interrupts.

Al sighs. 'Well, give Petey an answer, do you want us to bring you back a drink?'

Yes. But Justin can't bring himself to say it and instead shakes his head sulkily.

'OK, we'll be back in fifteen.'

Al gives him a comforting brotherly pat on his shoulder before they all leave him alone in the box to stew over Laurence and Jennifer and Bea and Chicago and London and Dublin and now Peter, and how exactly his life has ended up.

Two minutes later and already tired of feeling sorry for himself, he looks through the opera glasses and begins spying on the trickles of people seated below him who'd stayed in their seats for the interval. He spots a couple fighting, snapping at one another. Another couple kissing, reaching for their coats and then disappearing quickly to the exits. He spies a mother giving out to her son. A group of women laughing together. A couple saying nothing to one another or who have nothing to say to one another. He'd prefer the former. Nothing exciting. He moves to the boxes opposite. They are empty, everyone choosing to have their pre-ordered drinks in the nearby bar. He cranes his neck up higher.

How on earth can anyone see anything from there?

Here, there are a small number of people, like everyone else, just chatting. He moves along from right to left. Then stops. Rubs his eyes. Sure he is imagining it. He squints back through the opera glasses again and sure enough, there she is. With the old man. Every scene in his life was beginning to be like a page from *Where's Wally?*

She is looking through her opera glasses too, scanning the crowd below them both. Then she raises her opera glasses, moves slowly to the right and . . . they both freeze, staring at one another through the lenses. He slowly lifts his arm. Waves.

She slowly does the same. The old man beside her puts his glasses on and squints in his direction, mouth opening and closing the entire time.

Justin holds his hand up, intends to make a 'wait' sign. *Hold on, I'm coming up to you.* He holds his forefinger up, as though he's just thought of an idea. *One minute. Hold on, I'll be one minute,* he tries to signal.

She gives him the thumbs-up and he breaks into a smile.

He drops the opera glasses and stands up immediately, taking note of where exactly she is sitting. The door to the box opens and in walks Laurence.

'Justin, I thought maybe we could have a word,' he says politely, drumming his fingers on the back of the chair that separates them.

'No, Laurence, not now, sorry.' He tries to move past him.

'I promise not to take up too much of your time. Just a few minutes while we're alone. To clear the air, you know?' He opens the button of his blazer, smooths down his tie and closes his button again.

'Yeah, I appreciate that, buddy, I really do, but I'm in a really big hurry right now.' He tries to inch by him but Laurence moves to block him.

'A hurry?' he says, raising his eyebrows. 'But the interval is just about over and . . . ah,' he stops, realising. 'I see. Well, I just thought I'd give it a try. If you're not ready to have the discussion yet, that's understandable.'

'No, it's not that.' Justin looks through his opera glasses and up at Joyce, feeling panicked. She's still there. 'It's just that I really am in a hurry to get to somebody. I have to go, Laurence.'

Jennifer walks in just as he says that. Her face is stony.

'Honestly, Justin. Laurence just wanted to be a gentleman and talk to you like an *adult*. Something, it seems, you have forgotten how to be.

Though I don't know why I'm surprised about that.'

'No, no, look, Jennifer.' *I used to call you Jen. So formal now, a lifetime away from that memorable day in the park when they were all so happy, so in love.* 'I *really* don't have time for this right now. You don't understand, I have to go.'

'You can't go. The ballet is about to begin in a few minutes and your daughter will be onstage. Don't tell me you're walking out on her too, because of some ridiculous male pride.'

Doris and Al enter the box, Al's size alone completely crowding the small space and blocking his path to the door. Al holds a pint of cola in his hand and an oversized bag of crisps.

'Tell him, Justin.' Doris folds her arms and taps her long fake pink nails against her thin arms.

Justin groans. 'Tell him what?'

'*Remind* him of the heart disease in your family so that he may think twice before eating and drinking that crap.'

'What heart disease?' Justin holds his hands to his head while on the other side of him, Jennifer drones on and on in what sounds like Charlie Brown's teacher's voice. 'Wah, wah, wah' is all he hears.

'Your *father*, dying of a *heart attack*,' she says impatiently.

Justin freezes.

'The doc didn't say that it would necessarily happen to me,' Al moans to his wife.

'He said there was a good chance. If there's a history in the family.'

Justin's voice sounds to him as though it's coming from somewhere else. 'No, no, I really don't think you have to worry about that, Al.'

'See?' He looks at Doris.

'That's not what the doctor said, sweetheart. We have to be more careful if it runs in the family.'

'No, it doesn't run in the—' Justin stalls. 'Look, I really have to go now.' He tries to move in the crowded box.

'No, you will not,' Jennifer blocks him. 'You are not going anywhere until you *apologise* to Laurence.'

'It's really all right, Jen,' Laurence says awkwardly.

I call her Jen, not you!

'No, it's not, sweetheart.'

I'm her sweetheart, not you!

Voices come at him from all sides, wah wah wah, he is unable to make out the words. He feels hot and sweaty, dizziness grips him.

Suddenly the lights dim and the music begins and he has no choice but to take his seat again, beside a fuming Jennifer, an insulted Laurence, a silent Peter, a worried Doris and a hungry Al, who decides to munch loudly in his left ear, on the packet of potato chips.

He sighs and looks up at Joyce.

Help.

*   *   *

It seems the squabble in Mr Hitchcock's box has ended, but as the lights are going down, they are all still standing. When the lights lift again, they are all seated with stony faces, apart from the large man at the back, who is eating a large bag of crisps. I have ignored Dad all throughout the last few moments, choosing instead to invest my time in a crashcourse in lip-reading. If I have been successful, their conversation involved Carrot Top and barbecued bananas.

Deep inside, my heart drums like a *djembe*, its deep bass and slap reaching down into my chest. I feel it in the base of my throat, throbbing, and all because he saw me, he wanted to come to me. I feel relieved that following my instincts, however flighty, paid off. It takes me a few minutes to be able to focus on anything other than Justin, but when I calm my nerves slightly I turn my attention back to the stage where Bea takes my breath away and causes me to sniffle through her performance like a proud aunt. It occurs to me so strongly right now that the only people privy to those wonderful happy memories in the park are Bea, her mother, father . . . and me.

'Dad, can I ask you something?' I lean close to him and whisper.

'He's just after telling that girl that he loves her but she's the wrong girl,' he rolls his eyes. 'Eejit. The swan girl was in white and that one is in black. They don't look alike at all.'

'She could have changed for the ball. No one wears the same thing everyday.'

He looks me up and down. 'You only took your bathrobe off *one day* last week. Anyway, what's up with you?'

'Well, it's that, I, em, something has happened and, well . . .'

'Spit it out for Christsake, before I miss anything else.'

I give up whispering in his ear and turn to face him. 'I've been given something, or more, something very special has been *shared* with me. It's completely inexplicable and it doesn't make any sense at all, in an Our Lady of Knock kind of way, you know?' I laugh nervously and quickly stop, on seeing his face.

No, he doesn't know. Dad looks angry I've used Mary's apparition in County Mayo during the 1870s as an example of nonsense.

'OK, perhaps that was a bad example. What I mean is, it breaks every rule I've ever known. I just don't understand *why*.'

'Gracie,' Dad lifts his chin, 'Knock, like the rest of Ireland, suffered great distress over the centuries from invasion, evictions and famines, and Our Lord sent His Mother, the Blessed Virgin, to visit with His oppressed children.'

'No,' I hold my hands over my face, 'I don't mean why did Mary appear, I mean why has this . . . this *thing* happened to me? This thing I've been given.'

'Oh. Well, is it hurting anyone? Because if it's not and if you've been given it, I'd as soon stop callin' it a "thing" and start referring to it as a "gift". Look at them dancing. He thinks she's the swan girl. Surely he can see her face. Or is it like Superman when he takes the glasses off and suddenly he's completely different, even though it's as clear as day that it's the same person?'

A gift. I'd never thought of it like that. I look over at Bea's parents, beaming with pride, and I think of Bea before the interval, floating around with her flock of swans. I shake my head. No. No one is being hurt.

'Well, then,' Dad shrugs.

'But I don't understand *why* and *how* and—'

'What is it with people these days?' he hisses, and the man beside me turns round. I whisper my apologies.

'In my day, something *just was*. None of this analysis a hundred times over. None of these college courses with people graduating with degrees in Whys and Hows and Becauses. Sometimes, love, you just need to forget all of those words and enrol in a little lesson called "Thank You". Look at this story here,' he points at the stage. 'Do you hear anybody here giving out about the fact *she*, a *woman*, has been turned into a *swan*? Have you heard anything more ludicrous in your life?'

I shake my head, smiling.

'Have you met anyone lately who happens to have been turned into a swan?'

I laugh and whisper, 'No.'

'Yet look at it. This bloody thing has been famous the world over for centuries. We have non-believers, atheists, intellects, cynicists, *him*.' He nods his head at the man who shushed us. 'All kinds of what-have-yous in here tonight, but all of them want to see that fella in the tights end up with that swan girl, so she'll be able to get out of that lake. Only with the love of one who has never loved before, can the spell be broken. Why? Who the hell cares why? Do you think your woman with the feathers is going to ask *why*? No. She's going to say *thank you* because then she can move on and wear nice dresses and go for walks, instead of having to peck at soggy bread in a stinky lake every day for the rest of her life.'

I have been stunned to silence.

'Now, *whisht*, we're missing the performance. She wants to kill herself now, look? Talk about being dramatic.' He places his elbows on the balcony and leans in closer to the stage, his left ear tilted towards the stage more than his eyes, quite literally eavesdropping.

TWENTY-FIVE

During the standing ovation, Justin spies Joyce's father helping her into a red coat, the same one from their Grafton Street collision. She begins to move to her nearby exit with her father in tow.

'Justin,' Jennifer scowls at her ex-husband, who is more busy spying through his opera glasses up at the ceiling than at his daughter bowing on stage.

He puts the glasses down and claps loudly, cheering.

'Hey, guys, I'm going to go to the bar and keep some good seats for us.' He starts moving towards the door.

'It's already reserved,' Jennifer shouts after him, over the applause.

He holds his hand up to his ear and shakes his head. 'Can't hear you.'

He escapes and runs down the corridors, trying to find his way upstairs to the lower slips. The curtains must have fallen for the final time as people begin to exit their boxes, crowding the corridors and making it impossible for Justin to push past.

He has a change of plan: he'll rush to the exit and wait for her there. That way he can't miss her.

'Let's get a drink, love,' Dad says as we slowly amble behind the crowd exiting the theatre. 'I saw a bar on this floor.'

We stop to read some directions.

'There's the Amphitheatre bar, this way,' I say, looking out constantly for Justin Hitchcock.

A woman usher announces that the bar is open only for cast, crew and family members.

'That's great, we'll have some peace and quiet so,' Dad says to her, tipping his cap as he walks by. 'Oh, you should have seen my granddaughter up there. Proudest day of my life,' he says, putting his hand on his heart.

The woman smiles and allows us entry.

'Come on, Dad.' After we've bought our drinks, I drag him deep into the room to sit at a table in the far corner, away from the growing crowd.

'If they try to throw us out, Gracie, I'm not leaving my pint. I just sat down.'

I wring my hands nervously and perch on the edge of my seat, looking around for him. *Justin.* His name rolls around in my head, plays around my tongue like a contented pig in muck.

People filter out of the bar until all that is left are family, crew and cast members. Nobody approaches us again to usher us out, perhaps one of the perks of being with an old man. Bea's mother enters with the two unknown people from the box, and the chubby man I recognise. But no Mr Hitchcock. My eyes dart around the room.

'There she is,' I whisper.

'Who?'

'One of the dancers. She was one of the swans.'

'How do you know? They all looked the same. Even the nancy boy thought they were the same. Sure, didn't he profess his love to the wrong woman? The bloody eejit.'

There's no sign of Justin and I begin to worry that this is another wasted opportunity. Perhaps he has left early and isn't coming to the bar at all.

'Dad,' I say urgently, 'I'm just going to take a look around for somebody. Please do *not* move from this chair. I'll be back soon.'

'The only moving I'll be doing is this.' He picks up his pint and moves it to his lips. He takes a gulp of Guinness, closes his eyes and savours the taste, leaving a white moustache around his lips.

I hurry out of the bar and wander around the huge theatre, not sure where to start looking. I stand outside the nearby gents' toilets for a few moments but he doesn't appear. I look over at the box he was seated in but it's empty.

Justin gives up standing by the exit door as the last few people trickle by him. He must have missed her and he was stupid to think there was only one exit. He sighs with frustration. He wishes he could transport himself back in time to the day in the salon and relive the moment properly this time. His pocket vibrates, snapping him out of his daydream.

'Bro, where the heck are you?'

'Hi, Al. I saw the woman again.'

'The Sky News woman?'

'Yeah!'

'The Viking woman?'

'Yeah, yeah, her.'

'The *Antiques Roadshow* wo—'

'YES! For Christsake, do we have to go through this again?'

'Hey, did you ever think that maybe she's a stalker?'

'If she's a stalker, then why am I always chasing her?'

'Oh, yeah. Well, maybe you're the stalker and you don't know it.'

'Al . . .' Justin grits his teeth.

'Whatever, hurry back up here before Jennifer has a conniption fit. Another one.'

Justin sighs. 'I'm coming.'

He snaps his phone shut and takes one last look down the street. Among the crowd something catches his eye, a red coat. Adrenalin surges. He races outside, pushes past the slowly filtering crowd, his heart pounding, his eyes not budging from the coat.

'Joyce!' he calls. 'Joyce, wait!' he shouts louder. She keeps walking, unable to hear him.

He bumps and pushes, getting cursed at and prodded by people he pushes by until finally she's just inches from him.

'Joyce,' he says breathlessly, reaching out and grabbing her arm. She spins around, a face twisted in surprise and fright. A face of a stranger.

She hits him over the head with her leather bag.

'Ow! Hey! Jesus!'

Apologising, he slowly makes his way back to the theatre, trying to catch his breath, rubbing his sore head, cursing and grumbling to himself with frustration. He reaches for the main door. It doesn't open. He tries it again gently, then rattles it slightly a few times. Within seconds, he pulls and pushes the door with full force, kicking at the door with frustration.

'Hey, hey, hey! We're closed! Theatre's closed!' a member of staff informs him from behind the glass.

When I return to the bar, I thankfully find Dad sitting in the corner where I'd left him. Only this time he's not alone. Perched on the chair beside him, her head close to his as though in deep conversation, is Bea. I panic and rush over to them.

'Hi.' I approach them, terrified by what verbal diarrhoea may have slipped out of his mouth already.

'Ah, there you are, love. Thought you'd abandoned me. This nice girl came to see if I was OK, seeing as someone tried to throw me out again.'

'I'm Bea,' she smiles, and I can't help but notice how grown-up she has become. How self-assured and confident she is. I almost feel like telling her that the last time I'd seen her she was 'yay high', but I stop myself from gushing at her extraordinary transformation into adulthood.

'Hello, Bea.'

'Do I know you?' Frown lines appear on her porcelain forehead.

'Em . . .'

'This is my daughter, Gracie,' Dad butts in, and for once I don't correct him.

'Oh, Gracie,' Bea shakes her head. 'No. I was thinking of someone else. Nice to meet you.'

We shake hands and I hold on for a little too long perhaps, entranced by the feel of her real skin, not just a memory. I quickly let go.

'You were wonderful tonight. I was so proud,' I say breathily.

'Proud? Oh, yes, your father told me you designed the costumes,' she smiles. 'They were beautiful. I'm surprised I hadn't met you until now, we had been dealing with Linda for all the fittings.'

My mouth drops, Dad shrugs nervously and sips on what looks to be a new pint. A fresh lie for a fresh pint. The price of his soul.

'Oh, I didn't design them . . . I just . . .' You just what, Joyce? 'I just supervised,' I say dumbly. 'What else has he been telling you?' I nervously sit down and look around for her father, hoping this isn't the moment he chooses to enter and greet me in the midst of this ridiculous lie.

'Well, just as you arrived he was telling me about how he'd saved a swan's life,' she smiles.

'Single-handedly,' they both add in unison and laugh.

'Ha ha,' I force out and it sounds fake. 'Is that true?' I ask him doubtfully.

'Oh, ye of little faith.' Dad takes another gulp of Guinness. Seventy-five years old and he's already had a brandy and a pint: he'll be on his ear in no time. God knows what he'd be saying then. We'll have to leave soon.

'Well, you know what, girls, it's great to save a life, it really, really is,' Dad says from his high horse. 'Unless you've done it, you have no idea.'

'My father, the hero,' I smile.

Bea laughs at Dad. 'You sound exactly like my father.'

My ears perk up, 'Is he here?'

She looks around. 'No, not yet. I don't know *where* he is. Probably hiding from my mom and her new boyfriend, not to mention my boyfriend,' she laughs. 'But that's another story. Anyway he considers himself Superman—'

'Why?' I interrupt and try to rein myself in.

'About a month ago, he donated blood,' she smiles and holds her hands up. 'Ta-da! That's it!' She laughs. 'But he thinks he's some kind of hero that's saved somebody's life. I mean, I don't know, maybe he has. It's *all* he talks about. He donated

307

it at a mobile unit at the college where he was giving a seminar – you guys probably know it, it's in Dublin. Trinity College? Anyway, I wouldn't mind, but he only did it because the doctor was cute and for that Chinese thing, what do you call it? The thing where you save someone's life and they're forever indebted to you or something like that?'

Dad shrugs. 'I don't speak Chinese. Or know any. She eats the food all the time, though.' He nods his head at me. 'Rice with eggs, or something.' He ruffles his nose.

Bea laughs. 'Anyway, he figured if he was going to save someone's life he deserved to be thanked every day for the rest of his life by the person he *saved*.'

'How would they do that, then?' Dad leans in.

'By delivering a muffin basket, do his dry cleaning, a newspaper and coffee delivered to his door every morning, a chauffeur-driven car, front-row tickets to the opera . . .' She rolls her eyes and then frowns. 'I can't remember what else but they were ridiculous things. Anyway, I told him he may as well have a slave if he wants that kind of treatment, not save someone's life.' She laughs and Dad does too.

I make an *oh* shape with my mouth but nothing comes out.

'Don't get me wrong, he's a really thoughtful guy,' she adds quickly, misunderstanding my silence. 'And I was proud of him for donating blood as he's absolutely terrified by needles. He has a *huge* phobia,' she explains to Dad, who nods along in agreement. 'That's him there.' She opens her locket around her neck and if I have regained my power of speech, it is quickly lost again.

On one side of the locket is a photograph of Bea and her mother, and on the other side is the photograph of her and her father when she was a little girl, in the park on that summer day that is clearly imbedded in my memory. I remember how she jumped up and down with excitement and how it had taken us so long to get her to sit still. I remember the smell of her hair as she sat on my lap and pushed her head up against mine and shouted 'Cheeeeese!' so loudly she'd almost deafened me. She hadn't done that to me at all, of course, but I remember it with equal fondness as a day spent fishing with my father when I was a child, feel all the sensations of the day as clearly as the drink I now taste in my mouth and feel flowing down my throat. The cold of the ice, the sweetness of the mineral. It's all as real to me as the moments spent with Bea in the park.

'I'll have to put my glasses on to see this,' Dad says, moving closer and taking the gold locket in his old fingers. 'Where was this?'

'The park near where we used to live. In Chicago. I'm five years old there, with my dad, but I love this photograph. It was such a special day.' She looks at it fondly. 'One of the best.'

I smile too, remembering it.

'Photograph!' somebody in the bar calls out.

'Dad, let's get out of here,' I whisper while Bea is distracted by the commotion.

'OK, love, just after this pint—'

'No! Now!' I hiss.

'Group photo! Come on!' Bea says, grabbing Dad's arm.

'Oh!' Dad looks pleased.

'No, no no no no no.' I try to smile to hide my panic. 'We really must go now.'

'Just one photo, Gracie,' she smiles. 'We have to get the lady who's responsible for all these beautiful costumes.'

'No, I'm not—'

'Costume *supervisor*,' Bea corrects herself apologetically.

A woman on the other side of the group throws me a look of horror, on hearing this. Dad laughs. I'm stiff beside Bea, who throws one arm around me and the other arm around her mother.

'Everyone say Tchaikovsky!' Dad shouts.

'Tchaikovsky!' They all cheer and laugh.

I roll my eyes.

The camera flashes.

Justin enters the room.

The crowd breaks up.

I grab Dad, and run.

TWENTY-SIX

Back in our hotel room it's lights out for Dad, who climbs into bed in his brown paisley pyjamas, and for me, who is wearing more clothes in bed than I've worn for a long time.

The room is black, thick with shadows and still, apart from the flashing red digits in the time display panel at the bottom of the television. Lying flat and still on my back, I attempt to process the day's events. My body once again becomes the subject of much Zulu drumming as my heartbeat intensifies. I feel its pounding rebound against the springs in the mattress beneath me. Then the pulse in my neck vibrates so wildly it causes my ear drums to join in. Beneath my ribcage, it feels like two fists hammering to get out, and I watch the bedroom door and anticipate the arrival of an African tribe, ready to participate in the synchronised stamping of feet, at the end of my bed.

The reason for these internal war drums? Over and over again, my mind runs through the clanger

311

Bea dropped only hours ago. The words fell from her mouth just like a cymbal falling from its drum set. Since then it has rolled around the floor and only now lands face down on the ground with a crash, ending my African orchestra. The revelation that Bea's dad, Justin, donated blood a month ago in Dublin, the same month I fell down the stairs and changed my life for ever, plays over and over in my mind. Coincidence? A resounding yes. Something more? A shaky possibility. A *hopeful* possibility.

When is a coincidence just a coincidence, though? And when, if at all, should it be seen as something more? At a time like this? When I am lost and desperate, grieving for a child that was never born, and tending to my wounds after a defeated marriage? This, I have found, is the time when what was once clear has instead become cloudy, and what was once considered bizarre has now become a possibility.

It is during troubled times like these that people see straight, though others watch with concern and try to convince them that they can't. Weighted minds are just so because of all of their new thoughts. When those who have passed through their troubles and come out the other side suddenly embrace their new beliefs wholeheartedly, it is viewed with cynicism by others. Why? Because when you're in trouble you look harder for answers than those who aren't, and it's those answers that help you through.

This blood transfusion – is it *the* answer or merely an answer I'm looking for? I find that, usually, answers present themselves. They are not hidden under rocks or camouflaged among trees. Answers are right there, in front of our eyes. But if you haven't cause to look, then of course you will probably never find them.

So, the explanation for the sudden arrival of alien memories, the reason for such a deep connection to Justin – I feel it running through my very veins. Is this the answer that my heart is currently raging within me to realise? It hops up and down now, like Skippy, trying to get my attention, trying to alert me to a problem. I breathe in slowly through my nose and exhale, I close my eyes gently and place my hands over my chest, feeling the thump-thump, thump-thump that is raging within me. Time to slow everything down now, time to get answers.

Taking the bizarre as a given for just one moment, as people in trouble do: if I did indeed receive Justin's blood during my transfusion, then my heart is now sending his blood around my body. Some of the blood that once flowed through his veins, keeping him alive, now rushes through mine, helping to keep me alive. Something that came from his heart, that beat within him, that made him who he is, is now a part of me.

At first I shiver at the thought, goose bumps rising on my skin, but on further thought, I snuggle down into the bed and hug my body. I suddenly don't feel so lonely, feel glad of the company within me. Is this the reason for the connection I feel with him? That in flowing from his channels to mine, it enabled me to tune into his frequency and experience his personal memories and passions?

I sigh wearily, knowing nothing in my life makes sense any more, and not just since the day I fell down the stairs. I had been falling for quite some time before that. That day . . . that was the day I'd landed. The first day of the rest of my life, and quite possibly, thanks to Justin Hitchcock.

It has been a long day. The business at the airport, the *Antiques Roadshow*, then finally the clanger at the Royal Opera House. A tsunami of emotions has come crashing down upon me all in twenty-four hours, pulled me under and overwhelmed me. I smile now, remembering the events, the precious moments with Dad, from tea at his kitchen table to a mini-adventure in London. I offer a wide toothy grin to the ceiling above me and a thanks to beyond the ceiling.

From the darkness I hear a wheezing, short rasps drifting into the atmosphere.

'Dad?' I whisper. 'Are you OK?'

The wheezing gets louder and my body freezes.

'Dad?'

Then it's followed by a snort. And a loud guffaw.

'Michael Aspel,' he splutters through his laughter. 'Christ Almighty, Gracie.'

I smile with relief as his laughter intensifies,

becomes so much bigger than him that he almost can't bear it. I giggle at the sound of his laughter. He laughs harder on hearing me, and I at him. Our sounds fuel each other. The springs of the mattress beneath me squeak as my body shakes, causing us to roar even more. Thoughts of the umbrella stand, going live with Michael Aspel, the group cheering 'Tchaikovsky!' at the camera, the hilarity grows with each flickering scene.

'Oh, my stomach,' he howls.

I roll onto my side, hands on my belly.

Dad continues to wheeze and bangs his hand repeatedly on the side cabinet that separates us. I try to stop, the panic of a stiffening stomach sore but hilarious at the same time. I can't stop and Dad's high-pitched wheezing sets me off even more. I don't think I've ever heard him laugh so much and so heartily. From the pale light seeping through the window beside Dad, I see his legs rise in the air and kick around with glee.

'Oh. My. I. Can't. Stop.'

We wheeze and roar and laugh, sit up, lie down, roll around and try to catch our breaths. We stop momentarily and try to compose ourselves but it takes over our bodies again, laughing, laughing, laughing in the darkness, at nothing and everything.

Then we calm down and there is silence. Dad farts and we are off again.

Hot tears roll from the sides of my eyes and down my plumped cheeks, which ache from smiling and I squeeze them with my hands to stop. It occurs to me how close happiness and sadness are. So closely knitted together. Such a thin line, a thread-like divide that in the midst of emotions, it trembles, blurring the territory of exact opposites. The movement is minute, like the thin thread of a spider's web that quivers under a raindrop. Here in my moment of unstoppable cheek- and stomach-aching laughter, as my body rolls around, my stomach clenched, all the muscles taut, my body jumps about, is racked by emotion and therefore steps ever so slightly over the mark, and into sadness. Tears of sadness gush down my cheeks as my stomach continues to shake and ache with happiness.

I think of Conor and me; how quickly a moment of love was snapped away to a moment of hate. One comment to steal it all away. Of how love and war stand upon the very same foundations. How, in my darkest moments, my most fearful times, when faced, became my bravest. When feeling at your weakest you end up showing more strength, when at your lowest are suddenly lifted above higher than you've ever been. They all border one another, those opposites, and how quickly we can be altered. Despair can be altered by one simple smile offered by a stranger; confidence can become fear by the arrival of one uneasy presence. Just as Kate's son had wavered on the balance beam and in an instant his excitement had turned to pain. Everything is on the verge, always brimming the surface, a slight shake, a tremble sends things toppling. How similar emotions are.

Dad stops his laughter so abruptly it concerns me and I reach for the light.

Pitch-black so quickly becomes light.

He looks at me as though he's done something wrong, but is afraid to admit it. He throws the covers off his body and shuffles into the bathroom, grabbing his travel bag and hitting off everything in his path, refusing to meet my eyes. I look away. How quickly such comfort with someone can shift to awkwardness. How in the very second you reach a dead-end, moments when you are convinced you know exactly where you're going are altered. A realisation in less than a second. A flicker.

Dad makes his way back to bed wearing a different pair of pyjama bottoms and with a towel tucked under his arm. I turn off the light, both of us quiet now. Light so quickly becomes darkness again. I continue to stare at the ceiling, feeling lost again when only moments ago I'd been found. My answers of only minutes ago are again transformed into questions.

'I can't sleep, Dad.' My voice sounds childlike.

'Close your eyes and stare into the dark, love,' Dad responds sleepily, sounding thirty years younger too.

Moments later his light snores are audible. Awake . . . and then gone.

A veil hangs between the two opposites, a mere slip of a thing that is transparent to warn us or comfort us. You hate now but look through this veil and see the possibility of love; you're sad now but look through to the other side and see happiness. Absolute composure to a complete mess – it happens so quickly, all in the blink of an eye.

TWENTY-SEVEN

'OK, I've gathered us all here today because—'

'Somebody died.'

'No, Kate,' I sigh.

'Well, it sounds like— Ow,' she yelps as Frankie, I assume, physically harms her for her tactlessness.

'So are you all red-bused out of it?' Frankie asks.

I'm seated at the desk in my hotel room, on the phone to the girls who are huddled around the phone in Kate's house with me on loudspeaker. I'd spent the morning looking around London with Dad, taking photographs of him standing awkwardly in front of anything resembling anything English: red buses, post boxes, police horses, pubs, Buckingham Palace, and a completely unaware transvestite, as he was so excited to see 'a real one', who was nothing like the local priest who'd lost his mind and wandered the streets wearing a dress, in his home town of Cavan when he was young.

While I sit at the desk, he is lying on his bed watching a rerun of *Strictly Come Dancing*, drinking a brandy and licking the sour cream and onion off Pringles before depositing the soggy crisps in the bin.

'NICE!' he shouts at the television, responding to Bruce Forsyth's catchphrase.

I've called a conference call to share the latest news, or more for help and a plea for sanity strengthening. I may have gone one wish too far, but a girl can always dream. Kate and Frankie are huddled around Kate's home phone.

'One of your kids just puked on me,' Frankie says. 'Your *kid* just puked on me.'

'Oh, that is not puke, that's just a little dribble.'

'No, *this* is dribble . . .'

There's silence.

'Frankie, you are disgusting.'

'OK, girls, girls, please can you two stop, just this once?'

'Sorry, Joyce, but I can't continue this conversation until it is out of here. It's crawling around biting things, climbing on things, drooling on things. It's very distracting. Can't Christian mind it?'

I try not to laugh.

'Do not call my child "it". And no, Christian is busy.'

'He's watching football.'

'He doesn't like to be disturbed, particularly by you. Ever.'

'Well, you're busy too. How do I get it to come with me?'

There's a silence.

'Come here, little boy,' Frankie says uneasily.

'His name is Sam. You're his godmother, in case you've forgotten that too.'

'No, I haven't forgotten *that*. Just his name.' Her voice strains, as though she's lifting weights. 'Wow, what do you feed it?'

Sam squeals like a pig.

Frankie snorts back.

'Frankie, give him to me. I'll bring him in to Christian.'

'OK, Joyce,' Frankie begins in Kate's absence, 'I've done some research on the information you gave me yesterday and I've brought some paperwork with me, hold on.' I hear papers being ruffled.

'What's this about?' Kate asks, returning.

'This is about Joyce jumping into the mind of the American man, thereby possessing his memories, skills and intelligence,' Frankie responds.

'What?' Kate shrieks.

'I found out that his name is Justin Hitchcock,' I say excitedly.

'How?' Kate asks.

'His surname was in his daughter's biography in last night's ballet programme, and his first name, well, I heard that in a dream.'

There's silence. I roll my eyes as I imagine them giving each other *that* look.

'What the hell is going on here?' Kate asks, confused.

'Google him, Kate,' Frankie orders. 'Let's see if he exists.'

321

'He exists, believe me,' I confirm.

'No, sweetie, you see, the way these stories work is, we're supposed to think you're crazy for a while before eventually believing you. So let us check up on him and then we'll go from there.'

I lean my chin on my hand and wait.

'While Kate's doing that, I looked into the idea of sharing memories—'

'What?' Kate shrieks again. 'Sharing memories? Are you both out of your mind?'

'No, just me,' I say tiredly, resting my head on the desk.

'Actually, surprisingly enough, it turns out that you're not clinically insane. On that count, anyway. I went online and did some research. It turns out you're not alone in feeling that.'

I sit up, suddenly alert.

'I came across websites with interviews with others who have admitted to experiencing some-body else's memories and who have also acquired their skills or tastes.'

'Oh, you two are having me on. I knew this was a set-up. I knew it was out of character for you to drop by, Frankie.'

'This isn't a set-up,' I assure Kate.

'So you're trying to tell me honestly that you've magically acquired somebody *else*'s skills.'

'She speaks Latin, French and Italian,' Frankie explains. 'But we didn't say it was magically. *That* is ridiculous.'

'And what about tastes?' Kate is not convinced.

'She eats meat now,' Frankie says matter-of-factly.

'But why do you think these are somebody else's skills? Why can't she just have learned Latin, French and Italian by herself and decided that she likes meat all by herself, like a normal person? I suddenly like olives and have an aversion to cheese, does that mean my body has been possessed by an olive tree?'

'I don't think you're quite getting this. What makes you think olive trees don't like cheese?'

Silence.

'Look, Kate, I agree with you about the change of diet being a natural thing, but in all fairness, Joyce did learn three languages overnight without *actually* learning them.'

'Oh.'

'And I have dreams of Justin Hitchcock's private childhood moments.'

'Where the hell was I when all of this was happening?'

'Making me do the hokey cokey live on Sky News,' I huff.

I place the phone on loudspeaker and for the few minutes that follow, pace the room patiently and watch the time on the bottom of the television as both Frankie and Kate laugh heartily, on the other end.

Dad's tongue freezes mid-Pringle lick as his eyes follow me.

'What's that noise?' he finally asks.

'Kate and Frankie laughing,' I respond.

He rolls his eyes and continues licking his Pringles, attention back on a middle-aged male newsreader doing the rumba.

After three minutes, the laughter stops and I take them off loudspeaker.

'So as I was saying,' Frankie says, catching her breath, as though nothing had happened, 'what you're experiencing is quite normal – well, not normal, but there are other, eh . . .'

'Freaks?' Kate suggests.

'. . . *cases* where people have spoken of similar things. The only thing is, these are all people who have had heart transplants, which is nothing to do with what you've been through, so that blows that theory.'

Thump-thump, thump-thump. In my throat again.

'Hold on,' Kate butts in, 'one person says here that it's because she was abducted by aliens.'

'Stop reading my notes, Kate,' Frankie hisses. 'I wasn't going to mention her.'

'Listen,' I interrupt their squabbling, 'he donated blood. The same month that I went into hospital.'

'So?' Kate says.

'She received a blood transfusion,' Frankie explains. 'Not all that different to the heart transplant theory I just mentioned.'

We all go quiet.

Kate breaks the silence. 'OK, so, I still don't get it. Somebody explain.'

'Well, it's practically the same thing, isn't it?' I say. 'Blood comes from the heart.'

Kate gasps. 'It came straight from his heart,' she says dreamily.

'Oh, so now blood transfusions are romantic to you,' Frankie comments. 'Let me tell you about what I got from the Net. Due to reports from several heart transplant recipients claiming experiences of unexpected side effects, Channel Four made a documentary about whether it's possible that in receiving a transplanted organ, a patient could inherit some of their donor's memories, tastes, desires and habits as well. The documentary follows these people making contact with the donor families in the recipients' efforts to understand the new life within them. It questions science's understanding of how the memory works, featuring scientists who are pioneering research into the intelligence of the heart and the biochemical basis for memory in our cells.'

'So if they think that the heart holds more intelligence than we think, then the blood which is pumped from someone's heart could carry that intelligence. So in transfusing his blood, he transfused his memories too?' Kate asks. 'And his love of meat and languages,' she adds a little tartly.

Nobody wants to say yes to that question. Everybody wants to say no. Apart from me, who's had a night to warm to the idea already.

'Did *Star Trek* have an episode of this one time?' Frankie asks. 'Because if they didn't, they should have.'

'This can easily be solved,' Kate says excitedly. 'You can just find out who your blood donor was.'

'She can't.' Frankie, as usual, dampens her spirits. 'That kind of information is confidential. Besides, it's not as though she received all of his blood. He could only have donated less than a pint in one go. Then it's separated into white blood cells, red blood cells, plasma and platelets. What Joyce would have got, if Joyce received it at all, is only a part of his blood. It could even have been mixed with somebody else's.'

'His blood is still running through my body,' I add. 'It doesn't matter how much of it there is. And I remember feeling distinctly odd as soon as I opened my eyes in the hospital.'

A silence answers my ridiculous statement, as we all consider the fact that my feeling 'distinctly odd' had nothing to do with my transfusion and all to do with the unspeakable tragedy of losing my baby.

'We've got a Google hit for Mr Justin Hitchcock,' Kate fills the silence.

My heart beats rapidly. Please tell me I'm not making it all up, that he exists, that he's not a figment of my delusional mind. That the plans I've put in place already are not going to scare away some random person.

'OK, Justin Hitchcock was a hatmaker in Massachusetts. Hmm. Well, at least he's American. You have any knowledge of hats, Joyce?'

I think hard. 'Berets, bucket hats, fedoras, fisher-men hats, ball caps, pork-pie hats, tweed caps.'

Dad stops licking his Pringle again and looks at me. 'Panama hat.'

'Panama hat,' I repeat to the girls.

'Newsboy caps, skull caps,' Kate adds.

'Top hat,' Dad says, and I pass this down the phone once again.

'Cowboy hat,' Frankie says, sounding deep in thought. She snaps out of it. 'Wait a minute, what are we doing? Anybody can name hats.'

'You're right, it doesn't feel right. Keep reading,' I urge.

'Justin Hitchcock moved to Deerfield in 1774 where he served as a soldier and fifer in the Revolution . . . I should probably stop reading this. Over two hundred years old is probably too much of a sugar daddy for you.'

'Hold on,' Frankie takes over, not wanting me to lose hope. 'There's another Justin Hitchcock below that. New York sanitation department—'

'No,' I say with frustration. 'I already know he exists. This is ridiculous. Add Trinity College to the search; he did a seminar there.'

Tap-tap-tap.

'No. Nothing for Trinity College.'

'Are you sure you spoke to his daughter?' Kate asks.

'Yes,' I say through gritted teeth.

'And did anybody see you talking to this girl?' she says sweetly.

I ignore her.

'I'm adding the words, art, architecture, French, Latin, Italian to the search,' Frankie says over the tap-tap-tap sound.

'Aha! Gotcha, Justin Hitchcock! *Guest* lecturer at Trinity College, Dublin. The Faculty of Arts and Humanities. Department of Art and Architecture. Bachelor's degree, Chicago, Master's degree, Chicago, Ph.D. Sorbonne University. Special interests are History of Italian Renaissance and Baroque Sculpture, Painting in Europe in 1600–1900. External responsibilities include founder and editor of the *Art and Architectural Review*. He is the co-author of *The Golden Age of Dutch Painting: Vermeer, Metsu and Terborch*, author of *Copper as Canvas: Paintings on Copper 1575–1775*. He has written over fifty articles in books, journals, dictionaries and conference proceedings.'

'So he exists,' Kate says, as though she's just found the Holy Grail.

Feeling more confident now I say, 'Try his name with the London National Gallery.'

'Why?'

'I have a hunch.'

'You and your hunches.' Kate continues reading, 'He is a curator of European Art at the National Gallery, London. Oh my God, Joyce, he works in London. You should go see him.'

'Hold your horses, Kate. She might freak him out and end up in a padded cell. He might not even be the donor,' Frankie objects. 'And even if he is, it doesn't explain anything.'

'It's him,' I say confidently. 'And if he was my donor, then it means something to me.'

'We'll have to figure out a way to find out,' Kate offers.

'It's him,' I repeat.

'So what are you going to do about it?' Kate asks.

I smile lightly and glance at the clock again. 'What makes you think I haven't done something already?'

Justin holds the phone to his ear and paces the small office in the National Gallery as much as he can, stretching the phone cord as far as it will go on each pace, which is not far. Three and a half steps up, five steps down.

'No, no, Simon, I said *Dutch* Portraits, though you're correct as there certainly will be *much* Dutch portraits,' he laughs. 'The Age of Rembrandt and Frans Hals,' he continues. 'I've written a book about that subject so it's something I'm more than familiar with.' *A half-written book you stopped working on two years ago, liar.*

'The exhibition will include sixty works, all painted between 1600 and 1680.'

There is a knock on the door.

'Just a minute,' he calls out.

The door opens anyway and his colleague, Roberta, enters. Though young, in her thirties, her back is hunched, her chin pressed to her chest as though she is decades older. Her eyes, mostly cast downward, occasionally flicker upwards to meet his before falling again. She is apologetic for everything, as always, constantly saying sorry to the world, as though her very presence offends. She tries to manoeuvre her way through the obstacle course that is his cluttered office to reach his desk. This she does the same way as she does through her life, as quietly and as invisibly as possible, which Justin would find admirable if it weren't quite so sad.

'Sorry, Justin,' she whispers, carrying a small basket in her hand. 'I didn't know you were on the phone, sorry. This was at reception for you. I'll just put it here. Sorry.' She backs away, barely making a sound as she tiptoes out of the room and closes the door silently behind her. A silent whirlwind that spins so gracefully and slowly it hardly appears to move at all, failing to uproot anything that lies around it.

He simply nods at her and then tries to concentrate on the conversation, picking up where he left off.

'It will range from small individual portraits meant for the private home to the large-scale group portraits of members of charitable institutions and civic guards.'

He stops pacing and eyes the hamper suspiciously, feeling as though something is about to jump out at him.

'Yes, Simon, in the Sainsbury Wing. If there's anything else you need to know please do contact me here at the office.'

He hurries his colleague off the phone and hangs up. His hand pauses on the receiver, not sure whether to call for security. The small hamper seems alien and sweet, in his musty office, like a new-born baby in a cradle left on the dirty steps of an orphanage. Underneath the wicker handle, the contents are covered by a chequered cloth. He stands back and lifts it slowly, preparing to jump away at any moment.

A dozen or so muffins stare back at him.

His heart thumps and he quickly looks around his box-sized office, knowing nobody is with him, but his discomfort at receiving this surprise gift adds an eerie presence. He searches the basket for a card. Taped to the other side is a small white envelope. With what he realises now are shaking hands, he rips it rather clumsily from the basket. It hasn't been sealed and so he slides the card out. In the centre of the card in neat handwritten script it simply says:

Thank you...

TWENTY-EIGHT

Justin power-walks through the halls of the National Gallery, part of him obeying and the other part disobeying the 'no running in the halls' rule as he jogs three steps then walks three steps, jogs three steps and slows to a walk again. Goody Two-Shoes and the daredevil within him battling it out.

He spots Roberta tiptoeing through the hallway, making her way like a shadow to the private library where she has worked for the past five years.

'Roberta!' His daredevil is unleashed; disobeys the 'no shouting in the halls' rule, and his voice echoes and rebounds off the walls and high ceilings, deafening the ears of all in the portraits, loud enough to wilt van Gogh's sunflowers and to crack the mirror in the Arnolfini portrait.

It's also enough for Roberta to freeze and turn slowly, her eyes wide and terrified like a deer caught in the headlights. She blushes as the half-dozen members of the public turn to stare at her. Her gulp is visible from where he stands and

Justin's immediately sorry for breaking her code, for pointing her out when she wanted to be invisible. He stops his power-walking and tries to walk quietly along the floors, glide as she does, in an attempt to retract the noise he had made. She stands, stiff as a board and as close to the wall as possible like an elegant climber, clinging to the walls and fences, preferring shelter and not noticing its own beauty. Justin wonders if her behaviour is as a consequence of her career, or if being a librarian in the National Gallery had seemed attractive to her because of her way. He thinks the latter.

'Yes,' she whispers, wide-eyed and frightened.

'Sorry for shouting your name,' he says as quietly as he can.

Her face softens and her shoulders relax a little.

'Where did you get this hamper?' He holds it out to her.

'At reception. I was returning from my break when Charlie asked me to give it to you. Is there something wrong?'

'Charlie.' He thinks hard. 'He's at the Sir Paul Getty Entrance?'

She nods.

'OK, thank you, Roberta, I apologise for shouting.' He dashes off to the East Wing, his daredevil and good side clashing again in a remarkably confused half-run, half-walk combination, while the basket swings from his hand.

'Finished for the day, Little Red Riding Hood?' He hears a croaky chuckle.

Justin, noticing he was skipping along with the basket, stops abruptly and spins around to face Charlie, a security guard, over six foot tall.

'My, Grandmother, what an ugly head you have.'

'What do you want?'

'I was wondering who gave you this basket?'

'A delivery guy from . . .' Charlie moves over to behind his small desk and riffles through some papers. He retrieves a clipboard. 'Harrods. Zhang Wei,' he reads. 'Why? Something wrong with the muffins?' He runs his tongue over his teeth and clears his throat.

Justin's eyes narrow. 'How did you know they were muffins?'

Charlie refuses to meet his stare. 'Had to check, didn't I? This is the National Gallery. You can't expect me to accept a package without knowing what's in it.'

Justin studies Charlie, whose face has pinked. He spies crumbs stuck to the crevices at the corners of his mouth and slight traces down his uniform. He removes the chequered cloth from his hamper and counts. Eleven muffins.

'Don't you think it's odd to send a person eleven muffins?'

'Odd?' Eyes wander, shoulders fidget. 'Dunno, mate. Never sent muffins to anyone in my life.'

'Wouldn't it seem more obvious to send a *dozen* muffins?'

Shoulders shrug. Fingers fidget. His eyes study

everybody that enters the gallery, far more intently than usual. His body language tells Justin that he's finished with the conversation.

Justin whips out his cellphone as he exits to Trafalgar Square.

'Hello?'

'Bea, it's Dad.'

'I'm not talking to you.'

'Why not?'

'Peter told me what you said to him at the ballet last night,' she snaps.

'What did I do?'

'You interrogated him on his *intentions* all night.'

'I'm your father, that's my job.'

'No, what you did is the job of the Gestapo,' she fumes. 'I swear, I'm not speaking to you until you *apologise* to him.'

'Apologise?' he laughs. 'What for? I merely made a few enquiries into his past, in order to ascertain his agenda.'

'Agenda? He doesn't *have* an agenda!'

'So I asked him a few questions, so what? Bea, he's not good enough for you.'

'No, he's not good enough for *you*. Well, I don't care what you think of him, it's me that's supposed to be happy.'

'He picks *strawberries* for a living.'

'He is an *IT consultant*!'

'Then, who picks strawberries?' *Somebody picks strawberries*. 'Well, honey, you know how I feel about consultants. If they are *so amazing* at

336

something why don't they do it themselves, instead of just making money telling people?'

'You're a lecturer, curator, reviewer, *whatever*. If you know so much why don't you just build a building or paint a damn picture yourself?' she shouts. 'Instead of just bragging to everybody about how much you know about them!'

Hmm.

'Sweetheart, let's not get out of control now.'

'No, you are the one out of control. You will apologise to Peter and if you do not, I will not answer your phone calls and you can deal with your little dramas all by yourself.'

'Wait, wait, wait. Just one question.'

'Dad, I—'

'Did-you-send-me-a-hamper-of-a-dozen-cinnamon-muffins?' he rushes out with.

'What? No!'

'No?'

'No muffins! No conversations, no *nothing*—'

'Now, now, sweetheart, there's no need for double negatives.'

'I'll have no more contact with you until you apologise,' she finishes.

'OK,' he sighs. 'Sorry.'

'Not to *me*. To *Peter*.'

'OK, but does that mean you won't be collecting my dry cleaning on your way over tomorrow? You know where it is, it's the one beside the tube station—'

The phone clicks. He stares at it in confusion.

My own daughter hung up on me? I knew this Peter was trouble.

He thinks again about the muffins and dials again. He clears his throat.

'Hello.'

'Jennifer, it's Justin.'

'Hello, Justin.' Her voice is cold.

Used to be warm. Like honey. No, like hot caramel. It used to bounce from octave to octave when she heard his name, just like the piano music he'd wake on Sunday mornings to hear her play from the conservatory. But now?

He listens to the silence on the other end.

Ice.

'I'm just calling to see whether you'd sent me a hamper of muffins.' As soon as he's said it, he realises how ridiculous this call is. Of course she didn't send him anything. Why would she?

'I beg your pardon?'

'I received a basket of muffins to my office today along with a thank you note, but the note failed to reveal the sender's identity. I was wondering if it was you.'

Her voice is amused now. No, not amused, mocking. 'What would I have to thank you for, Justin?'

It's a simple question, but knowing her as he knows her, it has implications far beyond the words, and so Justin jumps up and snaps at the bait. The hook cuts through his lip and bitter Justin is back, the voice he grew so accustomed to during

338

the demise of their . . . well, during *their* demise. She has reeled him right in.

'Oh, I don't know, twenty years of marriage, perhaps. A daughter. A good living. A roof over your head.' He knows it's a stupid statement. That before him, after him and even without him, she had and always would have a roof, of all things, over her head, but it's spurting out of him now and he can't stop and won't stop, for he is right and she is wrong and anger is spurring on every word, like a jockey whipping his horse as they near the finish line. 'Travel all over the world.' *Whip-crack-away!* 'Clothes, clothes and more clothes.' *Whip-crack-away!* 'A new kitchen when we didn't need one, a *conservatory*, for Christsake . . .' And he goes on, like a man from the nineteenth century who'd been keeping his wife accustomed to a good life she would otherwise have been without, ignoring the fact that she had made a good living herself, playing in an orchestra that travelled the world, making several trips that he had accompanied her on.

At the beginning of their married life they had no choice but to live with Justin's mother. They were young and had a baby to rear, the reason for their hasty marriage, and as Justin was still attending college by day, bar tending at night and working at an art museum at the weekend, Jennifer had made money playing the piano at an upmarket restaurant in Chicago. At the weekends, she would return home in the early hours of the morning, her back sore and tendonitis in her middle finger, but that all went out of his mind when she'd dangled the line with that seemingly innocent question. She had known that this tirade would come and he gobbles, gobbles, gobbles, munches on the bait that fills his mouth. Finally running out of things they have spent the last twenty years doing together, and out of steam, he stops.

Jennifer is silent.

'Jennifer?'

'Yes, Justin.' Icy.

Justin sighs with exhaustion. 'So, was it you?'

'It must have been one of your other women, because it most certainly wasn't me.'

Click and she's gone.

Rage bubbles inside him. Other women. *Other women! One* affair when he was twenty years old, a fumble in the dark with Mary-Beth Dursoa at college, *before* he and Jennifer were even married, and she carries on as though he was Don Juan. In their bedroom, he'd even put a print of *A Satyr Mourning over a Nymph* by Piero di Cosimo, which Jennifer had always loathed but he had always hoped would send her subliminal messages. In the painting there is a young girl semi-clothed who on first glance seems asleep but on further viewing has blood seeping from her throat. A satyr is mourning her. Justin's interpretation of the painting is that the woman, mistrusting her husband's fidelity, followed him into the woods. He was hunting, not going astray as she thought, and shot her by accident, thinking her rustling in

340

the trees was an animal. Sometimes during his and Jennifer's darkest moments, when their hate raged during their toughest arguments, when their throats were red raw, their eyes stinging with tears, their hearts breaking from the pain, their heads pounding from the analysis, Justin would study the painting and envy the satyr.

Fuming, he charges down the North Terrace steps, sits down by one of the fountains, places the basket by his feet and bites into a muffin, scoffing it down so quickly he barely has time to taste it. Crumbs fall at his feet, attracting a flock of pigeons with intent in their beady black eyes. He goes to reach for another muffin but he is swarmed by overenthusiastic pigeons pecking at the contents of his basket, greedily. Peck, peck, peck – he watches dozens more flock towards him, coming in to land like fighter jets. Afraid of falling missiles from those that circle his head, he picks up his basket and shoos them away with all the butchness of an eleven-year-old.

He breezes in the front door of his home, leaving it open behind him, and is immediately greeted by Doris, with a paint palette in her hand.

'OK, so I've narrowed it down,' she begins, thrusting dozens of colours in his face.

Her long leopard-print nails are each decorated with a diamanté jewel. She wears an all-in-one snakeskin jumpsuit, and her feet wobble dangerously in patent lace-up ankle stilettos. Her hair is still its usual shock of red, her eyes catlike with inky eyeliner sweeping up from her corners of her eyes, her painted lips to match her hair remind him of Ronald McDonald. He watches them with severe irritation as they open and close.

The random words he hears are, 'Gooseberry Fool, Celtic Forest, English Mist and Woodland Pearl, all *calm* tones, would look so good in this room *or* Wild Mushroom, Nomadic Glow and Sultana Spice. The Cappuccino Candy is one of my faves but I don't think it'll work next to that curtain, what do you think?'

She waves a fabric in front of his face and it tickles his nose, which tingles with such intensity it senses the fight that is about to brew. He doesn't respond but takes deep breaths and counts to ten in his mind. And when that doesn't work and she keeps listing paint colours, he keeps on going to twenty.

'Hello? Justin?' She snaps her fingers in his face. 'Hel-lo?'

'Maybe you should give Justin a break, Doris. He looks tired.' Al looks nervously at his brother.

'But—'

'Get your sultana spice behind over here,' he teases and she whoops.

'OK, but just one more thing. Bea will love her room done in Ivory Lace. And Petey too. Imagine how romantic this will be for—'

'ENOUGH!' Justin screams at the top of his lungs, not wanting his daughter's name and the word romantic to share the same sentence.

Doris jumps and stops talking immediately. Her

hand flies to her chest. Al stops drinking, his bottle freezes just below his lips, his heavy breathing above the rim making ivory pipe music. Other than that, there's absolute silence.

'Doris,' Justin takes a deep breath and tries to speak as calmly as possible, 'enough of this please. Enough of this Cappuccino Nights—'

'Candy,' she interrupts, and quickly silences again.

'Whatever. This is a Victorian house, from the nineteenth century, not some painted lady from an episode of *Changing Rooms*.' He tries to restrain his emotions, his feelings insulted on behalf of the building. 'If you had mentioned Cappuccino Chocolate—'

'Candy,' she whispers.

'Whatever! To anyone during that time, you would have been instantly burned at the stake!'

She squeaks, insulted.

'It needs *sophistication*, it needs to be *researched*, it needs furniture *of* the period, colours *of* the period, not a room that sounds like Al's dinner menu.'

'Hey!' Al speaks up.

'I think it needs,' Justin takes a deep breath and says gently, 'somebody else for the job. Maybe it's just bigger than you thought it was going to be but I appreciate your help, really I do. Please tell me you understand.'

She nods slowly and he breathes a sigh of relief. Suddenly the paint palettes go flying across the room as Doris lets rip, 'You pretentious little bastaaaaard!'

'Doris!' Al leaps up out of his armchair, or at least, makes a great attempt to.

Justin immediately takes steps back as she walks aggressively towards him, pointing her sparkly animal-print nail at him, like a weapon.

'Listen here, you silly little man. I have spent the last two weeks researching this dump of a basement in the kinds of libraries and places you wouldn't even think *exist*. I've been to dark, dingy dungeons where people smell of old . . . things.' Her nostrils flare and her voice deepens, threateningly. 'I purchased every historic period paint brochure that I could get my hands on and applied the colours in accordance with the colour rules at the end of the nineteenth century. I've shaken hands with people you don't even wanna know about, I've seen parts of London *I* didn't even wanna know about. I've looked through books so old, the dust mites were big enough to hand them to me from the shelves. I have matched the Dulux colours as closely as I possibly could to your historic period paint and I've been to second-hand, third-hand, even *antique* stores and seen furniture in such disgusting derelict conditions, I almost set up the ISPCF. I've seen things crawling around dining-room tables and sat in such rickety chairs I could smell the black death that killed the last person who died sitting right in it. I have sanded down so much pine, I have splinters in places you don't wanna see. So.' She prods him in the chest with her dagger nail as she emphasises each word that finally backs him up against the wall. 'Don't. Tell. Me. That *this* is too big for me.'

She clears her throat and stands up straight. The anger in her voice is replaced with a vulnerable 'poor me' tremble. 'But despite what you said, I will finish this project. I will go on undeterred. I will do it in spite of you and I will do it for your brother, who might be dead next month and you don't even care.'

'Dead?' Justin's eyes widen.

With that, she turns on her heel and storms off into her bedroom.

She sticks her head out of the doorway. 'By the way, just so you know, I would have banged the door behind me VERY LOUDLY to show just how angry I am but it's currently out in the backyard ready for sanding and priming, before I paint it . . .' and this she spits out rebelliously, 'Ivory Lace.'

Then she disappears again, without a bang.

I shift from foot to foot nervously outside the open door of Justin's home. Should I press the bell now? Simply call his name into the room? Would he call the police and have me arrested for trespassing? Oh, this was such a bad decision. Frankie and Kate had persuaded me to come here, to present myself to him. They had pumped me up to such a point I had hopped in the first taxi that came my way to Trafalgar Square, to catch him at the National

Gallery before he left. I'd been so close to him as he'd been on the phone, heard his calls to people as he asked them about the basket. I'd felt oddly comfortable just watching him, without his knowing, unable to take my eyes off him, revelling in the secret thrill of being able to see him for who he is instead of viewing his life from his own memories.

His anger at whoever was on the phone – most likely his ex-wife, the woman with the red hair and freckles – convinced me it was the wrong time to approach him and so I'd followed him. *Followed*, not stalked. I'd taken my time while trying to build up the courage to talk to him. Would I mention the transfusion or not? Would he think I was crazy or be open to listening or, even better, open to believing?

But once on the tube, the timing again wasn't right. It was overcrowded, people were pushing and shoving, avoiding eye contact, never mind first-time introductions or conversations about studies into the possible intelligence of blood. And so after pacing up and down his road, feeling like both a school-girl with a crush and a stalker at the same time, I now find myself standing outside the door, with a plan. But my plan is once again being compromised as Justin and his brother Al begin to talk about something I know I shouldn't be hearing, about a family secret I am more than familiar with already.

I move my finger away from the doorbell, keep hidden from all the windows and I bide my time.

TWENTY-NINE

Justin looks to his brother in panic and searches quickly for something to sit on. He pulls over a giant paint tub and sits down, not noticing the wet white ring of paint around the top.

'Al, what was she talking about? About you being dead next month.'

'No, no, no,' Al laughs. 'She said, *might* be dead. That's distinctly different. Hey, you got away lightly there, bro. Good for you. I think that valium is really helping her. Cheers.' He holds up his bottle and downs the last of it.

'Hold on, hold on. Al, what are you talking about? There's something you haven't told me? What did the doctor say?'

'The doctor told me exactly what I've been telling you for the last two weeks. If any members of a person's immediate family developed coronary heart disease at a young age, i.e., a male under fifty-five years old, well then, we have an increased risk of coronary heart disease.'

'Have you high blood pressure?'

'A little.'

'Have you high cholesterol?'

'A lot.'

'So, all you do is make lifestyle changes, Al. It doesn't mean you're going to be struck down like . . . like . . .'

'Dad?'

'No.' He frowns and shakes his head.

'Coronary heart disease is the number-one killer of American males *and* females. Every thirty-three seconds an American will suffer some type of coronary event and almost every minute someone will die from it.' He looks at their mother's grandfather clock half-covered in a dust sheet. The minute hand moves. Al grabs his heart and starts groaning. His noises soon turn to laughter.

Justin rolls his eyes. 'Who told you that nonsense?'

'The pamphlets at the doc's office said so.'

'Al, you're not going to have a heart attack.'

'It's my fortieth birthday next week.'

'Yeah, I know.' Justin hits him playfully on the knee. 'That's the spirit, we'll have a big party.'

'That's what age Dad was when he died.' He lowers his eyes and peels the label from his beer.

'That's what this is about?' Justin's voice softens. 'Damnit, Al, that's what this is all about? Why didn't you say something earlier?'

'I just thought that I'd spend some time with

you before, you know, just in case . . .' His eyes tear up and he looks away.

Tell him the truth.

'Al, listen, there's something you should know.' His voice trembles and he clears his throat, trying to control it. *You've never told anyone.* 'Dad was under a huge amount of pressure at work. He had a lot of difficulties, financial and otherwise, that he didn't tell anyone. Not even Mom.'

'I know, Justin. I know.'

'You know?'

'Yeah, I get it. He didn't just drop dead for no reason. He was stressed out of his mind. And I'm not, I know that. But ever since I was a kid, I've had this feeling hanging over me that it's gonna happen to me too. It's been playing on my mind for as long as I can remember and now that my birthday's next week and I'm not in the greatest of shape . . . Things have been real busy at the business and I haven't been looking after myself. Never could do it like you could, you know?'

'Hey, you don't have to explain it to me.'

'Remember that day we spent with him on the front lawn? With the sprinklers? Just hours before Mom found him . . . Well, remember the whole family playing around?'

'They were good times,' Justin smiles, fighting back the tears.

'You remember?' Al laughs.

'Like it was yesterday,' Justin says.

'Dad was holding the hose and spraying us both.

349

He seemed in such good humour.' Al frowns with confusion and thinks for a while, then the smile returns. 'He'd brought Mom home a big bunch of flowers – remember she put that big flower in her hair?'

'The sunflower.' Justin nods along.

'And it was real hot. Do you remember it being real hot?'

'Yeah.'

'And Dad had his pants rolled up to his knees and his shoes and socks off. And the grass was getting all wet and his feet were all covered in grass and he just kept chasing us around and around . . .' He smiles into the distance. 'That was the last time I saw him.'

It wasn't for me.

Justin's memory flashes through the image of his father closing the living-room door. Justin had run into the house from the front yard to go to the bathroom; all that playing around with water was almost making him burst. As far as he knew, all the members of his family were still outside playing. He could hear his mom chasing and taunting Al, and Al, who was only five years old, screeching with laughter. But when he was coming downstairs, he spotted his dad coming out of the kitchen, walking down the hall. Justin, wanting to jump out and surprise him, crouched down and watched him from behind the banister.

But then he saw what was in his hand. He saw the bottle of liquid that was always locked away in the cabinet in the kitchen and only taken out on special occasions when his dad's family came over from Ireland to visit. When they all drank from that bottle they would change, they would sing songs that Justin had never heard before but that his dad knew every word of, and they would laugh and tell stories and sometimes cry. He wasn't sure why that bottle was in his dad's hands now. Did he want to sing and laugh and tell stories today? Did he want to cry?

Then Justin saw the bottle of pills in his hand too. He knew they were pills, because they were in the same container as the medicine Mom and Dad took when they were sick. He hoped his dad wasn't feeling sick now and he hoped he didn't want to cry. He watched as he closed the door behind him with the pills and bottle of alcohol in his hands. He should have known then what his dad was about to do but he didn't. Thinks of that moment over and over and tries to force himself to call out and stop him. But the nine-year-old Justin never hears him. He stays crouched on the stair, waiting for his dad to come out so he can jump out and surprise him. As time went by he began to feel that something wasn't right, but he didn't quite know why he felt that way and he didn't want to ruin the big surprise by checking on his dad.

After minutes that felt like hours, of nothing but silence from behind the door, Justin gulped and stood up. He could hear Al screaming with laughter outside. He could still hear Al laughing when he went inside and saw the green feet on the floor. He remembers the sight of those feet so vividly, Dad lying on the floor like a big green giant. He remembers following those feet and finding his dad on the floor, staring lifeless at the ceiling.

He didn't say anything. Didn't scream, didn't touch him, didn't kiss him, didn't try to help him because though he didn't understand much at that time, he knew that it was too late for help. He just slowly backed out of the room, closed the door behind him and ran out to the front lawn to his mom and younger brother.

Five minutes they had. Five more minutes of everything being exactly the same. He was nine years old on a sunny day with a mom and a dad and a brother, and he was happy and Mom was happy and the neighbours smiled at him normally like they did all the other kids, all the food they ate for dinner was made by his mom and when he was bad at school the teachers shouted at him, like they should. Five more minutes of everything being the same, until his mom went into the house and then it was all completely different, then everything changed. Five minutes later, he wasn't nine years old with a mom, a dad and a brother. He wasn't happy, neither was Mom, and the neighbours smiled at him with such a sadness he wished they didn't bother smiling at all. Everything they ate came from containers carried over by women that lived on the same street, who always looked sad too, and when he acted up at school the teachers just looked at him with that same face. Everyone had the same face. The five extra minutes wasn't long enough.

Mom told them Dad had suffered a heart attack. She told the entire family and anybody that came by with a home-cooked meal or pie.

Justin could never bring himself to tell anyone he knew the truth, half because he wanted to believe the lie and half because he thought his mother had started to believe it too. So he kept it to himself. He hadn't even told Jennifer, because saying it out loud made it true and he did not want to validate his father dying that way. And now, their mother gone, he was the only person who knew the truth about his dad. The story of their father's death that had been fabricated to help them had ended up hanging like a black cloud over Al and a burden for Justin.

He wanted to tell Al the truth right now, he really did. But how could it help him? Surely knowing the truth would be far worse, and he'd have to explain how and why he'd kept it from him all these years . . . But then he would no longer have to shoulder all the burden. Perhaps there would be finally some release for him. It could help Al's fear of heart failure and they could deal with it together.

'Al, there's something I have to tell you,' Justin begins.

The doorbell rings suddenly. A sharp sting of a ring that startles them both from their thoughts, smashing the silence like a sledgehammer through glass. All their thoughts shatter and fall to pieces on the ground.

'Is someone gonna get that?' Doris yells, breaking the silence.

Justin walks to the door with a white ring of paint around his behind. The door is already ajar and he pulls it open further. Before him, on the railings, hangs his dry cleaning. His suits, shirts and sweaters all covered in plastic. Nobody is there. He steps outside and runs up the basement steps to see who has left them there, but apart from the skip, the front lawn is empty.

'Who is it?' Doris calls.

'Nobody,' Justin responds, confused. He unhooks his dry cleaning from the railing and carries it inside.

'You're telling me that cheap suit just pressed the doorbell itself?' she asks, still angry at him from before.

'I don't know. It's peculiar. Bea was going to collect this tomorrow. I hadn't arranged a delivery with the dry cleaners.'

'Maybe it's a special delivery, for being such a good customer because by the looks of it, they dry cleaned your entire wardrobe.' She eyes his choice of clothes with distaste.

'Yeah, and I'll bet the special delivery comes with a big bill,' he grumbles. 'I had a little falling-out with Bea earlier; maybe she organised this as an apology.'

354

'Oh, you are a stubborn man.' Doris rolls her eyes. 'Do you ever think for a second that it's *you* who should be making the apologies?'

Justin narrows his eyes at her. 'Did you talk to Bea?'

'Hey, look, there's an envelope on this side,' Al points out, interrupting the beginnings of another fight.

'There's your bill,' Doris laughs.

Justin's heart immediately leaps to his mouth as he catches sight of the familiar envelope. He throws the pile of clothes down on the dust sheet and rips off the envelope.

'Be careful! These have just been pressed.' Doris takes them and hangs them from the door frame.

He opens the envelope and gulps hard, reading the note.

'What does it say?' Al asks.

'It must be a death threat, look at his face,' Doris says excitedly. 'Or a begging letter. Some of those are so much fun. What's wrong with them and how much do they want?' she giggles.

Justin takes out the card he received on the muffin basket earlier, and he holds the two cards together so that they make a complete sentence. Reading the words causes a chill to run through his body.

Thank you ... For Saving My Life.

THIRTY

I lie in the skip, breathless, heart beating at the speed of a humming bird's wings. I'm like a child playing hide and seek, with intense nervous excitement rolling around my tummy; like a dog on its back trying to rid itself of fleas. Please don't find me, Justin, don't find me like this, lying at the bottom of the skip in your garden, covered in plaster and dust. I hear his footsteps move further away, back down the steps to his basement flat and the door closes.

What on earth have I become? A coward. I chickened out and rang the doorbell to stop Justin telling the story about his father to Al and then, afraid of playing God to two strangers, I ran, leaped and landed in the bottom of a skip. How metaphorical. I'm not sure I'll ever be able to speak to him. I don't know how I'll ever find the words to explain how I'm feeling. The world is not a patient place: stories such as this are mostly for the pages of the *Enquirer* or double-page spreads in certain women's magazines. Beside my story would be a photograph of me, in my dad's kitchen, looking forlornly at the camera. With no make-up. No, Justin would never believe me if I told him – but actions speak louder than words.

Lying on my back, I stare up at the sky. Lying face down, the clouds stare right back down at me. They pass over the woman in the skip with curiosity, calling the stragglers behind them to come see. More clouds gather, eager to see what the others are grumbling about. Then they too pass over, leaving me staring at blue and the occasional white wisp. I almost hear my mother laughing aloud, imagine her nudging her friends to come have a look at her daughter. I imagine her peeping over a cloud, hanging over too far like Dad in the balcony at the Royal Opera House. I smile, enjoying this now.

Now, as I brush dust, paint and wood from my clothes and clamber out of the skip, I try to remember what other things Bea mentioned her father wanted to have done, by the person he saved.

'Justin, calm down, for creep's sake. You're making me nervous.' Doris sits on a stepladder and watches Justin pace up and down the room.

'I can't calm down. Do you not understand what this means?' He hands her the two cards.

Her eyes widen. 'You saved someone's life?'

'Yeah.' He shrugs and stops pacing. 'It's really

no big deal. Sometimes you just gotta do what you gotta do.'

'He donated blood,' Al interrupts his brother's failed attempt at modesty.

'*You* donated blood?'

'It's how he met Vampira, remember?' Al refreshes his wife's memory. 'In Ireland when they say, "Fancy a pint?" *beware*.'

'Her name is *Sarah* not Vampira.'

'So you donated blood to get a date.' Doris folds her arms. 'Is there nothing you do for the greater good of humanity or is it *all* just for yourself?'

'Hey, I have a heart.'

'Though a pint lighter than it was,' Al adds.

'I have donated plenty of my time to helping organisations – colleges, universities and galleries – which are in need of my expertise. Something I don't *have* to do, but which I have agreed to do *for them*.'

'Yeah and I bet you charge them per word. That's why he says "oops-a-daisies" instead of "shit" when he stubs his toe.'

Al and Doris dissolve into laughter, thumping and hitting each other in their fit.

Justin takes a deep breath. 'Let's get back to the matter at hand. *Who* is sending me these notes and running these errands?'

He begins pacing again and biting his nails. 'Maybe this is Bea's idea of a joke. She's the only person I had the conversation with about deserving thanks in return for saving a life.'

Please, don't be Bea.

'Man, you are selfish,' Al laughs.

'No.' Doris shakes her head, her long earrings whip against her cheeks with each movement, her back-brushed hairsprayed hair as still as a microphone head. 'Bea wants nothing to do with you until you apologise. No words can describe how much she hates you right now.'

'Well, thank God for that.' Justin continues pacing. 'But she must have told somebody or this wouldn't be happening. Doris, find out from Bea who she spoke to about this.'

'Huh.' Doris lifts her chin and looks away. 'You said some pretty nasty things to me before. I don't know if I can help you.'

Justin falls to his knees and shuffles over to her. 'Please, Doris, I'm begging you. I am so, so sorry for what I said. I had no idea how much time and effort you were putting into this place. I underestimated you. Without you, I'd still be drinking from a toothbrush holder and eating from a cat bowl.'

'Yeah, I meant to ask you about that,' Al interrupts his grovelling. 'You don't even have a cat.'

'So I'm a good interior designer?' Doris lifts her chin.

'A *great* designer.'

'How great?'

'Greater than . . .' he stalls. 'Andrea Palladio.'

Her eyes look to the left, look to the right. 'Is he better than Ty Pennington?'

'He was an Italian architect in the sixteenth century, widely considered the most influential person in the history of Western architecture.'

'Oh. OK. You're forgiven.' She holds out her hand. 'Give me your phone and I'll call Bea.'

Moments later they are all seated around the new kitchen table listening to Doris's half of the phone conversation.

'OK, Bea told Petey, and the costume supervisor for *Swan Lake*. And her father.'

'The costume supervisor? Do you guys still have the programme?'

Doris disappears to her bedroom and returns with the ballet programme. She flicks through the pages.

'No,' Justin shakes his head on reading her biography, 'I met this woman that night and it's not her. But her father was there? I didn't see her father.'

Al shrugs.

'Well, these people aren't involved in this, I certainly didn't save her life or her father's. The person must be Irish or have received medical attention in an Irish hospital.'

'Maybe her dad's Irish, or was in Ireland.'

'Give me that programme, I'm calling the theatre.'

'Justin, you can't just call her up.' Doris dives for the programme in his hand, but he dodges her. 'What are you going to say?'

'All I need to know is if her father is Irish or

was in Ireland during the past month. I'll make the rest up as I go along.'

Al and Doris look at each other worriedly while he leaves the kitchen to make the call.

'Did you do this?' Doris asks Al quietly.

'No way.' Al shakes his head, his chins wobbling.

Five minutes later Justin returns.

'She remembered me from last night and, no, it's not her or her father. So either Bea told somebody else or . . . it must be Peter fooling around. I'm gonna get that little kid and—'

'Grow up, Justin. It's not him,' Doris says sternly. 'Start looking elsewhere. Call the dry cleaners, call the guy who delivered the muffins.'

'I have already. They were charged to a credit card and they can't release the owner's details.'

'Your life is just one big mystery. Between the Joyce woman and these mysterious deliveries, you should hire a private investigator,' Doris responds. 'Oh! I just remembered.' She reaches into her pocket and hands him a piece of paper. 'Speaking of private investigators. I got this for you. I've had it for a few days but didn't say anything because I didn't want you going on a wild-goose chase and making a fool of yourself. But seeing as you're choosing to do that anyway, here.'

She hands him the piece of paper with Joyce's details.

'I called International Directory Enquiries and gave them the number of the Joyce person that showed up on Bea's phone last week. They gave me the address that goes with it. I think it'd be a better idea to find this woman, Justin. Forget this other person. It seems very odd behaviour to me. Who knows who's sending you these notes? Concentrate on the woman; a nice healthy relationship is what you need.'

He barely reads the page before putting it in his jacket pocket, totally uninterested, his mind elsewhere.

'You just jump from one woman to another, don't you?' Doris studies him.

'Hey, it could be the Joyce woman that's sending the messages,' Al pipes up.

Doris and Justin both look at him and roll their eyes.

'Don't be ridiculous, Al,' Justin dismisses him. 'I met her in a hair salon. Anyway, who says it's a woman that's doing this?'

'Well, it's obvious,' Al replies. 'Because you were given a *muffin basket*.' He scrunches up his nose. 'Only a woman would think of sending a muffin basket. Or a gay guy. And whoever it is, he or she – or maybe it's a he*she* – they know how to do calligraphy, which further backs up my theory. Woman, gay guy or tranny,' he sums up.

'*I* was the one who thought of the muffin basket!' Justin puffs. '*And* I do calligraphy.'

'Yeah, like I said. Woman, gay guy or tranny,' he grins.

Justin throws his hands up in exasperation and falls back in his chair. 'You two are no help.'

'Hey, I know who could help you.' Al sits up.

'Who?' Justin rests his chin on his fist, bored.

'Vampira,' he says spookily.

'I've already asked her for help. All I could see were my blood details in the database. Nothing about who received my donation. She won't tell me where my blood went and she won't ever speak to me again either.'

'On account of you running away from her after a Viking bus?'

'That had something to do with it.'

'Gee, Justin, you really have a beautiful way with women.'

'Well, at least *somebody* thinks I'm doing something right.' He stares at the two cards he's placed in the centre of the table.

Who are you?

'You don't have to ask Sarah straight out. Maybe you could snoop around a bit in her office,' Al gets excited.

'No, that would be wrong,' Justin says unconvincingly. 'I could get into trouble. I could get *her* into trouble and, besides, I've treated her so badly.'

'So a really lovely thing to do,' Doris says slyly, 'would be to drop by her office, and tell her you're sorry. As a friend.'

A smile slowly creeps onto each of their faces.

'But can you take a day off work next week, to go to Dublin?' Doris asks, breaking their evil moment.

'I've already accepted an invitation from the

National Gallery in Dublin to give a talk on Terborch's *Woman Writing a Letter*,' Justin says excitedly.

'What's the painting of?' Al asks.

'A woman writing a letter, Sherlock,' Doris snorts.

'What a boring story.' Al scrunches up his nose. Then he and Doris settle down and watch as Justin reads the notes over and over, hoping to decipher a hidden code.

'*Man Reading a Note*,' Al says rather grandly, 'Discuss.'

He and Doris crack up again as Justin exits the room.

'Hey, where are you going?'

'Man booking a flight,' he winks.

THIRTY-ONE

At seven fifteen the next morning, just before Justin leaves his flat for work, he stands poised at the front door, hand on the door handle.

'Justin, where's Al? He wasn't in bed when I woke up.' Doris shuffles out of her bedroom in her slippers and robe. 'What on earth are you doing now, you funny little man?'

Justin holds a finger to his lips, hushing her, and jerks his head in the direction of the door.

'Is the blood person out there?' she whispers excitedly, kicking off her slippers and tiptoeing like a cartoon character, to join him at the door.

He nods excitedly.

They press their ears up against the door and Doris's eyes widen. '*I can hear!*' she mouths.

'OK, on three,' he whispers and they mouth together, *One, two*— He pulls the door open with full force. 'HA! Gotcha!' he shouts, striking an attacker's pose and pointing his finger with more aggression than intended.

'Aaaah!' the postman screams with fright, dropping envelopes by Justin's feet. He fires a package at Justin and holds another parcel by his head in defence.

'Aaaah!' Doris shouts.

Justin doubles over as the package hits between his legs. He falls to his knees, his face turning red as he gasps for air.

They all hold their chests, panting.

The postman remains cowered, his knees bent, his head covered by a package.

'Justin,' Doris picks up an envelope and hits Justin across the arm, 'you idiot! It's the postman.'

'Yes,' he rasps, and makes choking sounds. 'I can see that now.' He takes a moment to compose himself. 'It's OK, sir, you can lower your package now. I'm sorry to have frightened you.'

The postman slowly lowers the parcel, fear and confusion in his eyes. 'What was that about?'

'I thought you were someone else. I'm sorry, I was expecting . . . something else.' He looks to the envelopes on the floor. Bills. 'Is there nothing else for me?'

His left arm starts to niggle at him again. Tingling as though a mosquito has bitten him. He starts to scratch. Lightly at first and then he pats his inner elbow, smacking the itch away. The tingling becomes more intense and he digs his nail into his skin, scratching over and over. Beads of sweat break out on his forehead.

The postman shakes his head and starts to back away.

'Did nobody give you anything to deliver to me?' He climbs back to his feet and moves closer, unintentionally appearing threatening.

'No, I said no.' The postman rushes up the steps. Justin looks after him, confused.

'Leave the man alone. You almost gave him a heart attack.' Doris continues picking up the envelopes. 'If you have that reaction to the real person, then you'll scare them off too. If you ever do meet this person, I advise you rethink the "Ha! Gotcha!" routine.'

Justin pulls up the sleeve of his shirt and examines his arm, expecting to find red lumps or a rash, but there are no marks on his skin apart from the scratch marks he has made himself.

'Are you on something?' Doris narrows her eyes. 'No!'

She shuffles back into the kitchen with a harrumphing sound. 'Al?' her voice echoes around the kitchen. 'Where are you?'

'Help! Help me! Someone!'

In the distance they hear Al's voice, muffled as though his mouth is stuffed with socks.

Doris gasps, 'Baby?' Justin hears the fridge door opening. 'Al?' She sticks her head in the fridge. She returns to the living room, shaking her head, alterting Justin to the fact that her husband was not in the fridge after all.

Justin rolls his eyes. 'He's outside, Doris.'

'Then for goodness' sake stop just standing there looking at me and help him!'

He opens the door and Al sits slumped on the ground at the base of the steps. Wrapped around his sweaty head, Rambo style, is one of Doris's tangerine headbands, his T-shirt is soaked with sweat, beads of perspiration run down his face, his legs are spandex-clad and crumpled underneath him, still in the same position as when he'd fallen.

Doris pushes by Justin aggressively, and charges towards Al. She falls to her knees. 'Baby? Are you OK? Did you fall down the stairs?'

'No,' he says weakly, his chins resting on his chest.

'No, you're not OK or no, you didn't fall down the stairs?' she asks.

'The first one,' he says with exhaustion. 'No, the second. Hold on, what was the first?'

She shouts at him now as though he is deaf. 'The first was, are you OK? And the second was, did you fall down the stairs?'

'No,' he responds, rolling his head back to rest it against the wall.

'To which one? Will I call an ambulance? Do you need a doctor?'

'No.'

'No what, baby? Come on, don't go to sleep on me, don't you dare go anywhere.' She slaps his face. 'You have to stay conscious.'

Justin leans against the door frame and folds

his arms, watching the two. He knows his brother is fine, lack of fitness being his only problem. He goes to the kitchen for some water for Al.

'My heart...' Al is panicking when Justin returns. His hands are scraping at his chest and he's gasping for air, stretching his head upwards and taking in gulps, like a goldfish reaching to the surface of the fish bowl for food.

'Are you having a heart attack?' Doris shrieks.

Justin sighs, 'He's not having a—'

'Stop it, Al!' Justin is interrupted by a screeching Doris. 'Don't you dare have a heart attack, do you hear me?' She picks up a newspaper from the ground, starts hitting Al across the arm with each word. 'Don't. You. Dare. Even. *Think*. Of. Dying. Before. Me. Al. Hitchcock.'

'Ow,' he rubs his arm, 'that hurts.'

'Hey, hey, hey!' Justin breaks it up. 'Give me that paper, Doris.'

'No!'

'Where did you get it?' He tries to grab it out of her hands but she dodges him each time.

'It was just there, beside Al,' she shrugs. 'Paperboy delivered it.'

'They don't have paperboys around here,' he explains.

'Then I guess it's Al's.'

'There's a coffee to-go too,' Al, finally getting his breath back, manages to say.

'A coffee-to-WHAT?' Doris screeches so loudly, a window from the neighbour's flat upstairs is banged closed loudly. This does not deter Doris. 'You bought a coffee?' She begins spanking him again with the newspaper. 'No wonder you're dying!'

'Hey,' he crosses his arms over his body protectively, 'it's not mine. It was outside the door with the newspaper when I got here.'

'It's mine.' Justin snatches the paper from Doris's hands and the coffee to-go that is on the ground beside Al.

'There's no note attached.' She narrows her eyes and looks from one brother to the other and back. 'Trying to defend your brother is only going to kill him in the long run, you know.'

'I might do it more often, then,' he grumbles, shaking the newspaper and hoping for a note to fall out. He checks the coffee cup for a message. Nothing. Yet he's sure it's for him and whoever left it there can't be long gone. He focuses then on the front page. Above the headline, in the corner of the page he notices the instruction, 'P. 42.'

He can't open it quick enough and battles with the oversized pages to get to the correct point. Finally he opens it up on the classified pages. He scans the advertisements and birthday greetings and is about to close the paper altogether and join Doris in blaming Al for feeding his caffeine habit, when he spots it.

'Eternally grateful recipient wishes to thank Justin Hitchcock, donor and hero, for saving life. Thank you.'

He holds his head back and howls with laughter. Doris and Al look at him with surprise.

'Al,' Justin lowers himself to his knees before his brother, 'I need you to help me now.' His voice is urgent, the pitch going up and down with excitement. 'Did you see anybody when you were jogging back to the house?'

'No.' Al's head rolls tiredly from one side to the other. 'I can't think.'

'Think.' Doris slaps his face lightly.

'That's not entirely necessary, Doris.'

'They do it in the movies when they're looking for information. Go on, tell him, baby.' She nudges him a little more lightly.

'I don't know,' Al whinges.

'You make me sick,' she growls in his ear.

'Honestly, Doris, that's really not helping.'

'Fine,' she folds her arms, 'but it works for Horatio.'

'By the time I got to the house, I couldn't breathe, let alone see. I don't remember anyone. Sorry, bro. Man, I was so scared. All of these black dots were in front of my eyes and I just couldn't see any more, I was getting so dizzy and—'

'OK,' Justin leaps to his feet and runs up the stairs to the front yard. He runs to the drive entrance and looks up and down the street. It's busier now; at seven thirty there is more life as people leave their homes to head for work and the traffic noise level has picked up.

'THANK YOU!' Justin shouts at the top of his

lungs, his voice breaking through the quiet. A few people turn around to look at him but most keep their heads down as a light drizzle of October London rain begins to fall while another man loses his mind on a Monday morning in the city.

'I CAN'T WAIT TO READ THIS!' He waves the newspaper around in the air, shouting up the road and down so that he can be heard from all angles.

What do you say to someone whose life you saved? Say something deep. Say something funny. Say something philosophical.

'I'M GLAD YOU'RE ALIVE!' he shouts.

'Eh, thanks.' A woman scurries past him with her head down.

'EM, I WON'T BE HERE TOMORROW!' Pause. 'IN CASE YOU'RE PLANNING ON DOING THIS AGAIN.' He lifts the coffee into the air and waves it around, sending droplets to jump from the small drinking hole and burn his hand. Still hot. Whoever it was, they weren't here that long ago.

'EM. GETTING THE FIRST FLIGHT TO DUBLIN TOMORROW MORNING. ARE YOU FROM THERE?' he shouts to the wind. The breeze sends more crispy autumn leaves parachuting from their branches to the ground, where they land running, make a tapping sound, and scrape along the ground until it's safe to stop.

'ANYWAY, THANKS AGAIN.' He waves the paper in the air and turns to face the house.

Doris and Al are standing at the top of the stairs, their arms folded, their faces a picture of concern. Al has caught his breath and composed himself but is leaning against the iron railings for support.

Justin tucks the newspaper under his arm, straightens himself up and tries to appear as respectable as possible. He puts his hand in his pocket and strolls back towards the house. Feeling a piece of paper in his hand, he retrieves it and reads it quickly before crumpling it in his hand and tossing it into the skip. He has saved a person's life just as he thought; he must focus on the most important matter at hand. He makes his way to the flat, trying to appear as dignified as possible.

From the bottom of the skip, beneath rolls of old tired smelly carpets, crushed tiles, paint tubs and plaster board, I lie in the discarded bath tub and listen as the voices recede and the door to the flat finally closes.

A crumpled ball of paper has landed nearby and as I reach for it, my shoulder knocks over a two-legged stool, which toppled onto me in my rush to leap into the skip. I locate the paper and open it up, smoothing out the edges. My heart starts its rumba beat again as I see my first name, Dad's address and his phone number scrawled upon it.

THIRTY-TWO

'Where on earth have you been? What happened to you, Gracie?'

'Joyce,' is my response as I burst into the hotel room, breathless and covered in paint and dust. 'Don't have time to explain.' I rush around the room, throwing my clothes into my bag, taking a change of clothes and hurrying by Dad, who's sitting on the bed, in order to get to the bathroom.

'I tried calling you on your hand phone,' Dad calls to me.

'Yeah? I didn't hear it ring.' I struggle to squeeze into my jeans, hopping around on one foot while I pull them up and brush my teeth at the same time.

I hear his voice saying something. Mumbles but no words.

'Can't hear you, brushing my teeth!'

Silence while I finish and then back to the room and he continues as though we didn't have five minutes of silence.

'That's because when I called it, I heard it ringing

here in the bedroom. It was on top of your pillow. Just like one of those chocolates the nice ladies here leave behind.'

'Oh. OK.' I jump over his legs to get to the dressing table and reapply my make-up.

'I was worried about you,' he says quietly.

'You needn't have been.' I hop around with one shoe on, while searching everywhere for the other.

'So I called downstairs to reception to see if they knew where you were.'

'Yeah?' I give up looking for my shoe and concentrate on inserting my earrings. My fingers are trembling with the adrenalin of the Justin situation and my fingers become too big for the task at hand. The back of one earring falls to the floor. I get down on my hands and knees to find it.

'So then I walked up and down the road, checking all of the shops that I know you like, asking all the people in them if they'd seen you.'

'You did?' I say, distracted, feeling carpet burns through my jeans as I shuffle around the floor on my knees.

'Yes,' he says quietly again.

'Aha! Got it!' I find it beside the bin below the dresser. 'Where the hell is my shoe?'

'And along the way,' Dad continues, and I hold back my aggravation, 'I met a policeman and I told him I was very worried, and he walked me back to the hotel and told me to wait here for you but to call this number if you didn't come back after twenty-four hours.'

'Oh, that was nice of him.' I open the wardrobe, still searching for my shoe, and find it still full of Dad's clothes. 'Dad!' I exclaim. 'You forgot your other suit. And your good jumper!'

I look at him, I realise for the first time since I entered the room, and only now notice how pale he looks. How old he looks in this new soulless hotel room. Perched at the edge of his single bed, he's dressed in his three-piece suit, cap beside him on the bed, his case packed or half-packed and sitting upright right beside him. In one hand is the photograph of Mum, in the other is the card the policeman gave him. The fingers that hold them tremble; his eyes are red and sore-looking.

'Dad,' I say as panic builds inside me, 'are you OK?'

'I was worried,' he repeats again in the tiny voice I'd as good as ignored since I'd entered the room. He swallows hard. 'I didn't know where you were.'

'I was visiting a friend,' I say softly, joining him on the bed.

'Oh. Well, this friend here was worried.' He gives a small smile. A weak smile and I'm jolted by how fragile he appears. He looks like an old man. His usual attitude, his jovial nature is gone. His smile disappears quickly and his trembling hands, usually steady as a rock, force the photo-frame of Mum and the card from the policeman back into his coat pocket.

I look at his bag. 'Did you pack that yourself?'

'Tried to. Thought I got everything.' He looks away from the open wardrobe, embarrassed.

'OK, well, let's take a look in it and see what we have.' I hear my voice and it startles me to hear myself speaking to him as though addressing a child.

'Aren't we running out of time?' he asks. His voice is so quiet, I feel I should lower mine so as not to break him.

'No,' my eyes fill with tears and I speak more forcefully than I intend, 'we have all the time in the world, Dad.'

I look away and distract those tears from falling by lifting his case onto the bed and trying to compose myself. Day-to-day things, the ordinary, the mundane is what keeps the motor running. How extraordinary the ordinary really is, a tool we all use to keep going, a template for sanity.

When I open the case I feel my composure slip again but I keep talking, sounding like a delusional 1960s suburban TV mother, repeating the hypnotic mantra that everything's just dandy and swell. I 'oh, gosh' and 'shucks' my way through his suitcase, which is a mess, though I shouldn't be surprised as Dad has never had to pack a suitcase in his life. I think what upsets me is the possibility that at seventy-five years old, after ten years without his wife, he simply doesn't know how to, or else my being missing for a few hours has prevented him from accomplishing it. A simple thing like that, my big-as-an-oak-tree,

380

steady-as-a-rock father cannot do. Instead he sits on the edge of the bed twisting his cap around in his gnarled fingers, liver spots like the skin of a giraffe, his fingers trembling in air as though wobbling on an invisible fingerboard and controlling the vibrato in my head.

Things have attempted to be folded but have failed, are crumpled in small balls with no order at all as though they have been packed by a child. I find my shoe inside some bathroom towels. I take my shoe out and put it on my foot without saying anything, as though it's the most normal thing in the world. The towels go back to where they belong. I start folding and packing all over again. His dirty underwear, socks, pyjamas, vests, his washbag. I turn my back to take his clothes from the wardrobe and I take a deep breath.

'We have all the time in the world, Dad,' I repeat. Though this time, it's for my own benefit.

On the tube, on the way to the airport, Dad keeps checking his watch and fidgeting in his seat. Every time the tube stops at a station, he pushes the seat in front of him impatiently as if to move it along himself.

'Have you to be somewhere?' I smile.

'The Monday Club. He looks at me with worried eyes. He's never missed a week, not even when I was in hospital.

'But today is Monday.'

He fidgets. 'I just don't want to miss this flight. We might get stuck over here.'

'Oh, I think we'll make it.' I do my best to hide my smile. 'And there's more than one flight a day, you know.'

'Good.' He looks relieved and even impressed. 'I might even make evening Mass. Oh, they won't believe everything I tell them tonight,' he says with excitement. 'Donal will drop dead when everybody listens to me and not to him for a change.' He settles back into his seat and watches out the window as the blackness of the underground speeds by. He stares into the black, not seeing his own reflection but seeing somewhere else and someone else a long way off, a long time ago. While he's in another world, or the same world but a different time, I take out my mobile and start planning my next move.

'Frankie, it's me. Justin Hitchcock is getting the first plane to Dublin tomorrow morning and I need to know what he's doing stat.'

'How am I supposed to do that, Dr Conway?'

'I thought you had ways.'

'You're right, I do. But I thought you were the psychic one.'

'I'm certainly not pyschic and I'm not getting anything about where he could be going.'

'Are your powers fading?'

'I don't have powers.'

'Whatever. Give me an hour, I'll get back to you.'

Two hours later, just as Dad and I are about to board, I receive a phone call from Frankie.

'He's going to be in the National Gallery tomorrow morning at ten thirty. He's giving a talk on a painting called *Woman Writing a Letter*. It sounds fascinating.'

'Oh, it is, it's one of Terborch's finest. In my opinion.'

Silence.

'You were being sarcastic, weren't you?' I realise. 'OK, well, does your Uncle Tom still run that company?' I smile mischievously and Dad looks at me curiously.

'What are you planning?' Dad asks suspiciously once I've hung up the phone.

'I'm having a little bit of fun.'

'Shouldn't you get back to work? It's been weeks now. Conor called your hand phone while you were gone this morning, it slipped my mind to tell you. He's in Japan but I could hear him very clearly,' he says, impressed with either Conor or the phone company, I'm not sure which. 'He wanted to know why the house hadn't got a For Sale sign in the garden yet. He said that you were supposed to do that.' He looks worried, as though I've broken a world-old rule and now the house will explode if it doesn't have a For Sale sign dug into the ground.

'Oh, I haven't forgotten.' I'm agitated by Conor's call. 'I'm selling it myself. I have my first viewing tomorrow.'

He looks unsure and he's right to because I'm lying through my teeth, but all I have to do is go through my books and call around my list of clients who I know to be looking for a similar property. I can think of a few straight away.

'Your company knows this?' His eyes narrow.

'Yes,' I smile tightly. 'They can take the photos and put the sign up in a matter of hours. I know a few people in the estate agent world.'

He rolls his eyes.

We both look away, in a huff, and just so I don't feel that I'm lying, while we shuffle along the queue to board the plane, I text a few clients I showed properties to before I took my leave to see if they're interested in a viewing. Then I ask my trusty photographer to take the shots of the house. Just as we take our seats on the plane, I have already arranged the photographs and For Sale sign for later today and a viewing appointment for tomorrow. Both teachers at the local school, she and her husband will view the house during their lunch break. At the bottom of the text is the mandatory 'Was so sorry to hear about what happened. Have been thinking of you. See you tomorrow, Linda xx.'

I delete it straight away.

Dad looks at my thumb working over the buttons on my phone with speed. 'You writing a book?'

I ignore him.

'You'll get arthritis in your thumb and it's not much fun, I can tell you that.'

I press send and switch the phone off.

'You really weren't lying about the house?' he asks.

'No,' I say, confidently now.

'Well, I didn't know that, did I? I didn't know what to tell him.'

Score one to me.

'That's OK, Dad, you don't have to feel in the middle of all this.'

'Well, I am.'

Score one to him.

'Well, you wouldn't have been if you hadn't answered *my* phone.'

Two one.

'You were missing all morning – what was I supposed to do, ignore it?'

Two all.

'He was concerned about you, you know. He thought you should see someone. A professional person.'

Off the charts.

'Did he now?' I fold my arms, wanting to call him straight away and rant about all the things I hate about him and that have always annoyed me. The cutting of his toenails in bed, his nose-blowing every morning that almost rattled the house, his inability to let people finish their sentences, his stupid party coin trick that I fake laughed to every time he did it, including the first, his inability to sit down and have an adult conversation about our problems, his constant walking away during our fights . . . Dad interrupts from my silent torture of Conor.

'He said you called him in the middle of the night, spurting Latin.'

'Really?' I feel anger surge. 'What did you say?'

He looks out the window as we pick up speed down the runway.

'I told him you made a fine fluent Italian-speaking Viking too.' I see his cheeks lift and I throw my head back and laugh.

All even.

He suddenly grabs my hand. 'Thanks for all this, love. I had a great time.' He gives my hand a squeeze and goes back to looking out the window as the green of the fields surrounding the runway goes racing by.

He doesn't let go of my hand, so I rest my head on his shoulder and close my eyes.

THIRTY-THREE

Justin walks through arrivals at Dublin airport on Tuesday morning, with his cellphone glued to his ear, listening once again to the sound of Bea's voice mail. He sighs and rolls his eyes before the beep, beyond bored now with her childish behaviour.

'Hi, honey, it's me. Dad. Again. Listen, I know you're angry with me, and at your age everything is oh-so-very-dramatic, but if you'd just listen to what I have to say, the odds are you'll agree with me and thank me for it when you're old and grey. I only want the best for you and I will not hang up this phone until I have convinced you...' He immediately hangs up.

Behind the barricade at arrivals is a man in a dark suit holding a large white placard with Justin's surname written in large capitals. Underneath are those two magical words, 'THANK YOU'.

Those words had captured his attention on billboards, newspapers, radio adverts and television adverts all day and every day, since the first note arrived. Whenever the words drifted from the lips of a passer-by, he did a double take, following them as though hypnotised, as though in them was contained a special encrypted code just for him. Those words floated in the air like the scent of freshly cut grass on a summer's day; more than a smell, they carried with them a feeling, a place, a time of year, a happiness, a celebration of change, of moving on. They transport him just as the hearing of a special song familiar from youth does, when nostalgia, like the tide, sweeps in and catches you on the sand, pulling you in and under when you least expect it, often when you least want it.

Those words were constantly in his head, *thank you, thank you, thank you*. The more he heard them and reread the short notes, the more alien they became, as though he was seeing the sequence of those particular letters for the first time in his life – like music notes, so familiar, so simple, but arranged in a different way, become pure master-pieces.

This transformation of everyday common things to something magical, this growing under-standing that what he perceived to be was not at all, reminded him of when he was a child and spent long silent moments staring at his face in the mirror. Standing on a footstool so that he could reach, the more intensely he stared, the more his face began to morph into one he was wholly unfamiliar with. It wasn't the face his mind had so stubbornly convinced him he had, but instead he saw the real him: eyes further apart than he'd thought, one eyelid lower than the other, one nostril also ever so slightly lower, the corner of one side of his mouth turning downward, as though there was a line going through the centre of his face and with the drawing of that line everything was dragged south, like a knife through sticky chocolate cake. The surface, once smooth, drooped and hung. A quick glimpse and it was unnoticeable. Careful analysis, before brushing his teeth at night, revealed he wore the face of a stranger.

Now he takes a step back from those two words, circles them a few times and views them from all angles. Just as with paintings in a gallery, the words themselves dictate the height at which they should be displayed, the angle from which they should be approached and the position from which they should best be contemplated. He has found the correct angle now. He can now see the weight they hold, like pigeons, *and* the messages they carry, oysters with their pearls, bees on dutious guard of their queen and honey, with their barbed stings attached. They have a sense of purpose, the strength of beauty and ammunition. Rather than a polite utterance heard a thousand times a day, 'Thank you' now has meaning.

Without another thought about Bea, he flips his phone closed and approaches the man holding the sign. 'Hello.'

'Mr Hitchcock?' The six-foot man's eyebrows

are so dark and thick Justin can barely see his eyes.

'Yes,' he says suspiciously. 'Is this car for a *Justin* Hitchcock?'

The man consults a piece of paper in his pocket. 'Yes, it is, sir. Is that still you or does it change things?'

'Ye-es,' he says slowly, contemplatively. 'That's me.'

'You don't seem so sure,' the driver says, lowering the sign. 'Where are you going this morning?'

'Shouldn't you know that?'

'I do. But the last time I let somebody in my car as unsure as you, I delivered an animal rights activist directly into an IMFHA meeting.'

Unfamiliar with the initials, Justin asks, 'Is that bad?'

'The President of the Irish Masters of Fox Hounds Association thought so. He was stuck at the airport with no car, while the lunatic I collected was splashing red paint around the conference room. Let's just say, in terms of a tip for me, it was what the hounds would call a "blank day".'

'Well, I don't think the *hounds* would call it anything, necessarily,' Justin jokes, 'unless they go "Ooo-ooo".' He lifts his chin and howls into the air, playfully.

The driver stares at him blankly.

Justin's face flushes. 'Well, I'm going to the National Gallery.' Pause. 'I'm *pro* the National Gallery. I'm going to talk about painting, not turn people into canvases as a method of venting my frustration. Though if my ex-wife was in the audience I'd run at her with a paint brush,' he laughs, and the driver responds with another glare.

'I wasn't expecting anybody to greet me,' Justin yaps at the chauffeur's heels, out of the airport into the grey October day. 'Nobody at the Gallery informed me you'd be here,' he tests him as they hurry across the pedestrian walkway through the parachuting raindrops, which pull on their emergency cords as they plummet towards Justin's head and shoulders.

'I didn't know about the job until late last night when I got a call. I was supposed to be going to my wife's aunt's funeral today.' He roots around his pockets for the car parking ticket and slides it into the machine to validate it.

'Oh, I'm sorry to hear that.' Justin stops wiping away the raindrop parachuting casualties that have landed with a shplat on the shoulders of his brown corduroy jacket, and looks at the driver grimly, out of respect.

'So was I. I hate funerals.'

Curious response. 'Well, you wouldn't be alone in thinking that.'

He stops walking and turns to face Justin with a look of intense seriousness on his face. 'They always give me the giggles,' he says. 'Does that ever happen to you?'

Justin is unsure whether to take him seriously or not but the driver doesn't crack even the slightest

391

smile. Justin pictures his father's funeral, goes back to when he was nine years old. The two families huddled together at the graveyard, all dressed head to toe in black like dung beetles around the dirty open hole in the ground where the casket was placed. His dad's family had flown over from Ireland, bringing with them the rain, which was unconventional for Chicago's hot summer. They stood beneath umbrellas, he close to his Aunt Emelda, who held the umbrella in one hand and another tightly on his shoulder, Al and his mother beside him under another umbrella. Al had brought along a fire engine, which he played with while the priest talked about their father's life. This annoyed Justin. In fact, everything and everybody annoyed Justin that day.

He hated Aunt Emelda's hand being there on his shoulder, though he knew she was trying to be helpful. It felt heavy and tight, as though she was holding him back, afraid he'd escape from her, afraid he'd scuttle into the big hole in the ground where his father was going.

He'd greeted her that morning, dressed in his best suit, as his mother had requested in her new quiet voice, which Justin had to put his ear to her lips to hear. Aunt Emelda had pretended to be psychic just as she always did when they met one another after their long stints apart.

'I know just what you want, little soldier,' she'd said in her strong Cork accent, which Justin could barely understand and was never sure whether she'd just broken into a song or was speaking to him. She'd rummaged in her oversized handbag and dug out a soldier with a plastic smile and a plastic salute, quickly peeling off the price, and with it ripping off the soldier's name before handing it to him. Justin stared down at Colonel Blank, who saluted him with one hand and held a plastic gun in the other, and immediately mistrusted him. The blank-shooting plastic gun got lost in the heavy pile of black coats by the front door as soon as he'd pulled open the packet. As usual, Aunt Emelda's psychic powers had been tuned into the desires of the wrong nine-year-old boy, for Justin had not wanted this plastic soldier on this day of all days, and he couldn't help but imagine a young boy across town waiting for a plastic soldier for his birthday and instead being handed Justin's father by the tuft of his jet-black hair. However, he accepted her thoughtful gift with a smile as big and sincere as Colonel Blank's. Later that day, as he stood beside the hole in the ground, maybe for once Aunt Emelda could read his mind as her hand gripped him tighter and her nails dug into his bony shoulders as though holding him back. For Justin had thought about jumping into that damp dark hole.

He thought about what it would be like in the world down there. If he could escape the strong hand of his Corkonian aunt and leap into the hole before anybody could catch him, maybe when the ground was closed over on top of them, like a grass carpet being rolled over, they would both be together. He wondered if they would have their own cosy world under the ground. He could have him all to himself, without having to share him with Mom or Al, and there they could play and laugh together, where it was darker. Maybe Dad just didn't like the light; maybe all he wanted was for the light to go away so that it wouldn't make his eyes squint and his fair skin burn and freckle and itch, as it always did when the sun came out. When that hot sun was in the sky it annoyed his dad, and he would have to sit in the shade while he and his mom and Al would play outside, Mom getting browner and browner by the day, his dad getting paler and more irritated by the heat. Maybe a break from the summer was all he wanted; for the itch and the frustration of light to go away.

As his casket was lowered into the hole, his mother let out howls that made Al cry too. Justin knew that Al wasn't crying because he missed his dad, he was crying because he was scared of Mom's reaction. She started crying when his grandma, his father's mother's sniffles became loud wails, and when Al started crying it broke the hearts of the entire congregation to see the young child left behind in tears. Even Dad's brother, Seamus, who always looked like he wanted to laugh, had a trembling lip and a vein that jutted out of his neck like a body-builder, which made Justin think there was another person inside Uncle Seamus, just bursting to get out if Uncle Seamus would let him.

People should never start crying. Because if they start . . . Justin felt like shouting out for them all to stop being so stupid; that Al wasn't crying because of his dad. He wanted to tell them that Al had little idea of what was really going on. He'd been concentrating on his fire engine all day and occasionally looking to Justin with a face so full of questions that he had to keep turning away.

There were men in suits that carried his dad's casket to this place. Men that weren't his uncles or his dad's friends. They weren't crying like everyone else, but they weren't smiling either. They didn't look bored but they didn't look interested. They looked as though they had been to Dad's funeral a hundred times already and they didn't care so much that he had died again but also didn't mind having to make another hole, carry him again and bury him again. He watched as the men with no smiles threw handfuls of soil onto the coffin, making drumming sounds against the wood. He wondered if that would wake his dad up from his summer slumber. He didn't cry like everyone else because he felt assured that Dad had finally escaped the light. His dad would no longer have to sit alone in the shade.

Justin realises the driver is staring at him intently. His head moves in close as though he's awaiting the answer to a very personal question concerning a rash and whether Justin has ever had one too.

'No,' Justin says quietly, clearing his throat

and adjusting his eyes to the world of thirty-five years later. Time travel of the mind; a powerful thing.

'That's us over there.' The driver presses the button on his keys and the lights of an S-class Mercedes light up.

Justin's mouth drops. 'Do you know who organised this?'

'No idea.' The driver holds the door open for him. 'I just take the orders from my boss. Thought it was unusual having to write "Thank You" on the sign. Does that make sense to you?'

'Yes, it does but . . . it's complicated. Could you find out from your boss who's paying for this?' Justin sits into the back seat of the car, places his briefcase on the floor beside him.

'I could try.'

'That would be great.' *I'll have gotcha then!* Justin relaxes into the leather chair, stretches his legs out fully and closes his eyes, barely able to hold back his smile.

'I'm Thomas, by the way,' the driver introduces himself. 'I'm here for you all day so wherever you want to go after this, just let me know.'

'For the entire day?' Justin almost chokes on his free bottle of chilled water, which was waiting for him in the hand rest. He saved a rich person's life. Yes! He should have mentioned more to Bea than muffins and daily newspapers. A villa in the South of France. What an idiot he was not to have thought more quickly.

'Would your company not have organised this for you?' Thomas asks.

'No.' Justin shakes his head. 'Definitely not.'

'Maybe you've a fairy godmother you don't know about,' Thomas says, deadpan.

'Well, let's see what this pumpkin's made of,' Justin laughs.

'Won't get to test it in this traffic,' Thomas says, braking as they enter Dublin traffic, worsened by the grey rainy morning.

Justin presses the button on the door for heated seats and reclines as he feels his back and behind warming. He kicks off his shoes, reclines his chair and relaxes in comfort as he watches the miserable faces of those in buses glaring sleepily out of the fogged-up windows.

'After the Gallery, do you mind bringing me to D'Olier Street? I need to visit somebody in the blood donor clinic.'

'No problem, boss.'

The October gust huffs and puffs and attempts to blow the last of the leaves off the nearby trees. They hang on tight, like the nannies in *Mary Poppins*, who cling to the lampposts of Cherry Tree Lane in a desperate attempt to prevent their airborne competition from blowing them away from the big Banks job interview. The leaves, like many people this autumn, are not yet ready to let go. They cling on tight to yesterday, unable to have controlled their change in colour but, by God, putting up a fight before giving up the place that has been their home for two seasons. I watch as one leaf lets go, dances around in the air before falling to the ground. I pick it up and slowly twirl it around by its stalk in my hand. I'm not fond of autumn. Not fond of watching things so sturdy wither as they lose against nature, the higher power they can't control.

'Here comes the car,' I comment to Kate.

We're standing across the main road from the National Gallery, behind the parked cars, shaded by the trees rising above and over the gates of Merrion Square.

'You paid for *that*?' Kate says. 'You really are nuts.'

'Tell me something I don't know. Actually, I paid half. That's Frankie's uncle driving – he runs the company. Pretend you don't know him if he looks over.'

'I don't know him.'

'Good, that's convincing.'

'Joyce, I have never seen that man in my life.'

'Wow, that's *really* good.'

'How long are you going to keep this up, Joyce? The London thing sounded fun but really, all we know is that he donated blood.'

'To me.'

'We don't know that.'

'I know that.'

'You can't know that.'

'I can. That's the funny thing.'

She looks doubtful and stares at me with such a look of pity, it makes my blood boil.

'Kate, yesterday I had carpaccio and fennel for my dinner, and I spent the evening singing along to practically all the words of Pavarotti's *Ultimate Collection*.'

'I still don't understand how you think that it's this Justin Hitchcock man that's responsible for it. Remember that film *Phenomenon*? John Travolta just suddenly became a genius overnight.'

'He had a brain tumour that somehow increased his ability to learn,' I snap.

The Mercedes pulls up by the gates of the Gallery. The driver gets out of the car to open the door for Justin and he emerges, briefcase in hand, a beam from ear to ear, and I'm happy to see that next month's mortgage payment has gone to good use. I shall worry about that, and everything else in my life, when the time comes.

He still has the aura I felt from the day I first laid my eyes on him in the hair salon – a presence that makes my stomach walk a few flights of stairs and then climb the final ladder to the ten-metre diving platform at the Olympics final. He looks up at the Gallery, around at the park, and with that strong jawline he smiles, a smile that causes my stomach to do one bounce, two bounce, three bounce, before attempting the toughest dive of all, a reverse one-point-five somersault and then one, two, three and a half twists before entering the water, with a belly flop. My unsophisticated entry into the water shows I am not a seasoned nervous wreck. The dive, while terrifying, was quite pleasant and I'm open to taking those steps again.

The leaves around me rustle as another soft breeze blows and I'm not sure if I imagine that it carries to me the smell of his aftershave, the same scent as from the hair salon. I have a brief flash of him picking up a parcel wrapped in emerald-green paper, which sparkles under Christmas tree lights and surrounding candles. It's tied with a large red bow and my hands are momentarily his as he unties it slowly, carefully peels back the tape from the paper, taking care not to rip it. I am struck by his tenderness for the package, which has been lovingly wrapped, until his thoughts are momentarily mine and I am in on his plans to pocket the paper and use it on the unwrapped presents he has sitting out in the car. Inside is a bottle of aftershave and a shaving set. A Christmas gift from Bea.

'He's handsome,' Kate whispers. 'I support your stalking campaign one hundred per cent, Joyce.'

'It's not a stalking campaign,' I hiss, 'and I'd have done this if he was ugly.'

'Can I go in and listen to his talk?' Kate asks. 'No!'

'Why not? He's never seen me; he won't recognise me. Please, Joyce, my best friend believes she is connected to a complete stranger. At least I can go and listen to him to see what he's like.'

'What about Sam?'

'Do you want to mind him for a little while?'

I freeze.

'Oh, forget that,' she says quickly. 'I'll bring him in with me. I'll stay down the back and leave if he disturbs anyone.'

'No, no, it's OK. I can mind him.' I swallow and paste a smile on my face.

'Are you sure?' She looks unconvinced. 'I won't stay for the entire thing. I just want to see what he's like.'

'I'll be fine. Go.' I push her away gently. 'Go in and enjoy yourself. We'll be fine here, won't we?'

Sam puts his socked toe in his mouth in response.

'I promise I won't be long.' Kate leans into the stroller, gives her son a kiss and dashes across the road and into the Gallery.

'So . . .' I look around nervously. 'It's just you and me, Sean.'

He looks at me with his big blue eyes and mine instantly fill.

I look around to make sure nobody has heard me. I mean Sam.

Justin takes his place at the podium in the lecture hall in the basement of the National Gallery. A packed room of faces stares back at him and he is in his element. A late arrival, a young woman, enters the room, apologises and quickly takes a place among the crowd.

'Good morning, ladies and gentlemen, and thank you so much for making it here on this rainy morning. I am here to talk about this painting. *Woman Writing a Letter*, by Terborch, a Dutch Baroque artist from the seventeenth century who was largely responsible for the popularisation of the letter theme. This painting – well, not this painting alone – this genre of letter-writing is a personal favourite of mine, particularly when in this current age it seems a personal letter has almost become extinct.' He stops.

Almost but not quite, for there's somebody sending me notes.

He steps away from the podium, takes one step towards the audience and looks at the crowd, suspicion written upon his face. His eyes narrow as he studies his audience. He scans the rows, knowing that somebody here could be the mystery note-writer.

Somebody coughs, snapping him out of his trance, and he is back with them again. He is mildly flustered but continues where he left off.

'In an age when a personal letter has almost become extinct, this is a reminder of how the great masters of the Golden Age depicted the subtle range of human emotions affected by such a seemingly simple aspect of daily life. Terborch was not the only artist responsible for these images. I cannot go further on this subject without paying lip-service to Vermeer, Metsu and de Hooch, who all produced paintings of people reading, writing, receiving and dispatching letters, which I have written about in my book *The Golden Age of Dutch Painting*:

Vermeer, Metsu and Terborch. Terborch's paintings use letter-writing as a pivot on which to turn complex psychological dramas and his are among the first works to link lovers through the theme of a letter.'

He studies the woman who arrived a little late as he says half of this and another young woman behind her for the second half, wondering if they are reading deeper into his words. He almost laughs aloud at himself at his assumption that, first, the person whose life he saved would be in this room; secondly, that it would be a young woman; and thirdly, attractive. Which makes him ask himself what exactly was he hoping to come out of this current drama?

I push Sam's stroller into Merrion Square, and we're instantly transported from the Georgian centre of the city to another world, shaded by mature trees and surrounded by colour Burned oranges, reds and yellows of the autumn foliage litter the ground and, with each gentle breeze, hop alongside us like inquisitive robin redbreasts. I choose a bench along the quiet walk and turn Sam's stroller around so that he faces me. In the trees bordering the walk I hear twigs snapping as homes are being constructed and lunch prepared.

I watch Sam for a while, as he strains his neck to see the remaining leaves that refuse to surrender their branch, far above him. He points a tiny finger up at the sky and makes sounds.

'Tree,' I tell him, which makes him smile, and his mother is instantly recognisable.

The vision has the same effect as a boot hitting my stomach. I take a moment to catch my breath.

'Sam, while we're here we should really discuss something,' I say.

His smile widens.

'I have to apologise for something,' I clear my throat. 'I haven't been paying much attention to you lately, have I? The thing is . . .' I trail off and wait until a man has passed us by to continue. 'The thing is,' I lower my voice, 'I couldn't bear to look at you . . .' I trail off as his grin widens.

'Oh, here.' I lean over, remove his blanket and press the button to release his safety straps. 'Come up here to me.' I lift him out of the buggy and sit him on my lap. His body is warm and I hug him close. I breathe in the top of his head, candy, his wispy hairs so silky like velvet, his body so chubby and soft in my arms, I want to squeeze him tighter. 'The thing is,' I say quietly to the top of his head, 'it broke my heart to look at you, to cuddle you like I used to, because each time I saw you, I remembered what I'd lost.' He looks up at me and babbles in response. 'Though how could I ever be afraid to look at you?' I kiss his nose. 'I shouldn't have taken it out on you but you're not mine, and that's so hard.' My eyes fill and I let the tears fall. 'I wanted to have a little boy or girl so that just like when you smile, people could say, oh look, you're the picture of your mummy, or maybe that the baby would have my nose or my eyes because that's what people say to me. They say I look like my mum. And I love hearing that, Sam, I really do, because I miss her and I want to be reminded of her every single day. But looking at you was different. I didn't want to be reminded I'd lost my baby every single day.'

'Ba-ba,' he says.

I sniffle. 'Ba-ba gone, Sam. Sean for a boy, Grace for a girl.' I wipe my nose.

Sam, uninterested in my tears, looks away and studies a bird. He points a chubby finger again.

'Bird,' I say through my tears.

'Ba-ba,' he responds.

I smile and wipe my eyes as yet more stream down.

'But there's no Sean or Grace now.' I hug him tighter and let my tears fall, knowing that Sam won't be able to report my weeping to anybody.

The bird hops a few inches and then takes off, disappearing into the sky.

'Ba-ba gone,' Sam says, holding his hands out, palms up.

I watch it fly into the distance, still visible like a speck of dust against the pale blue sky. My tears stop. 'Ba-ba gone,' I repeat.

'What do we see in this painting?' Justin asks.

Silence as everyone views the projected image.

'Well, let us state the obvious first. A young woman sits at a table in a quiet interior. She is writing a letter. We see a quill moving across a sheet of paper. We do not know what she is writing but her soft smile suggests she is writing to a loved one or perhaps a lover. Her head tilts forward, exposing the elegant curve of her neck . . .'

While Sam is back in his buggy, drawing circles on paper with his blue crayon, or more likely, banging out dots on the paper, sending wax shrapnel all over his buggy, I produce my own pen and paper from my bag. I take my calligraphy pen in my hand and imagine I'm hearing Justin's words from across the road. I don't need to see the work of the *Woman Writing a Letter* on the canvas for it has been painted in my mind after Justin's years of intensive study during college and again during research for his book. I begin to write.

As part of a mother/daughter bonding activity when I was seventeen years old, during my goth phase, when I had dyed black hair, a white face and red lips that were victim to a lip-piercing, Mum enrolled us both in a calligraphy class at the local primary school. Every Wednesday at seven p.m.

Mum read in a rather new-age book that Dad didn't agree with that through partaking in activities with your children they would more easily, and of their own accord, open up and share things about their lives, rather than being forced to in a face-to-face, formal and almost interrogative-style sit-down, which Dad was more accustomed to.

The classes worked and, though I moaned and groaned when learning this uncool task, I opened up and told her all. Well, almost all. The rest she had the intuition to guess. I came away with a deeper love, respect and understanding of my mother as a person, a woman and not just as a mum. I also came away with a skill in calligraphy.

I find that when I put pen to paper and get into the rhythm of quick upward flicks, just as we were taught, it takes me back to those classes, transports me to those classrooms where I sat with my mother.

I hear her voice, I smell her scent and I replay our conversations, sometimes awkward as, because I'm seventeen, we dance around the personal, but we talk about it in our own way, finding a way of getting to the point in spite of that. It was a perfect activity for her to choose for me at seventeen, better than she ever knew. Calligraphy had rhythm, roots in Gothic style, it was written in the vigour of the moment and it had attitude. A uniform style of writing, but one that was unique. A lesson to teach me that conformity may not quite mean what I once thought that it had meant, for there are many ways to express oneself in a world with boundaries, without overstepping them.

Suddenly I look up from my page. 'Trompe l'oeil,' I say aloud with a smile.

Sam looks up from his crayon banging and regards me with interest.

*   *   *

'What does that mean?' Kate asks.

'Trompe l'oeil is an art technique involving extremely realistic imagery in order to create the optical illusion that the depicted objects really exist, instead of being two-dimensional painting. It's derived from French, *trompe* meaning "trick" and *l'oeil* meaning "eye",' Justin tells the room. 'Trick the eye,' he repeats, looking around at all the faces in the crowd.

Where are you?

THIRTY-FOUR

'So how did that go?' Thomas the driver asks as Justin gets back into the car after his talk.

'I saw you standing at the back of the room. You tell me.'

'Well, I don't know much about art but you certainly knew how to talk a lot about one girl writing a letter.'

Justin smiles and reaches for another free bottle of water. He's not thirsty but it's there, and it's free.

'Were you looking for somebody?' Thomas asks.

'What do you mean?'

'In the crowd. I noticed you looking around a few times. A woman, is it?' he grins.

Justin smiles, and shakes his head. 'I have no idea. You'd think I was crazy if I told you.'

'So, what do you think?' I ask Kate as we walk around Merrion Square and she fills me in on Justin's lecture.

'What do I think?' she repeats, strolling slowly behind Sam's buggy. 'I think that it doesn't matter if he ate carpaccio and fennel yesterday because he seems like a lovely man anyway. I think that no matter what your reasons are for feeling connected to him or attracted to him, they're not important. You should stop all this running around and just introduce yourself.'

I shake my head. 'No can do.'

'Why not? He seemed to be interested when he was chasing your bus down the road, and when he saw you at the ballet. What's changed now?'

'He doesn't want anything to do with me.'

'How do you know that?'

'I know.'

'*How?* And don't tell me it's because of some mumbo-jumbo thing you saw in your tea leaves.'

'I drink coffee now.'

'You hate coffee.'

'*He* obviously doesn't.'

She does her best not to be negative but looks away.

'He's too busy looking for the woman whose life he saved; he's no longer interested in me. He had my contact details, Kate, and he never called. Not once. In fact, he went so far as to throw them in a skip, and don't ask me how I know that.'

'Knowing you, you were probably lying in the bottom of it.'

I keep tight-lipped.

Kate sighs. 'How long are you going to keep this up?'

I shrug. 'Not much longer.'

'What about work? What about Conor?'

'Conor and I are done. There's nothing more to say. Four years of separation and then we'll be divorced. As for work, I've already told them I'm going back next week – my diary is already full with appointments – and as for the house – shit!' I pull up my sleeve to find my watch. 'I have to get back. I'm showing the house in an hour.'

A quick kiss and I run for the nearest bus home.

'OK, this is it.' Justin stares out of the car window and up to the second floor, which houses the blood donor clinic.

'You're donating blood?' Thomas asks.

'No way. I'm just paying somebody a visit. I shouldn't be too long. If you see any police cars coming, start the engine.' He smiles, but it is unconvincing.

He nervously asks for Sarah at reception and is told to wait in the waiting room. Around him men and women on their lunch breaks from work sit in their suits and read the newspapers, waiting to be called for their blood donations.

He inches closer to the woman beside him, who's flicking through a magazine. He leans over her shoulder and as he whispers, she jumps.

'Are you sure you want to do this?'

Everyone in the room lowers their papers and magazines to stare at him. He coughs and looks away, pretending somebody else said it. On the walls around him are posters encouraging those in the room to donate, and there are also thank you posters of young children, survivors of leukaemia and other illnesses. He has already waited half an hour and checks his watch every minute, conscious he has a plane to catch. When the last person leaves him alone in the room, Sarah appears at the door.

'Justin.' She isn't icy, she isn't tough or angry. Quiet. Hurt. That's worse. He'd rather she was angry.

'Sarah.' He stands to greet her, is locked in an awkward half-embrace and a kiss on one cheek, which turns into two, a questionable third but is aborted and almost becomes a kiss on the lips. She pulls away, ending the farcical greeting.

'I can't stay long, I have to get to the airport for a flight, but I wanted to call by and see you face to face. Can we talk for a few minutes?'

'Yes, sure.' She enters the reception and sits down, arms still folded.

'Oh.' He looks around. 'Don't you have an office, or something?'

'This is nice and quiet.'

'Where is your office?'

Her eyes narrow with suspicion and he gives up that particular line of questioning and quickly takes a seat beside her.

'I'm here, really, to apologise for my behaviour the last time we met. Well, every time we met and every moment after that. I really am sorry.'

She nods, waiting for more.

Damn it, that's all I had! Think, think. You're sorry and . . .

'I didn't mean to hurt you. I got very distracted that day with those crazy Vikings. In fact, you could say I've been distracted by crazy Vikings almost every day for the last month or two and, uh . . .' *Think!* 'Could I go to the men's room? If you wouldn't mind. Please.'

She looks a little taken aback but directs him. 'Sure, it's straight down the hall at the end.'

Standing outside, which has a newly hammered 'For Sale' sign attached to the front wall, Linda and her husband, Joe, are pressing their faces up against the window and gawking into the living room. A protective feeling comes over me. Then as soon as it comes, it vanishes. Home is not a place – not this place, anyway.

'Joyce? Is that you?' Linda slowly lowers her sunglasses.

I give them a big wobbly smile, reaching into my pocket for the bunch of keys, which is already minus my car keys and furry ladybird that used to be on Mum's set. Even the set of keys have lost their heart, their playfulness; all they have now is their function.

'Your hair, you look so different.'

'Hi, Linda. Hi, Joe.' I hold out my hand to greet them.

Linda has other plans and reaches out to offer me a huge, tight hug.

'Oh, I'm so sorry for you.' She squeezes me. 'Poor you.'

A nice gesture, if perhaps I'd known her a bit longer than to show her three houses over a month ago, and even then she'd done the same with her hands on my practically flat stomach on learning I was pregnant. My body suddenly becoming everybody else's property, I'd found entirely annoying during my only month of being able to talk about it.

She lowers her voice to a whisper. 'Did they do that at the hospital?' She eyes my hair.

'Eh, no.' I laugh. 'They did that at the hair salon,' I chirp, my usual Lady of Trauma coming back to save the day. I turn the key in the door and allow them to enter first.

'Oh,' she breathes excitedly, and her husband smiles and takes her hand. I have a flashback of Conor and me ten years ago, coming to view the house, which had just been deserted by an old lady who had lived alone for the previous twenty years. I follow my younger self and him into the house and suddenly they are real and I am the ghost, remembering what we saw and listening to our conversation, replaying the moment again.

It had reeked inside, had old carpets, creaking floors, rotting windows and wallpaper that was so old it had just gone out of fashion for the third time round. It was disgusting and a money pit, and we loved it as soon as we stood where Linda and her husband stand right now.

We had it all ahead of us back then, when Conor was the Conor I loved and I was the old me; a perfect match. Then Conor became who he is now and I became the Joyce he no longer loved. As the house became more beautiful, our relationship became uglier. We could have lain on a cat-hair-infested rug on our first night in our home back then and would have been happy, but then every minute detail of what was wrong in our marriage we attempted to fix by getting a new couch, repairing the doors, replacing the draughty windows. If only we'd put that much time and concentration into ourselves; self-improvement rather than home improvement. Neither of us thought to fix the draught in our marriage. It whistled through the growing cracks while neither of us was paying attention until we both woke up one morning with cold feet.

'I'll show you around downstairs, but, em,' I look up at the nursery door, no longer vibrating as it had when I first returned home. It is just a door, quiet and still. Doing what a door does. Nothing. 'I'll let you wander around upstairs by yourselves.'

'Are the owners still living here?' Linda asks.

I look around. 'No. No, they're long gone.'

*   *   *

415

As Justin makes his way down the hall to the toilet, he examines each of the names on the doors, looking for Sarah's office. He has no idea where to start but maybe if he can find the folder that deals with blood taken from Trinity College in early autumn, then he'll be closer to finding out.

He sees her name on the door, raps on it gently. When he hears no response he enters and closes it quietly behind him. He looks around quickly, piles of folders on the shelves. He runs immediately to the filing cabinets and starts rifling through them. Moments later the door knob turns. He drops the file back into the cabinet, turns towards the door and freezes. Sarah looks at him, shocked.

'Justin?'

'Sarah?'

'What are you doing in my office?'

You're an educated man, think of something smart.

'I took a wrong turn.'

She folds her arms. 'Why don't you tell me the truth now?'

'I was on my way back and I saw your name on the door and I thought I'd come in and have a look around, see what your office is like. I have this thing, you see, where I believe that an office really represents what a person is like and I thought that if we're to have a future tog—'

'We're not going to have a future.'

'Oh. I see. But if we *were* to—'

'No.'

He scans her desk and his eyes fall upon a photograph of Sarah with her arms around a young blonde girl and a man. They pose happily together on a beach.

Sarah follows his gaze.

'That's my daughter, Molly.' She tightens her lips then, angry at herself for saying anything.

'You have a daughter?' He reaches for the frame, pauses before touching it and looks to her for permission first.

She nods, lips loosening, and he takes it in his hands.

'She's beautiful.'

'She is.'

'How old is she?'

'Six.'

'I didn't know you had a daughter.'

'You don't know a lot of things about me. You never stuck around long enough on our dates to talk about anything that wasn't about you.'

Justin cringes, his heart falls. 'Sarah, I'm so sorry.'

'So you said, so sincerely, right before you came into my office and started rooting around.'

'I wasn't rooting—'

Her look is enough to stop himself from telling another lie. She takes the photo frame from his hands, gently. Nothing about her is rough or aggressive. She is filled with disappointment; not for the first time an idiot like Justin has let her down.

'The man in the photo?'

She looks sad as she studies it and then places it back on the table.

'I would have been happy to tell you about him before,' she says softly. 'In fact, I remember trying to on at least two occasions.'

'I'm sorry,' he repeats, feeling so small he almost can't see over her desk. 'I'm listening now.'

'And I'm sure I remember you telling me you had a flight to catch,' she says.

'Right,' he nods, and makes his way to the door. 'I am so truly, very, very sorry. I am hugely embarrassed and disappointed in myself.' And he realises he actually means it from the bottom of his heart. 'I am going through some strange things at the moment.'

'Find me someone who isn't. We all have crap to deal with, Justin. Just please do not drag me into yours.'

'Right.' He nods again and offers another apologetic, embarrassed smile before exiting her office, rushing down the stairs and into the car, feeling two foot tall.

THIRTY-FIVE

'What's that?'

'I don't know.'

'Just give it a wipe.'

'No, you do.'

'Have you seen something like that before?'

'Yeah, maybe.'

'What do you mean, maybe? You either have or you haven't.'

'Don't get smart with me.'

'I'm not, I'm just trying to figure it out. Do you think it will come off?'

'I've no idea. Let's ask Joyce.'

I hear Linda and Joe mumbling together in the hallway. I've left them to their own devices and have been standing in the galley kitchen, drinking a black coffee and staring out at my mother's rose bush at the back of the garden and seeing the ghosts of Joyce and Conor sunbathing on the grass during a hot summer with the radio blaring.

'Joyce, could we show you something for a moment?'

'Sure.'

I put the coffee cup down, pass the ghost of Conor making his lasagne specialty in the kitchen, pass the ghost of Joyce sitting in her favourite armchair in her pyjamas, eating a Mars bar, and make my way to the hall. They are on their hands and knees examining the stain by the stairs. My stain.

'I think it might be wine,' Joe says, looking up at me. 'Did the owners say anything about the stain?'

'Eh . . .' My legs wobble slightly and for a moment I think my knees are going to go. I lean out to hold on to the banister and pretend to lean down and look at it more closely. I close my eyes. 'It's been cleaned a few times already, as far as I know. Would you be interested in keeping the carpet?'

Linda makes a face while she thinks, looks up and down the stairs, through the house, examining my choice of décor with a ruffled nose. 'No, I suppose not. I think wooden floors would be lovely. Don't you?' she asks Joe.

'Yeah,' he nods. 'A nice pale oak.'

'Yeah,' she agrees. 'No, I don't think we'd keep this carpet.' She turns her nose up again.

I haven't intended to keep the owners' details from them deliberately – there's no point as they'll see it on the contract anyway. I had assumed they

420

knew that the property was mine, but it was their misunderstanding, and as they poked holes in the decorations, the choice of room layout, and funny noises and smells they weren't used to but that I had stopped noticing by now, I didn't think it would be necessary to make them uncomfortable by pointing it out now.

'You seem keen,' I smile, watching their faces aglow with warmth and excitement at finally finding a property they felt at home in.

'We are,' she grins. 'We have been so fussy up till now, as you well know. But now the situation has changed and we need to get out of that flat and find somewhere bigger as soon as we can, seeing as we're expanding, or I'm expanding,' she jokes nervously, and it's only then that I notice her small bump beneath her shirt, her belly button hard and protruding against the fabric.

'Oh, wow . . .' Lump to throat, wobble of knees again, eyes fill, please let this moment be over quickly, please make them look away from me. They have tact and so they do. 'That's fantastic, congratulations,' my voice says cheerily, and even I can hear how hollow it is, so devoid of sincerity, the empty words almost echo within themselves.

'So that room upstairs would be perfect.' Joe nods to the nursery.

'Oh, of course, that's just wonderful.' The 1960s surbuban housewife is back as I gosh, gee-whizz and shucks my way through the rest of the conversation.

'I can't believe they don't want any of the furniture,' Linda says, looking around.

'Well, they're both moving to smaller property and their belongings just won't fit there any more.'

'But they're not taking *anything*?'

'No,' I smile, looking around. 'Nothing but the rose bush in the back garden.'

And a suitcase of memories.

Justin falls into the car with a giant sigh.

'What happened to you?'

'Nothing. Could you just drive directly to the airport now, please? I'm a little behind time.' Justin places his elbow on the windowledge and covers his face with his hand, hating himself, hating the selfish miserable man he has become. He and Sarah weren't right for one another but what right had he to use her like that, to bring her down with him into his pit of desperation and selfishness?

'I've got something that will cheer you up,' Thomas says, reaching for the glove compartment.

'No, I'm really not in the—' Justin stops, seeing Thomas retrieve a familiar envelope from the compartment. He hands it over to him.

'Where did you get this?'

'My boss called me, told me to give it to you before you got to the airport.'

'Your boss.' Justin narrows his eyes. 'What's his name?'

Thomas is silent for a while. 'John,' he finally replies.

'John Smith?' Justin says, his voice thick with sarcasm.

'The very man.'

Knowing he'll squeeze no information from Thomas, he turns his attention back to the envelope. He circles it slowly in his hand, trying to decide whether to open it or not. He could leave it unopened and end all of this now, get his life back in order, stop trying to use people, take advantage. Meet a nice woman, treat her well.

'Well? Aren't you going to open it?' Thomas asks.

Justin continues to circle it in his hand.

'Maybe.'

Dad opens the door to me, his iPod in his ears, the control pad in his hand. He looks my outfit up and down.

'OOH, YOU LOOK VERY NICE TODAY, GRACIE,' he shouts at the top of his voice, and a man walking his dog across the road turns to stare. 'WERE YOU OUT SOMEWHERE SPECIAL?'

I smile. Light relief at last. I put my finger on my lips and take the earphones out of his ears.

'I was showing the house to some clients of mine.'

'Did they like it?'

'They're going to come back in a few days to measure. So that's a good sign. But being back over there, I realised there are so many things that I have to go through.'

'Haven't you been through enough? You don't need to sob for weeks just to make yourself feel OK about it.'

I smile. 'I mean that I have to go through *possessions*. Things I've left behind. I don't think they want a lot of the furniture. Would it be OK if I stored it in your garage?'

'My woodwork studio?'

'That you haven't been in for ten years.'

'I've been in there,' he says defensively. 'Oh, all right then, you can put your things in there. Will I ever get rid of you at all, at all?' he says with a slight smile on his face.

I sit at the kitchen table and Dad immediately busies himself, filling the kettle as he does for everyone who enters the kitchen.

'So how did the Monday Club go last night? I bet Donal McCarthy couldn't believe your story. What was his face like?' I lean in, excited to hear.

'He wasn't there,' Dad says, turning his back to me as he takes a cup and saucer out for himself and a mug for me.

'What? Why not? And you with your big story to tell him! The cheek of him. Well, you'll have next week, won't you?'

He turns around slowly. 'He died at the weekend. His funeral's tomorrow. Instead we spent the night talking about him and all his old stories that he told a hundred times.'

'Oh, Dad, I'm so sorry.'

'Ah, well. If he hadn't have gone over the

weekend, he would have dropped dead when he'd heard I met Michael Aspel. Maybe it was just as well,' he smiles sadly. 'Ah, he wasn't such a bad man. We had a good laugh even if we did enjoy getting a rise out of one another.'

I feel for Dad. It is such a trivial thing compared with the loss of a friend, but he had been so excited to share his stories with his great rival.

We both sit in silence.

'You'll keep the rose bush, won't you?' Dad asks finally.

I know immediately what he's talking about. 'Of course I will. I thought that it'd look good in your garden.'

He looks out the window and studies his garden, probably deciding where he'll plant it.

'You have to be careful with moving, Gracie. Too much shock causes a serious, possibly a grave decline.'

I smile sadly. 'That's a bit dramatic, but I'll be fine, Dad. Thanks for caring.'

He keeps his back turned. 'I was talking about the roses.'

My phone rings, vibrates along the table and almost hops off the edge.

'Hello?'

'Joyce, it's Thomas. I just left your young man off at the airport.'

'Oh, thank you so much. Did he get the envelope?'

'Eh, yeah. About that: I gave it to him all right

425

but I've just looked in the back seat of the car and it's still there.'

'What?' I jump up from the kitchen chair. 'Go back, go back! Turn the car around! You have to give it to him. He's forgotten it!'

'You see, the thing is, he wasn't too sure on whether he wanted to open it or not.'

'What? Why?'

'I don't know, love! I gave it to him when he got back into the car before we got to the airport, just like you asked. He seemed very down and so I thought it'd cheer him up a bit.'

'Down? Why? What was wrong with him?'

'Joyce, love, I don't know. All I know is he got into the car a bit upset so I gave him the envelope and he sat there looking at it and I asked him if he was going to open it and he said maybe.'

'Maybe,' I repeat. Had I done something to upset him? Had Kate said something to him? 'He was upset when he came out of the Gallery?'

'No, not the Gallery. We stopped off at the blood donor clinic on D'Olier Street before the airport.'

'He was donating blood?'

'No, he said he had to meet somebody.'

Oh my God, maybe he'd discovered it was me who'd received his blood and he wasn't interested.

'Thomas, do you know if he opened it?'

'Did you seal it?'

'No.'

'Then there's no way of my knowing. I didn't see him open it. I'm sorry. Do you want me to

426

drop it at your house on the way back from the airport?'

'Please.'

An hour later I meet Thomas at the door and he gives me the envelope. I can feel the tickets still inside and my heart falls. Why didn't Justin open it and take it with him?

'Here, Dad.' I slide the envelope across the kitchen table. 'A present for you.'

'What's in it?'

'Front-row seats to the opera for next weekend,' I say sadly, leaning my chin on my hand. 'It was a gift for somebody else, but he clearly doesn't want to go.'

'The opera.' Dad makes a funny face and I laugh. 'It's far from operas I was raised,' though he opens the envelope anyway as I get up to make some more coffee.

'Oh, I think I'll pass on this opera thing, love, but thanks anyway.'

I spin round. 'Oh, Dad, why? You liked the ballet and you didn't think that you would.'

'Yes, but I went to that with you. I wouldn't go to this on my own.'

'You don't have to. There are two tickets.'

'No, there aren't.'

'There definitely are. Look again.'

He turns the envelope upside down and shakes it. A loose piece of paper falls out and flutters to the table.

My heart skips a beat.

Dad props his glasses on the tip of his nose and peers down at the note. '"Accompany me",' he says slowly. 'Ah, love, that's awful nice of you—'

'Show me that.' I grab it from his hands, disbelievingly, and read it for myself. Then I read it again. And again and again.

'Accompany me? Justin.'

THIRTY-SIX

'He wants to meet me,' I tell Kate nervously, as I twirl a string from the end of my unravelling top around my finger.

'You're going to cut off your circulation, be careful,' Kate responds, motherly.

'Kate! Did you not hear me? I said he wants to meet me!'

'And so he should. Did you not think that this would eventually happen? Really, Joyce, you've been taunting the man for weeks. And if he did save your life, as you're insisting he did, wouldn't he want to meet the person whose life he saved? Boost his male ego? Come on, it's the equivalent to a white horse and a shiny suit of armour.'

'No it's not.'

'It is in his male eyes. His male *wandering* eyes,' she spits out aggressively.

My eyes narrow as I study her closely. 'Is everything OK? You're beginning to sound like Frankie.'

'Stop biting your lip, it's starting to bleed. Yes, everything's great. Just hunky-dory.'

'OK, here I am,' Frankie makes her announcement as she breezes through the door and joins us on the bleachers.

We are seated on a split-level viewing balcony at Kate's local swimming pool. Below us Eric and Jayda splash noisily in their swimming class. Beside us Sam is sitting in his stroller, looking around.

'Does he ever do anything?' Frankie watches him suspiciously.

Kate ignores her.

'Issue number one for discussion today is why do we have to constantly meet in these places with all these *things* crawling around?' She looks at all the toddlers. 'What happened to cool bars, new restaurants, shop openings? Remember we used to go out and have *fun*?'

'I have plenty of fucking fun,' Kate says a little too defensively and loudly. 'I am just one great big ball of fucking fun,' she repeats, and looks away.

Frankie doesn't hear the unusual tone in Kate's voice, or does hear it and decides to push anyway. 'Yes, at dinner parties for other couples who haven't been out for a month either. For me, that's not so fun.'

'You'll understand when you have kids.'

'I don't plan to have any. Is everything OK?'

'Yes, she's "hunky-dory",' I say to Frankie, using my fingers as inverted commas.

'Oh, I see,' Frankie says slowly and mouths 'Christian' at me.

I shrug.

'Is there anything you want to get off your chest?' Frankie asks.

'Actually, yes.' Kate turns to her with fire in her eyes. 'I'm tired of your little comments about my life. If you're not happy here or in my company, then piss off somewhere else, but just know that it'll be without me.' She turns away, her cheeks flushed with anger.

Frankie is silent for a moment as she observes her friend. 'OK,' she says perkily and turns to me. 'My car is parked outside; we can go to the new bar down the road.'

'We're not going anywhere,' I protest.

'Ever since you left your husband and your life has fallen apart, you've been no fun,' she says to me sulkily. 'And as for you, Kate, ever since you got that new Swedish nanny and your husband's been eyeing her up, *you've* been absolutely miserable. As for me, I'm tired of hopping from one night of meaningless sex with handsome strangers to another, and having to eat microwave dinners alone every evening. There, I've said it.'

My mouth falls open. So does Kate's. I can tell we are both trying our best to be angry with her but her comments are so spot on, it's actually quite humorous. She nudges me with her elbow and chuckles mischievously in my ear. The corners of Kate's lips begin to twitch too.

'I should have got a manny,' Kate finally says.

'Nah, I still wouldn't trust Christian,' Frankie responds. 'You're being paranoid, Kate,' she assures her seriously. 'I've been around there, I've seen him. He adores you and she is not attractive at all.'

'You think?'

'Uh-huh,' she nods, but when Kate looks away, mouths 'gorgeous' to me.

'Did you mean all that you said?' Kate says, brightening up.

'No.' Frankie throws her head back and laughs. 'I *love* meaningless sex. I need to do something about the microwave dinners, though. My doctor says I need more iron. OK,' she claps her hands, causing Sam to jump with fright, 'what's this session's meeting been called for?'

'Justin wants to meet Joyce,' Kate explains, and snaps at me, 'Stop biting your lip.'

I stop.

'Ooh, great,' Frankie says excitedly. 'So what's the problem?' She sees my look of terror.

'He's going to realise that I'm me.'

'As opposed to you being . . . ?'

'Someone else.' I bite my lip again.

'This is really reminding me of the old days. You are thirty-three years old, Joyce, why are you acting like a teenager?'

'Because she's in love,' Kate says, bored, turning to face the swimming pool and clapping her coughing daughter, Jayda, whose face is half under the water.

'She can't be in love.' Frankie rolls her nose up in disgust.

'Is that normal, do you think?' Kate, beginning to get worried about Jayda, tries to get our attention.

'Of course it's not normal,' Frankie responds. 'She hardly knows the guy.'

'Girls, eh, stop for a minute,' Kate tries to butt in.

'I know more about him than any other person will ever know,' I defend myself. 'Apart from himself.'

'Eh, lifeguard.' Kate gives up on us and calls gently to the woman sitting below us. 'Is she OK, do you think?'

'Are you in love?' Frankie looks at me as though I've just said I want to have a sex change.

I smile just as the lifeguard crashes into the water to save Jayda and a few kids scream.

'You'll have to take us over to Ireland with you,' Doris says with excitement, placing a vase on the kitchen windowsill. The flat is almost finished and she's arranging the finishing touches. 'They could be a nutcase and you'd never know. We need to be nearby just in case something happens. They could be a murderer, a serial stalker who dates people and then kills them. I saw something like that on *Oprah*.'

Al begins hammering nails into the wall and Justin joins in with the rhythm, gently and repeatedly

433

bashing his head against the kitchen table in response.

'I am not taking you both to the opera with me,' Justin says.

'You took me along on a date with you when you and Delilah Jackson went out.' Al stops hammering and turns to him. 'Why should this be any different?'

'Al, I was twelve years old.'

'Still,' he shrugs, returning to his hammering.

'What if she's a celebrity?' Doris says excitedly. 'Oh my God, she could be! I think she is! Jennifer Aniston could be sitting in the front row of the opera and there could be a place free beside her. Oh my God, what if it is?' She turns to Al with wide eyes. 'Justin, you *have* to tell her I'm her biggest fan.'

'Whoa, whoa, whoa, hold on a minute, you're starting to hyperventilate. *How on earth* have you come to that conclusion? We don't even know if it's a woman. You are obsessed with celebrities,' Justin sighs.

'Yeah, Doris,' Al joins in. 'It's probably just a normal person.'

Justin rolls his eyes. 'Yeah,' he imitates his tone, 'because celebrities aren't normal people, they're really underworld beasts that grow horns and have three legs.'

With that both Al and Doris pause from their hammering and hanging duties to stare at him.

'We're going to Dublin tomorrow,' Doris says

with an air of finality. 'It's your brother's birthday and a weekend in Dublin, in a very nice hotel like the Shelbourne Hotel – I've, I mean *Al* has always wanted to stay there – would be a perfect birthday present for him, from you.'

'I can't afford the Shelbourne Hotel, Doris.'

'Well, we'll need somewhere close to a hospital in case he has a heart attack. In any case, we're all going!' She claps her hands excitedly.

THIRTY-SEVEN

I'm on my way into the city to meet Kate and
Frankie for help on what to wear to tonight's
opera, when my phone rings.

'Hello?'

'Joyce, it's Steven.'

My boss.

'I just received another phone call.'

'That's really great but you don't have to call
me when that happens.'

'It's another complaint, Joyce.'

'From who and about what?'

'That couple you showed the new cottage to
yesterday?'

'Yes?'

'They've pulled out.'

'Oh, that's a shame,' I say, lacking all sincerity.
'Did they say why?'

'Yes, in fact they did. It seems a certain person
in our company advised them that to recreate the
look of the period cottage properly, they should

437

demand that the builders carry out excess work. Guess what? The builders weren't entirely interested in their list that included,' I hear paper rustling and he reads aloud, '"Exposed beams, exposed brickwork, log-burning stove, open fires . . ." The list goes on. So now they've backed out.'

'It sounds reasonable enough to me. The builders were recreating period cottages without any period features. Does that make sense to you?'

'Who cares? Joyce, you were only supposed to let them in to measure for their couch. Douglas had sold this place to them already when you were . . . out.'

'Evidently, he didn't.'

'Joyce, I need you to stop turning our clients away. Do you need to be reminded that your job is to *sell*, and if you're not doing that then . . .'

'Then what?' I say haughtily, my head getting hot.

'Then nothing,' he softens. 'I know you've had a difficult time,' he begins awkwardly.

'That time is over and has nothing to do with my ability to sell a house,' I snap.

'Then sell one,' he finishes.

'Fine.' I snap my phone shut and glare out the bus window at the city. A week back at work and already I need a break.

'Doris, is this really necessary?' Justin moans from the bathroom.

'Yes!' she calls. 'This is what we're here for. We

438

have to make sure you're going to look right tonight. Hurry up, you take longer than a woman to get changed.'

Doris and Al are sitting on the end of their bed in a Dublin hotel, not the Shelbourne, much to Doris's dismay. It is more of a Holiday Inn, but it's central to the city and shopping streets and that's good enough for her. As soon as they'd landed earlier that morning, Justin had been all set to show them around the sites, the museums, churches and castles, but Doris and Al had other things on their minds. Shopping. The Viking tour was as cultured as they got and Doris had howled when water had sprayed her in the face on entry into the River Liffey. They'd ended up rushing to the nearest rest room so that Al could wash the mascara out of her eye.

There were only hours to go until the opera, until he would finally discover the identity of this mystery person. He was filled with anxiety, excitement and nerves at the thought of it. It would be an evening of sheer torture or pleasantries depending on his luck. He had to figure out an escape plan if his worst-case scenario was to play out.

'Oh, hurry up, Justin,' Doris howls again and he fixes his tie and exits the bathroom.

'Work it, work it, work it!' Doris whoops as he strolls up and down the bedroom in his best suit. He pauses in front of them and fidgets awkwardly, feeling like a little boy in his communion suit.

He is greeted by silence. Al, who has been shovelling popcorn in his mouth at a serious speed, also stops.

'What?' he says nervously. 'Something wrong? Something on my face? Is there a stain?' He looks down, studying himself.

Doris rolls her eyes and shakes her head. 'Ha-ha very funny. Now seriously, stop wasting time and show us the real suit.'

'Doris!' Justin exclaims. 'This is the real suit!'

'That's your best suit?' she drawls, looking him up and down.

'I think I recognise that from our wedding.' Al's eyes narrow.

Doris stands up and picks up her handbag. 'Take it off,' she says calmly.

'What? Why?'

She takes a deep breath. 'Just take it off. Now.'

'These are too formal, Kate.' I turn my nose up at the dresses she has chosen. 'It's not a ball, I just need something . . .'

'Sexy,' Frankie says, waving a little dress in front of me.

'It's an opera, not a nightclub.' Kate whips it away from her. 'OK, look at this. Not formal, not slutty.'

'Yes, you could be a nun,' Frankie says sarcastically.

They both turn away and continue to root through the rails.

'Aha! I got it,' Frankie announces.

'No, I've found the perfect one.'

They both spin round with the same dresses in their hand, Kate holding one in red, Frankie holding the black. I chew on my lip.

'Stop it!' they say in unison.

'Oh my God,' Justin whispers.

'What? You've never seen a pink pinstripe before? It's divine. Worn with this pink shirt and this pink tie, oh, it would be perfect. Oh, Al, I wish you'd wear suits like this.'

'I prefer the blue,' Al disagrees. 'The pink is a bit gay. Or maybe that's a good idea in case she turns out to be a disaster. You can tell her your boyfriend's waiting for you. I can back you up on that,' he offers.

Doris stares at him with loathing. 'See, isn't this so much better than that other thing you were wearing? Justin? Earth to Justin? What on earth are you looking at? Oh, she's pretty.'

'That's Joyce,' he whispers. He had once read that a blue-throated hummingbird had a heart rate of one thousand two hundred and sixty beats per minute, and he'd wondered how on earth anything could survive that. He understood now. With each beat, his heart pushed out blood and sent it flowing around his body. He felt his entire body throb, pulsate in his neck, his wrists, his heart, his stomach.

'That's Joyce?' Doris asks, shocked. 'The phone woman? Well, she looks . . . *normal*, Justin. What do you think, Al?'

Al looks her up and down and nudges his brother. 'Yeah, she looks real *normal*. You should ask her out once and for all.'

'Why are you both so surprised she looks normal?' Thump-thump. Thump-thump.

'Well, sweetie, the very fact that she exists is a surprise,' Doris snorts. 'The fact that she's *pretty* is damn near a miracle. Go on, ask her out for dinner tonight.'

'I can't tonight.'

'Why not?'

'I've got the opera!'

'Opera shopera. Who cares about that?'

'You have been talking about it non-stop for over a week. And now it's opera shopera?' Thump-thump. Thump-thump.

'Well, I didn't want to alarm you before but I was thinking about it on the plane on the way over and . . .' she takes a deep breath and touches his arm gently, 'it can't be Jennifer Aniston. There's just going to be some old lady sitting in the front row waiting for you with a bouquet of flowers that you don't even want, or some overweight guy with bad breath. Sorry, Al, I don't mean you.' She touches his arm apologetically.

Al misses the insult he's so upset about the bombshell she's dropped. 'What? But I brought my autograph book!'

Justin's heart beats the speed of a humming-bird's heart, his mind now at the speed of its wings. He can barely think, everything is happening too fast. Joyce, far more beautiful up close than he remembers, her newly short hair soft around her face. She is beginning to move away now. He has to do something quick. *Think, think, think!*

'Ask her out tomorrow night,' Al suggests.

'I can't! My exhibition is tomorrow.'

'Skip it. Call in sick.'

'I can't, Al! I've been working on this for months, I'm the damn curator, I *have* to be there.' Thump-thump, thump-thump.

'If you don't ask her out, I will.' Doris pushes him.

'She's busy with her friends.'

Joyce starts to move away.

Do something!

'Joyce!' Doris calls out.

'Jesus Christ.' Justin tries to turn round and scarper in the other direction but both Al and Doris block him.

'Justin Hitchcock,' a voice says loudly and he stops trying to break through their barrier and slowly turns round. The lady standing beside Joyce is familiar. She has a baby in a stroller beside her.

'Justin Hitchcock.' The girl reaches her hand out. 'Kate McDonald.' She shakes his hand firmly. 'I was at your talk last week in the National Gallery. It was incredibly interesting,' she smiles. 'I didn't know you knew Joyce,' she smiles brightly and elbows Joyce. 'Joyce, you never said! I was at Justin Hitchcock's talk just last week! Remember I told

443

you? The painting about the woman and the letter? And the fact that she was writing it?'

Joyce's eyes are wide and startled. She looks from her friend to Justin and back again.

'She doesn't know me, exactly,' Justin finally speaks up and feels a slight tremble in his voice. The adrenalin is surging through him so much he feels as if he's about to take off like a rocket through the department store's roof. 'We've passed one another on many occasions but never had the opportunity to meet properly.' He holds out his hand. 'Joyce, I'm Justin.'

She reaches out to take his hand and static electricity rushes through as they get a quick shock from one another.

They both let go quickly. 'Whoa!' She pulls back and cradles her hand in the other, as though burned.

'Oooh,' Doris sings.

'It's static electricity, Doris. Caused when the air and materials are dry. They should use a humidifier in here,' Justin says like a robot, not moving his eyes from Joyce's face.

Frankie cocks her head and tries not to laugh. 'Charming.'

'I tell him that all the time,' Doris says angrily.

After a moment, Joyce extends her hand again to finish the handshake properly. 'Sorry, I just got a—'

'That's OK, I got it too,' he smiles.

'Nice to meet you, finally,' she says.

They remain holding hands, just staring at one another. A line of Doris, Justin and Al standing opposite Joyce's party of three.

Doris clears her throat noisily. 'I'm Doris, his sister-in-law.'

She reaches diagonally over Justin and Joyce's handshake to greet Frankie.

'I'm Frankie.'

They shake hands. While doing so, Al reaches over diagonally to shake hands with Kate. It becomes a hand-shaking marathon as they all greet at once, Justin and Joyce finally releasing hold of one another.

'Would you like to go for dinner tonight with Justin?' Doris blurts out.

'Tonight?' Joyce's mouth drops.

'She would *love* to,' Frankie answers for her.

'*Tonight*, though?' Justin turns to face Doris with wide eyes.

'Oh, it's no problem, Al and I want to eat alone anyway,' she nudges him. 'No point being the gooseberry,' she smiles.

'Are you sure you wouldn't rather stick to your *other* plans tonight?' Joyce says, slightly confused.

'Oh, no,' Justin shakes his head, 'I'd love to have dinner with you. Unless of course *you* have plans?'

Joyce turns to Frankie. 'Tonight? I have that *thing*, Frankie . . .'

'Oh, no, don't be silly. It doesn't really make a difference now, does it?' She widens her eyes. 'We can have drinks any other time.' Frankie waves her hand dismissively. 'Where are you taking her?' She smiles sweetly at Justin.

'The Shelbourne Hotel?' Doris says. 'At eight?'

'Oh I've always wanted to eat there,' Kate sighs. 'Eight suits her fine,' she responds.

Justin smiles and looks at Joyce. 'Does it?'

Joyce seems to consider this, her mind ticking at the same rate as his heart.

'You're *absolutely* sure you're happy to cancel your other plans for tonight?' Frown lines appear on her forehead.

Her eyes bore into his and guilt overcomes him as he thinks of whoever he is currently making arrangements to stand up.

He gives a single nod and is unsure of how convincing it seems.

Sensing this, Doris begins to pull him away. 'Well, it was wonderful to meet you all but we really better get back to shopping. Nice to meet you, Kate, Frankie, Joyce sweetie.' She gives her a quick hug. 'Enjoy dinner. At eight. Shelbourne Hotel. Don't forget now.'

'Red or black?' Joyce holds up the two dresses to Justin, before he's pulled away.

He considers this carefully. 'Red.'

'Black it is, then,' she smiles, mirroring their first and only conversation from the hair salon, the first day they met.

He laughs and allows Doris to drag him away.

THIRTY-EIGHT

'What the hell did you do that for, Doris?' Justin asks as they walk back towards their hotel.

'You've gone on and on about this woman for weeks and now you've finally got a date with her. What's so wrong with that?'

'I have *plans* tonight! I can't just stand the person up.'

'You don't even know who they are!'

'It doesn't matter, it's still rude.'

'Justin, seriously, listen to me. This whole Thank You message thing could honestly be somebody playing a cruel joke.'

He narrows his eyes with suspicion. 'Is it?'

'I honestly don't know.'

'I have no idea,' Al shrugs, beginning to pant.

Doris and Justin slow down immediately, taking baby steps.

Justin sighs.

'Would you rather risk going to something where you have no idea what or who to expect? Or go to dinner with a pretty lady, who you are absolutely crazy about and have been thinking about for weeks?'

'Come on,' Al joins in, 'when's the last time you felt like this about anyone? I don't even think you were like this with Jennifer.'

Justin smiles.

'So, bro, what's it gonna be?'

'You should really take something for that heartburn, Mr Conway,' I can hear Frankie telling Dad in the kitchen.

'Like what?' Dad asks, enjoying the company of two young ladies.

'Christian gets that all the time,' Kate says, and I hear Sam's babbling echo around the kitchen.

Dad babbles back at him, imitating his nonwords.

'Oh, it's called, em . . .' Kate thinks, 'I can't remember what it's called.'

'You're the same as me,' Dad says to her. 'You've got CRAFT too.'

'What's that?'

'Can't. Remember. A. Fuc—'

'OK, I'm coming!' I call down the stairs to Kate, Frankie and Dad.

'Yahooo!' Frankie hollers.

'OK, I've got the camera ready!' Kate calls.

Dad starts making trumpet noises as I walk down the stairs and I start to laugh. I keep an eye on Mum's photo on the hall table as I walk down the steps, maintaining eye contact with her all the way as she looks up at me. I wink at her as I pass.

As soon as I step into the hall and turn to them in the kitchen, they all go quiet.

My smile fades. 'What's wrong?'

'Oh, Joyce,' Frankie whispers as though it's a bad thing, 'you look beautiful.'

I sigh with relief and join them in the kitchen.

'Do a twirl.' Kate films with the video camera.

I spin in my new red dress while Sam claps his podgy hands.

'Mr Conway, you haven't said anything!' Frankie nudges him. 'Isn't she beautiful?'

We all turn to face Dad, who has gone silent, eyes filled with tears. He nods up and down quickly, but no words come.

'Oh, Dad,' I reach out and wrap my arms around him, 'it's only a dress.'

'You look beautiful, love,' he manages to say. 'Go get him, kiddo.' He gives me a kiss on the cheek and hurries into the living room, embarrassed by his emotion.

'So,' Frankie says smiling, 'have you decided whether it's going to be dinner or the opera tonight?'

'I still don't know.'

'He asked you out to dinner,' Kate says. 'Why do you think he'd rather go to the opera.'

'Because firstly, *he* didn't ask me out for dinner. His sister-in-law did. And I didn't say yes. *You* did.' I glare at Kate. 'I think it's killing him not knowing whose life he saved. He didn't seem so convinced at the end, before he left the shop, did he?'

'Stop reading so much into it,' Frankie says. 'He asked you out so go out.'

'But he looked guilty to be standing the opera date up.'

'I don't know,' Kate disagrees. 'He seemed to really want you at that dinner.'

'It's a tough decision,' Frankie summarises. 'I would *not* like to be in your shoes.'

'Hey, they're my shoes,' Kate says, insulted. 'Why can't you just come clean and tell him that it's you?'

'My way of coming clean was supposed to be him seeing me at the opera. This was going to be it, the night he found out.'

'So go to dinner and tell him that it was you all along.'

'But what if he goes to the opera?'

We talk in circles for a while longer, and when they leave, I discuss the pros and cons of both situations with myself until my head is spinning so much I can't think any more. When the taxi arrives, Dad walks me to the door.

'I don't know what you girls were in such deep conversation about but I know you've to make a decision about something. Have you made it?' Dad asks softly.

'I don't know, Dad.' I swallow hard. 'I don't know what the right decision is.'

'Of course you do. You always take your own route, love. You always have.'

'What do you mean?'

He looks out to the garden. 'See that trail there?'

'The garden path?'

He shakes his head and points to a track in the lawn where the grass has been trampled on and the soil is slightly visible beneath. 'You made that path.'

'What?' I'm confused now.

'As a little girl,' he smiles. 'We call them "desire lines" in the gardening world. They're the tracks and trails that people make for themselves. You've always avoided the paths laid down by other people, love. You've always gone your own way, found your own way, even if you do eventually get to the same point as everybody else. You've never taken the official route,' he chuckles to himself. 'No, indeed you haven't. You're certainly your mother's daughter, cutting the corners, creating spontaneous paths, while I'd stick to the routes and make my way the long way round.' He smiles as he reminisces.

We both study the small well-worn ribbon of trampled grass across the garden leading to the path.

'Desire lines,' I repeat, seeing myself as a little girl, as a teenager, a grown woman, cutting across that patch, each time. 'I suppose desire isn't linear. There is no straightforward way of going where you want.'

'Do you know what you're going to do now?' he asks as the taxi arrives.

I smile and kiss him on his forehead. 'I do.'

THIRTY-NINE

I step out of the taxi at Stephen's Green and immediately see the crowds flowing towards the Gaiety Theatre, all dressed in their finest for the National Irish Opera's production. I have never been to an opera before, have only ever seen one on television, and my heart, tired of a body that can't keep up with it, is pounding to get out of my body and run into the building itself. I'm filled with nerves, with anticipation, and with the greatest hope I have ever felt in my life, that the final part of my plan will come together. I'm terrified that Justin will be angry that it's me, though why he would be, I've run through a hundred thousand times in my head and can't seem to come to any rational conclusion.

I stand halfway between the Shelbourne Hotel and the Gaiety Theatre, no less than three hundred yards between them. I look from one to the other, close my eyes and don't care how stupid I look in the middle of the road as people pass by me on this Saturday night. I wait to feel the pull. Which way to go. Right to the Shelbourne. Left to the Gaiety. My heart drums in my chest.

I turn to the left and stride confidently toward the theatre. Inside the bustling entrance foyer, I purchase a programme and make my way to my seat. No time for pre-performance drinks; if he shows up early and sees I'm not here I would never forgive myself. Front-row tickets – I could not believe my luck but I had called the very moment the tickets had gone on sale to secure these precious seats.

I take my seat in the red velvet chairs, my red dress falling down either side of me, my purse on my lap, Kate's shoes glistening on the floor before me. The orchestra are directly in front of me, tuning and rehearsing, dressed in black in their underworld of fabulous sounds.

The atmosphere is magical, the balconies drip from the side. Thousands of people buzzing with excitement, orchestra fine-tuning and striving for perfection, lots of bodies moving around, balconies like honeycombs, the air rich with perfumes and aftershaves, pure honey.

I look to my right at the empty chair and shiver with excitement.

An announcement explains that the performance will begin in five minutes, that those who are late will be forbidden entry until a break, but are able to stay outside and watch the performance on the screens until the ushers tell them it is an appropriate time to enter.

Hurry, Justin, hurry, I plead, my legs bouncing beneath me with nerves.

Justin speed-walks from his hotel and up Kildare Street. He is just out of the shower but already his skin feels moist, his shirt sticks to his back, his forehead glistens with sweat. He stops walking at the top of the road. The Shelbourne Hotel is directly beside him, the Gaiety Theatre two hundred yards to his right.

He closes his eyes and takes deep breaths. Breathes in the fresh October air of Dublin city. *Which way to go. Which way to go.*

The performance has begun and I cannot take my eyes off the door to my right-hand side. Beside me is an empty seat whose very presence sends a lump to my throat. While onstage a woman sings with such emotion, much to my neighbours' annoyance beside and behind me, I can't help but turn my head to face the door. Despite the announcement, a few people have been permitted entry and have moved quickly to their seats. If Justin does not come now, he may not be able to be seated until after the interval. I empathise with the woman singing before me, for the mere fact that, after all this time, a door and an usher being the only things separating us, is an opera in itself.

I turn round once more and my heart skips a beat as the door beside me opens.

*   *   *

Justin pulls on the door and as soon as he enters the room, all heads turn to stare at him. He looks around quickly for Joyce, his heart in his mouth, his fingers clammy and trembling.

The maître d' approaches. 'Welcome, sir. How can I help you?'

'Good evening. I've booked a table for two, under Hitchcock.' He looks around nervously, takes a handkerchief out of his pocket and dabs at his forehead nervously. 'Is she here yet?'

'No, sir, you are the first to arrive. Would you like me to show you to your table or would you rather have a drink before?'

'The table please.' If she arrives and sees he isn't at the table, he will never forgive himself.

He is led to a table for two in the centre of the dining room.

He sits in the chair that has been held out for him and immediately servers flow to his table, pouring water, laying his serviette on his lap, bringing bread rolls.

'Sir, would you like to see the menu or would you like to wait for the other party to arrive?'

'I'll wait, thank you.' He watches the door and takes this moment of being alone to calm himself.

It has been over an hour. There have been a few moments when people have entered and been shown their seats but none of those people have been Justin. The chair beside me remains empty and cold. The woman next to it, glances occasionally at it and at me who is twisted round, eye obsessively and possessively on the door, and she smiles politely, sympathetically. It brings tears to my eyes, a feeling of utter loneliness, in a room full of people, full of sound, full of song, I feel utterly alone. The interval begins, the curtain lowers, the house lights are raised and everybody stands up and exits to the bar, outside for cigarettes or to stretch their legs.

I sit and I wait.

The more lonely I feel, the more hope that springs in my heart. He may still come. He may still feel this is as important to him as it is to me. Dinner with a woman he's met once or an evening with a person whose life he helped save, a person who has done exactly what he wished and thanked him in all the ways he asked.

Perhaps it wasn't enough.

'Would you like to see the menu now, sir?'

'Em,' he looks at the clock. She's a half-hour late and his heart sinks but he remains hopeful. 'She's just running a little late, you see,' he explains.

'Of course, sir.'

'I'll have a look at the wine menu, please.'

'Of course, sir.'

The woman's lover is ripped from her arms and she pleads for him to be let go. She wails and howls and hollers in song, and beside me the woman sniffles. My eyes fill too, remembering Dad's face of pride when he saw me in my dress.

'Go get him,' he said.

Well, I didn't. I've lost another one. I've been stood up by a man who'd rather have dinner with me. As nonsensical as it should be, it is crystal clear to me. I wanted him to be here. I wanted the connection I felt, that he caused, to be the thing that brought us together, not a chance meeting in a department store, a few hours before. It seems so fickle for him to choose me over something far more important.

Perhaps I am viewing this the wrong way, though. Perhaps I should be happy he chose dinner with me. I look at my watch. Perhaps he is there right now, waiting for me. But what if I leave here and he arrives, missing me? No. I am best to stay put and not confuse matters.

My mind battles on, as events do on stage.

But if he is at the restaurant now, and I am here, then he is alone, has been alone for over an hour. Why then, wouldn't he give up on a date with me and run a few hundred yards to seek out the mystery date? Unless he has come. Unless he took one look through the door, saw that it was me and refused to come in. I am so overwhelmed by the thoughts in my head I tune out of the act, too muddled, completely ambushed by the questions in my head.

Before I know it, the opera is over. The seats

are empty, the curtains are down on the stage, the lights are up. I walk out to the cold night air. The city is busy, filled with people enjoying their Saturday night out. My tears feel cold against my skin as the breeze hits them.

Justin empties the last of his second bottle of wine into his glass and slams it back onto the table unintentionally. He has lost all co-ordination by now, he can barely read the time on his watch but he knows it's gone past a reasonable hour for Joyce to show.

He has been stood up.

By the one woman he's had any sort of interest in since his divorce. Not counting poor Sarah. He had never counted poor Sarah.

I am a horrible person.

'I'm sorry to disturb you, sir,' the maître d' says politely, 'but we have received a phone call from your brother, Al?'

Justin nods.

'He wanted to pass on the message that he is still alive and that he hopes you are, em, well, that you're enjoying your night.'

'Alive?'

'Yes, sir, he said you would understand, as it's twelve o'clock. His birthday?'

'Twelve?'

'Yes, sir. I'm also sorry to tell you that we are closing for the evening. Would you like to settle your bill?'

Justin looks up at him, bleary-eyed, and tries to nod again but feels his head loll to one side.

'I've been stood up.'

'I'm sorry, sir.'

'Oh, don't be. I deserve it. I stood up a person I don't even know.'

'Oh. I see.'

'But they have been so kind to me. So, so kind. They gave me muffins and coffee, a car and a driver, and I've been so horrible to him or her.' He stops suddenly.

It might be still open!

'Here.' He thrusts his credit card at him. 'I might still have time.'

I stroll around the quiet streets of the neighbourhood, wrapping my cardigan tighter around me. I told the taxi driver to let me out round the corner so that I could get some air and clear my head before I return home. I also want to be rid of my tears by the time Dad sees me, who I'm sure is currently sitting up in his armchair as he used to do when I was younger, alert and eager to find out what had happened, though he would pretend to be asleep as soon as he heard the key in the door.

I walk by my old house, which I successfully managed to sell only days ago, not to the eager Linda and Joe, who found out it was my home and were afraid my bad luck was an omen for them and their unborn child, or more, that the stairs that caused my fall, would perhaps be too dangerous for Linda during her pregnancy. Nobody takes responsibility for their actions, I notice. It wasn't the stairs, it was me. I was rushing. It was my fault. Simple as that. Something I'm going to have to dig deep to forgive, as it shall never be forgotten.

Perhaps I've been rushing through my whole entire life, jumping into things head first without thinking them through. Running through the days without noticing the minutes. Not that the times when I slowed down and planned ever gave any more positive results. Mum and Dad had planned everything for their entire lives: summer holidays, a child, their savings, nights out. Everything was done by the book. Her premature departure from life was the one thing they had never bargained on. A blip that knocked everything off course.

Conor and I had teed-off straight for the trees and had bogeyed, big time.

The money for the house is to be halved and shared between Conor and me. I will have to start hunting for something smaller, something cheaper. I have no idea what he will do – an odd realisation.

I stop outside our old home and stare up at the red bricks, at the door we argued about what colour to paint, about the flowers we'd thought deeply about before planting. Not mine any more, but the memories are; the memories can't be sold. The building that housed my once-upon-a-time dreams stands for someone else now, as it did for the people before us, and I feel happy to let it go. Happy that was another time and that I can begin again, anew, though bearing the scars of before. They represent wounds that have healed.

It's midnight when I return to Dad's house and behind the windows is blackness. There isn't a single light on, which is unusual, as he usually leaves the porch light on, particularly if I'm out.

I open my bag to get my keys and bump against my mobile phone. It lights up to show I have missed ten calls, eight of which are from the house. I had it on silent at the opera and, knowing that Justin didn't have my number, I didn't think to look at it. I scramble for my keys, my hands trembling as I try to fit the key into the lock. They fall to the ground, the noise echoing in the silent dark street. I lower myself to my knees, not caring about my new dress, and shuffle around the concrete, feeling for the metal in the darkness. Finally, my fingers touch upon them and I'm through the door like a rocket, turning on all the lights.

'Dad?' I call in the hallway. Mum's photograph is on the floor, underneath the table. I pick it up and place it back where it belongs, trying to stay calm, but my heart is having its own idea.

No answer.

I walk to the kitchen and flick the switch. A full cup of tea sits on the kitchen table. A slice of toast with jam, with one bite taken from it.

'Dad?' I say more loudly now, walking into the living room and turning on the light.

His pills have all been spilled on the floor, all the containers opened and emptied, all the colours mixed.

I panic now, running back through the kitchen, through the hall, and run upstairs, turning on all the lights as I yell at the top of my lungs.

'DAD! DAD! WHERE ARE YOU? DAD, IT'S ME, JOYCE! DAD!' Tears are flowing now; I can barely speak. He is not in his bedroom, or the bathroom, not in my room or anywhere else. I pause on the landing, trying to listen in the silence to hear if he's calling. All I can hear is the drumbeat of my heart in my ears, in my throat.

'DAD!' I yell, my chest heaving, the lump in my throat threatening to seize my breath. I've nowhere else to look. I start pulling open wardrobes, searching under his bed. I grab a pillow from his bed and breathe in, holding it close to me and instantly soaking it with tears. I look out the back window and into the garden: no sign of him.

My knees too weak to stand, my head too clouded to think, I sink onto the top stair on the landing and try to figure out where he could be.

Then I think of the spilled pills on the floor and I yell the loudest I have *ever* shouted in my life. 'DAAAAAAD!'

Silence greets me and I have never felt so alone. More alone than at the opera, more alone than in an unhappy marriage, more alone than when Mum died. Completely and utterly alone, the last person I have in my life, taken away from me.

Then.

'Joyce?' A voice calls from the front door, which I've left open. 'Joyce, it's me, Fran.' She stands there in her dressing gown and slippers, her eldest son standing behind her with a flashlight in his hand.

'Dad is gone.' My voice trembles.

'He's in the hospital, I was trying to call y—'

'What? Why?' I stand up and rush down the stairs.

'He thought he was having another heart—'

'I have to go. I have to go to him.' I rush around searching for my car keys. 'Which one is he in?'

'Joyce, relax, love, relax.' Fran's arms are around me. 'I'll drive you.'

FORTY

I run down the corridors, examining each door, trying to find the correct room. I panic, my tears blinding my vision. A nurse stops me and helps me, tries to calm me. Knows instantly who I'm talking about. I shouldn't be allowed in at this time but she can tell I'm distraught, wants to calm me by showing me he's all right. She allows me a few minutes.

I follow her down a series of corridors and finally she leads me into his room. I see Dad lying in bed, tubes attached to his wrists and nose, his skin deathly pale, his body so small under the blankets in the bed.

'Was that you making all that fuss out there?' he asks, his voice sounding weak.

'Dad.' I try to remain calm but my voice comes out muffled.

'It's OK, love. I just got a shock, is all. Thought my heart was acting up again, went to take my pills but then I got dizzy and they all fell. Something to do with sugar, they tell me.'

'Diabetes, Henry,' the nurse smiles. 'The doctor will be around to explain it all to you in the morning.'

I sniffle, trying to remain calm.

'Ah, come here, you silly sod.' He lifts his arms towards me.

I rush to him and hug him tight, his body feeling frail but protective.

'I'm not going anywhere on you now. Hush, now.' He runs his hands through my hair and pats my back comfortingly. 'I hope I didn't ruin your night, now. I told Fran not to bother you.'

'Of course you should have called me,' I say into his shoulder. 'I got such a fright when you weren't home.'

'Well, I'm fine. You'll have to help me, though, with all this stuff,' he whispers. 'I told the doctor I understand but I don't really,' he says, a little worried. 'He's a real snooty type.' He ruffles up his nose.

'Of course I will.' I wipe my eyes and try to compose myself.

'So, how did it go?' he asks, perking up. 'Tell me all the good news.'

'He, em,' I purse my lips, 'he didn't show up.' My tears start again.

Dad is quiet; sad then angry, then sad again. He hugs me again, tighter this time.

'Ah, love,' he says gently. 'He's a bloody fool.'

FORTY-ONE

Justin finishes explaining the story of his disastrous weekend to Bea, who is sitting on the couch, her mouth open in shock.

'I can't believe I missed all this. I'm so bummed!'

'Well, you wouldn't have missed it if you'd been talking to me,' Justin teases.

'Thank you for apologising to Peter. I appreciate it. He appreciates it.'

'I was acting like an idiot; just didn't want to admit my little girl was all grown up.'

'You better believe it,' she smiles. 'God,' she thinks back to his story, 'I still can't imagine somebody sending you all that stuff. Who could it be? The poor person must have waited and waited for you at the opera.'

Justin covers his face and winces. 'Please stop, it's killing me.'

'But you chose Joyce, anyway.'

He nods and smiles sadly.

'You must have really liked her.'

'She must have really not liked me because she didn't show up. No, Bea, I'm over it now. It's time to move on. I hurt too many people in the process of trying to find out. If you can't remember anyone else you told, then we'll never know.'

Bea thinks hard. 'I only told Peter, the costume supervisor and her father. But what makes you think it wasn't either of them?'

'I met the costume supervisor that night. She didn't act like she knew me, and she's English – why would she have gone to Ireland for a blood transfusion? I called her and asked her about her father. Don't ask.' He sees off her glare. 'Anyway, turns out her father's Polish.'

'Hold on, where are you getting that from? She wasn't English, she was Irish,' Bea frowns. 'They both were.'

Thump-thump. Thump-thump.

'Justin,' Laurence enters the room with cups of coffee for him and Bea, 'I was wondering when you have a minute, if we could have a word.'

'Not now, Laurence,' Justin says, moving to the edge of his seat. 'Bea, where's your ballet programme? Her photograph's in it.'

'Honestly, Justin.' Jennifer arrives at the door with her arms folded. 'Could you please just be respectful for one moment. Laurence has something he wants to say and you owe it to him to listen.'

Bea runs to her room, pushing through the battling adults, and returns waving the programme in her hand, ignoring them. As does Justin.

He grabs it from her and flicks through it quickly. 'There!' he stabs his finger on the page.

'Guys,' Jennifer steps in between them, 'we really have to settle this now.'

'Not now, Mum. Please!' Bea yells. 'This is important!'

'And this is not?'

'That's not her.' Bea shakes her head furiously. 'That's not the woman I spoke to.'

'Well, what did she look like?' Justin is up on his feet now. Thump-thump. Thump-thump.

'Let me think, let me think.' Bea panics. 'I know! Mum!'

'What?' Jennifer looks from Justin to Bea with confusion.

'Where are the photographs we took of the first night I stood in for Charlotte in the ballet?'

'Oh, em—'

'Quick.'

'They're in the corner kitchen cupboard,' Laurence says, frowning.

'Yes, Laurence!' Justin punches the air. 'They're in the corner kitchen cupboard! Go get them, quick!'

Alarmed, Laurence runs into the kitchen, while Jennifer watches him with an open mouth. There is much shuffling of papers while Justin paces the floor at top speed and Jennifer and Bea watch him.

'Here they are.' He offers them forward and Bea snaps them out of his hand.

Jennifer tries to interject but Bea and Justin's speech and movements are on fast forward.

Bea shuffles through the photos at top speed. 'You weren't in the room at the time, Dad. You had disappeared somewhere but we all got a group photo and, here it is!' She rushes to her dad. 'That's them. The woman and her father, at the end.' She points.

Silence.

'Dad?'

Silence.

'Dad, are you OK?'

'Justin?' Jennifer moves in closer. 'He's gone very pale, get him a glass of water, Laurence, quick.'

Laurence rushes back to the kitchen.

'Dad.' Bea clicks her fingers in front of his eyes. 'Dad, are you with us?'

'It's her,' he whispers.

'Her who?' Jennifer asks.

'The woman whose life he saved.' Bea jumps up and down excitedly.

'*You* saved a woman's life?' Jennifer asks, shocked. '*You?*'

'It's Joyce,' he whispers.

Bea gasps. 'The woman who phoned me?'

He nods.

Bea gasps again. 'The woman you stood up?'

Justin closes his eyes, and silently curses himself.

'You saved a woman's life and then *stood her up?*' Jennifer laughs.

'Bea, where's your phone?'

470

'Why?'

'She called you, remember? Her number was in your phone.'

'Oh, Dad, that was ages ago. My phone log only holds ten recent numbers. That was weeks ago!'

'Damnit!'

'I gave it to Doris, remember? She wrote it down. You called the number from your flat!'

You threw it in the skip, you jerk! The skip! It's still there!

'Here.' Laurence runs in with the glass of water, panting.

'Laurence.' Justin reaches out, takes him by the cheeks and kisses his forehead. 'I give you my blessing. Jennifer,' he does the same and kisses her directly on the lips, 'good luck.'

He runs out of the apartment as Bea cheers him on, Jennifer wipes her lips with disgust and Laurence wipes the spilled water from his clothes.

As Justin sprints from the tube station to his house, rain pours from the clouds like a cloth being squeezed. He doesn't care, he just looks up to the sky and laughs, loving how it feels on his face, unable to believe that Joyce was the woman all along. He should have known. It all makes sense now, her asking him if he was sure he wanted to make new dinner plans, her friend being at his talk, all of it!

He turns the corner into his drive and sees the

skip now filled to the brim with items. He jumps in and begins sorting through it.

From the window, Doris and Al stop packing their suitcases and watch him with concern.

'Damnit, I really thought he was getting back to normal,' Al says. 'Should we stay?'

'I don't know,' she replies worriedly. 'What on earth is he doing? It's ten o'clock at night – surely the neighbours will call the cops.'

His grey T-shirt is soaked through, his hair slicked back, water drips from his nose, his trousers are stuck to his skin. They watch him whooping and hollering as he throws the contents of the skip onto the ground beside it.

FORTY-TWO

I lie in bed, staring at the ceiling, trying to process my life. Dad is still in hospital undergoing tests and will be home tomorrow. With nobody around, it has forced me to think about my life and I have worked my way through despair, guilt, sadness, anger, loneliness, depression, cynicism and have finally found my way to hope. Like an addict going cold turkey, I have paced the floors of these rooms with every emotion bursting from my skin. I have spoken aloud to myself, screamed, shouted, wept and mourned.

It's eleven p.m., dark, windy and cold outside as the winter months are fighting their way through, when the phone rings. Thinking it's Dad I hurry downstairs, grab the phone and sit on the bottom stair.

'Hello?'

'It was you all along.'

I freeze. My heart thuds. I move the phone from my ear and take a deep breath.

'Justin?'

'It was you all along, wasn't it?'

I'm silent.

'I saw the photograph of you and your father with Bea. That's the night she told you about my donation. About wanting thank yous.' He sneezes.

'Bless you.'

'Why didn't you say anything to me? All those times I saw you? Did you follow me or . . . or, what's going on, Joyce?'

'Are you angry with me?'

'No! I mean, I don't know. I don't understand. I'm so confused.'

'Let me explain.' I take a deep breath and try to steady my voice, try to speak through the heartbeat that is currently at the base of my throat. 'I didn't follow you to any of the places we met so please don't be concerned. I'm not a stalker. Something happened, Justin. Something happened when I received my transfusion and *whatever* that was, when your blood was transfused into mine, I suddenly felt connected to you. I kept turning up at places you were at, like the hair salon, the ballet. It was all a coincidence.' I'm speaking too fast now but I can't slow down. 'And then Bea told me you'd donated blood around the same time that I'd received it and . . .'

'What?'

I'm not sure what he means.

'You mean, you don't know for sure if it is my blood that you received? Because I couldn't find out, nobody would tell me. Did somebody tell you?'

'No. Nobody told me. They didn't need to. I—'

'Joyce.' He stops me and I'm immediately worried by his tone.

'I'm not some *weird* person, Justin. Trust me. I have never experienced what I have over the past few weeks.' I tell him the story. Of experiencing his skills, his knowledge, of sharing his tastes.

He is quiet.

'Say something, Justin.'

'I don't know what to say. It sounds . . . odd.'

'It is odd, but it's the truth. This will sound even worse but I feel like I've gained some of your memories too.'

'Really?' His voice is cold, far away. I'm losing him.

'Memories of the park in Chicago, Bea dancing in her tutu on the red chequered cloth, the picnic basket, the bottle of red wine. The cathedral bells, the ice-cream parlour, the seesaw with Al, the sprinklers, the—'

'Whoa, whoa, whoa. Stop now. Who are you?'

'Justin, it's me!'

'Who's told you these things?'

'Nobody, I just know them!' I rub my eyes tiredly. 'I know it sounds bizarre, Justin, I really do. I am a normal decent human being who is as cynical as they come but this is my life and these are the things that are happening to me. If you don't believe me then I'm sorry and I'll hang up and go back to my life, but please know that this is not a joke or a hoax or any kind of set-up.'

He is quiet for a while. And then, 'I want to believe you.'

'You feel something between us?'

'I feel that.' He speaks very slowly as though pondering every letter of every word. 'The memories, tastes and hobbies and whatever else of mine that you mentioned, are things that you could have seen me do or heard me say. I'm not saying you're doing this on purpose, maybe you don't even know it, but you've read my books; I mention many personal things in my books. You saw the photo in Bea's locket, you've been to my talks, you've read my articles. I may have revealed things about myself in them, in fact I know I have. How can I know that you knowing these things is through a transfusion? How do I know that – no offence – but that you're not some lunatic young woman who's convinced herself of some crazy story she read in a book or saw in a movie? How am I supposed to know?'

I sigh. I have no way of convincing him. 'Justin, I don't believe in anything right now, but I believe in this.'

'I'm sorry, Joyce,' he begins to end the conversation.

'No, wait,' I stop him. 'Is this it?'

Silence.

'Aren't you going to even try to believe me?'

He sighs deeply. 'I thought you were somebody

else, Joyce. I don't know why because I'd never even met you, but I thought you were a different kind of person. This . . . this I don't understand. This, I find . . . it's not right, Joyce.'

Each sentence is a stab through my heart and a punch in my stomach. I could stand hearing this from anyone else in the world but not him. Anyone but him.

'You've been through a lot, by the sound of it, perhaps you should . . . talk to someone.'

'Why don't you believe me? Please, Justin. There must be something I can say to convince you. Something I know that you haven't written in an article or a book or told anyone in a lecture . . .' I trail off, thinking of something. No, I can't use that.

'Goodbye, Joyce. I hope everything works out for you, really I do.'

'Hold on! Wait! There is one thing. One thing that only you could know.'

He pauses. 'What?'

I squeeze my eyes shut and take a deep breath. Do it or don't do it. Do it or don't. I open my eyes and blurt it out, 'Your father.'

There's silence.

'Justin?'

'What about him?' His voice is ice cold.

'I know what you saw,' I say softly. 'How you could never tell anyone.'

'What the hell are you talking about?'

'I know about you being on the stairs, seeing

him through the banisters. I see him too. I see him with the bottle and the pills closing the door. Then I see the green feet on the floor—'

'STOP IT!' he yells, and I'm shocked to silence.

But I must keep trying or I'll never have the opportunity to say these words again.

'I know how hard it must have been for you as a child. How hard it was to keep it to yourself—'

'You know nothing,' he says coldly. 'Absolutely nothing. Please stay away from me. I don't ever wish to hear from you again.'

'OK.' My voice is a whisper but it is to myself as he has already hung up.

I sit on the steps of the dark empty house and listen as the cold October wind rattles the building.

So that's that.

One Month Later

FORTY-THREE

'Next time we should take the car, Gracie,' Dad says as we make our way down the road back from our walk in the Botanics. I link his arm and I'm lifted up and down with him as he sways. Up and down, down and up. The motion is soothing.

'No, you need the exercise, Dad.'

'Speak for yourself,' he mutters. 'Howya, Sean? Miserable day isn't it?' he calls across the street to the old man on his Zimmer frame.

'Terrible,' Sean shouts back.

'So what did you think of the apartment?' I broach the subject for the third time in the last few minutes. 'You can't dodge it this time.'

'I'm dodging nothing, love. Howya, Patsy? Howya, Suki?' He stops and bends down to pat the sausage dog. 'Aren't you a cute little thing,' he says, and we continue on. 'I hate that little runt. Barks all bloody night when she's away,' he mutters, pushing his cap down further over his eyes as a great big gust blows. 'Christ Almighty, are we gettin' anywhere at all, I feel like we're on one of those milltreads with this wind.'

'Treadmills,' I laugh. 'So come on, do you like the apartment or not?'

'I'm not sure. It seemed awful small and there was a funny man that went into the flat next door. Don't think I liked the look of him.'

'He seemed very friendly to me.'

'Ah, he would to you, and all.' He rolls his eyes and shakes his head. 'Any man would do for you now, I'd say.'

'Dad!' I laugh.

'Good afternoon, Graham. Miserable day, isn't it?' he says to the neighbour passing.

'Awful day, Henry,' Graham responds, shoving his hands in his pockets.

'Anyway, I don't think you should take that apartment, Gracie. Hang on here a little longer until something more appropriate pops up. There's no point in taking the first thing you see.'

'Dad, we've seen ten apartments and you don't like any of them.'

'Is it for me to live in or for you?' he asks. Up and down. Down and up.

'For me.'

'Well, then, what do you care?'

'I value your opinion.'

'You do in your— Hello there, Kathleen!'

'You can't keep me at home for ever, you know.'

'For ever's been and gone, my love. There's no

482

budging you. You're the Stonehenge of grown-up children living at home.'

'Can I go to the Monday Club tonight?'

'Again?'

'I've to finish off the game of chess I started with Larry.'

'Larry just keeps positioning his pawns so that you'll lean over and he can see down your top. That game will never end.' Dad rolls his eyes.

'Dad!'

'What? Well, you need to get more of a social life than hanging around with the likes of Larry and me.'

'I like hanging around with you.'

He smiles to himself, pleased to hear that.

We turn into Dad's house and sway up the small garden path to the front door.

The sight of what's on the doorstop stops me in my tracks.

A small hamper of muffins, covered in plastic wrapper and tied with a pink bow. I look at Dad, who steps right over them and unlocks the front door. His movement makes me question my eyesight. Have I imagined them?

'Dad! What are you doing?' Shocked, I look around behind me but nobody's there.

Dad winks at me, looks sad for a moment and then gives me a great big smile before closing the door in my face.

I reach for the envelope that is taped to the

plastic and with trembling fingers slide the card out.

Thank you...

'I'm sorry, Joyce.' I hear a voice behind me that almost stops my heart and I twirl round.

There he is, standing at the garden gate, a bouquet of flowers in his gloved hands, the sorriest look on his face. He is wrapped up in a scarf and winter coat, the tip of his nose and cheeks red from the cold, his green eyes twinkling in the grey day. He is a vision; he takes my breath away with one look, his proximity to me almost too much to bear.

'Justin . . .' Then I'm utterly speechless.

'Do you think,' he takes a step forward, 'you could find it in your heart to forgive a fool like me?' He stands at the end of the garden, beside the gate.

I'm unsure what to say. It's been a month. Why now?

'On the phone, you hit a sore point,' he says, clearing his throat. 'Nobody knows that about my dad. Or knew that. I don't know how you did.'

'I told you how.'

'I don't understand it.'

'Neither do I.'

'But then I don't understand most ordinary things that happen everyday. I don't understand what my daughter sees in her boyfriend. I don't understand how my brother has defied the laws of science by not turning into an actual potato chip. I don't know how Doris can open the milk carton with such long nails. I don't understand why I didn't beat down your door a month ago and tell you how I felt . . . I don't understand so many simple things, I don't know why this should be any different.'

I take in the sight of his face, his curly hair covered by a woolly hat, his small nervous smile. He studies me back and I shiver, but not from the cold. I don't feel it now. The world has been heated up entirely for me. How kind. I thank beyond the clouds.

Frown lines appear on his forehead as he looks at me.

'What?'

'Nothing. You just remind me so much of somebody right now. It's not important.' He clears his throat, smiles, trying to pick up where he left off.

'Eloise Parker,' I guess, and his grin fades.

'How the hell do you know that?'

'She was your next-door neighbour who you had a crush on for years. When you were five years old you decided to do something about it and so you picked flowers from your front yard and brought them to her house. She opened the door before you got up the path and stepped outside wearing a blue coat and a black scarf,' I say, pulling my blue coat around me tighter.

'Then what?' he asks, shocked.

'Then nothing.' I shrug. 'You dropped them on the ground and chickened out.'

He shakes his head softly and smiles. 'How on earth . . . ?'

I shrug.

'What else do you know about Eloise Parker?' He narrows his eyes.

I smile and look away. 'You lost your virginity to her when you were sixteen, in her bedroom when her mom and dad were away on a cruise.'

He rolls his eyes and lowers the bouquet so that it faces the ground. 'Now you see, *that* is not fair. You are not allowed to know stuff like that about me.'

I laugh.

'You were christened Joyce Bridget Conway but you tell everyone your middle name is Angeline,' he retaliates.

My mouth falls open.

'You had a dog called Bunny when you were a kid.' He lifts an eyebrow, cockily.

I narrow my eyes.

'You got drunk on poteen when you were,' he closes his eyes and thinks hard, 'fifteen. With your friends Kate and Frankie.'

He takes a step closer to me with each piece of knowledge and that smell, the smell of him I've dreamed to be near gets closer and closer.

'Your first French kiss was with Jason Hardy when you were ten, who everyone used to call Jason Hard-On.'

I laugh.

'You're not the only one who's allowed to know stuff.' He takes a step closer and can't move any nearer now. His shoes, the fabric of his thick coat, every part of him touches me.

My heart takes out a trampoline and enrols in a marathon session of leaping. I hope Justin doesn't hear it whooping with joy.

'Who told you all of that?' My words touch his face in a breath of cold smoke.

'Getting me here was a big operation,' he smiles. '*Big*. Your friends had me run through a series of tests to prove I was sorry enough to be deemed worthy of coming here.'

I laugh, shocked Frankie and Kate could finally agree on something, never mind keeping anything of this magnitude a secret.

Silence. We are so close, if I look up at him my nose will touch his chin. I keep looking down.

'You're still afraid to sleep in the dark,' he whispers, taking my chin in his hand and lifting it so that I can look nowhere else but at him. 'Unless somebody's with you,' he adds with a small smile.

'You cheated on your first college paper,' I whisper.

'You used to hate art.' He kisses my forehead.

'You lie when you say you're a fan of the *Mona Lisa*.' I close my eyes.

'You had an invisible friend named Horatio until you were five.' He kisses my nose and I'm about

487

to retaliate but his lips touch mine so softly, the words give up, fainting before they reach my voice box and sliding back to the memory bank where they came from.

I am faintly aware of Fran exiting her house and saying something to me, of a car driving by with a beep, but everything is blurred in the distance as I get lost in the moment with Justin, as I create a new memory for him, for me.

'Forgive me?' he says as he pulls away.

'I have no choice but to. It's in my blood,' I smile, and he laughs. I look down at the flowers in his hands, which have been crushed between us. 'Are you going to drop these on the ground too and chicken out?'

'Actually, they're not for you.' His cheeks redden even more. 'They're for somebody at the blood clinic who I really need to apologise to. I was hoping you would come with me, help explain the reason for my crazy behaviour, and maybe she could explain a few things to us in turn.'

I look back to the house and see Dad spying at us from behind the curtain. I look to him questioningly. He gives me the thumbs-up and my eyes fill.

'He was in on this too?'

'He called me a worthless silly sod and an up-to-no-good fool.' He makes a face and I laugh.

I blow Dad a kiss as I begin slowly to walk away. I feel him watching me, and feel Mum's eyes on me too, as I walk down the garden path, cut across the grass and follow the desire line I had created as a little girl, out onto the pavement leading away from the house I grew up in.

Though this time, I'm not alone.

Cecelia Ahern

Making the everyday magical

Inside:

- Cecelia answers your questions on her books and the inspirations behind her writing

- Keep up to date with Cecelia's latest news on her website

- Don't miss Cecelia's other bestsellers

Q&A with Cecelia

We gave you the chance to ask Cecelia questions about her books and the inspirations behind her writing. There was a great response and so we couldn't fit them all in here. But why not visit the website to read some more.

Where did you get your inspiration from? I absolutely love your work and have all of your books. *Yvonne Blasius*

It is very difficult for me to say what exactly inspires me and where exactly I get my ideas from. The obvious answer is: life. I absorb everything around me. All the people I've met and all the places I've been, all the stories I've heard, music, books, absolutely anything and everything inspires me. I find that I'm constantly day dreaming, constantly imagining and creating scenarios in my head. I'm a creative person and so I allow my mind to wander, to go off on tangents, to take pathways off the beaten track and get lost. I ask questions and look for answers and then I try to think of more answers. I'm always open to new possibilities, to hearing the other side of the story, and then I like creating the third side of the story that nobody has thought of, or that perhaps people have thought of but have never thought through fully. I watch people, I listen to people, I try to see the world from their eyes. I like to view things from a different angle. I like climbing inside peoples heads and trying to imagine everything from their point of view. I can sit still for hours on end, staring at a wall, my body totally still but my mind going on the greatest adventures. I think that's just the way I am. Being a writer is a natural thing because it's something that's not forced. I don't try to think of ideas, ideas come to me. I don't try to create characters, they introduce themselves to me. I'm emotional and through the very action of feeling, I'm immediately inspired because it brings me to another place and connects me to writing.

I started to read *Thanks for the Memories* after having a miscarriage and it touched my heart so much that it made me cry but seemed to help. Had you been through it? Because you wrote everything that I felt. Thank you. *Rebecca Martins*

Thank you. I think it's important when I'm writing to really feel my way through the story. If I write something because I think it's sad or moving then it's really not good enough. I have to feel sad, I have to feel moved. I have to dig deep and use my own experiences of having felt loss, loneliness and deep sadness in order to be able to tell the story accurately. If I have a deep understanding of my character, then I have a deep understanding of their journey. Joyce's journey was one of loss and of grief and what grief is made up are a whole series of emotions – loneliness, deep sadness, anger, despair, feeling a lack of direction, confusion, feeling left behind – that as humans we all experience on a daily basis. And while all our journeys are different and we all deal with circumstances in different ways, what ties us together is our ability to feel the same emotions. My stories are very much emotion driven. It's so important to me that I do these feelings justice, knowing that people reading my books have possibly experienced what I'm writing about – particularly the issue of miscarriage where so many women suffer, and most of them secretly – means that I work so hard to make sure I'm writing about the subject accurately. My books of course are a means of entertainment and escapism, but if they can be of any comfort or help to somebody who is suffering then that is an amazing gift for me as a writer.

I was wondering how old were you when you knew you wanted to be an author? I am deciding between interior design, being an author (I love your books – I hope if I choose to be an author my books are half as good as yours!) or a photographer. Thanks for

answering and please keep writing - I absolutely LOVE your books!!
Kendall Tate

Funnily enough, I never knew that I wanted to be an author. Ever since I was seven or eight, I've been writing diaries every day, writing songs, poems, short stories. When I was fourteen I attempted my first novel, *Beans on Toast and a Bottle of Beer*, which I never managed to finish as school exams called. I knew from a young age that I wanted to do a Communications course at college that I'd heard about. It was very broad and practical and it involved documentary making, creative writing, journalism, radio production etc. Since an early age, if I was angry I felt compelled to write, when I was happy I felt compelled to write. Despite studying Journalism and Media Communications which involved a certain amount of writing, I still wasn't focused on getting into writing for a career. I wanted to do film production. But when I had finished college and I'd started writing *PS, I Love You*, it took over my life. I wrote all night and slept all day. I didn't leave the house for three months until the book was finished and I knew within the first week that it was something special. With my mother's encouragement I sent a few chapters away hoping for some advice. What I ended up getting months later was a book deal! Incredible! So what I'm saying is, writing is a passion, not just a profession. I would write if I wasn't published. I would write on my own time, all of the time and so if you wake up in the morning and feel compelled to do something, then that's what you should do.

How do you find all your ideas? How do you manage to create all these universes? How do you write? *Laëtitia Montassier*

Unlike some writers I don't have a daily routine for writing. Some people like to write nine-to-five, or have a specific word count that they like to achieve per day. I just like to write when I feel the moment's right, when I feel like I've something to say, when the characters are ready to move ahead with the story. Thankfully, when I'm in the zone and I get swept away by the story, my hours could be all day, all night, and this could go on for weeks, consuming all of my time. Then I could take a few days off and do nothing but recharge my batteries. I think I'm an all-or-nothing writer. I have to immerse myself in the world that I'm creating. I find it difficult to have created this new world, with new characters, spend such intense moments with them, and then have to put the pen down in order to take a lunch break. That system doesn't work for me. I like to write long hand. I love physically writing, I love the feel of pen on paper, I love the flow of ideas from my mind, from my heart, onto the paper. It feels like a very natural way to tell a story, whereas writing purely on a computer feels very mechanical, as though there's a block between me and the story. After I write a chapter, I type a chapter and edit it as I go along, shaping the story and further developing the characters. When I write I have to see the picture in front of me, I always believe that if I can see it – and most importantly feel it – then I can write it. I smell the scents I'm writing about, I feel the emotions my characters are feeling, I see the rooms they're in. I totally immerse myself in the stories I tell and live the journey along with my characters.

I just want to ask a very simple question – do you believe in happily ever afters? *Caren Ong Yu Sze*

My books have often been compared to modern fairy tales and when I heard this at first, I didn't know whether I was comfortable with that description. What I feel about fairy tales is that, though uplifting, they are often unrealistic and the female characters are eventually rescued and whisked off into the sunset so that finding a man is their happily ever after. This isn't how I like stories to be, this isn't how I see real life. In my books my characters are on journeys of self-discovery. I introduce them to the reader just as they've hit their lowest point. I like to catch them before they fall and help carry them along through their journey. In *PS, I Love You* we met Holly after she'd just lost Gerry; in *If You Could See Me Now* it was when Elizabeth had been left with a child to care for and she was at breaking point; for Sandy in *A Place Called Here* it was when she literally lost herself and her way in life; and in *Thanks for the Memories* it was when Joyce lost her child.

For me, a happy ending is when the person feels as though they're able to face the day, when they feel that they can get through the moments and they're happy to be alive. It's not about finding the man of your dreams, it's about finding the happiness within ourselves. Instead of being rescued by other people, my characters – through the help of friends and family – rescue themselves. They create their own futures. That, for me, is a happy ending, and I suppose that's what makes my stories 'modern fairy tales' and I'm comfortable with that now.

Dear Cecelia Ahern, when is your next book coming out and what is the title of that book? I love your books and I am waiting for your next book to be published. *Karlya Kang*

My next and sixth novel is called *The Gift* and it will be published October in Ireland and the UK. It's a story based around Christmas time that deals with the theme of time – how it's the most precious thing that we have and how often we take time, and whom we spend it with, for granted. The world is speeding up, people are increasingly busy, there's a pressure to balance work life with family life. So many people have said to me, "Oh if I could just be in two places at once," or "If I could just clone myself, I'd be able to get things done." Well my mind wandered, as it always does and I wondered, if we could be in two places at once, where would we choose to be? This story is about how a man called Lou Suffern has three opportunities to be in two places at the same time, and how he learns a harsh lesson about what's important. Because my books always carry a message, I thought they'd lend themselves well to this fable style story. I adore Christmas stories, the magical feel of the period of time, where we at times revert to feeling like children again. It's also one of the busiest times of the year for people, pressures mount and for some, not so enjoyable as families are thrown together and old wounds are reopened. It felt like the perfect period to base the story around and a time when messages are learned and people take stock of their lives as they gather with family and friends as the year comes to an end.

What do you find most rewarding about writing novels? *Kayla Kirby*

Apart from the personal enjoyment that I get from writing novels, I love meeting and talking to my readers and hearing their feedback and listening to their personal. This gives me such encouragement to see that people connect with my work, that people enjoy and appreciate what I do and it also makes me eager to please my readers each time I write a new book. I always say that I write for myself because I'm so passionate about it and it gives me such joy but the most amazing thing is to know that one little idea that I've had while lying in bed, or making a coffee, or doing the washing or just going about the ordinary things in my life, can affect the lives of others all around the world, whether it's just for a moment of entertainment or a moment of comfort. Despite where we're from or what we've been through, despite never meeting in the past or never possibly meeting in the future, that we can all be connected by a story, that we're never alone, is such a rewarding thought.

Keep up to date with Cecelia!

WHERE RAINBOWS END

Rosie and Alex – best friends or soulmates?

Since childhood, Rosie and Alex have stuck by each other through thick and thin. But they're suddenly separated when Alex and his family move from Dublin to America. Rosie is lost without him. Then, just as she is about to join Alex in Boston, she gets life-changing news – news that will keep her at home in Ireland.

Their magical connection remains but can their friendship survive the years and miles – as well as new relationships? And always at the back of Rosie's mind is whether they were meant to be more than just good friends all along. Misunderstandings, circumstances and sheer bad luck have kept them all apart – until now. But will they gamble everything – including their friendship – on true love? And what twists and surprises does fate have in store for them this time …?

'A heart-warming, completely absorbing tale of love and friendship'
Company

'A winner' *Glamour*

www.cecelia-ahern.com

978-0-00-726082-9 • £6.99

Save 10%

when you buy direct from
HarperCollins – call 08707 871724.

Free postage and packing
in the UK only.

IF YOU COULD SEE ME NOW

**What if love was right there in front of you
– you just couldn't see it?**

Elizabeth Egan is too busy for friends. As a reluctant mother to her sister Saoirse's young son Luke and with her own business to run, every precious moment is made to count.

But with Saoirse crashing in and out of their lives, leaving them both reeling, Luke and Elizabeth are desperately in need of some magic.

Enter Ivan. Wild, spontaneous and always looking for adventure, Ivan changes Elizabeth in ways she could never have imagined. With her newly open eyes and heart, Elizabeth sees what she's been missing all along.

As for Ivan, he thought he was there to help Luke, not Elizabeth – or himself …

'Captivating' *Irish Independent*

'Enchanting and unexpected' *You*

www.cecelia-ahern.com

978-0-00-726081-2 • £6.99

Save 10%

when you buy direct from
HarperCollins – call 08707 871724.

Free postage and packing
in the UK only.